FENCING WITH DANGER

Pavel Lubov's True Story

by

Helene Vorce-Tish

PublishAmerica
Baltimore

First Printing

This is a work of fiction set in a background of history. Public personages both living and dead may appear in the story under their right names. Scenes and dialogue involving them with fictitious characters are of course invented. Any other usage of real people's names is coincidental. Any resemblance of the imaginary characters to actual persons, living or dead, is entirely coincidental.

ISBN: 1-4241-3426-9
PUBLISHED BY PUBLISHAMERICA, LLLP
www.publishamerica.com
Baltimore

Printed in the United States of America

My very special thanks to my friends James Richardson and Irene Swope for information and for giving so generously of their time.

For
my dear friend
Eleanor — Tish
Helen Vance

AUTHOR'S NOTE

The main characters in this book are real; however, I have used pseudonyms for a number of them and changed the last names of others to protect their privacy. This book is mainly a work of nonfiction. I have taken some liberties to build up suspense and add to the dramatic effect of the story without changing the true events in the lives of Pavel and Natasha Lubov.

TO STEPAN DANILOV

My Grandfather

Grandfather, a part of my life
Always within me
Always guiding me
Keeping me focused
Keeping me strong and determined
Through all these terrible times

"Never mind competition. In this life you don't compete with others—you compete with yourself. Find the inner strength to overcome the things you have to go through in this life. Stay strong in spite of all the things you have to endure."

Stepan Danilov

We are the People
See our banners
Raised high for freedoms
A new way of life
Fill our baskets with truths
And we will harvest them.
For all to enjoy
People of the Earth
Believe! Believe! Believe!

Helene Vorce-Tish

Table of Contents

Chapter 1

Pavel watched the train pull into the Moscow station. This would be the moment of his freedom, freedom from that cursed army. For the past three years, he had been forced to live and march to the tune of the Communist Party. Yes, cursed was the word. He was filled with anger as the word "army" crossed his mind. Instead of boarding a train, he felt like rushing to Moscow square and yelling to the crowds, "Wake up! Tramp down the Communists! Live your lives in freedom!"

But he knew this wasn't the right time. To make people listen, you had to talk and convince them that the communist government was restricting their human rights and making slaves of their minds. His mind filled with bitterness as he thought of his past three forced years in the Russian army. Now, the question was which way to go? He didn't have much. No money. No job. That was exactly his position, but still and then his eyes turned to watch the people pushing toward the platform.

Not many people were boarding the train for Lipetsk, Pavel noticed as he brushed the thick dark hair from his eyes. He climbed the steps up to the platform and sat down in a seat toward the back of the car. At this point, he was too angry and too bitter to talk to anyone. Besides, you never knew who worked with the KGB or was a staunch party member.

At that moment, Pavel noticed a conductor walking rapidly through the train, checking identifications and anything that appeared out of the ordinary.

The conductor reached out his hand for the man's identification and ticket. "Pavel Lubov? You are going to Lipetsk?"

"Yes," Pavel answered, frowning as he handed the conductor his identification and ticket for Lipetsk. He turned away from the uniformed conductor and gazed intently at the tall buildings of Moscow as they moved rapidly past the window.

In a few hours he would be back home. He rubbed his hands together in eagerness. Where would all this bitterness take him? He was never a staunch party member. He hated communism and what it had done to the country. He wanted to become involved in a party that felt the same way. Fight for freedoms. Was this safe? What the hell did he care about safety?

Just as he turned back to the window, a tall man grabbed him by the shoulders. It was his friend, Ivan. Pavel gasped in surprise! It was unbelievable to see him, right here on the train! They used to play together as children.

"Kogo ya vizhul Pavel Lubov! It's great to see you. What a surprise to see you here and right here on this train! Just coming home?"

Pavel stood up and embraced his old friend. "Ivan Dimitri! What a homecoming for me to see you! We've got lots to talk about."

"Out of the army for good?"

"Yes, out of the a-rm-y for good!" Pavel said bitterly.

"I can understand that. I'd be angry, too. I've heard plenty about the army."

"Say, how are my mother and father doing? It's difficult to tell just from reading their letters."

"Doing pretty well. Say, I'm going with a fine girl now. Her name is Marina. We may get married this fall."

"That's great, Ivan. Where are you working now?"

"Same place. The steel factory in Lipetsk. Maybe I can get you a job there. What do you think?"

"No thanks, Ivan," Pavel responded with stern determination. He clenched his hands as he spoke. By God, this was the last thing he wanted to do! "I've been thinking about this for a long time now."

"What will you do, then? Jobs aren't all that easy to find."

"My mind is made up. I plan to go over to the university tomorrow and make some plans." Pavel knew that he couldn't get anywhere by doing labor in the steel company even though this is where his parents worked. But the idea ground against his plans to get a good job and join a political party to work against the Communist Party that he had grown to hate.

"That will be tough. Most students go directly from high school and also pass stiff examinations. And, remember you are twenty years old now."

"So, I'm twenty. I'm determined to do it. I didn't pass the exams when I was finishing high school, but now, I don't have to take the exams since I've served in the army. I think I can make it!"

"Okay, but can you afford it?" Anton knew that Pavel's parents were poor like everyone else in Russia.

Pavel felt the anger rising in his chest. He hated people who tried to direct him, especially out of what he felt dedicated to do. "Well, I can count on forty rubles a month from the government for books. I'll get some job working nights or weekends."

"You're sure determined. You sound like what your grandfather used to say. I remember him. We were just kids then."

Pavel felt angry. Was this the way to come home? Having someone tell him what he should do next? But this was his old friend, Ivan. People were obviously used to letting the government plan their lives—just don't step out of line. Well, to hell with that, he thought!

"My grandfather talked to me about many things. Before I went into the service, I was thinking about what I was going to do with my life. Like a lot of other kids that age, for me the things that older people say to you don't really have much meaning. Once he said, 'Never mind competition. You don't compete with others, you compete with yourself.' At that time, I wondered what he was talking about. I was only seventeen. Now, I'm beginning to realize what he meant."

"You'll soon have the chance to find out, Pavel. My younger brother, Andrey, plans to go to the university in several years. He's doing very well in school."

Several hours later, the train pulled into the station in Lipetsk. Pavel rose quickly and hurried through the cars. Ivan smiled at his friend's eagerness.

As they moved through the crowds at the station, Pavel broke into a big smile at the sight of his old pal, Ivan. How great to see him! They used to go to sporting events together as teenagers.

Anton looked in amazement as he hurried to greet Pavel. "What a surprise to see you! How does it feel to be free and out of the army?'"

"The army," Pavel said with disgust. "How can I ever forget those camps? Do you remember the lies that the government fed us? We were supposed to have the strongest, the best fit army in the world. Maybe it was the largest, but certainly not the best equipped and trained. I would call it a drunken bunch of untrained people!"

"Yes, I was in the army, too! You had to think like a criminal or you wouldn't survive. The officers encouraged us to steal. It was like being with a pack of wolves. You even had to learn to howl like a wolf!"

"Sounds bad. Let's catch the bus for home. You coming with us, Anton? " Ivan asked. "You said you wanted to borrow some tools."

Anton nodded and motioned Pavel to come with them. "You live in the same apartment building. Right?"

"Okay, but I'm going to get off at the store on the way home. Haven't eaten since I left camp early this morning."

"Go to it, fellow!" Anton called after him.

It seemed strange to Pavel to be back and moving around among the people on the streets. Until just this morning, army officers were ordering him around. "Get up, you stupid bastards!" Always they were called "stupid bastards." He had to put all this behind him.

Pavel jumped off the bus about a block away from the store. He heard some shouting and screaming. A large crowd was fighting and pushing in front of the food store. Suddenly, two men appeared carrying wooden clubs. They started hitting the people in front of them in the attempt to get ahead.

Then, Pavel heard a young boy call out in pain. He hurried toward him, pushing people away as he hurried through the crowd. One old woman was trying to get away from the crowd. Her head was bleeding, and she was shaking as she wove unsteadily back down the street.

"There is a little bread left, but I cannot get it!" she cried in dismay.

Pavel turned to help her reach a bench. How horrifying, he thought. The people have probably been waiting for hours. Now, they have turned on each other. They have no one to help them! Can't the damn government get anything right? Pavel thought angrily to himself. They just care about power and control.

The youngster that was crying out for help lay exhausted on the pavement. The men with the clubs had left him, believing he was dead. Now, people were stepping over him in their rush to get some food.

"What are you doing, you murderers?" Pavel yelled at the men. "What the hell is the matter with you?"

"The young punk wouldn't get out of the way," one of the men shouted.

In his anger, Pavel yelled back, "You're nothing but a piece of shit!" Pavel turned to run after him. But the men had left the scene and were lost in the crowded street. He vowed he would never let this go unavenged.

Pavel kneeled down beside the boy and carefully raised his head. Some blood was running from his nose.

"Is that you, Ivan?" the boy asked.

"Ivan?"

"Yes, Ivan is my brother."

"Your brother? Oh, my God. You must be Andrey, Ivan's brother." And here, he had just left Ivan on the bus. Ivan and his mother, Olga were neighbors in the same apartment building as Pavel's mother and father.

The boy was still alive, but he had several bad bruises on his forehead and deep cuts on the sides of his head. Of all times and places to find Andrey, lying out here on the street like a piece of garbage, Pavel thought angrily. Another man noticed the young boy struggling to breathe.

"Come, I'll help you get him home. I'm Alex. I saw what happened. People lost their tempers when the store ran out of bread." He turned to make sure no one was listening. "But you don't read about any of this in the newspapers or see it on television."

When they reached the apartment house where Pavel and his friends lived, they carried Andrey up the outside stairs to the second floor.

Andrey's mother opened the door and stared in disbelief at her son. "What happened? What happened?'" she cried in despair. "Who did this to my son?"

"The crowd in front of the store started fighting, Mrs. Dimitri. Some men were beating people with clubs," Pavel explained, his face red with anger.

"The crowd just went crazy when the store ran out of bread. Some of the people had been standing in line for hours," said Alex.

"So what? I stand in line for hours lots of days!" Olga cried in despair as the men carried the boy to the couch.

Andrey began to move his head slowly, moaning deeply in pain. Then, he opened his eyes, looked at his mother and seemed to fall off into a deep sleep.

"Where is Ivan? He should be back here."

"He is stopping over at Anton's place for a few minutes."

"Go quickly down to the first floor, Pavel. Dr. Korotch is probably home. He is very old, but maybe he can help."

A few minutes later, Pavel returned with the elderly doctor. The old man was breathing heavily from climbing the many stairs. He sat down by the couch and began to take the boy's pulse. "Get cold cloths and put them on your son's head, Mrs. Dimitri," he instructed. "I have some antiseptic to put on the cuts."

"How is he, Doctor? Is he going to be all right?"

The doctor waited for what seemed like an interminable amount of time before he answered. He shook his head slowly. "Andrey probably has a concussion. Only time will tell if he'll come out of the coma. I am very sorry, Mrs. Dimitri. I'll do the best I can for him."

Pavel watched Olga place some cloths on Andrey's head. Her face was strained and filled with worry and concern. What would Ivan think when he got home? He was not the type to react foolishly or suddenly. Usually, he was quiet and accepted things as they came along. But this was different. This was his brother.

"These things happen too often, Pavel. People turn on each other in anger. They don't realize what they're doing! If you hadn't come along just at that moment, he would have died. You saved him!" Olga held a handkerchief against her face as she sobbed uncontrollably, her shoulders rising and falling in grief.

"You saved him!" The words permeated Pavel's mind. He held his head in his hands. But would Andrey live? Could he live a normal life after this or would he be consumed with hate and revenge like so many others? Where would it all lead to—submission or civil war?

Olga tried to get some response from Andrey. He had always been such strong, determined boy, but now he lay so limp and unresponsive on the coach as though he were in a deep, deep sleep.

Pavel could see how worried she was about her son. For a while he talked about some of the childhood games he use to play with Andrey. But then, their eyes would turn back to Andrey, lying so still, so lifeless…and the terrible reality settled down on them like a final sentence with no hope.

A few minutes later, Ivan rushed into the room. His face was filled with anxiety. Someone outside the building had told him about

16

Andrey. He knelt down by his brother's side and held him close to him. His eyes were filled with tears.

"What beast did this to Andrey? What beast? I'll find him! I'll kill him, if it's the last thing I do!" Ivan moved quickly to the door. Pavel tried to stop him.

"Get away from me!" he shouted. "This is my fight!"

"Listen, Ivan! If you start a fight with these men, you could end up in prison for years. This won't help Andrey. He needs our help!"

But words at this time meant nothing to Ivan. He rushed to the door.

Pavel called again from the hallway. "Stop! Wait a minute!" But Ivan refused to listen and dashed down to the street.

This wasn't like Ivan! He had never seen Ivan so angry, so out of control. He had already just seen the anger and mobs of people out of control on the streets near the store. Now, it was his friend, Ivan. Pavel gripped his hands in dismay. The Dimitri's had been neighbors in this apartment house for many years. It was not like Ivan to dash out to the street, ready for a fight. He had never been a person of sudden anger and quick action, more reserved and quiet like his father who had just been laid to rest a year.

Just as he started to go back to the Dimitri apartment, Pavel's father appeared in the hallway. His arms were outstretched to greet his son. "Pavel, come here to your father. It's good to see you safe and well."

Pavel embraced his father. They held each other for a few minutes, then stepped back to look into each other's eyes. Pavel brushed the tears away with his sleeve. This was the moment he had been waiting for all these years, but the words choked in his throat.

The wrinkles in Valentin's face moved with emotion as he smiled at his son with pride. "Come, look and see who's here!" Valentin's eyes darted back and forth with enthusiasm.

Pavel wanted to tell his father about Andrey, but then he glanced past his father. Standing by the window was a very attractive young woman. It was Lidiia! His love, who was waiting for him, wanting him!

At the sight of Pavel, she hurried across the room and gave him a warm hug and raised her lips to his. Her face reflected the joy she felt at seeing him again.

17

"So, you're finally home! I've missed you so much. How are you?" Her questions came in a rush of girlish excitement. She was almost twenty, but looked much younger. Her long blonde hair was drawn back from her face.

Pavel felt overwhelmed. Everything seemed to be happening all at once. Pavel turned and wiped his forehead. He searched for the words and the control that he usually had within himself. He reached out and drew Lidiia close to him. This beautiful girl had been waiting for him. His travel case was filled with her letters that professed her love for him, and he often tossed at night thinking of holding her in his arms.

"What are you planning to do now, Pavel? Get a job or what?"

"Well, like I was explaining in my last letter, I've got to get a profession. I plan to enroll in the university. Maybe study languages. Depends on what the counselor recommends, Lidiia. But, I really believe that it's the best thing to do. "

He could see the disappointment in her face. Maybe she was thinking about settling down and getting married. They had to talk. But he couldn't think about that right now. The shock of seeing Andrey almost beaten to death was still before his eyes. Would the boy die? What would his mother do?

"What's the matter, Pavel?" His father's sharp words tore through his feelings like a sharp knife. "Ask Lidiia to sit down. I'll go and get some sweets from the kitchen."

"It won't be easy, Pavel. You'll be competing against seventeen year-old students, and most of them already have a background in the English language."

Pavel nodded. "Yes, I know. And I know it won't be easy, but still I've got to do this before I can even think about a future for us—" He stopped talking when his father entered the room with the plate of sweets.

He rose quickly and told his father what had happened to Andrey at the store and how badly Andrey had been beaten.

Valentin shook his head. His eyes darted around the room as though searching for a solution. "Your mother will be home any minute now. She can go to Olga and help her. We must be able to do something."

Later, when Lidiia rose to leave, she brushed Pavel's cheek with a slow kiss and searched his face for a response. But she found only dismay and trouble in his eyes.

18

"I'll get in touch with you, Lidiia," Pavel promised. "We have lots to talk about, but this is a bad time right now."

Valentin watched Lidiia walk down the hall. He glanced at Pavel with a slow smile. "She'd make a nice girl for you, son. You should think about that. You're twenty years old now."

A few minutes later, Marina appeared hurrying toward them with a sack of groceries. She had married Valentin over twenty-five years ago when she was very young. She still had the complexion and vitality of a girl in her early thirties.

She almost dropped the groceries when she saw Pavel coming from the doorway. "My son, you are home at last!" She lay the packages on the table and moved rapidly to embrace her son. "Oh, I've missed you so much! You just can't imagine."

"Yes, and it's great for me to be home again and out of that cursed army."

"Say, wasn't that Lidiia I saw just crossing the street? She must have just come from this apartment! I'll bet she was excited to see you."

"Yes, but a terrible thing has happed here, Mother. On the way home today from the station, I saw a large crowd rioting in front of that neighborhood food store. They were very angry. Then I heard screams and saw two men beating a young boy because he was in their way. It was Andrey, Mrs. Dimitri's boy! He was supposed to pick up some milk on the way home from school."

Pavel stopped suddenly and drew in his breath sharply. "Dr. Korotch is with him. He thinks Andrey has had a concussion. He's in a coma !"

Valentin quickly motioned to his wife. "We've got to do something for them! Marina, go with Pavel to help Olga. See what you can do."

When they entered the Dimitri's apartment, Olga was crying quietly. Marina embraced her and tried to comfort her. She said that the doctor would be back later. Her face was filled with despair.

They looked at the silent figure of Andrey on the couch. There was no sign of movement. Slowly, the boy's face seemed to soften into oblivion. He neither heard nor understood. Pavel glanced around the room. He felt the dark despair slowly coming towards them from the shadows near the window. It was getting late. Where was Ivan? He should be back by now. Pavel was determined to find him. They had been so close through the years, especially in high school. Ivan was always the quiet one, but Pavel was different. He liked to plan activities and tried to persuade Ivan to be more active. But still, they liked to plan what they thought were adventures together, jumping off steep rocks and yelling to scare the girls or pretending that they had encountered a very wild bear.

Pavel quietly slipped from the room and hurried down the street. Someone would know where he was. He had to find him before he got in a fight with the men who beat Andrey.

It was late. Almost midnight, and Pavel had been searching the streets for any sign of Ivan. Suddenly, just ahead, he saw a tall dark figure walking swiftly toward a bar that was still open. He was sure it was Ivan!

"Hey, Ivan what are you doing?'

Ivan turned around quickly. He frowned at Pavel. "What are *you* doing here? Get out of the way. I'm going into this bar and get the man who beat up Andrey."

"How?"

"I'll show you *how!*" Ivan pushed the door open. He moved quickly through the room toward a group of men drinking beer in a dark corner of the bar. Quickly, he swung at one of the men.

Pavel could see the flash of a knife in Ivan's hand. Maybe he could stop this fight if he moved fast enough.

A tall, burly man rose from his chair. He wavered as he moved toward Ivan. "You son of a bitch! You come to me because your brother doesn't know how to fight!" His speech was thick from drinking the beer.

"My brother is just a kid, you drunken fool! I know who you are. You're Yakov, the troublemaker. Now, you're a murderer!"

At those words, the man lunged toward Ivan and reached for his knife. But Ivan was quicker and knocked the man down on the floor.

Ivan would probably kill him! He lips were moving, and he was leaning over Yakov. Revenge was hot on his breath!

At that moment, the back door banged open. The manager rushed toward the two men. "Get out! Get out! Both of you. Else I'll call the police." He motioned to Ivan and Pavel to leave. Ivan started to object, but Pavel quickly pushed him away.

"Let's go! Let's get the hell out of here!"

"I'm going to get him! My brother is dying because of that son of a bitch!" He glared at Pavel and slipped the knife back into his pocket.

"Let's get the hell home. We can't fight him and all his friends. Besides, you know the Russian legal system. These men would probably bribe the militia or the judge. Then what? You could end up spending the rest of your life in prison."

"So? I can't let this man get away with this. His name is Yakov. Don't forget his name, Pavel. If he should kill me, go for him. And show him no mercy. Rip him apart!"

The words echoed in Pavel's mind as they made their way back to the apartment. No one was out in the street. Just the darkness that filled the air and the madness of the night. He had just left the insanity and inefficiency of the Russian army and now here he was involved in a street war. "Rip him apart!" Where would all this revenge take him?

Chapter 2

Pavel woke early the next morning. There was no sunlight coming through the windows. His mother and father had already left for work at the Lipetsk Steel Factory. They were very poor. Still, his father had worked very hard to make the small apartment comfortable for the family and had made a wooden separation that divided the two rooms. They had one cupboard, one very large box for their clothes, a small television set, and a big round table in the middle of the room. There was no hot water or shower. Neighbors all shared a lavatory down the hall.

Pavel rose and glanced at his watch. It was time to catch the bus and head for the university. As he remembered, the buildings were on a hill overlooking the Voronezh River and the city below.

He felt the emotion rising within him as he saw the buildings and students hurrying to classes. How often he had thought and dreamed about studying at this university. His grandfather had pointed out the advantage of an education to him many times, but Pavel was too young to really understand.

He hurried into the building, anxious to see the rooms along the hallways that had been a part of his feelings all during his years in the army. This would be a new beginning. He was old enough now to realize that his future was in his hands. It was up to him. This would take a lot of determination. The decision was strong and moving in his mind.

Pavel found the office of admissions near the end of the hall. A kind, dark-haired woman greeted him and motioned for him to sit down. She studied his papers carefully.

"I'm Ira Akhmatova," she announced, smiling pleasantly over a pair of dark-rimmed glasses. "What courses are you thinking about taking here at the university?"

Pavel pushed some dark strands of hair from his forehead. "I'm not sure. Maybe teaching, but I don't know in what field. I like to read, and I read a lot."

"Well, perhaps you would like to study mathematics or science."

"Maybe literature?" Pavel began.

"No, that's a girl thing, because girls like to sit and just read for hours. Ninety-five percent of the girls that are admitted to the university go into that field. Can you afford the time to read so many books?"

The question was important. Pavel studied the alternatives and his answer carefully. That didn't sound like an alternative. He knew he would need to get a part-time job. Did he have the time to read many, many books?

"We have Russian and world history. It is mostly about Soviet history, starting around 1917."

Pavel knew he certainly did not want to study about the Communist Party. He had strong beliefs that the Communist Party was a sadistic, fascist organization. Because of his grandparents' accounts, he knew that the Communist Party had done terrible things.

"Then, the only thing left we have to offer you is in the department of foreign languages, basically, English."

"In school we studied German," Pavel began slowly. "I know absolutely nothing about English."

"Well, then, that is the best opportunity for you. You know something about the other subjects, but you know nothing about English. This is a good place for you to start," Olga said encouragingly.

Something began to move inside Pavel. He felt it beginning to form in his mind. It stirred his thinking. Studying a completely different language presented a greater challenge for him. But would it be too difficult? No! He knew he could do it! He looked up and smiled, relieved that he had made a decision. "I agree. That's a good idea, Mrs. Akhmatova. I'll study English and take the English courses."

Pavel turned and walked back down the hall, his decision moving out in front of him. Was this the right decision? Well, he had made up his mind.

He stepped outside and sat down on a bench to wait for the next bus. Another half an hour. From this position on the hill, he could see a magnificent view of the city and the Voronezh River. It would make a beautiful painting if the artist would ignore the view of the huge steel plant nearby with its tall chimneys and concentrate on the trees and winding river.

Then, Pavel remembered his decision to study English. He moved the idea around in his mind. There was little doubt in Pavel's mind that to be proficient in the English language would take all of his strength and all of his abilities.

Suddenly, his grandfather's face seemed to emerge from the morning mist rising from the river."Let me tell you, Pavel. Listen carefully," his grandfather advised. "Don't choose the easiest way. If you go the easiest way, maybe you can achieve greater results, but it doesn't teach you very much. If you take the most difficult path, you will become a better person."

His grandfather's words often came to him when he was confused and unsure of which way to go. He respected and loved his grandfather. Now, his grandfather's words filled his mind and fired his determination.

At that moment, he heard a voice coming from behind him. He turned around. It was Skitt, a young high school student that lived in Pavel's apartment house. Pavel was surprised to see someone he knew approaching him with a big smile.

"So you are coming here to school, too, Pavel?"

"Yes, I just enrolled."

"Good for you. I'm going to study science."

"Fine. You should do well in that field. You said you made good grades in science and math in high school."

"Maybe I will become a great Russian scientist, and the Communist Party will reward me for my accomplishments and..." Skitt stopped suddenly when he noticed Pavel's frown and obvious disapproval.

"Don't talk to me about Communism, Skitt," Pavel said, gripping his hands with anger. "You are very young, but I would fight to my last breath to do away with Communism in Russia."

"Why do you say that, Pavel? Have people have told you bad things about Communism? That doesn't make it so!"

"No, what I know about Communism is what I've heard and seen first hand. I will tell you this, but keep it to yourself, Skitt. You should know that Stalin kept thousands and thousands of men in labor camps in Siberia because they were enemies of the people or because they were traitors. That is what the Communist Party told the people. Those were all lies."

"Lies? How do you know that, Pavel? This is what my teachers told us! Now, they can't be wrong—or our history books either!"

Pavel shook his head and leaned forward. "Listen! You've got to listen! I learned from my mother that my father's father died a terrible death in one of the purges in 1938. When my grandmother, Karolina, married my Grandfather, Andrey Lubov, he had a son by a previous marriage. He had a very good job as manager in the horse yard. At that time, everything was drawn by horse. His job was considered to be very important. It was a better job than most people had in the neighborhood. Andrey was arrested by the KGB because somebody took a pencil and punctured the eyes in the Stalin portrait that hung over his desk in his office."

"He was arrested because of what someone else had done? Are you sure about that, Pavel?" Skitt said frowning and shaking his head.

"Well, it's the absolute truth." Pavel tried to control his anger. Why couldn't Skitt understand? "It was a terrible, terrible thing to do, Skitt. Somebody had already reported what had been done to the portrait before my grandfather could do anything about it. At that time, some person who had bad feelings toward you would just say some lie, and the KGB would come and arrest the whole family."

"Did they take your grandmother away, too?"

"No they took Andrey and his teenage son away. Why? Nobody knows. There are too many questions and not enough answers. At that time there was no trial. Once you were arrested, you just vanished. Nobody knows anything about you, whether you are dead or alive. That's how the Communist Party kept people in great fear and controlled them. They didn't kill just a few people. Millions died."

"What happened to your grandfather and his son?"

"The only thing I learned was that in the late 30s after his arrest, my grandfather was transported to a Siberian labor camp. A man saw him boarding a train—the same train that they used to transport cattle. He said that he saw my grandfather standing by the train, holding his son. He kissed the boy goodbye and tried to be brave for the sake of his son who was crying and clinging to him. What happened to him or his son, nobody seemed to know. My grandmother was pregnant at the time. My father was born months later. She never remarried."

"That's a cruel story," said Skitt staring down at his feet. "Somebody does something to a little portrait and the man and his son die. That's terrible."

"Yes, the craziness didn't stop. It went on and on for decades and decades. My grandmother wouldn't talk about what happened because she still had this deep, deep fear of being executed if she said anything."

"How terrible it must have been for your grandmother!" Demitri said as he quickly wiped the tears from his eyes with his sleeve.

Then, Pavel could see that the boy was greatly moved. His dark eyes were filled with sorrow. "Yes, Skitt, this story still haunts me. I never saw a picture of my grandfather. Maybe at the time he was arrested the KGB took away all his possessions so the family wouldn't remember him. So if you ask me about Communism, I can tell you plenty. But, Skitt, this is a true story. It really happened. It has helped me in making decisions and understanding our history. I hope it will help you. I know you will do well here at the university. You're a serious student! Good luck!"

Skitt smiled and gave Pavel a quick slap on the back as he hurried into the university.

Pavel decided to take a walk along the river. Typical for early September, the day had started out very cold, but now the sun was shining brightly, casting shadows through the branches of the trees. Here, everything seemed so serene and in its proper place. So natural. Then, he thought of Yakov. A man would beat a young boy almost to the point of death just to get him out of the way. And what would happen next? He felt sure that Yakov would soon find Ivan. One or the other of them would probably end up dead. Revenge usually drove a man to destruction.

He knew that Ivan wanted to get married. He never was interested in an education or Russian politics. Up to now, he had been a quiet man, only interested in a job, food on the table and a family. For himself, he wanted an education, but making money was not of primary importance. Politics? He frowned and spat on the ground.

26

Well, that was different. He wanted to support a political party or movement that would bring more freedoms for the people.

Suddenly, there was a movement in the branches over his head. It was a squirrel jumping from branch to branch. The little fellow raced down the truck of the tree to get a drink of water near the river's edge.

Pavel kneeled down by the river bank and watched the squirrel until it finished drinking the water. Then, he picked up a stone and threw it out across the river. Large circles of water formed where the stone had dropped. Pavel looked intently at the circles spreading out across the river. In a way, it was like many ideas or concepts. As the idea spread, no one questioned the truth. It often engulfed a whole nation. Like Communism. Like wars. Then hatred and destruction. The people would become like slaves in bondage. Pavel swore to himself it wouldn't happen. He wouldn't let it happen.

It was getting dark, Pavel noticed. He had just time to catch the bus. He was looking forward to meeting some of his friends late that afternoon. They would just be getting out of work around five-thirty.

Where were they supposed to meet? At a bar about a half mile from his apartment building. Ivan had made the connections.

"Don't worry," Ivan had promised. "I'll get our old group together, and we'll have a hell of a good time."

Pavel hurried toward the old bar. In some ways, he was not surprised that it had not changed over the past few years. No money. People drank liquor the same as always, but often it was home-made wine, a little beer. Sometimes, they all pitched in for a bottle of vodka and just passed the bottle around.

Ivan was the first to arrive. "I guess we both have something to celebrate, Pavel. I got out of the army about four months ago."

"What are you doing now that you are a free man again?"

"Hey, wait a minute, man. Free? Not the way I feel about this communist government. It was all pushed down our throats since the time we were kids."

" So what can we do about it? I think it's better to forget about it!"

"I'm thinking of joining a political party that feels the same way I do. Or get a group together and start our own party!"

"Not so fast, Pavel. Listen, everywhere you go you will be restricted and watched by the KGB. You'll soon find out. Even television stations and newspapers are monitored."

27

Pavel frowned. "Maybe so. But there are ways."

"And besides that, you can't buy the books and tapes you want," Ivan said angrily as he pounded on the table.

So people were beginning to realize this, Pavel thought as he turned it over in his mind. Probably, talking about it quietly in the corners of bars and over tables in the privacy of their kitchens.

At that moment, a tall, muscular man strode rapidly through the bar and grabbed Pavel by the shoulders. He looked down into Pavel's puzzled frown.

"Hey, friend, don't you remember me? I'm your old pal, Maksim Romano."

Pavel's face broke into a big smile. He brushed his dark hair from his forehead as though to clear his memory. "Yes, of course. I didn't recognize you with that dark beard."

Maksim glanced over at Ivan. "Let's order some beer for our pal. So you're out of the army? What do you plan to do now?"

"Well, I enrolled at the university this morning. I plan to study English. Maybe teach. But I don't know about that for sure."

"How do your parents feel about your going to the university?"

"They're all for it. They even want to give me some money, but I won't take it. I know how hard they work, so I'll get a part-time job."

"Well, I'm getting along okay at the steel factory and plan to marry Karolina in the spring. That's what you should do. Get a job and get married. That's the way to go!" His voice sounded insistent.

But Pavel shook his head. He felt irritated at his friend's words. He felt the anger starting to rise in his throat. But, Maksim was his friend. He meant no harm. "Maybe so, but…" Pavel stopped abruptly when he caught sight of three men entering the bar.

"Look, who's here! Boris, Romanov, and Yaroslav. Do you remember them, Pavel?" Ivan asked, pleased that he was able to get the old group together.

"Sure, I remember. We used to play together when we were kids. We all used to go down to the river and swim."

"Yes, sometimes, we would help some of the neighbors harvest their crops in the field. After that, your grandfather would often take us down to the river for a swim after we worked real hard," Zhupey added thoughtfully.

The two men sat there quietly, their eyes fixed at nothing in particular, lost in the maze of the past. Suddenly, Maksim glanced over at Pavel. His eyes lighted up with a sudden recollection. "As I remember, once you said that your grandfather was in the war?"

"Yes, Grandfather Stepan. Did I ever tell you about when he was taken to a crematorium in a German prison camp? Well, at one time, Stepan couldn't find any job. He started stealing in the flea market, so he was put in jail. While he was in prison, World War II began. The prisoners were not freed or liberated. They were all taken to the front to fight. The guards took the prisoners to the front lines and stationed themselves just two yards behind them to watch the line of prisoners. If they refused to shoot or turned to run away, the guards shot them. Yes, they shot their own people at the war front.

"The guards gave them rifles and told them, 'There's the enemy. You attack them. If you die, you die, but you're not supposed to be taken prisoner, and you're not supposed to turn around and run.'"

"Those were some orders!" Maksim exclaimed. "So what did your grandfather do then?"

"One day, Stepan, along with some other Russians, was surrounded by the Germans. They were taken as prisoners and transported to Germany in cattle trucks. Everybody ended up in the prison camp.

"One day, the Germans ordered them to take off all their clothes and form a line. They were taken to a crematorium. Stepan was naked as he stood in line. The guards constantly watched them. Then, for one split moment, the guard's attention was distracted. He turned away. Stepan ran to escape through the little side door that they used to bring in fuel for the furnaces. A few men ran with him. They knew it was their last chance.

"Stepan heard some shots. The Germans searched for the prisoners and captured some of them, but Stepan hid in the tall grass until the sun went down. From that time on, he hid in the woods or the bushes during the day. He moved and traveled at night."

"He was lucky to get out of that camp alive and get away!" Ivan exclaimed. "That's a story you'd never forget! And what a wonderful man your grandfather was. I know I'll never forget him!"

"Pavel studied the faces of his friends. He had not seen Romanov, Yaroslav or Zhupey since they were youngsters playing in the fields and swimming in the river. "What have you guys been doing all these years? I haven't seen any of you since you were about twelve."

"We tried about the same things as everyone else, I guess," Romanov said, rubbing his forehead. "We went to the university for a few years, then got a job. The instructors were very demanding. It was too much. At least for me, anyway. I decided I'd better get to work and make some money."

"Let's get another round of beer," Ivan suggested.

"Good idea!" Maksim said with enthusiasm. He threw some money on the table. Then he stood up and gathered the rest of the money that was thrown on the table. He walked across the room to the bar.

A minute later, Maksim was back with the foaming mugs. The men picked them up eagerly.

"Say, what have you been doing the past few years?" Zhupey asked.

"First, there was the army. Now, I've got a job helping to repair some old buildings down by the river."

"Speaking of the army, I'll bet your grandfather was glad to come home and get on with his life after that experience. Right, Pavel?" Ivan asked.

"Well, first of all, he had one tough time getting home. First, he grabbed some clothes that a woman had hung out on a line to dry. He waited until the woman had gone back into the house and then grabbed the clothes. When the woman came back from the house, she saw him. Stepan thought sure she would inform the Germans, but she didn't do that. Instead, she gave him some food and clothing. He was surprised that this woman would do this because she was German and her husband was in the war, fighting the Russians. But she let him stay for the night in her house.

"Stepan left and started on his long journey back to Russia. One day, he saw some tanks moving. As he watched the tanks moving across the field, he realized that Germans didn't usually move across the fields. Then he saw that they were not German tanks. He went out to meet them. I can remember my grandfather telling me, 'I went out into the field and put my hands up in the air to surrender. I was just looking into their faces and the signs on the tanks. I knew then they were not Germans or Russians. They were Americans!

"At that time, the Americans were picking up stray prisoners all across Germany. They had temporary camps for prisoners. My grandfather remembered that he was treated extremely well. He was given lots of food and was not treated like a prisoner or animal. After all his experiences in Russian and German prisons, he didn't expect to be treated like a human in that camp. But that paradise didn't last long—just a few weeks.

"Then the allies turned them back to Russia. The Russians took Stepan to another camp which was a labor camp for prisoners. There they were treated like dirt. It was the same reason. He was a traitor. If a Russian soldier was captured during the war, he was considered a traitor. The government also invented all kinds of reasons to put men in prison. They made them work fifteen hours a day, and they didn't have to pay them. At that time in Russia, there weren't enough men to do the manual labor in the country."

"I never heard that part of your grandfather's story before," Maksim began thoughtfully. "No wonder your family has such bad feelings against Stalin and the Communist Party. But I'll say this. Your grandfather sure had a lot of grit."

"Well, Pavel, now you are back with the rest of us. What do you think of our Russian society? Do you approve of the government?" Maksim questioned, searching Pavel's face for some indication of his attitude.

"Listen, the government is saying we are the builders of the most advanced society in the world. But look around you. The people don't look like builders of the most advanced society. The streets are filled with Russians walking and standing around, mostly drunk! Now, Brezhnev is in power. Every day there are pompous speeches on the television about our achievements, yet the grocery stores are empty."

"Yes, lies and more lies and more brainwashing," Zhupey agreed.

"People are beginning to talk about change," Maksim began. Communist Party, changes in the government. In the past, no one would dare to say anything against the Communist Party."

"That's right. The Communist Party was everywhere—running our lives and coming down on people with a heavy boot." Pavel emphasized "Communist" with a particularly bitter tone.

Maksim did not miss the bitterness. "What would you do, Pavel? You sound like you hate Communism."

31

"We need changes. Nothing is working. We're told a bunch of lies. All the time. Lies! Lies!"

"Yes, a lot of people are saying that. So far it's just quiet talk. Getting nowhere!"

"They've got to do more than that, Maksim!" Pavel's voice rose in fierce determination. "What the hell! Are we a society of wimps and mice?"

"I agree with you, Pavel. All the way," Ivan agreed, pounding his fist on the table. "In fact, I'm thinking of either starting a political party or joining one that's not a lap-dog for the Communists."

"Better be careful," Zhupey warned, "Else the KGB will drag you down to headquarters and beat you up. It happens all the time!" Zhupey exclaimed, his face getting red with anger.

"To hell with the KGB!" Pavel exclaimed. He noticed Zhupey was looking anxiously toward the men at the bar.

"Okay, okay, calm down," Zhupey said. He had noticed a tall man glancing in their direction. The man certainly wasn't there when Maksim had gone to get more beer. Who was he? Had he been listening in on their conversations?

"You worried about that guy at the bar overhearing us? Forget it. He's just another Russian getting drunk." But Pavel took another look and choked on his beer. He had seen him somewhere before.

Zhupey looked up to see Pavel staring at the man. Pavel's eyes were steel-blue and calculating as the man approached their table.

"Do you remember me? I'm Yakov," he said forcefully, banging his fist on the table as he spoke. "Now, you tell your friend, Ivan, that I'm going to get him. Like this!" Yakov slipped a knife out of his pocket and drew it across Pavel's throat.

The group at the table rose quickly to intervene. Ivan sprang into action and forced himself on Yakov. But Yakov was quicker. He dashed through the room and made a quick leap up the stairs and out the door.

"Let's go after him!" Ivan shouted. "We'll make borscht out of him!"

Pavel remembered that Ivan had a quick temper. Ready to fight. "No, wait, Ivan. If we go after him now, he'll get his gang of ruffians together for a street fight, and we'll all end up in jail."

"His gang? What are you talking about?"

"Ivan's younger brother was attacked by this man in front of a food store. The crowd was mad because the store had sold out of bread. Andrey was up further in the line. Yakov was angry and pushed Andrey down and started beating him. He almost killed the kid! Then he ran off with a gang of ruffians."

"How is the boy doing now?" Ivan asked deeply concerned.

"Still in a coma."

"I remember the day," Ivan recalled. I had returned home earlier with Ivan. You wanted to get some snacks and cheese at the store."

"Then, when Ivan got home, he was ranging mad and went to look for Yakov. I followed him and caught up with him just as he was entering a bar. Ivan and Yakov got into a fight, and the manager ordered Ivan and me out of the place," said Pavel.

"Was Yakov alone?"

"No, he was with a group of very sinister-looking men. They're up to no good, believe me."

"Let's have some more beer," Ivan suggested.

"Not for me," Pavel answered as he felt down into his pockets. "I've got to get on home."

"I'll go with you. I live near your apartment," Ivan suggested.

"Hey, let's all walk together for a ways. Just to make sure that Devil is not around," Maksim said as he looked around the table.

A few minutes later, they left the bar. The streets were dark and deserted. A few shopkeepers were just closing their stores. The lights shown through the smoke-stained windows and cast eerie shadows on the black pavement.

They walked together for about three long blocks. Then Andrey stopped and looked around. "Say, I think it would be best if we walked the rest of the way with you. No trouble."

"No, no. Ivan and I will be just fine. A street fight would cause too much attention. Yakov is far away by now," Pavel assured them.

After they left, Pavel began to feel uneasy. He heard footsteps. Every time they stopped, the footsteps stopped. He felt a slow fear creeping up his neck.

"Do you hear someone following us?" Pavel asked.

Ivan stopped and looked around. "I think you're imagining things." But his voice did not sound convincing.

Suddenly, some shouts came from a store just ahead of them. Several men dashed out of the door. They had a few sacks of food with them. The store keeper was in fast pursuit. "Help me! Help me!" he yelled pleadingly.

Pavel and Ivan chased the two men and threw them down to the pavement. They struggled to get away, but the racket had aroused some other storekeepers. Soon, a crowd gathered.

A black car sped down the street. Several policemen grabbed the men and pushed them into the police car.

"How can I thank you both," the shopkeeper began. "Here take some bread and sausage for your families."

He turned and put some of the food in a sack for each of them

"Which way are you going now?"

Pavel motioned to the two-story apartment down the street.

They walked on together. When they reached the corner, Pavel noticed some men standing around drinking wine or sharing a little vodka.

Soon, they reached the old shopkeepers 's place where he said he rented an upstairs room. He thanked them all over again.

"This night has sure turned around," Ivan said. "Here we were, hearing footsteps and thinking this guy, Yakov, and his followers were after us."

"Yes, and then we end up getting those two thieves. That storekeeper was sure grateful."

They parted just before reaching Pavel's apartment building.

Pavel noticed that the old women who had been sitting out on the benches were just leaving. It was time to prepare dinner. Undoubtedly, they had been visiting and gossiping all day as usual. They seemed to know everything about the people who lived in the apartment building. They knew he had a girl friend, Lidiia, who was waiting for him to come home from the army. He imagined that they wondered if they were still together.

Did he know himself? That was the problem. He had to put the pieces of his life together. Lidiia. The university. Join some party that opposed Communism? There was a burning feeling and a new determination rising in his chest. What should he do?

Chapter 3

Pavel rose early after a fitful night of broken sleep. He must find a part-time job to support himself or forget his university plans. It was just that simple. But for him, there was no turning back.

Around noon, Pavel returned to the apartment. He had found a part-time job at a bottling factory. He planned to work in the evenings or long hours on the weekends.

His father was home early that day. He was very pleased with Pavel's news. "Hmm, a bottling factory? That sounds good!"

Pavel smiled to himself. He knew that Valentin was thinking about the beer at the bottling factory. Some free beer. That was it.

"Well, you're doing fine, Pavel. You went to the right place! Be sure and bring some homework back with you. I'll help you with it!"

A few minutes later, there was a loud knock at the door. It was Ivan. He seemed angry. Did someone tell him about Yakov's threats in the bar?

"I heard all about Yakov! Anton told me," Ivan said. He clenched his hands into tight fists as he spoke. "That son of a bitch holding a knife to your throat! I would have killed him on the spot!"

Pavel stood up in anger and leaned over Ivan. "Yea, they deserved that! But I'd be damned to be the one to do it! Next, you'd have a gang chasing you. Then they'd stab you a thousand times and leave you to die in your own blood in the streets."

"Ah, Pavel," Ivan sighed. "Always thinking of consequences. Consequences. Consequences. But what about right now?"

"Think about it, Ivan. You have your whole life ahead of you," Valentin emphasized, reaching over to touch Ivan on the shoulder. "Think about Valerie."

"Okay, I know I have to think of those things," Ivan said, wiping the sweat from his forehead. "I know. I know. And there's Andrey, too. He's feeling better now and had a little broth last evening. I'd better get back and help out at home."

On Monday morning, Pavel hurried to the bus stop. His first class met at eight-thirty. He had been looking forward to this day for a long time. Even the sun was shining brightly. The bus pulled up to the curb, and Pavel gave the driver a smile and wave.

When Pavel reached the university, a small group of students was just going into the building. They were supposed to meet in the language classroom. Pavel noticed how young they looked and so relaxed as they laughed and joked with each other. Soon, he would be one of them, but for him it was a lifetime opportunity and commitment. No jokes filled his mind that morning.

Pavel was assigned to take linguistics, phonetics, written and spoken English, grammar and the different methods of teaching. It was the usual load of classes. Each class lasted about one and a half hours.

After the morning classes, Pavel decided to go to the language lab and listen to some tapes and concentrate on the dialogues which were recorded in perfect English. His homework was to listen to the tapes and memorize the dialogue as well as learn the phonetics and the stresses on the words. He would need to spend a lot of time here. But he was sure he could to this. He was determined to learn the English words. Anytime any doubt crept into his mind, he tossed his head and set his jaw firmly, determined to move on.

Pavel found the best method was to write down the sentences from the tape, break the sentences into fragments and then put in the stresses, the intonation and the phonetics. The next day, the teacher, Tatyana Tsipko, checked the students' homework. She called on different pupils to recite the dialogue correctly.

Pavel immediately noticed to his chagrin that his classmates already knew how to pronounce most of the words correctly. They had studied English in high school. He realized that he would have to struggle to keep up with the others.

Weeks passed, and now Pavel was deeply concerned. He was falling further and further behind the other students in his class. Something was very wrong. His friends had warned him that it would be difficult since his classmates had studied English in high school. Finally, a thought circled around and around in his mind and tormented him. He was not used to being the worst student in the class. He had to do something. But what?

Before he had time to map out a strategy, Pavel saw a familiar face through the bus window. He hurried off the bus. It was Lidiia striding confidently toward a waiting car. When she saw Pavel, she signaled for her friend to leave.

How attractive she looked in the close-fitting skirt and jacket! Why hadn't he noticed that before? he asked himself. Of course, she was much younger then. But still.

"Hello, Pavel! Just finishing your classes for the day?"

"Yes, Lidiia," Pavel said, brushing her cheek with a kiss. He put his arm around her as they walked across the street. "Come with me and let's get some coffee." How lucky he was to have met her just like this. He had been waiting to have this chance to talk with her.

"How is Andrey?" she asked after they had settled at a table and ordered the coffee. "I've been really worried about him since I called and talked to your father last evening. You were out looking for a part-time job then."

"Much better. We are all so relieved. His mother hasn't slept or eaten anything since this happened. He's out of his coma now and improving."

"I'm so glad you called me yesterday and told me all that was going on. Like Yakov threatening Ivan and even you in the bar. How terrible!"

"Yes, I'm not at all convinced that Ivan will put all this behind him and forget about revenge. He is very angry when he talks about it like he's ready to look for Yakov and kill him. But I wish he would let it go!"

"And for Andrey, too." Lidiia added. " Say, how are your classes going?"

"Not well at all. The other students are way ahead of me," Pavel said, looking down as he stirred the steaming liquid. His feelings were about as dark as the coffee's at that moment. He suddenly looked away. He didn't want Lidiia to see how bad he felt.

"Don't let it get you down, Pavel. You knew it would be tough."

Pavel shook his head in discouragement. He couldn't find the words to explain his feelings.

"You know, I think your pride has been hurt! You're not used to being at the bottom of the class! I guess you'll have to study that much harder."

"You're right. I know it won't be easy, but I've got to make it!" He glanced quickly at Lidiia. He wanted to spend more time with her. It would be difficult with the hours of study and his part-time job.

"I'm sure you'll do better, Pavel. It will just take time."

Pavel felt her warm, sympathetic smile. Her blue eyes reflected the caring and concern for him. Yes, Lidiia was a beautiful girl in so many ways.

"Remember, a few months ago, when you were in the army, you wrote how much you missed doing things together? Like the picnics in the park?"

"The picnics in the park." Pavel let the words drift through his mind. Those afternoons were strong in his memory. Just the two of them. Alone. Together. He remembered exploring her lips and soft cheeks. The warmth of the grass beneath their bodies. "And the..."

"And the sweet red wine we drank, Pavel."

Pavel sighed. "Yes, I remember those days."

"I want to go to the park. Come on! Let's go to the park. I have a little bottle of wine here in my bag."

"You don't have to work this afternoon?" Lidiia worked at the neighborhood preschool.

"No. The classes let out early today. The board is having a meeting."

When they reached the park, Pavel began to feel the difference. Those days they were much younger and had no concerns. He remembered that he used to chase Lidiia around the bushes and then draw her close to him when he had captured her. The air had been filled with their laughter.

Now, the grass was turning brown from the lack of sun and rain. It was late September. There was no sun today to keep them warm.

Lidiia raised the wine to her lips and passed the bottle to Pavel. She glanced up at him and looked for the sparkle that used to always dance in his blue eyes. Not the same, she decided. She knew that he was worried about his classes. She would help him forget about all that for awhile.

"Let me taste the wine on your lips," she teased.

Pavel put his arms around her. They fell back on the ground. The parched grass made a crunching sound beneath their bodies.

They stayed in each other's arms for a long time, kissing and caressing. Pavel softly touched her ear with his tongue and whispered gently, how good it was to be back together again.

Pavel put his arm around Lidiia as they walked away from the park. How beautiful she was and how soft was her fine hair. "I love you, Lidiia. It will always be like this."

They parted at the corner. The afternoon with Lidiia had lifted his spirits.

That evening at dinner, Valentin noticed that his son was laughing more and in a lighter mood. Then he saw a lipstick smear on his shirt collar. "Looks like you did something besides studying this afternoon, Pavel. Some new girl friend?"

"Oh, no, Father. Not some other girl. I happened to run into Lidiia after I got off the bus this afternoon."

"That's good. Lidiia is a nice girl. I hope you will think about settling down with her."

Pavel looked up in surprise. But his thoughts returned to his class. He would reorganize his day. He would spend five hours a day studying. And work very hard. But then, a lot of other students were working very hard.

Later that evening, Elsa stopped by the apartment to see Marina. Elsa lived on the first floor. She brought, Katyn, her ten-month-old baby with her.

The child seemed to be quite attentive as she listened to her mother speak. Katyn tried to say a few words. Pavel suddenly had an idea. How was this child learning to say those words?

"Your child is beginning to say some words, Olga. I wonder if she understands what they mean?" Marina asked with interest.

"She didn't understand at first. She was just repeating what my husband and I were saying. But now, she asks for 'Da, Da', 'Ma, Ma' and 'Ba, Ba' for her bottle. Little things like that."

Suddenly, a thought came to Pavel. It seemed to spiral around and around in his brain. Later, he believed that it must have been a revelation.

As he made himself a cup of coffee. He was convinced. I am like a baby learning a language, he thought.

Pavel rubbed his eyes as though to wipe away the worry that had been tantalizing him. Now, he had a plan. He would study the English language like a baby learning to speak. First, he would listen to the English pronunciation of certain words even though he didn't know the meaning of the words. Then, he would learn the meanings and begin to combine the words into sentences. Pavel felt resolute.

Now, he was confident when he was called to read in class. He stood without hesitation. The other students didn't look down at their books in disgust when he spoke. Even his instructor nodded her head in approval as he read.

Once Viktor called out to him as he left the classroom, "Hey, Pavel, you've certainly surprised me! You're doing great now."

"Thanks, Vik. I sure was worried about it for a long time."

"You getting some extra help?"

"Me? Help? I don't have any money to get extra help. Even, if I called out, 'Help, help!' there would be no help."

Viktor laughed and walked away, shaking his head.

Still, Pavel knew that the real test would come in another month. The mid-term exam was scheduled for October twentieth. Would he succeed? He had to. But still? What if?

Chapter 4

Today was an important day. Pavel hurried to get dressed. He was filled with a strong feeling of anticipation, an almost overpowering will to succeed on this morning of mornings. The day of his first semester exams. He had been studying at least five hours a day using the method he had devised along with the methods his instructor had taught him. Would this be enough to move him up in his standing with the class?

That morning he didn't stop to chat with any of the other students in the classroom. He wanted to get there early so that he could study a little before the class commenced. He had only one thought in his mind. He had to succeed.

Finally, it was his time to read. The instructor called on him to read a long dialogue in English as well as a piece that he was supposed to have written on an assigned subject. He was unaware of some of the perplexed glances of some of the students in the class. But he knew he was reading smoothly, pronouncing the words carefully and correctly.

A few hours later, the exams were finished and the class was dismissed. Pavel knew it would be late afternoon before the results of the exam would be announced. Pavel decided to stay around the university and wait. It was too important to him to leave. Anyway, the fresh air outside would feel good after the long strain in the classroom that morning.

As he climbed down the long stairs from the university, a voice called out to him. It was Viktor, his classmate. "Wait a minute, Pavel!" he called out. "Tell me, friend, what have you been doing these past weeks to improve so much? Are you studying with a private tutor or something?"

"No such thing, Viktor. I have no money for that. You think I have improved? I hope the teacher believes the same thing."

"There is no doubt about it. Tell me the truth. What put the fire into you to change so fast? What happened?"

"Well, I made a rule for myself to study five hours a day. I'm really determined to improve." Pavel frowned as he remembered how poorly he had read before. "I had to do something, the way I was going!"

"But your pronunciation is so good. And your sentences that you wrote for your paper are so much more complex. I'm really impressed."

"Thanks a lot, Viktor. Well, we'll see what happens. I'm going to wait around here today to get the results of the test and study for my other classes."

"Good luck, Pavel. I've got to run."

It was a cold day, but not too cold to walk around outside. Pavel glanced up at the tall, gray buildings of the university. He had been studying here for over three months. It was his life now.

Pavel didn't tell his friend about his own method of studying English. Also, at night, he would secretly listen in bed to the BBC broadcasts on the radio. He knew it was forbidden to Russians, but the announcers spoke such correct English that listening to them was a real help.

The wind began to sweep up across the Voronezh River. In September when Pavel first started his classes, the light wind would kick up the currents and allow the sun to cast long rays of light in the sprays of water. Now, it was different. The sun hardly shone through the thick clouds, and the river looked dark and gray. A few birds, unmindful of the cold air, flew by, sweeping lower as they passed over the university grounds. Something stirred within Pavel's memory. It was a movie he had seen on television a long time ago. A small plane had made the crossing of the Atlantic Ocean and had dipped to acknowledge the enthusiastic crowd that stood waiting for it to land at a small airport in France. Why did the memory of that movie and the birds dipping near him over the university grounds have such a significance for him, he asked himself.

Before he could contemplate the matter any further, another classmate approached him. It was Grigori.

"Hey, how come you're still here, Pavel? I'll bet you're waiting for the results of the exam. I'm sure you did well. Me, I'm not so sure." Grigori shook his head and looked down at his hands.

"Here, I have a little bread and cheese. Let's sit down up close to the building by the trees where it is warmer."

Grigori accepted the bread gratefully. "There is so little in the stores today. Say, why are you rubbing your leg there, Pavel? Don't tell me you were wounded making time in the army?"

Pavel glanced up in scorn at the word "army." "Yeah, I was making time with a bunch of drunks and criminals. Let me tell you about what happened to me in the a-r-m-y." Pavel stressed the words with sarcasm.

"Oh, come on, now. The television tells everybody what a great army we have—the great Soviet Army."

"Don't I know it! They are all lies. It was just about six months ago that a fellow by the name of Skitt went berserk. The officers had been picking on him every day. Like making him scrub the same floor over and over again. When he finished, they would pour some filth from a bucket and make him do it all over again. Other times, they would rape him repeatedly. One day, Skitt was out near the guard tower and just went berserk. He started shooting different men at random. Before they could stop him, Skitt had killed seventeen men. He was able to escape into the nearby woods."

"Then what happened to him? " Grigori asked.

"Some of us were ordered to go out into the woods and bring him in. I was shot in the leg, but Skitt really didn't know what he was doing. The officers had tormented him day after day for such a long time. He didn't know what he was doing!"

"Sounds like he just broke," Grigori said in dismay. "I had no idea things were that bad in the service."

"Be thankful, friend, that you passed your entrance exams high enough so that you didn't have to go into the army."

"I should have been studying harder these past few weeks. But here comes someone. I think they've announced the results of the exam."

They both hurried up the stairs and down the long hallway of the university. A few students who had waited for the results of the exam were just leaving. Pavel opened the envelope containing his grades. He had passed very high and now ranked third in his class.

Grigori had not done as well. He had received a B for the semester, but seemed satisfied since he had not studied very much. He glanced at Pavel's grades. "Look, your hands are shaking."

"Yeah, just like an old man's," Pavel agreed with a grin.

"Getting that grade meant a lot to you. I can sure see that."

"When you start out at the bottom, you have to work very hard and hope you can make the grade," Pavel emphasized, trying not to let his feelings pour into his conversation.

Hours later, Pavel couldn't even remember leaving the university or going on the bus back to the old neighborhood. He could picture himself standing up in class and reading the English words, but it seemed like he was standing there alone with a sea of words encircling him, encouraging him to read on.

Everything had worked out the way he had planned, he thought as he walked up to his grandmother's apartment. Karolina had refused to move when the family had located a larger apartment. She wanted to stay in the same neighborhood with the furniture and her few dishes that held the memories for her. In a way, Pavel figured, it was her security, especially after her husband, Andrey Lubov, had been taken away by the KGB, during one of Stalin's purges. For years, she had lived in fear. Karolina refused to talk about what happened to anyone. Even Pavel. What security did she have during those years after Valentin was born, some eight months after her husband had been arrested?

Pavel would have good news for her today, he thought. It would be sure to please his grandmother. He had stopped at the corner to get her a few groceries. It would save her the trip.

Karolina opened the door before Pavel could knock. Her wrinkled face broke into a wide smile at the sight of her grandson. "Kogo ya vizhu!" she exclaimed. "It's good to see you. I have a cup of hot tea for you."

"That sounds great on such a cold day!" Pavel exclaimed. "Say, I have good news! I just got my grade in my language class. My semester grade is an A. Remember, I was having problems since the other students had studied English in high school and knew a whole lot more than I did?"

"I am proud of you, Pavel. Very proud. Just think, my grandson, studying at the University of Lipetsk!"

"Well, this is just the beginning. There is more. A lot more."

"I know," Karolina nodded wisely. "But it will all come. Mark my words, it will all come."

44

Before Pavel left, he brought in some wood and coal for the stove. He knew it was very heavy for her fragile arms and body to carry into the house, so he tried to get over to her apartment as often as he could to help her. How many more years would she be around anyway? he thought. Still, he hoped that he brought her some moments of happiness during his visits.

His thoughts of Karolina and her words of encouragement were still on his mind that evening as he walked the few blocks to a local disco. And so were the warmth and praise from his parents when he showed them the results of his examination.

Valentin had exclaimed loudly, "Look, what a fine son I have here. Mama. He's the best. Soon, he will be at the top of his class!"

When Pavel entered the disco, it was crowded and noisy. He searched through the people standing near the bar. The air was filled with smoke, but he could still see the lovely face of Lidiia moving toward him. Her lips formed the words, "Pavel, Pavel."

He reached for her hand to lead her to a table. "Come, let's have a glass of vodka, Lidiia. I have some important news for you! Let's sit down."

"Vodka! You have expensive tastes tonight, Pavel."

"Yes, I deserve it!" he answered with a proud toss of his head. "Look what I got on my language exam today. It's the semester final."

Lidiia's eyes widened as she stared at the report. Her eyes filled with soft tears. "Oh, you are to be congratulated! I'm proud of you!"

"Well, it has not been easy, Lidiia. I've had to study many hours."

"Don't I know that, sweetheart. Study. Study. Study. I hardly get a chance to be with you. Do you know that?" Lidiia's lips pursed in a pout, but soon she smiled at Pavel and moved closer to hold his hand under the table.

Pavel thought they would talk together about his studies and maybe about their future, but Lidiia turned the subject to her day at the preschool. Four children had been very ill with coughs and being a nurse as well as their teacher, she had to give them medications.

Pavel shook his head impatiently. "Wait a minute, Lidiia, I want to talk to you about us."

"Us? How can we have a future when you are going to school?"

"It will be all right. You have your job, and so, I go to school."

Lidiia rubbed her forehead in confusion. "What are you saying?"

"I am asking you to marry me, Lidiia. I love you and want you near me all the time. Not just meeting at a disco to see each other. It won't be like that."

"What will it be like, Pavel?"

"We will live together always and share our love together."

"Forever?"

"Yes, forever. It is time for us to begin. What do you say?"

"I've waited for you for a long time. All the time you were in the army, but I never knew how we could plan a future together."

"I know. It wasn't easy for either of us. And I hated being in that damned army and being away from you."

"Now, you are going to the university. I guess it's what you want, Pavel. It is important to you."

Pavel nodded. He had a burning desire to finish his education. "I don't have much to offer you right now, Lidiia. But we will have each other. Soon, things will be different."

Pavel searched her eyes for her reaction. Her eyes were filled with love, but he didn't see the questioning, the uncertainty pushing into the soft tears that were overwhelming her with emotion. He only saw the love and the *yes* forming on her lips.

Chapter 5

During the next few months following their marriage, Pavel was busy going to school, and Lidiia was teaching preschool classes. The months passed quickly. Sometimes, Pavel asked himself if they were really in love. Sometimes, he felt that Lidiia was drawing away from him because he had to study so much. But he tried to put these dark thoughts out of his mind and push forward.

The first couple to visit Pavel and Lidiia several months after their marriage was Ivan and Allery. They were newlyweds themselves and were living down the hall with Ivan's mother. It took years for a couple to get an apartment in Russia. Pavel and Lidiia were no exception. They were living with Pavel's parents. They shared meals together, and their lives were a mixture of sharing and trying to understand each other. Could this be the problem between them? Pavel often wondered.

That day, Pavel had just returned from the university and was surprised to find his old friends, Ivan and Allery, talking with Lidiia in the living room. He was pleased that Ivan had put the idea of revenge behind him. Still, Ivan continued to talk about Yakov, but it wasn't with the anger and hatred like before.

"So how is married life going for you?" Pavel asked as he sat down next to the couple.

Ivan started to speak, hesitated and then drew Allery close to him. "Well, we haven't had any quarrels," he said with a mischievous smile.

"No, and he's a great kisser," Allery added. She looked as though she were going to add to that compliment, but stopped as the color began to spread across her fair cheeks.

Pavel quickly turned to Lidiia. "Come on, Lidiia. Let's have some beer to celebrate our marriages! Aren't there a couple of bottles in the kitchen that I brought home from the bottle factory last night or did Papa drink it up?"

"Papa went to bed early last night, and yes, we have two bottles here."

"So how is it going with you and Lidiia, Pavel? How are you managing having to study so many hours every day and…"

"And half the night!" Lidiia interrupted from the kitchen, her voice strong with emotion.

"Oh, you better change your ways, Pavel. That doesn't sound so good. Not for a newlywed," Ivan advised.

"Well, it isn't so bad. We're getting along all right, although Lidiia complains about my studying so much."

"What do you expect to do when you finish your courses? Teach?"

Pavel rubbed his forehead as he thought over Ivan's question. "Probably. I'm not sure."

"Better think about it, Pavel! As a teacher you'll be one of the lowest paid in Lipetsk. You should be one of the government officials and live in a big house and drive a fancy car. Think about attending party meetings to get ahead!"

Pavel was on his way to the kitchen, but stopped and turned around at this remark. His face turned red with anger. "Over my dead body would I become a part of their damn Communist Party! I've heard enough of their lies about our fine Communist society!"

Lidiia looked up from her glass of beer and stared at Pavel. Her forehead was lined with worry. "Come, Allery, I don't want to listen to politics. I want to show you a new recipe that I got from the mother of one of my students today. I tasted a sample of the cake today, and it was very good."

Allery followed Lidiia out to the kitchen. "I don't like to hear the men talk about the way things are going either. Everything is okay. So we are all poor. My mother says that's the way it's always been. If you have more money than other people, you know the KGB or the government will call you in and question you. Where did you get all this money? So who wants that?"

"That's true enough, but I wish Pavel would just get a job and go to work. We need the money to raise a family. I'm not sure yet, but I might be pregnant. I'm worried about it! Now, we'd be better off if he got a job like Ivan." Lidiia glanced anxiously toward the living room. She did not want her husband to hear.

"Still, a baby would be wonderful, Lidiia! Does Pavel know?"

"I'm not going to tell him until I'm sure. He's so determined to go to school. What should I do?"

"It is important that you get along now and support him. Let me tell you, it is important for your marriage. My mother and father are divorced, and my mother has had to struggle all her life."

Ivan glanced in the direction of the kitchen, but couldn't hear the conversation. "I don't think the girls like to hear us talk against communism."

"My parents are the same way. Big changes scare people a lot. They don't like something new. It might be good. It could be something terrific, but many people are fearful. They follow their emotions."

"So what do you think? What do you think is going to happen?"

"I think changes are bound to come. Here we sit, about two hundred and fifty miles from Moscow. We live in a fairly large city. We are not ignorant as the KGB would like us to be. For years, we have done what we were told and said nothing. I think it is time to make a move for more freedoms." Pavel stood up with determination, clenching his fits. "You know, we are not alone. Many people are beginning to feel the same way."

"Yes, even Dr. Korotch here in this building talks like you do. He was imprisoned years ago. Tortured by the KGB. Now, he is writing about his experiences."

"Is that so?" Pavel asked with real interest. "So, my friend, what do you think?"

"I don't think much is going to change. Seriously, I have enough to worry about. Like getting food and milk on the table. Then when the children come, there will be no time for things like that. Believe me, Pavel, it takes all of a man's efforts to provide for a family."

"A family? You're talking about a family already?"

"Yes, don't you want children? Like I said, a man has to provide for his family—take care of them."

At these words, Allery came out from the kitchen. "Of course, Pavel and Lidiia want a family. So do we. Maybe not right away, but soon."

Ivan put his arm around Allery and tenderly brushed her long hair away from her face. "We must go. Take care of yourselves. Come over and see us. How about next Saturday evening?"

"I have to work very late on weekends, but we will come over very soon, I promise you." He glanced at Lidiia to see her reaction. It was clear that she was troubled. He knew she had been unhappy that they didn't have the time to go and visit their friends very often. And he knew that it was important to them both for him to make the time to visit with their friends.

When Ivan and Allery had gone, Pavel turned to Lidiia. "I'm sorry that I have had to spend so much time studying. We will go out more. I will find the time, I promise you."

But that night, Pavel studied late in the only room they had to themselves. Lidiia tried to sleep, but she tossed and turned for several hours.

"I wish you'd turn out that damn light! How can I sleep with that light shining in my eyes? I'm sick to death of your constant studying."

Pavel turned in the bed and tried to kiss her. "I'm sorry. Here let me put this cloth over your eyes." Why was she so cross, he asked himself. He wanted to feel her soft body next to him and hold her closely. Maybe it was all his fault because he had to spend so many hours studying. Why couldn't she understand? Didn't she want the same things he wanted? But maybe she didn't. She couldn't understand his hatred of communism and how the KGB had destroyed some of his family. Which way to go? He pushed those thoughts out of his mind like the movement of a rapid stream. His book that he was reading for his English language class had fallen to the floor. He picked it up and started to concentrate again. Lately, he had been traveling to Moscow to buy other books to read like *Sophie's Choice* and a few of Charles Dickens' novels.

It was obvious to Lidiia that Pavel had returned to his studying. She quickly turned away from him. How could he be so inconsiderate, she thought, especially since she might be pregnant. But she hadn't told him. What would he say? Would he be angry or would he be happy for them both? Lidiia turned away from the bright light and slept uneasily until the first rays of dawn moved silently into the room.

Another month passed. Lidiia was sure she was pregnant now. Some mornings she felt very sick and ate very little food or no food at all before going to the school. Marina was beginning to ask questions, but Lidiia decided not to confide in her or anyone. How could she explain her feelings?

But Marina was sure she could see all the signs of a pregnant woman. Didn't Pavel realize that Lidiia was pregnant? Why didn't he say something to her? Still, Marina didn't want to interfere. She hoped that Pavel and Lidiia would talk about these things together. She wanted their marriage to succeed, and a family would certainly bring them all closer together. Her forehead wrinkled into a deep frown. But, what could she do?

Finally, one day, she decided to say something. It was late in the afternoon. She heard Pavel at the door just returning from school.

"Is Lidiia sick or something?"

"Why, Mom, why do you ask that? She seems to be fine."

"If she is so fine, then why is she sick almost every morning and doesn't eat anything for breakfast. No bread or milk?"

"I didn't realize that. I leave before she goes to work most of the time. I will talk to her."

That night, Pavel placed his books on the stand and turned to Lidiia. He put his arms around her and kissed her softly on her lips. "My beautiful wife. My darling, Lidiia." He slowly moved his hand over her body, drawing her close to him. "Are you feeling well? Or are you just tired lately?"

Lidiia started to cry softly. She let the tears fall against his cheeks.

He held her face between his hands and carefully wiped the tears away. "Something is wrong. What is it? Tell me."

"I'm afraid to. I don't know what you will think if I tell you. I don't know if you will be happy or angry."

"Why would I be angry?"

"Because we have no room or time for anyone else right now."

"Lidiia!" Pavel almost shouted. "Are you pregnant?"

"Are you angry? It just happened. It just happened, Pavel. I couldn't help it. We couldn't help it."

"Oh, my darling, Lidiia, don't worry. We'll be just fine. We have Mom and Papa and your family. They will help us to care for the baby. And it is time for us to start a family." Pavel started to smother her with kisses. He wanted her to feel happy and secure with him.

For the first time in weeks, Lidiia felt the comfort of Pavel speaking softly to her, telling her how much he loved her and stroking her forehead slowly with his hand. She felt secure as she nestled up to him. And now, Pavel wanted the baby as much as she did.

Several months later, Pavel passed Ivan in the hallway. "Hey, my friend, you must keep your promise. We are having some friends over tomorrow evening. Bring some beer from your bottle factory. How about it?"

"Okay, for a little while."

"How is Lidiia and your parents? Are they well?"

"Lidiia is pregnant. We are expecting a baby this coming fall."

"That is wonderful news, Pavel. You will be completing your first year this spring. Right?"

"Yes. The days are passing by so fast. Soon I will be taking my final semester exams."

Pavel turned away and walked toward his apartment. He knew no one would be home. And it was a good thing to be alone, he thought, as he sat down in a chair in the living room. He stared down at his hands as though the lines on his palms would reveal some hidden truths. What had taken place during this past year? Immediately after he had decided on a concentrated plan of five hours a day for study and to begin a new method of learning the language, his life had taken a new direction. He was sure of it—he had felt this driving force and direction almost every day. And it was during this time that he felt a miracle had started. He had begun thinking about the presence of God in his life because during this time, he had risen from the bottom of the class to the top. What was the reason, he asked himself. Maybe it was because he had been studying so hard, or because he had some hidden talent deep within himself. But as absurd as it might sound, he still thought it was some kind of miracle that was sent to him from above.

Pavel walked over to the window and leaned out over the ledge. A small child was walking along with his *babushka*, his grandmother, and he shouted a greeting to Pavel. He smiled and waved his hand. Pavel smiled and waved back. Soon, he would have a child of his own to take for a walk.

The weather had been warmer than usual. A few birds had returned to the city anticipating an early spring, the same spring that Pavel was anticipating. This year, would end his first semester, and the promise of a new future—a future that moved out in front of him. Little did he know it would take him far beyond the borders of Soviet Russia.

Chapter 6

It had been three years since Pavel had looked out the window of his apartment and waved to the little boy that was walking with his grandmother. Now, he had a child of his own. He was named Stepan after Pavel's much-admired grandfather. It was Grandfather Stepan who had talked to Pavel and given him the determination to move forward in his life. Stepan had dark hair and some of the same facial expressions of his father. Pavel thought that Marina spoiled him, but she strongly protested and wanted her own way, saying after all, she was the grandmother.

"That is the prerogative of a grandmother. He is a fine boy. Look how he is growing so tall. And he is so active, I can hardly keep up with him!"

It was also three years ago, at the time of his first semester exams, that an event happened that virtually changed the course of his life. He could still picture that day so clearly in his mind. He remembered that he was at the university, waiting with his friends for his turn to speak.

"Grigori, I heard that the dean and many important people are coming to hear us speak. Why do you think that is so?"

"I know they aren't coming to hear me speak, Pavel, because I am barely passing now."

Pavel shrugged. "We can only do our best. We've all worked very hard."

"Yes, that's true," Viktor agreed, "but you've really sweated. When you started out you were really struggling with the pronunciation and putting your ideas together. At the time, I wondered if you were going to make it, but you are a real determined cuss."

Pavel smiled. "What else could I do? It was sink or swim!"

"Well, you sure did go for it! When you get up to speak in class I don't understand half of it because your sentences are so complex, particularly the words you use. Your vocabulary is amazing!"

"I've been reading a lot of books in the original English."

"Where did you buy them?"

"In Moscow, Viktor. I take the train to Moscow whenever I have a little money, and buy some books."

They were interrupted with a signal from one of the teachers. It was Pavel's turn to take his exams.

He was surprised to discover that Dean Akhmatova and other important members of the faculty had all come to witness these final exams.

"Just listen to this young student speak English," Dean Akhmatova whispered to her colleague. "He started out at the bottom of the class. He is a real phenomenon here at the university!"

It was a few days later, Pavel learned that he had passed and now ranked at the top of his class. It filled him with a special kind of excitement because now his life had a purpose. He knew he could succeed. He was confident. He was sure. And it filled him with a kind of wonder at how this had all come to him, Pavel Lubov, a very poor young man who previously had no talent whatsoever.

That day of his exams those three years ago was deeply engraved in his mind. But Lidiia did not share his enthusiasm. She began to push and try to persuade him to forget this idea of going to school and putting in hours of study every day. Pavel knew she did not understand his determination or his ideas of working with his friends for a new, freer Russia.

He was thankful that his parents did not interfere with their arguments. Did they have a blind trust in his ideas or did they believe he was doing the right thing by going to the university? Still, most Russian parents were proud of their children who were studying at the University of Lipetsk.

Lidiia came from a large family. Everyone helped to take care of the baby. She continued to work at the school. Often Pavel stayed over at the school library to study. Marina and Lidiia prepared the meals together. Stepan would play on the floor with his toys and sometimes climb up on Valentin's lap. Since Pavel was their only child, Stepan was their first and only grandchild. They were delighted when he first started to speak before he was a year old.

"I think he takes after his papa," Valentin declared. "I think he will be smart like Pavel and go to the university." He glanced at Marina and Lidiia but only Marina nodded her approval.

Valentin was concerned about the couple, but he decided the best thing would be to keep silent. In the fall, they would have been married for four years, but now it seemed that Pavel and Lidiia were constantly arguing. That was no way for a married couple to live, especially with a young son to raise.

Valentin was just finishing his beer when Pavel opened the door. He was carrying a stack of books with him.

"Papa, are you enjoying the beer that I brought home last night?"

"Yes, son. I'm sure glad you're loading beer bottles on the trucks." He smacked his lips appreciatively. "That's a good job you have there. Don't let go of that job!"

Pavel smiled and laughed at Valentin. "I'm surprised you like the beer. Never knew you enjoyed drinking before!"

Valentin pretended to throw the bottle at his son. "Never knew I liked to drink? You show me a Russian that doesn't like to drink, and I'll tell you he's no Russian. Maybe like you. You don't understand, Ne Nash!"

"That's the truth. The streets are full of those Russians and…"

Before he could finish, there was a loud knock at the door. It was Andrey, Ivan's brother. He had been running and his breath came in short gasps. His eyes were wild with terror.

"Ivan found the man who beat me up three years ago, and they got in a fight! I think the man is dead!"

"Andrey, Andrey! What happened!"

"Ivan heard this man talking and laughing about what had happened that day. He said some young punk tried to get ahead of him in line at the food store. He was drinking wine with some other men down at the corner. Ivan was furious when he heard this and started to attack him. The man pulled out a knife. They fought over the knife. Then the militia arrived!"

"Did you see all this happen yourself?"

"No. Someone came to our apartment and told us what had happened. I ran down to the street. The militia were dragging Ivan away."

"What makes you think Ivan killed the man?" Pavel asked searching the young boy's face.

"Because I saw them carrying the man away. He looked dead to me. My mother and Marina are terrified."

"Is the baby home, too?"

"No, he's staying with Allery's mother this week while Allery works."

Lidiia put down a kettle in the kitchen and hurried down the hall. She could hear loud hysterical crying coming from the apartment. Her heart reached out for Olga and Allery.

Pavel turned to Andrey. "I'll go with you. I've got to try and help Ivan."

The streets were filled with people just returning from work. Andrey knew where the militia had taken Ivan. He had seen the militia beating him and dragging him through the streets to a car.

When they got to the station, there was only one officer on duty.

"What do you want?" he demanded as he glared angrily at Pavel.

"I understand an Ivan Dimitri was brought in here."

"Ivan, yes," the man drawled. "A street ruffian. A murderer."

"A murderer? The man beat up this boy here, Andrey, three years ago and almost killed him. He lay in a coma for almost a week."

"So you say, so you say. People say anything."

"Is the man still alive?"

"He is not expected to live."

"Can we see Ivan?" Andrey asked, his lips beginning to quiver. "He's my brother, sir."

The officer stood up quickly placing his hands on his hips. "See him? Nobody sees people in the jail. Go on back to your mother, boy!" He slammed his fist on the desk and looked angrily at Pavel and Andrey.

Pavel put his arm around Andrey and led him away. "I will come back here tomorrow. I'll try to find someone to help us. Go home, quickly, Andrey. I will see you later."

But would he be able to help Ivan? Pavel clasped his head in his hands trying to force an answer, a name, somebody. Without realizing it he was walking in the direction of Maksim's apartment. Would he know of someone that could defend Ivan?

He was lucky to find Maksim at home. He had just gotten home from work.

"Pavel, come on in! Good to see you, friend. I haven't seen you since your son was born. How is he doing?"

"Fine, really fine. Growing fast. I decided to stop by because our neighbor is in trouble. Just this afternoon, he got in a knife fight with a man in the streets. The man may not live. My friend was arrested. I tried to see him, but the militia refused."

"That's typical. What's your friend's name?"

"Ivan Dimitri. He has a wife, Allery, and a baby." Pavel shook his head just thinking about the young family.

Maksim nodded in sympathy. "What was the fight about?"

"This man, his name is Yakov, beat up Ivan's younger brother three years ago. He was only fourteen then. Andrey was in a coma for three days."

"So, Ivan ran into him?"

"Yes, he heard Yakov talking to a man about what had happened. He was drinking and laughing about it!"

"No wonder he was angry. Right now, I can't think of anyone who can help." Maksim paused and started to walk back and forth in the room. He noticed his friend's dismay and troubled face. "Wait a minute. You know that old Doctor Korotch that lives on the first floor of your apartment? Maybe he can do something for you."

"Doctor Korotch?" Pavel asked in surprise.

"Yes, he knows a lot of people in the city. He's not as old as he looks. Korotch was imprisoned for years, even survived his sentence of working in the uranium mines."

"That's a death sentence. Hardly anyone survives that! Undoubtedly, he's in bad shape after all the exposure to radiation. I'll go and talk to him. Maybe I can find him at home tonight."

The lights were just coming on in the buildings when Pavel reached the street. Some of the windows of the shops were covered with steam from the cold, damp weather. Through the window, he could see the last customer making a hurried purchase. As the man left the shop, the lights cast eerie shadows through the steamed pane of the closing door.

Pavel reached his apartment house just before dark. He wondered how Vladimir Korotch would be able to help. The man seemed so thin and frail yet he opened his door for Pavel with a vigorous swing that was totally surprising.

"Come in, come in. What can I do for you?"

Pavel explained what had happened and Ivan's arrest.

"Andrey and his mother and Allery are terrified!"

"I can imagine. I remember how Andrey was so badly beaten. He pulled through, but for a while I wondered if he would make it."

The man seemed lost in thought, and Pavel wondered if he were capable of helping him. He was supposed to be around fifty-five years old, but because of all that he had suffered from the irradiation from the mines, he looked around eighty. His eyes seemed sunken into a mass of wrinkled yellow skin.

Suddenly, he looked up and his expression changed. His face was alert, and he leaned forward with determination. "I know an attorney who owes me a favor. I'll go to see him in the morning. Come back after your classes tomorrow afternoon. I may have good news for you."

"Thanks, Doctor. I didn't know where to turn."

"Let me know if I can help the family in any way. I have a little money. Not much, but perhaps..."

"I'll let you know. I'm going upstairs now. My wife is with Allery and Olga. Of course, they are very upset."

"It's a terrible thing that happened!" the doctor agreed looking up and down the hallway as though expecting further trouble.

When Pavel reached the Dimitri apartment, Lidiia was preparing some food for the family in the kitchen, but it was obvious that no one was hungry.

"Where is Andrey?" Olga asked. "I thought he was with you."

"We tried to see Ivan at the jail, but the militia refused. I told him to go on home, and I'd try to find someone that could help us. He should be home soon. I wouldn't worry. Remember, he's seventeen now."

Suddenly, there was a knock at the door. It was a KGB officer demanding to search the apartment.

Pavel stared at him in amazement. "What are you looking for, officer?"

"We have talked to Yakov, the man Ivan tried to kill. He said Ivan is writing pamphlets against the government. He's a dirty spy."

"That's absurd!" Allery exclaimed. "He's just an ordinary factory worker. He doesn't know anything about politics or want anything to do with politics!"

"Who are you, miss?"

"I'm his wife, Allery."

The officer took out a pad of paper and started writing down their names.

"Anyone else live here?"

"Yes, I do!" Andrey suddenly burst into the room. "What are you doing here?"

The KGB officer glared at Andrey. "Listen, kid, you don't ask me questions. And who in the hell are you?"

"I'm Andrey Dimitri. Ivan's brother. That man, Yakov, beat me up three years ago! I almost died!"

"I don't know anything about that. So just shut up now. I'm going to look around here. Keep out of my way!"

Olga sat down on the couch and waved her hands helplessly. Lidiia tried to comfort her.

The officer walked through the small apartment opening drawers, pulling out the furniture and looking in the closets. He didn't bother to put anything back. Papers were strewn across the floor. When he left, the apartment looked like a moving tornado had exploded its fury and hatred through the rooms.

Marina looked around the apartment and began to cry hopelessly.

Pavel sat down next to Olga and took her hands into his. "I'm going to try and get you some help. Doctor Korotch says he is going to contact somebody tomorrow morning."

"What can he do?" Olga asked helplessly.

"I don't think he would say anything if he didn't have some ideas, Olga."

"Look at the mess that KGB officer made in our place! He had no right to say that Ivan is a spy. No right, Pavel! I'd like to shoot him right in the gut!"

"Slow down, Andrey. We have enough problems right now without you getting in trouble with the KGB."

"I don't care. What right have they got to come here and treat us like that?"

"It's always been that way with the KGB and the Communists. Russian citizens don't have any rights. No rights at all!" Pavel spoke with vehemence. Then he glanced at Andrey. He must be careful what he said because this young boy in his despair could get into deep trouble. Andrey had a quick temper and was totally unlike his

59

brother, Ivan. Pavel figured it was due to some of the Italian blood that he had inherited from his father. He was a handsome young man with dark hair and eyes and a flashing smile. Some day before long, Pavel figured, the girls would all be falling in love with him.

"We must be careful what we say and do, Andrey. Tomorrow, I will see you after my classes, and I hope I will have found someone that can help Ivan. Just try and stay calm."

"If you don't, I'm going down and get Ivan out of jail if I have to shoot it out with the militia. I have friends who will do as I say!" Andrey said defiantly as Pavel left the room. "And I will get my revenge on that Yakov, I promise you!"

Chapter 7

It was early morning, and Ivan, although he had eaten very little food since he was imprisoned yesterday afternoon, could only think of his wife and baby. How scared Allery and his mother must feel. Why did he get in a fight with Yakov? Why did he end up killing him? He tossed the desperation that filled his mind back and forth. He knew what had happened. Out of his anger at hearing his brother ridiculed, he had struck back at the man who had beat up Andrey. He didn't realize that the man had a knife. But when he saw the shiny weapon being thrust at him, he grabbed at it and thought only of killing this man, this man with the evil smirk on his face and his rotten teeth grinning at him in defiance. Now, his heart reached out to Allery. He wanted to hold her in his arms and comfort her. Reassure her that everything would be all right. But he knew deep within himself, there was no way out. He knew of no one who could help.

Ivan pressed his head against the steel bars in front of him. He could picture his beautiful wife holding out her arms to him! He remembered how she used to sit in front of a mirror, carefully brushing her long dark hair that reached down to her waist. Sometimes, he would come up behind her and take the brush from her hands and slowly smooth her hair between his fingers. Then, he would kiss her tenderly and watch her face break into a smile. When would he be able to hold her in his arms again? And there was his precious little baby boy! When he smiled, his fair little face was filled with a special light of happiness. Yesterday morning, he had held him and rocked him gently in his arms. What was he doing now? What would his mother do when he cried for his papa? There was no comfort for him. There was no comfort for his Allery.

Ivan had heard last night that Yakov would probably survive. That in itself was good news, so that he would not be charged with murder. He hoped that his brother would not do anything foolish. The family was suffering enough. At seventeen, Andrey was rash and often impulsive. He had a quick temper.

Late that morning, a strange face appeared before his cell. The guard unlocked the door and allowed the man to enter.

"You cannot stay long, Mr. Zaharoff. Remember, this is a favor."

Yuri Zaharoff nodded in agreement. "Your friend, Vladimir Korotch, came to see me this morning. I am a lawyer. He is concerned about you and your family. I told him I would do what I could for you."

"I am grateful for that, Mr. Zaharoff. I heard last night that Yakov is expected to live, so what will happen to me now?"

"There is another problem. Yakov has accused you of being a spy and writing pamphlets against the government."

"That's ridiculous! Absolutely ridiculous," Ivan said shaking his head in despair at that news. "I've never had any interest in politics."

"Don't be discouraged. There are things we can do."

"Will the militia listen to me if I tell them that Yakov beat up Andrey three years ago?"

"Maybe. Maybe not."

"What can you do?"

"There are ways to deal with the judge. Your friend Vladimir Korotch has influential friends who have some money. Be quiet and say nothing." Mr. Zaharoff rose to leave at the sight of the guard approaching the cell. His five minutes were up, and if he didn't have some influence with the militia officer, he wouldn't have been able to talk to Ivan in the first place.

Lidiia found it almost impossible to console Allery. She worried and worried what would happen to her husband. "Please try and eat a little. You need to keep up your strength. It is important. Do it for, Ivan!"

"What's the use?" she asked despondently. "I know what they do to men they think are writing and talking against the government."

"Dr. Korotch is trying to get us some help, Allery. He has a lot of influential friends."

"I don't know what he can do. I don't know what he can do for my Ivan." Allery started to shake and cry uncontrollably.

Olga turned from the stove. "Here, eat some of this borscht I've made for us. It's hot and nourishing."

At that moment, there was a knock at the door. Allery sat up startled. What if it were the KGB? What did they want here again? It was a good thing that Andrey wasn't home.

But it was not a KGB officer. It was Pavel just returning from his classes.

"I have good news! Doctor Korotch has a lawyer friend who is going to try and help Ivan. He has been over to the jail already. But, Lidiia, I think we'd better go and find what's wrong with Stepan. I just heard him crying when I came into the hallway."

Pavel entered the room, Stepan reached out his arms for his father. "What's got you all upset, little fella?"

"Oh, it's really nothing," Allery tried to sound reassuring. "Some neighbors were in here talking about what happened in the street yesterday, and they saw Ivan being arrested. We told them about the KGB searching Olga's apartment. I guess all the loud voices scared Stepan. He'll be all right."

But Lidiia wasn't so sure. She took the child into her arms and went into the kitchen to warm up a cup of milk.

Pavel decided to go downstairs and visit with the doctor. Maybe he had some more information about Ivan's fate.

He found the man lying on the couch, his yellow withered hands fingering the blanket fitfully. He tried to sit up when Pavel entered the room.

"Just a minute; I want to sit up."

"I didn't mean to bother you, Vladimir. Stay where you are."

"That's all right. You were asking before what we could do for Ivan. I think we can get the KGB off his back for now and maybe dismiss his case."

"You mean this lawyer can accomplish this?" Pavel asked in amazement.

"We'll see. Yuri is talking about bribing the judge. I have a few influential friends with some money."

"I know it's done all the time, but money...well, money. That's a hard thing to get, you know."

"Rest assured, but keep it quiet. Don't tell anyone at this point. Not even the Dimitris. We will try our best."

"I can't begin to thank you, Vladimir. Lidiia and my mother are trying to help them as much as we can."

Fortunately, his parents didn't ask him any questions about what the doctor had said, Pavel recalled as he walked into the university language lab the next morning. His homework assignment was to listen to the English dialogue on tape. By now, it was not difficult for him to understand and memorize the words.

After a while, a very pretty girl came and sat down next to him to wait her turn to listen to the tape. He had seen her before. Once, he had helped her with a homework assignment. Her name was Anna Snegova.

"I notice your pronunciation is improving a lot, Anna. What have you been doing?"

"I have a friend, Ivanio Batisti, that I have been seeing. He is a foreign national and speaks excellent English."

"Is that so!" Pavel exclaimed in surprise. "What's he doing in Lipetsk?"

"He works for a company in Italy that has a contract with the Lipetsk Steel Company."

"So he's Italian."

"Yes, he's Italian and very good looking! But the trouble is, he will only be here for about two years." Anna turned away and pursed her lips in a deliberate pout." Just listening to him helps me with my English."

"Well, that's too bad he'll be here only two years. Still, you can have a lot of fun in two years!"

Anna pretended to resent this and tossed her long blonde hair as she rose from her chair. "Let me know when you're through with the tape, Pavel."

"I'm sorry, I didn't mean to hurt your feelings. I was just teasing. Really, I envy you for having a friend that speaks English. I wish I knew someone that I could converse with in English."

"He's not the only foreign national here in the city. Matt James works for the Lloyd Steel Company in England. Matt is also working with a contract with the Lipetsk Steel Company. Matt James is a good friend of Karolina Kanturia. The girl in our language class. Interesting, hmm, Pavel?"

"Yes, absolutely. Here, I'm through with the tape."

Pavel walked out of the lab, writing himself a mental note to talk with Anna some more. He would enjoy talking with these men and getting the experience of speaking English in casual conversations. It would be a great opportunity.

It was late afternoon when Pavel reached the apartment building. Andrey was just ahead of him on the stairs. He seemed full of energy and bounding with enthusiasm. Pavel thought that was strange since the family was under so much stress worrying about Ivan.

"What's up? You have such a happy expression on your face."

"I got some good news today at school. I passed very high on my exams, so now I can go to the university in the fall!"

"That's wonderful news, Andrey! Congratulations!" Pavel was pleased to hear this report. This should certainly cheer his mother — a new direction for the whole family. He hoped this would help Andrey to focus on his future and not try to get revenge on Yakov.

When he entered the door to his apartment, only Lidiia was home. She was just changing her clothes after a day at the preschool.

Pavel decided that since they were alone he would tell her about Matt James and Ivanio Batisti. He couldn't keep back his enthusiasm to meet them, but he was surprised at Lidiia's reaction to the idea.

"Foreign nationals! I wouldn't think you would want anything to do with them. What for, anyway?"

"Just to visit with them. It would be a good chance for me to practice my English. Good for you too, Lidiia."

"Now, why would it be good for me, Pavel? Just tell me why in the world it would be good for me!"

"It's an excellent opportunity to learn some English. After all, English is the language that is spoken in business circles all over the world!"

"So what? We're not in those business circles. You could get in a lot of trouble seeing those foreign nationals."

"Trouble? I'm not worried about trouble. I just want a chance to practice the language."

"Well, you don't need to see them. I don't want anything to do with them," Lidiia was almost shouting with anger.

Pavel shook his head and decided to go into the bedroom to see if Stepan were awake, but the child was asleep, his head nestled against a soft toy that his grandmother had given him. He was growing so fast. This fall he would be three years old.

But while the child was doing so well, he and Lidiia were having problems. This fall they would have been married four years. If only his wife could understand his desire for an education. His need to study. Their arguments had become angrier and more frequent. There must be something he could do, he thought, as he watched his wife get ready to go out to the store.

A few weeks later, Ivanio invited him and Anna to dinner. Anna had stopped him after class and told him about the invitation. Lidiia was invited, but she was not interested in meeting the foreigners. She had tried to discourage Pavel, but finally gave up.

Ivanio lived in an apartment much like Pavel's. Anna had arrived earlier right after classes and was busy in the kitchen preparing dinner.

"So you are a student at the university studying English like Anna?" Ivanio began. "How many more years before you finish your courses?"

"A little over two years."

"Anna tells me you have a wife and a little boy. You know they are welcome here. I would like to meet them."

Pavel was impressed with the man's excellent vocabulary and pronunciation of English. "I appreciate that. Lidiia has a cold and isn't feeling well, but you will meet her another time."

Ivanio smiled and glanced toward the kitchen. Anna was preparing lasagna. The aroma of the tomato sauce and the cheese was filling the room.

"I see that your girl friend has learned how to cook some Italian food, Ivanio. You are lucky. The food is delicious!"

"I'm surprised you speak such good English, Pavel. You must be an excellent student."

"He's at the top of our class. When I first met Pavel, he was having a difficult time since he didn't study English like I did in high school."

"I understand you were in the Russian army?"

"And what an army it was!" Pavel continued to explain his experiences in the service then turned to Ivanio's business in Lipetsk.

"I am here because the company I work for in Italy has a contract with the Lipetsk Steel Company. The company is buying our steel coating technology because they want to build a shop to produce refrigerators. They need the technology to coat the steel."

"So they are buying the technology and the equipment?"

"Exactly. Our company in Italy manufactures refrigerators and washing machines. I am here for about two years to help the Lipetsk Steel Company install the equipment and teach the Russian workers how to use it."

"I understand that there is another man, Matt James, that is also working with the company."

"Yes, he's British. We are all good friends. He has a girlfriend that I guess you know. Her name is Karolina Kanturia."

"She's in our language class. I would like to meet this Matt James."

"You shall, you shall. Say, would you like a glass of wine? This is the real stuff, not your homemade brew that you Russians make."

"Well, maybe a little. I don't drink much, myself."

"That's a surprise! I thought all Russians drank a lot."

"I guess that's true enough."

"Pavel works at a factory on weekends and loads bottles on the trucks. He takes beer home to his father."

"Yes, Papa likes his beer. He likes to drink. But me, I drink very little. He calls me a Ne Nash!"

Pavel started to laugh. It was contagious, and soon they were all exploding with laughter at this serious, intelligent Russian being called a Ne Nash!

"What is Matt James doing at the steel company?"

"Matt works for the Lloyd Steel Company in England. He is over here to install three rolling mills. He's a very interesting person. It would be good for you to meet Matt. I will arrange a time with him, and we'll all get together real soon."

With that promise in his mind, Pavel left Ivanio's apartment and started walking home. As he neared the apartment house, he was surprised to see Vladimir Korotch just entering the building.

"Wait a minute, Vladimir! Do you have any news about Ivan?"

"Come on into my apartment. I have something to tell you."

"Are you getting enough to eat? You've looked thinner these past few weeks. Are you sure you are all right?"

"Well, that's the way it is. Some days I feel like eating. Other days I don't."

Pavel nodded in sympathy. "Is Yakov still in the hospital?"

"No. In fact, Yuri Zaharoff, Ivan's lawyer, had some business in the courthouse yesterday, and he ran into Yakov."

"Yakov! You mean he's not in jail for his part in the fight and using a knife? And what about his beating up Andrey and almost killing him?"

"You can forget all that. Yakov smiled right in Yuri's face and said he was free to leave."

"I can't believe it! After all that he did. And how Andrey suffered. We didn't think he would live."

"It was all done with a bribe. And that's our next step. Ivan will be free in a few weeks. The same way."

Bribes and bribes and more bribes, Pavel thought as he left the apartment. That was the way the legal system worked. Men like Yakov were free to go. What was going to happen to the Russian society? It was a dangerous path and only getting worse. What place would he have in this turmoil that was a mockery of justice?

Chapter 8

Fall was in the air Pavel noticed as he got off the bus near the university. The summer had gone by swiftly. Stepan would soon be three years old. He had tried to spend more time with his family, but time would not give in to him. Like a stern parent, time was demanding and relentless. There was always work at the bottling factory, the hours at the university, the lab work and the studying. By now, he had read many books in English. His appetite was insatiable.

During the holidays and a few weekends, Marina offered to take care of Stepan so that the couple could get away and be together. Marina never said anything, but Pavel knew she was worried about them. Did Lidiia notice this? He wondered. She didn't seem to understand his needs to study, to finish his education and move out into the world. Sometimes Lidiia would burst out with anger and shake her head. "Why don't you just go and get a job?" she demanded.

Pavel was disgusted at her demands. No one could tell him he couldn't spend time with Ivanio Batisti and Matt James. A few times, Lidiia relented and went with him. Once, Matt and Karolina stopped by the apartment. That particular evening, Valentin had been drinking beer and was very funny. They had laughed together at his jokes. But that was a month ago, and now Lidiia began to object to getting together again. She continually worried that they were headed straight into trouble. Sometimes the KGB beat people to death for not obeying their orders.

Pavel continued to scoff at this idea until the day he was called into the dean's office at the university. Ira Akhmatova frowned at him when he entered her office on the ground floor of the university.

"I wanted to speak to you. We have noticed that you have been spending time with some foreign nationals. I strongly discourage you from having anything to do with them." Her usual brown friendly eyes were focused on Pavel's face with stern disapproval.

"Dean Akhmatova, I am only seeing them to practice my English, and..."

"You're a young, promising student and seeing these foreign nationals will only hurt your future career. It is very important that you stop seeing them."

"They are just friends. I am not doing anything criminal or doing anything against the government," Pavel protested.

But the Dean persisted in her disapproval, and Pavel left her office disturbed and all the more disgusted at her attitude. He resolved not to say anything about this to Lidiia. Maybe the whole thing would pass over and be forgotten, yet he knew that wasn't likely. He had a feeling that he was in trouble.

For a while after being called into the dean's office, he made excuses not to get together with Ivanio and Matt. His friends couldn't understand what was going on. Ivanio called on the phone several times and said, "What's wrong? What's happened? We don't see you anymore. Are you sick or something?"

What was he supposed to tell him? One day he was friends with the man, and the next day he was making up excuses not to see him or Matt James. Was he supposed to tell them that Dean Akhmatova told him that he couldn't meet with them? So for a while, he told Ivanio and Matt that he was under some pressure.

He knew the university had no right to forbid him to see these friends. He decided not to listen to them. Still, the pressure began to grow as the year turned the corner into 1985.

A few months later, Dean Akhmatova called Pavel into her office again to warn him about seeing those people. This time there were several other department heads in her office.

Pavel was annoyed. Again, he repeated his innocence of doing anything against the government or the Communist Party.

Soon, Dean Akhmatova realized that Pavel would not listen to her. She knew he was continuing to see those men, since the KGB watched every move of a foreigner and gave the reports to the university.

The pressure began to intensify until he was called into the KGB office at the university. Pavel up to this time, wasn't aware that it was their office. They had another name on a little plate over the office: "Society for Helping University Students." But it was the KGB office.

When Pavel entered the room, he noticed two men talking together in an animated discussion. Mr. Lomonosov moved deliberately in his chair to face Pavel. He appeared to be in his late thirties. His tie hung loosely around his neck. The other man moved over to stand by the window. He had a very bald head and thick, horn-rimmed glasses.

Mr. Lomonosov glared at Pavel disapprovingly. "We know that you are friends with these foreign nationals. What you probably don't know is that they're foreign spies. They are spying here for their military. They are at the steel plant, and they're trying to steal our technology."

The other man, Mr. Zhukovsky, stepped forward and faced Pavel. "We are telling you to stop meeting with them. They might be using you for those purposes."

"Mr. Zhukovsky, we are just friends. That's all. Sometimes, we just meet and talk about movies, music or something like that. There are no military secrets to discuss. After all, who am I to know anything about technological or military secrets? I am just a student practicing my language. That's all."

It was obvious to Pavel that these men could not be convinced of his intentions, and their accusations were total nonsense. As he left the room, he was convinced that this was one of the KGB methods to scare and control people, and he decided to ignore their demands. To hell with them! Stupid idiots!

It was February when Ivan was released from prison. The money had been paid, and he was jubilant at the thought of returning home to his wife and child. Pavel was with him as they walked away from the prison office.

"I feel like I am walking through the streets of freedom!" Ivan declared, stretching his arms high in the air.

"You are walking through the streets toward your home," Pavel corrected.

"Why so solemn? This is a great day!"

"I understand that, but it's a question of how much freedom you'll have. Remember, the KGB has a file on you now. I should know about that, Ivan!"

"What do you mean, old friend? What have you been up to? I have had very little news locked up in that coup!"

"Two girls in my class are friends with some foreign nationals. One of the men is from Italy and the other one is from England. They have contracts with the Lipetsk Steel Plant. I've become friends with them. It gives me a good opportunity to practice my English, you know."

"So you got in trouble over that?" Ivan asked in disbelief.

"Absolutely. Dean Akhmatova has called me into her office several times to warn me. Then the KGB called me into their office. They have a little office right in the university—of all places! This Mister Lomonosov says those foreigners are spies. He said I could be accused of helping the foreign spies in the country, and there could be criminal charges!"

"What are you going to do about it?"

"Nothing. It's all total nonsense! Can you imagine me, Pavel Lubov, a poor student at the university, a spy helping the Italians?"

"Yeah, that is crazy. But it sounds like the way the KGB operates. Believe me, I don't want to see their faces again!"

When Pavel and Ivan reached the apartment house, it was late afternoon. Allery and Olga were excited to see him. Tears flowed down Allery's face as she embraced her husband.

"I am so grateful to you and Doctor Korotch for getting my Ivan out of prison. I can't thank you enough!"

Later, when Pavel entered his apartment, Marina looked up surprised when she saw Pavel with his usual armful of books. "I thought you would be late coming home with Ivan. He must have been ready to leave when you got there."

"Yes, and Ivan is one happy man to get home and be with his family."

"Well, that's good news. But I've been concerned about you. Aren't you risking a lot by seeing Ivanio and Matt? Lidiia is so against it."

"I don't think the KGB has the right to tell me what people I can choose as my friends. It is utter nonsense to believe that I am consorting with spies or working against the Russian government."

Marina studied Pavel's determined face."I understand, but why don't you just quit seeing them and avoid all this trouble?"

"Mama, I won't let them do this to me. I won't let them pull those scare tactics on me. I'm going to do what I want to do in my life. I am determined to get my education and begin working for freedom from communism and this wretched government."

Marina sighed. "Well, I will say this. I still don't understand why the KGB is causing so much trouble. And I hope they will leave you alone now."

Pavel decided that since Lidiia wasn't home and Stepan was sleeping that he would go downstairs and talk to Vladimir Korotch. The old man was making himself a cup of tea when Pavel knocked at the door.

"Ivan got home today. I walked with him from the prison."

"That must have been a long walk!"

"He wanted to walk and taste the fresh air and sunshine. We stopped at my friend's apartment for a while on the way home."

Before Pavel decided to confide in Vladimir Korotch about his conflicts with the KGB, he searched the man's face to see if he were well enough to listen to his problems. Vladimir had suffered so much in his life from his days in prison and working in the uranium mines.

As Pavel explained his situation with the KGB, Vladimir nodded sympathetically. "Still, you know that men have been sentenced to camps like Perm-35 for more than fifteen years for consorting with foreign nationals and foreign intelligence. You must be careful."

"I had two grandfathers who also suffered in prison camps, Korotch. I understand the terrible brutality of the KGB and the Communist system."

"Yes, Pavel, this is a sick society that even an old doctor cannot fix. I do not know the remedy for it, but I have personally experienced the symptoms of a society that is crumbling and falling apart with a serious illness."

"Lidiia doesn't want me to see my friends anymore, but I'm not doing anything wrong. And, not only that, but I won't let the KGB tell me I can't see these people. What right have they to tell me what to do and run my life?"

"Ah, yes, you are young," Korotch sighed. "Of course, these are different times. Maybe you can get away with more now. I was arrested for talking against the Communist Party with some doctors in my home. I was reported by a man who brought his friend with him. He was a journalist and went back to his office and talked about me. I was arrested and taken away from my wife who was just three months pregnant!"

"Then what happened?"

"I protested. The prison authorities demanded evidence that the KGB wanted. I had not been consorting with foreign intelligence, so I had nothing to tell them. They beat me and threw me naked into a freezing cold isolation cell. I almost died. I told them in the beginning I was a medical doctor. Finally, they questioned some of my friends who verified my statements. Then, I was sent to another camp."

"You were not released then?"

"No, one of the prison officers had it in for me. At this camp, we often had to work in temperatures below forty-one degrees. Even the barracks had ice on the ceilings. I can remember that the guards had to count us at the end of the day. They shouted, 'Scum, scum, line up!' And we felt like scum. Maggots the size of angle worms crawled in the meat, and the mattresses were filled with insects."

"Didn't they ever acknowledge that you were a doctor?'"

"Acknowledgment was not one of their virtues. There was no honor or decency in the camp."

"Sounds like the Russian army."

"Not quite, my friend. The rule of the camp was survival. The men survived by bribes to get easier jobs or more scraps of food. But the worse thing at that camp was the "count" at the end of the day. If the count wasn't right, or they believed someone was missing, they would make us all lie face down in the snow until they got it right. Often by that time, it was late and dark, and the wind was still cold and icy. Then, we got only a bowl of something like thin cabbage soup."

Pavel frowned at these words. "Then, I understand, you were sent to work in the uranium mines."

"I was there almost a year. One of my friends, whose brother had a lot of influence in the government, arranged for my release. Otherwise, I would not be alive today after all my exposure to radiation. Now, I look like I'm Death in Life."

Pavel's eyes filled with sympathy as he looked at Valadimir. He knew the man was not old, just in his fifties, but he looked like a very old man. When he spoke about the horrors of the camp, his yellowed skin would shake with emotion. Only his eyes revealed a sharp keenness that peered out from between the heavy folds of his eyelids. As Pavel listened to the man recall the past, he could see the deep intelligence casting out pictures from his mind.

"Yes, death in life. Do you recall Coleridge's, "The Rime of the Ancient Mariner"? Listen, see if I can remember the words.

The many men, so beautiful!
And they all dead did lie:
And a thousand thousand slimy things
Lived on; and so did I.

I closed my lids, and kept them closed,
And the balls like pulses beat;
For the sky and sea, and the sea and the sky
Lay like a load on my weary eye,
And the dead were at my feet.

"I skipped a couple of verses, I think, but yes, Pavel, that's how it was. That's how I felt when I was working at the uranium mines."

"Wasn't Coleridge an English poet? I'm surprised that you are familiar with that poem."

"My mother was English. She used to read some of the English classics to me when I was a young boy."

"You were very fortunate. Here, I am just learning English and reading some of the classics. Now, according to the poet, didn't the ancient mariner kill the albatross which was supposed to be a bird of good luck? Then he finally blessed all the creatures and survived, and his penance was to tell the story the rest of his life to anyone who would listen?"

"That's right. That's what happened. Only the analogy is not the same. Most of the men in the camps were innocent, not like the mariner. They had been accused of crimes against the state. Now, maybe I am like the ancient mariner. I live on with my skinny hands and glittering eye to tell my story. My hope is that before I die I will see the beginning of changes in Russia. New freedoms and a new way of life. At that time, I will pass my legacy on to you, Pavel and..."

Valadimir was suddenly interrupted by the sounds of loud banging coming from the floor above. "It sounds like someone knocking on a door."

Pavel sprang from his seat and dashed for the stairs. When he entered the hallway, he saw three KGB officers entering his apartment.

Only Lidiia and the baby were home. She stood as though she were paralyzed with fear and terror. The officers said that they had come to search the apartment. They moved ruthlessly through the rooms, tossing books and papers onto the floor. Their loud voices and shouts of command echoed through the long hallway. Then they returned to the living room and noticed Pavel standing by the door.

"You're under arrest!" they announced, grabbing his arm and forcing him to go with them. "We've put up with enough of your nonsense. You will see what happens to people who disobey!"

That night, Lidiia went to bed with strong feelings moving around through her mind. She tossed around and around and could not sleep. What was going to happen next in her life?

Her thoughts moved over the past few months. Often, Pavel would turn on the radio, and she could hear the music coming from the BBC broadcast. He had listened to the British station many nights. It was forbidden to Russians to listen to this station, but Pavel wanted to listen to the programs. He said it helped him with his English pronunciation. Now, she only reflected back on those times when Pavel was lying next to her. She felt that he was moving in a different world. The voices of the BBC were turned off. They were not in the room. But somehow she could see herself with her young son encircled with the strange words and the world of the BBC. Was Pavel living in this different world—a world where freedoms were taken for granted? If he should take her hand, she wasn't sure she wanted to follow him. She was afraid. Where would he take her?

Chapter 9

Lidiia had not heard from Pavel in several days. She was seething with anger. How could he do this to her, she asked herself over and over again. What sense was it for him to continue to see those foreign nationals? Why did he refuse to follow the orders of the KGB? It was making life so difficult for them. They had been having heated arguments over the situation. And it was all over his desire to study languages and complete his education. What a waste, she thought. Here, he could have been working all these years. And life would have been so much simpler for both of them. Why couldn't he be like Ivan and be content with just making a living and following the guidelines of the Communist Party?

But Pavel saw things differently. He refused to allow the officers to control his life. As he waited in the jail to be called into the KGB office, his mind was exploding with anger at the gall of these men to tell him what he could and could not do and prevent him from making friends with a couple of people who weren't Russian.

On the third day after his arrest, Pavel was taken into the KGB office. This time, their voices were not quiet and persuading.

"You have refused to obey our demands that you stop seeing these foreign nationals, so I guess we have to show you that we can do something about it!" Mr. Zhukovsky shouted. The other man quickly moved forward and struck Pavel on the throat and head and knocked him backwards onto the floor. Pavel's head hit the hard cement. Blood rushed from his nose. He choked and passed out. The guards dragged him back to his cell.

A half hour later, Pavel slowly started to regain consciousness and realize that he was back in his cell again. Then, he remembered what had happened. In spite of the excruciating pain in his throat and head, he was angrier than before. What right did they have to strike him and treat him like a common criminal? If he gave in to them, he would not be the same person again. He would invariably become a slave to their rotten system.

A few hours later, they came for him and began the questioning all over again, demanding that Pavel follow their orders.

"I hear what you are saying, but I do not understand your requests. I'm just a student practicing my language with these men."

"Let me tell you something. We have been watching this Ivanio Batisti. We know that one time he took a trip to Moscow and from the window of the train, he was seen watching some military operations and taking some notes, even some photos," Mr. Zhukovsky emphasized, staring at Pavel through his thick glasses.

"I can't understand that, Mr. Zhukovsky. That train leaves from Lipetsk at eleven at night and arrives in Moscow at six in the morning, so the train is traveling to Moscow at night and in total darkness. Ivanio can't watch anything or take notes or photos."

"Oh, is that so?" Zhukovsky responded sarcastically.

"Yes, I'm telling you the truth. I have taken the train to Moscow several times to buy books."

Mr. Zhukovsky pretended to shake his head in disbelief. Pavel knew that he had surprised them with his own knowledge and that they had made a mistake.

Finally, the officers decided to let him go with more warnings and threats. Pavel knew that if they had any other charges or recourse, he would have been taken back to jail.

When Pavel went home later that day and told Lidiia what had happened to him, she was upset and angry. How could he have been so stupid to allow himself to get in that position? Just because he had insisted on visiting with the Italian and Englishman?

Pavel tried to explain. "You see, this KGB officer tried to tell me that Ivanio Batisti and Matt James were spies. Their explanations were ridiculous. They made a big mistake."

"You are the one that made the mistake in the first place! You know what you are doing? You're going to get me in trouble. Pretty soon, they will come and take me away and interrogate me! I don't think you know what you are doing!"

"I know exactly what I am doing! The KGB is just trying to break me. They know those two men aren't spies."

But the arguments continued over the next few months. When Pavel tried to explain what Lomonosov and Zhukovsky were doing, Lidiia wouldn't listen. He knew that when he refused to comply with the orders of the KGB, the officers believed that meant he was a rebel. He was against them. To Pavel, this was just another one of their usual methods to scare and control people.

Many times, he tried to explain to Lidiia what the Communist Party was doing to Russia and how the KGB through the years had controlled the thinking and life of the Russian people through fear. Through fear, they could control the very society which they were slowly destroying.

However, these were not Lidiia's concerns. She turned away from these discussions. Her concern was whether there was enough bread and milk in the grocery store and whether there was enough money to buy those things. At the time, Pavel did not really blame her for this, but on the other hand, Lidiia didn't really care about communism and about the beginning of unrest and questioning that was happening in the country. To Pavel, it seemed as though she was looking at the world through different eyes.

The spring of 1985 passed quickly. Everyone turned back to their usual ways of living and making do with less and less, yet Ivan was thankful he was a free man able to provide enough food for his wife and child. The baby, Ivan, was three and a half years old now, active and continually asking questions.

Though this whole experience of being threatened and held in prison was terrifying, in some ways it had brought the family together. Now, every moment was so precious, so meaningful. Even in the darkness of the night when he held his wife close to him as she slept, he felt their love encircling them, and it seemed as though his very soul reached out to hold those moments. Sometimes, he would wake suddenly, and the fear would drench his body, the fear that all this love would be taken away from him.

But as the days passed, the warmth of the spring brought new hope for him and Marina. She had found a job working in a large store. There was always someone who could watch Ivan. Sometimes, Olga would take him and Stepan to the park, so they could play together.

It was warm enough now for the old women to sit out on the benches in front of the apartment house and exchange the news that they had heard or created in their own minds. One old woman, Karolina, seemed to be a paragon of information. The others would lean forward, their dark eyes snapping to hear the latest gossip.

"I tell you, things are not going well between Pavel and Lidiia Lubov," Karolina offered wisely with a nod of her head.

"I think you are right. Someone told me they have heard loud voices coming from that apartment sometimes," Galina agreed.

"What do you think will happen?"

"I hope they don't break up. They have that lovely child, Stepan. What a smart youngster!"

"Takes after his father. Look how Pavel studies so hard. I heard him speaking English to someone yesterday. He has a real talent for languages," Karolina said with authority.

"Maybe so, but that doesn't bring in the bread and the milk."

"It may bring us more intelligent leaders. God knows we need them."

Galina was startled to hear the divine mentioned. Religion was not welcome anymore. The party had tried to sweep it away in the dust and the corners, but the old remembered and didn't forget. Where else could they turn? she thought.

Lidiia rarely stopped to talk to the old women. They were busy gossiping as usual she noticed as she walked passed them on the way to the park to look for Olga and the children. Undoubtedly, they had heard Pavel and herself quarreling sometimes. She suspected anything she said to them would be discussed after she left, so she drew the hurt feelings within herself and avoided their eyes.

It was late in the afternoon, and she knew Stepan would be ready to come home with Valentin and Marina. Sometimes, she wondered if the child was affected by the quarreling.

Her fears were allayed when she heard Stepan's childish laughter just ahead on the path to the park. "Oh, Mama, look what I found today in the park!"

"What did you find, Stepan?"

"A toad. A toad. He just woke up from his winter's nap."

"That's very nice. He does look sleepy. I think you should return him to his mama, though."

"Can't I keep him, please, please?" Stepan pleaded, his blue eyes searching his mother's face for approval.

Ivan was jumping around excitedly and poking at the toad with his finger.

"Grandma, can I have him if Stepan can't keep him? Please?"

"No, he's mine, Ivan. You can see he likes me. Just look at his eyes! So what do you say, Mama?"

"Maybe for a little while, but I don't think he will do well in our place."

Stepan stopped outside the apartment to put some dirt into a large bowl. "This will be Toady's house."

Lidiia shrugged and carried the bowl up the stairs for the little boy.

When they reached the hallway, Lidiia was startled to see two KGB officers knocking on their door. She felt the terrible fear returning and sweeping through her body. What did they want now? Why didn't they leave them alone?

Before she could say anything, the officers were demanding to see the apartment. "We have come to search your place."

"Why have you come back? Two men were here five months ago. They found absolutely nothing."

"That was five months ago, Mrs. Lubov. Your husband continues to see those foreign nationals."

Lidiia was about to answer them, but they brushed her aside and proceeded to search the rooms. They didn't notice Stepan when he placed the bowl on the window sill in the bedroom. Then, the boy looked into the stern face of the officer and his uniform and ran to his mother for protection.

"Mama, Mama, what are those bad men doing in our place?"

"We are not bad!" the officer said shouting at the child. "You're father is bad. He is working against our government!"

Stepan turned to Lidiia for an answer, but she just held him close to her.

An hour later, the KGB left the apartment. Again, it was left in a mess. They had found Pavel's radio and took it away with them.

"That's m-m-y papa's," Stepan whimpered, but the officer only frowned at him and pushed him to one side. He hurried to check on his new pet toad. To his sorrow, he found the bowl smashed on the floor. They had smashed the toad with their big boots.

Lidiia tried to comfort him, but Stepan cried uncontrollably and wouldn't listen to her. "M-m-my ne-ew toad is de-de-dead," he stuttered. He ran through the apartment looking at the mess, then sat down and cried when he picked up the squashed toad. "M-my n-n-ew pet!" His small body shook with sorrow and fright.

Before the rest of the family had returned from work, Lidiia had straightened the apartment, but she was unable to console Stepan. He continued to sit despondently on the couch ignoring Lidiia's attempts to read to him or amuse him with his toys.

Lidiia decided there was no use in berating Pavel when he came home. She was exhausted from their arguments and began to think in her darkest moments that maybe they didn't have any future together.

As the days passed, Pavel was the first to notice that Stepan was not speaking clearly and stuttered most of the time. "What has happened to the boy? Something has been going on here to affect him like this."

"Now, you are beginning to realize what the effect of these searches of our apartment by the KGB have on him and the family. I insist, I demand that you stop seeing those foreign nationals. Then, they will leave us alone. You must do it for us or I will..." Lidiia suddenly stopped. She reached out and grabbed the back of a chair for support and realized that her anger was driving her forward, completely out of control.

"Stop it! Stop it!" Pavel shouted. "You accuse me of causing problems with our son. What are you doing, yourself? You expect me to put my tail between my legs and go on like some beaten dog? I should let the KGB do this to me? Just like they try to break other people? Just like they did to my grandparents? I won't give in to them. They are just trying to destroy me!"

Suddenly, there was a sound at the door. Marina and Valentin were just returning from work. They immediately noticed the tension in the room and the anger in their children's faces. Stepan was crying softly in the corner. Marina picked him up and tried to sooth him. The room became very silent. Everyone drew in their feelings and took up their lives where they had abandoned them.

It was a late summer evening when Ivan noticed some of his friends having a drink of wine not far from the park. He was on his way home from work and had been congratulating himself on his good fortune—such a beautiful wife and fine son. His mother had been ill, so Allery had been staying home more to care for Ivan. But Olga was getting better now.

Some music was drifting through an open window. A sentimental Italian song. It stirred his feelings, and his thoughts turned to Allery again. How beautiful she was in her white, flowing nightgown last evening! She had worn it on their wedding night when they had come together for the first time. What an angel she was. What an angel! And Ivan was the result of that love. They had created him together!

"Come on over here, Ivan! Have a drink with us." It was Maksim.

Ivan started to move toward the group. He rarely drank these days. Pavel's father had even called him a Ne Nash once! Mainly, he didn't have time. And mainly, he wanted to get home to his wife and child.

"Here's a glass for you. A toast to your health, my friend!"

"It is good to see you again, Maksim. How is your new wife?"

"Karolina is fine. She and Allery work at the same store now."

"How old is your son, Ivan?"

"He just turned four last week. Doesn't seem possible. But, I must get on home. It's getting late." Ivan knew that Allery was making his favorite dish tonight for his birthday. A special Russian stew. It had been difficult for her to get the meat and the vegetables. It had entailed getting up very early and standing in a long line.

He hurried through the streets. It was a Saturday night. Many people were crowding into the stores, mainly to look around since few had any rubles to buy anything.

Suddenly, Ivan heard sounds of gunfire, and people shouting. There was no time for Ivan to duck for cover. He fell on his face, the blood running in swirling pools on the pavement. He tried to raise himself up, to grab for something to save himself. His last thoughts were for his wife. A scene passed before his eyes. It was Allery standing there with outstretched arms. But he could not go to her. He slowly turned his head and saw the glaring eyes of Yakov staring at him as the man fired another round of bullets into his body. A small smirk formed on his lips.

"Goodbye, you son of a bitch!" he yelled as he disappeared running toward a vacant building.

Chapter 10

For Allery, life seemed to be crumbling all around her. As the days passed, she seemed to be walking in darkness. There was no direction or meaning. She had Ivan to fill her arms, but it was not the same sweet understanding and love as she had known with Ivan.

People came and tried to comfort her with words like, "It was all so senseless. He was a good man. He was well liked."

Pavel's old grandmother, Karolina, told her that he was in God's hands, resting in peace. But Allery, herself, could not live in peace. Ivan was gone. What did it all mean? How could she put her life back together again?

Soon after she had talked to Karolina, the old lady died so naturally and peacefully that the contrast between her passing and Ivan's violent death was maybe like the contrasts of life itself.

Andrey had turned into a quiet, withdrawn young man. He took refuge in his studies, and Allery was thankful for that. At least, he wasn't out looking for revenge. She hoped that when he had moved out of his grief, he would eventually put all this behind him. For herself, she felt as though she had no life of her own and no way to turn.

Then about a month later, she learned that Lidiia and Pavel were going to divorce and live apart. Lidiia wanted the apartment that Karolina had occupied, so Pavel agreed. She told Allery that she was convinced that Pavel's problems with the KGB was affecting their son. Allery knew they had been having problems almost from the beginning of their marriage, so their separating was not a surprise. They didn't seem in tune with each other.

Pavel and his mother continued to try and assist Allery and Olga, but finally Allery decided to go back to live with her family. She needed the support of her parents and sisters.

In some ways, Pavel thought it was a relief to have separated from Lidiia. Now, the quarrels had retreated back into the walls, and only faint whispers woke him at night or appeared on the pages of the book while he was studying. After a while, they disappeared, and he was at peace with himself. He continued to see the foreign nationals until the middle of the year when they had completed their contract with the Lipetsk Steel Company.

But Marina and Valentin were concerned about their son, especially Marina. "Pavel keeps to himself too much, Valentin. He doesn't go out to see any of his friends. Just sits back there and studies all the night. Do you think he regrets breaking up with Lidiia?"

"I doubt that. They didn't see things the same way. She saw things her way, and he saw things his way. They weren't alike. Two different people walking two different roads."

"Yes, but I thought maybe a wife would be good for him. Now he is so quiet."

"Mama, he's always been quiet. Maybe because he is the only child, he's had more time to think. He's developed habits to be by himself."

"Well, he used to spend weekends with his grandparents, and all the children used to get together there. It was good for him."

"He will find his way. In another year, he will have completed his education at the university. Maybe soon he will find himself a girl and settle down."

Strains of this conversation reached Pavel in the back bedroom. He lifted up his head to say something, but leaned back over his books again. He knew he was certainly in no hurry to begin a new relationship. It had been six months now since Lidiia had moved from the apartment.

He was thinking about this conversation again when he was riding the bus to Troyekurovo, the small rural village outside of Lipetsk. Students were supposed to go to the nearby villages and help harvest the crops on the collective farms. Sitting opposite him was another young student. She was very attractive. She was lovely with such fair soft skin and fine features. Her dark eyes sparkled when she talked to her friends sitting next to her. They called her "Natasha."

Natasha. Natasha. Pavel let the words drift silently over his tongue. Well, maybe he thought. He decided he would put this all to the test. By chance his leg was extended across the aisle, and his foot was almost under her feet. At that moment she was just sitting there, evidently day dreaming and looking out of the window at the passing countryside.

Somehow a crazy idea came into Pavel's mind. Okay, he said to himself, if all of a sudden she moves and steps on my foot, then this girl is the one for me. If not, I'll just forget about it.

At that exact moment that Pavel was running this plan through his mind, her foot moved suddenly on top of his foot. A crazy idea, he knew, but somehow the idea agreed with him.

When they got off the bus, he walked over to her. "I think I've seen you around the university. What are you studying?"

"English. I decided to be an English teacher. But I'm finding that the language is very difficult."

"That's what I am studying. I will be through in almost six months." Pavel spoke the words in English to try her out. See what she could understand.

"Oh, you speak perfect English!" Natasha exclaimed in Russian. "I find it very difficult to express myself easily in English."

"I can help you. I have some books in English that I can loan you. I bought them in Moscow."

Natasha was very impressed. After a while, she stopped and asked, "Do you like rock music?"

"Yes, I'm very fond of rock music. In fact, I've been collecting rock tapes for the past couple of years."

"Have you? Some students get together, dance, and play rock music in one of the rooms after school on Friday. Maybe I will see you there sometime?" Natasha made the effort to say the last few words in English.

Pavel was pleased. "That sounds good. Maybe I'll drop by on Friday after my last class. I could bring along some of my tapes."

A few days later, Pavel hurried to the room that was supposed to be where students got together and listened to the music. But, he was disappointed. Natasha was not there. He sat down and glanced through the tapes. He noticed that many were popular Italian songs like, "Amore No," and "Il Tempo Se Me Va."

Suddenly, he looked up and saw Natasha walking over toward him. "Do you like them? Here are two popular performers, Pupo and Adriano Celentano."

Pavel nodded and started to talk about some of the tapes he had collected. "Sometime, maybe you could come over to my place and listen to them. I live with my parents in an apartment on Gazima Street."

"I would like to do that." She was very impressed with Pavel's knowledge of music, especially rock.

As the music began again, Pavel moved out to a space and Natasha followed. Pavel noticed that her face filled with a special light as she listened to the words of the song and began to dance to the beat of the music.

What a beautiful young girl, Pavel thought. Her face is so expressive. She reaches out for the same things I do.

"Let's go out and walk along the river," Pavel suggested when the students began to leave. He wanted to find out more about her.

The day was very warm for fall, but the mist rising from the river rose and cooled the air. The sun sent shafts of light through the trees. The path along the river was exceptionally beautiful today, but for Pavel and Natasha their eyes were only on each other.

They started out speaking in English. At first the words came easily, tumbling out in their eagerness to be understood.

"I come from a large family, Natasha explained. "I came to the university right after high school. I have several more years."

"Do you have a boyfriend?"

"No, maybe because I am too shy. I don't know. But that's what some of my friends say."

That's very true, Pavel thought as he noticed that when she spoke she often cast her eyes down with a slight smile. But her shyness reflected something special about her. A certain thoughtfulness.

"Well, I am an only child. I live in a two-story red-brick apartment house. There are always a lot of people outside the apartment house. Somebody brought in some sand where the kids can play and make sand castles out in front."

"Do you have a girlfriend?"

"No, but I was married for about five years. We divorced about six months ago. I have a little boy almost four and a half years old. Are you surprised?"

"I don't know. I hadn't thought about that." Natasha tried to continue in English, but stopped suddenly and began to speak in Russian. "I can't find the English words to say what I mean."

"That's all right. Let's just walk and talk about music. I can see you love it as much as I do."

Suddenly, they saw a tall young man approaching them on the path. He was carrying several books. It was Andrey!

He put his arms around Pavel in a warm embrace. "How good to see you, Pavel! I haven't seen you in several weeks!"

"Good to see you, too, Andrey! How is your mother now?"

"It has not been easy for her. Sometimes she is very lonely. I guess I'm not much help to her. I have to study so much of the time." Andrey sighed with regret.

"Does Allery come over with the baby?"

"Sometimes, but remember, she has to work. The baby is over four years old now!" He looked questioningly at Natasha.

"Oh, this is Natasha. She is also a student at the university. I met her on the bus going over to Troyekurovo where we helped the people on the farms." Pavel smiled to himself at his private scheme of seeing if this attractive girl would place her foot on his foot, and then he would try to start going out with her. Someday, he would tell her about this, and they would laugh together.

Andrey nodded in recognition. She was a beautiful girl. If they were right for each other, it would be good for Pavel. His mother often talked about the tragedy of his marriage with Lidiia. They had not been right for each other, even though she was such an attractive girl, and she had given him a beautiful son. They were not right for each other.

As Andrey walked passed them, Natasha looked up at Pavel, her eyes filled with questions. "Who is Allery? What happened? He seemed so sad when he mentioned his mother being so lonely."

Pavel explained that Andrey's brother was murdered in the streets near his home. His words were filled with pain as he told how Yakov had beaten Andrey into unconsciousness and how Ivan had tried to find Yakov and get his revenge.

"So Ivan got into a knife fight with Yakov over what he did to Andrey? Then Yakov wanted revenge on Ivan for putting him in prison for a while?"

"That's right."

"Do you think Andrey will still try to avenge his brother's death?"

"We hope he will be so busy with his studies that it will keep his mind occupied. Andrey has become very quiet and reserved. He used to have a real temper. Quite different from his brother, Ivan, who was usually pretty calm, except, of course, when it came to his brother's beating. That, he couldn't tolerate."

"I'm sure his mother and Allery have suffered a lot from this tragedy."

They walked on together, very thoughtful and thinking and commenting about the little child left behind without his father. And how much Ivan had loved his wife and little boy.

Pavel didn't want that afternoon to end that way. He was hoping that he might find a moment to hold her and kiss her softly on the lips. He wanted to find out if her eyes would light with a new softness when he touched her.

But it was soon time to leave because Pavel had to return to the university and study at the language lab for a few hours. Natasha promised to meet him again when her class was out on the following Tuesday. They would meet near the benches out in front of the university.

On the way to the university that Tuesday morning, Natasha thought about what Pavel had told her of his life. What did it mean? He had been in the army, married and had a young son. She had seen him around the university, but before now she hadn't paid much attention to him. Big, tall men with a strong muscular build had always attracted her before, but Pavel was slender and not as tall. Still, Pavel was much more intelligent than the men she had met in her classes. And he had a certain way of seriously discussing something, then finishing the sentence with a clever remark and a quick smile. His ideas had a way of entering her mind and compelling her to think of him.

Natasha was late. Her teacher kept the class over an extra twenty minutes. She was worried that Pavel would have left to study in the library or somewhere else. But he was still waiting near the benches as she bounded down the steep steps from the university.

"I'm sorry. You know, it's bad enough to have to go to that class where we are studying the history of Marxism and Communism, and then to have this teacher keep us overtime!"

"So you share my feelings about Communism? Why don't you just drop that course?"

"That's fine advice to give a young student!" she laughed. "You know we have to study that stuff in order to pass the exams. I just want to take the English and literature courses. And they don't offer many courses on those subjects."

"Yes, it is a pain. Next time I go to Moscow, I will get you some English books. In the meantime, you can borrow some of mine. I'll show them to you when you come to my place."

Natasha's face shone with pleasure. "I would like to see them and some of the tapes you have. I don't know much about the modern groups."

"You don't have a tape or record player in your family's apartment?"

"No, our family is very poor. We just have a radio, and you know they don't play modern music. Just Communist songs devoted to Lenin and the Communist Party." Her voice dropped at the words, "Communist Party."

Pavel could sense the disdain in her voice. The disapproval. Here was a girl who was aware of the affect of communism on the people. "Let's go for a walk along the river. I think we might find the last of a few wild flowers in the woods." But Pavel really wanted to be alone with her.

The path down to the river was steep, but worn from the footsteps of many people coming to view the beautiful scenery along its banks. It was quiet at this time of the year as though the river was enjoying the warmth of the sun on its surface. "Look, there is a flower just beginning to bloom." Pavel picked it and held the pink petals in his hands."It's as soft and delicate as your cheeks," he said standing close to her.

She looked down at the flower and then turned to look up into his eyes. They held a deep caring and sincerity.

Pavel took her gently in his arms and kissed her softly on her lips. Yes, as he had hoped, her eyes were filled with a special warmth. "I am so glad that you came into my life, Natasha."

They walked along in silence for a while. Natasha didn't know what to say. "That's so nice of you to tell me that. For myself, I don't know what to say. Everything between us has happened so fast."

Before they parted that afternoon, Natasha promised that she would go home with him on the bus the following week and see his tape collection. This intelligent, serious man had come into her life so quietly. But she began to realize that when she wasn't with him, she had a certain loneliness, a longing to be with him and a longing to share with him the music they both loved.

The next week went by very slowly for Pavel. He was looking forward to showing Natasha his books and tape collection and sharing some of his life with her. Although the apartment was very plain and small, this is where he had spent most of his life.

Natasha was surprised at Pavel's very large collection of music. He showed her the books he was reading about the different groups and singers—all so new and interesting to Natasha. They listened to the hard rock music of the sixties and the seventies. Pink Floyd. At the university when the students got together, they mostly played the sweet music from Italy.

"What will you do when you finish your courses at the university, Pavel?"

"I guess I will teach English in some school. What do you plan to do?"

"The same thing, only I have two more years, you know."

They were sitting on some cushions on the floor. Slowly, he moved closer and put his arm around her, drawing her slender body close to his. He looked into her eyes. They were sparkling and encouraging. He began to kiss her and hold her tighter. He could feel her young body and soft breasts against him.

Suddenly, there was a knock at the door. Pavel knew it was not time for his parents to be returning from work. He was surprised to find Valadimir Korotch standing anxiously in the hall.

"I am very sorry to intrude, but I thought you would want to know that the militia picked up Yakov today. He claims again that Andrey is a spy against the government, just like Ivan, and that's why he killed Ivan. The KGB came and searched the apartment again. I hope they didn't come to your apartment?"

"No, but I don't think they'll bother me because my foreign friends left Russia some months ago. And that was the reason they were after me."

"I hope you are right, but I think once you are on the files of the KGB, it will be some time before they leave you alone."

Pavel shrugged and turned to Natasha. "This is my friend, Natasha, Doctor Korotch. He lives in an apartment downstairs. Natasha is also a student at the university and is studying to be an English teacher."

Valadimir recognized immediately why Pavel was attracted to the young woman. She had a certain youth and shyness about her, yet when she spoke she had the intelligence of an inquiring mind—one that Pavel could surely relate to in conversations.

They discussed music for a while, and then Valadimir said he had to leave and return to his apartment to get some rest.

"Well, it's good that the KGB wasn't here today," Valadimir remarked as he walked away, but the worried concern still remained on his forehead.

"What's this all about, Pavel? I don't understand why he is talking to you about the KGB. I didn't know you were being questioned by them."

"It's all because I used to visit two foreign nationals from Italy and England. Two girls from my classes were going with them, and they introduced me. I spent quite a bit of time with Matt and Ivanio, mainly just to practice English. They became good friends of mine. The KGB didn't like my seeing them. They claimed the men were spies. Those men left the country some time ago. I can't believe I have anything to worry about now."

"Is that all that happened?"

"Basically, that's all that happened. I can't understand what those fools were doing. After all, just because I was being friends with some people who weren't Russian, they had to cause me all that trouble."

As Natasha left the apartment, she could still sense the uneasiness in Pavel's voice. Dr. Korotch's warning seemed to follow her as she walked down the hallway. When she was with Pavel, she didn't want to leave. She felt a strong stirring within her that felt good and warm. As these thoughts filled her mind, the warning of Korotch came slowly into her troubled feelings. Was her life taking a different turn? Was it where she wanted to go?

Chapter 11

It was in the fall of 1986 that Pavel started teaching at the Plekhanovo High School in Lipetsk. At that time, Pavel was teaching English classes, and Natasha was still attending the University of Lipetsk.

One evening, Pavel was watching Gorbachev speaking on television. Suddenly, there was someone calling his name and knocking at the door. It was Andrey. Pavel hadn't seen him for almost a month now.

"Come on in, Andrey, listen to Gorbachev."

Andrey looked disinterested and made a face.

Pavel ignored his indifference. "You know, it doesn't look like Gorbachev wants to bring about big changes. He doesn't mean to change the structure of our society or the Communist Party. He just wants some reforms to improve the party and to improve our economy within the Communist system."

"I don't think we need to improve the Communist system," Andrey said in a determined voice.

Pavel stared at Andrey in amazement. "That's a surprise coming from you! After all the militia and the system did to your brother. Then, they ended up releasing Yakov? I don't understand."

"Maybe I just want to stay healthy. The KGB has warned me and searched our apartment several times. One of the officers advised me to start going to party meetings. If I do this, they will get off my back. You can't imagine how my mother is suffering."

"I understand that, Andrey, but you can't let the KGB run your life for you."

"I know that, but I'm not sure what to do about them. Anyway, I have a night class and have to get going. Are you still going with Natasha?"

"Still going with her?" Pavel emphasized the words "still" with a note of surprise in his voice. "Of course. I'm crazy about her!"

Andrey laughed at his friend's enthusiasm and turned to leave. "I hope I find a beautiful girl like that!"

Those words sounded in Pavel's ears after he left. He had always believed that this tall, dark, Italian-looking kid would have all the girls chasing after him, but Andrey had become quiet and morose after his brother's death.

Pavel was troubled about Andrey, but he finally went back to watch the television program. When it was over, he sat down and turned the problems over and over in his mind. It was clear that Gorbachev didn't want to change the Communist system. But as Pavel watched Gorbachev speak, he saw the expression on the man's face change. At one point, the confidence on his face faded. Where was the country headed, Pavel asked himself.

The next day, Natasha decided to stop by the apartment on her way home from the university. It was late in the afternoon, and Pavel had just returned from teaching at the high school. Valentin was not home yet, but Marina was enjoying an afternoon with Stepan. Stepan was talkative and very bright. He was five years old now and was already learning to read.

Marina had bought him a large stuffed black bear for his birthday. Stepan was delighted with the him and always held him on his lap when his grandmother read to him.

"Bruno is learning to read, too, babushka! Look how he follows along with every word you say. Look at him. But I think he's hungry now. Can he have a sweet? Please, please, babushka?"

Marina laughed at her grandson's enthusiasm. "Are you sure it is Bruno that wants the sweet, or is it Stepan that wants the sweet?"

"Well, he looks very hungry, but he will share the candy with me. Just look at him. He's rubbing his tummy!"

"What's that you said, son?" Pavel asked as he placed some books on the table.

"Bruno wants some candy. He just said so."

"Okay, maybe we can find a piece for you, too, if you're good."

"I'm always good, Papa. Since I turned five years old, I forgot how to be bad. Ivan isn't five yet, and he gets in trouble sometimes."

Natasha followed Pavel into the room. "So this is your son? I think he resembles you in many ways. He has your blue eyes and some of the same expressions."

"Yes, I agree. Stepan does favors me a lot."

"You named him Stepan? Is that a family name or just a favorite name?"

94

"Oh, no, he was named after my grandfather, Stepan Danilov. I admired him a great deal. In fact, he was a great influence in my life."

"In what way, Pavel?"

"He always told me to never quit and to keep on striving."

"Stepan quit playing with his toys and looked up at the mention of his great-grandfather's name. "Tell me the story of Grandfather Stepan, Papa."

"Your grandfather escaped from a German concentration camp during the second World War just before he was supposed to be killed in the crematorium. He was standing in line with the other prisoners when he found the opportunity to escape. He ran naked through the fields, hiding in the tall grass during the day and suffering from the cold at night. Then he found some clothes hanging on a line near a home. Can you believe that a German woman fed him and gave him some clothes? Her own husband was fighting in the front lines. But he kept on moving, determined to get back home."

"Grandfather must have been very brave. I'm glad I was named after him."

"What happened to him when he got back to Russia?" Natasha asked.

"He had to go back to prison because he had been captured by the Germans and was considered a traitor!"

"How terrible! Those were the Stalin days. But how did your grandfather influence your thinking?"

"When I was growing up, he would say to me, 'Never mind competition. In this life, you don't compete with other people, you compete with yourself.' He said that there were certain tests that you have to go through in life, and if you don't meet those tests, you lose, and you lose not against the others, but you lose against yourself."

"I can see that it was his determination to meet challenges that have been so important to you."

"Yes, he was talking about finding your inner strength to move ahead in spite of any obstacles."

"Well, your son has inherited a fine name from a fine man. I wonder what obstacles you will have to overcome in the future?"

"Probably, plenty," Pavel acknowledged. "But come, Gorbachev is going to be on television again. I think he is supposed to make an important speech." He turned back to look at his son. Stepan had fallen asleep holding Bruno closely against his chest. There were little traces of candy in the corners of his mouth.

"Such a good boy, Stepan," Marina said as she smoothed the hair from the youngster's forehead. "Lidiia says she will bring him over to spend next weekend with us. It is still nice outside. Maybe Marina will bring Ivan over and we can all go to the park and let them play together."

When Pavel turned on the television, Gorbachev was speaking because he was presiding at the party congress. "Look, Natasha, every day his face seems to change. I think the man is lost. You can almost see the panic in his face."

"I think he is losing control. He wanted to make some reforms, and now he seems lost. Maybe he can't handle what is going on in Russia."

"Everything is moving so fast. These are new times. Still, Andrey was over here the other day. He said the KGB advised him to start going to party meetings. He wasn't sure what he was going to do!"

"Maybe he just wants to keep out of trouble. The family certainly has been through a lot of trouble!"

"Yes, that's so, but that doesn't sound like Andrey. He's never gone along with something he didn't agree with—that's not his nature. More defiant, I'd say, than a blind follower of the party."

"What does he know about the party?"

"The stuff we are all fed in school. Until recently, the terrible crimes of Stalin have not been revealed to the people, yet the television has continued to glorify the Communist Party and what it is doing for the people. And look! Now, we have trouble getting enough food on the table."

"How do you know that Andrey doesn't agree with the ideas of the party?"

"You should have heard him talk after the KGB came the first time and searched their apartment. He said if the militia didn't release his brother, he would go with some friends and kill them all. He was filled with revenge."

At that moment, Valentin entered the door. He was tired from working all day. "You shouldn't have quit working at that bottling factory, Pavel." He went into the kitchen and returned with a bottle of beer. "My last one! What a life for a hard-working Russian!"

Pavel shrugged. "Well, that's a shame, Papa, but it was important that I finish up at the university and get a job. Maybe Valadimir Korotch still has some beer in his apartment left over from the old days."

"Ha, Valadimir! You must be crazy. That sick old fellow hasn't had any beer since the KGB sent him off to the prison camps. He's long since forgotten what beer tastes like!" Valentin shook his head sadly, muttering to himself.

Pavel motioned to Natasha. "Let's go over and see how Olga is doing now."

"Just for a while. They're expecting me home for dinner."

When they reached the end of the hallway, Andrey was just leaving. "I'm going out for a while. Going to meet some guys for a drink. Want to come along?"

"No, not this time, Andrey."

He had left the door ajar. Olga was sitting in a chair in front of a very small television set. She moved some books to one side on the couch for them to sit down. The ash trays on the coffee table were filled with cigarette butts. One was still burning and curling into a line of fine white ashes. On a nearby table, some old cracked plates still held the traces of gravy and crumbs of bread. In the corner were sacks of old garbage. Pots and pans were piled around the kitchen counter, but there were no signs of cooking or food.

Olga turned off the television and turned to the couple with a weak smile. She glanced around the apartment. "I have not been feeling so well."

"Have you been going to work?" Pavel asked, searching Olga's face for some answers.

"Oh, yes. That's about all."

"Are you sick?"

"Not really sick, sick. Just not up to doing much."

It was apparent to Pavel that things were not going as usual. "How are Allery and Ivan?"

"Fine. She will be here this weekend. Ivan and Stepan can play together."

"And Andrey?"

"Andrey." Olga shook her head sadly. "He has started going to some party meetings. I know they mean nothing to him. Just nothing."

"Maybe he is going to them just to keep out of trouble."

"Not Andrey. He's never been afraid of trouble before. When he isn't studying, he's going out to meet some other university students. Sometimes, they talk against the party when they stop by here. They try to convince Andrey not to go to meetings and remind him what happened to his brother under the system."

"What about Yakov? Where is he now?"

"Well, you remember he was picked up again by the militia after he killed Ivan. He was held for a while and then released. Maybe it was bribes, maybe it was because they believed his lies about Andrey. Who knows?" Olga's lips quivered as she spoke. She shook her head and looked down. She was trying very hard to control her emotions, but they kept pushing to the surface, demanding to loosen in a flood of tears.

"How many times I have cried for Ivan! But I try to keep up for Allery's and Ivan's sake. Poor child growing up without a father!"

Natasha put her arms around Olga. "Sometimes, life can be so hard, so cruel. Try to find comfort in your grandchild. He is such a fine little boy."

"And we will find more time to spend with the children and plan some good times together," Pavel promised. "But now, we have to go. Marina wants you to come over for dinner. She has made a hearty soup and fresh bread."

Olga didn't move. It was as though she didn't hear Pavel. Her eyes trailed out toward the window. There was no light in her gray eyes.

"How much she has suffered," Pavel explained to Natasha before she left to return home. "First, her husband was killed in a street demonstration years ago. Then Ivan. Now, Andrey is so difficult to understand. I wonder how we can help him, Natasha."

Pavel turned and walked back down the hallway. He decided to ask Marina to go and see Olga. He was sure she would come for dinner then. It would be good for her to have some company.

When Pavel entered the apartment, Stepan was just waking up. He came out of the bedroom, dragging his favorite little blanket.

"Papa, when I grow up I want to be brave just like my grandpa."

Pavel reached down and picked the child up in his arms. "You will be, Stepan. You will be."

At that moment, Marina came into the living room with Olga. They walked toward the table together. Pavel noticed that Olga was smiling. Marina had made her laugh a little. Mama is so wonderful working with people, he thought. She is so sympathetic and kind-hearted.

"Good hot soup!" Valentin exclaimed with enthusiasm as Marina placed the bowls on the table.

"Better than the beer, huh, Papa?"

"Never better. What beer does to the Russian, fuel does for the furnace!"

They all laughed heartily at Valentin's comparison. Pavel was about to answer when the phone rang. It was Maksim Romano. He wanted Pavel to meet him and several other men for coffee and discuss a business idea.

"I don't know what it is all about, Mama. Maybe interesting. Maybe not." The coffee shop was dimly lit, and the air was heavy with cigarette smoke. It was around eight o'clock, and the long brown tables that filled the small room were virtually empty now. Only a group of men remained in the shop. They swallowed the strong coffee rapidly as they talked.

They looked up when Pavel entered the room and watched him make his way to the table.

Pavel felt they were quietly appraising him with their eyes. Maksim was the only man in the group he recognized.

"Come sit down, Pavel. I want you to meet Sergey Tokaloff and Igor Sviatoslav. They are interested in opening up a disco club for young people here in the city. I know how much you love music, so I suggested to them that you might be interested in their venture."

"Tell me about yourself," Tokaloff began. "What are you doing now?"

"I started teaching English, Russian, history and literature at Plekhanovo High School this fall. I have a large collection of rock tapes."

"You know quite a bit about the music and the rock groups?"

"That's right."

"Then, here's what I have in mind. I am planning to open a disco. It will be privately operated. I think there is a real need for a place for young people to dance and listen to music here in the city. I need a D.J. That's where you would come in. Alex would be the sound manager, and Lana Rurik will be the light and sound manager. Sergey Dnieper may also agree to help us out as a D.J."

"It would bring in extra money, Pavel," Maksim encouraged.

"Well, of course, money is important, but this is something that really interests me. Tell me more. What music will we play, Tokaloff?"

"The KGB will give us a list of songs that we will be allowed to play. Of course, pop is played on the television and radio, but rock and roll will not be allowed. As you know, the government wants Russia to be completely separated from the West."

"I don't know what we will do. There isn't that much music we can play. You and I know that all the music that comes from the West is considered anti-Soviet."

"That's true. We'll have to decide what to do as we go along."

"I would like to bring in some other things. I believe it would be beneficial to the young people to tell them about the poets and writers who have written such powerful stories about their experiences. The government is now beginning to release some of those stories."

"Yes, we can find them written in some of the magazines like *Moskva, Neva* and *Yunost*. I know someone who has made copies of Solzhenitsyn's, *One Day in the Life of Ivan Denisovich* and *The Gulag Archipelago*. Maybe we can also bring in some of the paintings of our artists that are becoming well-known."

"Sounds like a good idea. Plan on getting started the first of the year. We'll get together again and talk some more."

After they had left, Maksim turned to Pavel. "So how is teaching going?"

"It is okay, but I'm not sure this is for me. You see, I replaced a teacher that had been on maternity leave for almost a year. Some of those students have missed out on almost a full year of foreign languages. I have to bring them up to the level that they should have been when I first started teaching the class."

"What about the lower grades? Do you teach any of them?"

"Yes, I teach grades four to eleven and have about six classes a day. I am very proud of my fourth graders. I can do a lot with them and spark some interest in them because they are just starting to study English."

"So you are not sure you want to continue to teach?"

"If something else comes along, I might be interested in changing jobs."

On the way home, all those ideas kept moving around in Pavel's mind. The music he listened to at home played on his imagination. He wanted to bring it to the young people and open their minds. He wanted to use a microphone and tell them about the people who were writing about their experiences and had suffered under an oppressive Communist system. Some of the best poets and writers had been forced underground. Many were just beginning to rise up and tell their story.

If he stopped teaching, what would he do? Natasha and he had become closer. Many times, their thoughts seemed to fuse into one. She understood him so well. And he looked forward to each moment they could be together. Once, she had puzzled him when they had talked about marriage. "I don't know about marriage, Pavel. I'm not so sure. So many of my friends who have married are not happy. Before they got married, they were so much in love, but now there seems to be only problems."

He pushed those thoughts away. There was no hurry. Too much lay ahead. The promise of the disco. Promoting the words of the poets and the writers. The old people either didn't care or understand. But hope lay with the young people and changes he hoped would make life more meaningful and where the people would not be oppressed by the KGB and the Communist Party.

As Pavel approached the apartment, the words from the popular song, "Revolution," moved powerfully into his mind. They kept pace with him as he walked, and he didn't know why.

Revolution, you taught us not to believe in Gods
You taught us to believe in the power of evil
How many worlds are we burning per hour?
All for the sake of your sacred fire.

We know that this wretched life is simply not able
to give you all you want. No, no, no
But we believe that we now can change if...
Yes, yes, yes

He wondered why this particular song had come into his mind. Which direction would they all travel? Whatever it was, he wanted to be there. He wanted to be a part of it. But he had to help Andrey find a way. Maybe he owed it to Ivan. He had to show Andrey a direction before he did something drastic. With his temper, anything could happen!

Chapter 12

A few months after the disco opened, it became apparent to Pavel that they needed new tapes, new music. One night, he went to Tokaloff and complained. He knew that Tokaloff had a keen business sense. He typified the young Russian who was eager to move out and explore the possibilities of a freer market.

"Tokaloff, we've got to get more music, different music, or the young people will get bored and not come."

"Well, you know the KGB has given us a list of tapes, and that's all we're supposed to play."

"Think about it, my friend. We haven't had the turn-out the last few weeks. Why don't we play some heavy metal for a change?"

Tokaloff began to turn this idea around in his mind. "We can try that. Tomorrow evening you take the microphone. Speak out a little. Here are some copies of a few selections from the *Moskva* magazine. They feature several writers who describe their terrible experiences in the prison camps. Try it out. See what you can do to interest the people."

The next day, Pavel arrived early to look around the club. He was pleased at the new sign out in front, "**Ulybka**." In English it meant "The Smile." The disco itself could seat around one hundred people. There was a bar and a little place to dance. Adjoining this room was a large hall. They planned to use this room for exhibitions and recitals.

In the beginning, they had convinced the authorities that this would be a good place for young people to meet and find good entertainment. Pavel and Tokaloff explained that young people had a lot of talent, and there wasn't a place for them to show that talent. They planned to invite new artists to display their work in the hall. Writers and poets could read their stories and poetry.

Tokaloff told Pavel that he envisioned the club would have an atmosphere something like Paris was at the beginning of the past century where writers would gather in the sidewalk cafes and discuss their views.

That evening, Pavel played some heavy metal tapes, and Tokaloff studied the reaction of the young people. He stood out in the crowd. He was extremely tall with sharp facial features as though they had been chiseled and refined.

It was past nine o'clock when Tokaloff handed the microphone to Pavel. "Everyone is having a good time, but I think we need to break things up a little."

"Good evening. I am Pavel Lubov and the D.J. for *Ulybka*. We named the club *Ulybka* because we believe that our club will bring a smile into your evening entertainment. We also want to feature new writers and poets that live and work among you. Tonight, I want to talk about Yakov Pasternak, the author of *Doctor Zhivago*. He received the Nobel Prize for literature in 1958, and look what happened to him. He was thrown out of Russia! That shouldn't have happened. We need to respect our writers and poets, just like some of you who write want to be recognized. Why is it important? Because no society will succeed if its best talent is suppressed. Look, yes, you can buy this book at the bookstore. Read it for yourself."

At this point, Pavel turned and put on a tape of the band DDT, *Revolution*. The words blared out to the crowd that was gathered around the microphone. "We know that this wretched life is simply not able to give you all you want, but we believe that we now can change it…Yes, Yes, Yes."

Soon, everyone took up the words. Their voices rang with enthusiasm through the club. At the close of the evening, many people stopped on the way out to talk to Tokaloff.

"We had a great time!" one couple commented. "Keep it up! We liked that tape of DDT much better than that soft pop. Get some more of that!"

After they had left, Pavel turned to Tokaloff. "Well, what did you think? Is this the way we want to go with the club? The young people are asking for more than soft pop."

Tokaloff stopped and carefully considered Pavel's suggestions. "Well, there're some problems. We don't have many other tapes. You know how much I want the disco to succeed, but are we taking some risks playing music like DDT?"

"Risks, risks?" Pavel's voice started to rise. "We can't worry about risks if we want to attract the young people. Maybe a little at a time?"

"Well, I guess that sounds about right."

Pavel wanted to say more, but it could wait. In his mind, he was already many months ahead. After all, if he didn't talk about what was happening to noted Russian poets and writers who would? If he didn't play the music that pointed the way of the future to those that came to the club who would?

One late afternoon the club had two visitors, members of the Komsomol, the Communist Youth League of the city. That day, Pavel had decided to stop by and look over some tapes that he planned to use that evening. He was surprised to find Tokaloff engrossed in a serious conversation with Vadim Chernovil, a member of the Komsomol.

"I like your club here, Mr. Tokaloff. This is a good place for young people."

"Pavel, show Mr. Tokaloff the hall where we have some paintings. This is all the work of our young people here in Lipetsk."

Mr. Chernovil nodded in approval when he saw the works of the young artists. "We are very pleased that you are exhibiting some of their paintings and giving them the opportunity to read their poems. You are doing a very good job. You are helping us by providing entertainment for the young people in the city."

But Pavel knew he was walking on a very narrow line. Now, every evening, he played, along with other tapes and records, some of the Russian underground music. It was definitely anti-Soviet. The lyrics told the listeners to get up and do something. What are you going to do this evening? Go to bed and sleep? Go out into the streets—a new day is breaking, a day for freedoms and a better life. People were looking for a way to go. Pavel felt this movement in everything around him. He wanted to be a part of what was stirring in Russia.

The disco was becoming very popular with the younger crowd of Lipetsk.

After a few months, Pavel realized it was important for him to get more tapes. A friend suggested to him that he might be able to buy some underground tapes in Moscow. He decided to leave on the eleven o'clock train just before the weekend. Natasha agreed to meet him at the disco, and they would leave a little early that evening.

It was eight o'clock when Natasha arrived at the club. She decided to go to the bar first. She didn't want to make Pavel nervous, especially if he were talking to the people with the microphone.

Natasha noticed that it was almost time for Pavel to take a break and let Sergey Dnieper take over as D.J. She moved toward a table near the bar and wondered how long it would be before Pavel would be free to join her.

A man at the bar looked up from his glass of beer and saw this beautiful young girl who had just entered the disco. His eyes followed her as she walked across the room. Her slender body moved gracefully as she walked. For a moment, she was the only one in the place for him. Great shape. He was lucky. She was alone.

"Excuse me, miss, would you like to dance to this one?"

"I'm sorry, I—I'm waiting for someone," Natasha blushed and stammered. She had never been in a disco or bar alone before.

"Wait a minute, mister. This gal is spoken for," Pavel said as he hurried over to the table. He ordered a beer for them both.

The man walked away. Just my bad luck again, he thought. I should have flipped a coin on the bar. Maybe it would have told me to forget it. I should have known a beautiful dame like that has a boyfriend.

"I'm glad you got here early. Maybe we can dance a little before we have to go to the station."

"I got some good news today. I wanted to tell you that I just received my grades for winter term. They are high enough that I can apply for a scholarship this coming spring semester!"

"Wonderful! Congratulations! I can imagine your parents are very pleased with that news."

"How is Stepan? "

"He is fine. Growing so fast. Can you come over this weekend? We are taking Ivan and Stepan to a puppet show. Then, we are all going to get together at our place for dinner. Mama and Allery are going to put it all together."

"Maybe I can get over for a while. I have something else to tell you. On the way over, I passed a building where they were having a party meeting. I heard their loud voices and hurried by, but I recognized one voice—it was Andrey's! Then I saw him coming out of the door. I don't believe he saw me."

Pavel frowned. "I didn't think he meant it when he said he was going to start going to party meetings. But come on. Let's dance. It gives me the chance to hold you close to me."

As they moved with the music, he felt Natasha's soft breasts next to him. Dnieper was playing a romantic love song. Maybe someone told him that Pavel was dancing with Natasha. What a beautiful woman, what a beautiful woman, he thought as he held her closer. He reached down and smoothed her hair away from her forehead, then slowly traced her cheek with his finger. He wanted to kiss her, but he would wait until they left the club together.

Dnieper was supposed to take over the rest of the evening. The man owned him a favor.

They walked together under the quiet street lights. A full moon was shining in the sky and cast a softness across Natasha's face. Pavel stopped and embraced her and began to move his lips slowly across her cheek. They sought each other's lips with a youthful eagerness.

Soon, they could see the lights of an approaching truck. Tokaloff had promised Pavel that he would leave the disco for a little while and take them to the train station. The surrounding streets were quiet at this time of night. Only a few drunken men were slowly weaving their way back to their apartments.

Natasha was looking forward to going to Moscow. She had been there only once before several years ago.

As the train slid out from the station, she tried to look out of the window.

"You can't see anything at all," Natasha said in a disappointed tone.

"That exactly proves the point I made with the KGB officer."

"What point?"

"Remember I told you that the KGB had arrested me and tried to tell me that my Italian friend was a spy? Well, they also said that they had seen this man on this very train taking photos from the window and taking notes at what he saw. That was supposed to prove to me that he was a spy!"

"How ridiculous!"

"Yes, I caught them in their own lies!"

"Do you know how to get to that place in Moscow where they sell the underground tapes?"

"Yes, I don't think it will be difficult to find. When you come over this weekend, I want you to listen to Pink Floyd's, *The Dark Side of the Moon*. It is a great tape. Roger Waters wrote the words. You will notice that the pronunciation of the words is excellent. Listening to tapes like this will help you with your English."

"Thanks for those books you got for me. They're helping a lot."

"See? I'm the best friend you ever had!"

"Well, I don't know," Natasha drawled, her eyes sparkling with amusement.

In spite of the jerking of the train at different stops, they both fell fast asleep long before the train pulled into the station in Moscow.

It was a gray, overcast day for early spring. The station was crowded with travelers hurrying to make another train. In the midst of all this congestion, an elderly man with crippled, bent legs was pushing himself along on a dolly cart. His face showed the strains of his exertion from trying to move through the many people. They hurried by him, pushing and knocking against the cart.

"Look at that poor man!" Natasha called to Pavel. "He needs a wheelchair."

"It's a sad situation for disabled people. Most disabled people are put into internats somewhere outside of Moscow. Maybe someday, there will be better planning for the disabled, and they will have ramps and elevators for them."

"I hope so. Then disabled people, like wheelchair users and even the blind, can travel and shop in the stores."

Pavel stopped to inquire what bus to take to The Rock Laboratory. This was the place where he hoped to find some underground tapes for the disco.

The bus let them off several blocks away from the laboratory. It was a very large building. The office was just to the right of the long hallway.

A tall, large-framed man rose from his desk to meet them. "I'm Mr. Makarenko. I was expecting you. Your friend, Sergey Tokaloff told me you were coming today. What can I do for you?"

"I am looking for some tapes of underground bands that we could use in our disco. I understand that you are a management company for these bands."

"That's true. Come. I will show you our sound-recording studio. This studio is entirely independent of any other studio. The bands like to come here and record, and we help them find places to perform."

"Is this the only place in Moscow that records the underground bands?"

"Yes. We do all the recording. Since our studio operates independently of everyone else, the bands are attracted to this laboratory."

"I need some recommendations. I want some tapes of bands that would go over well in our disco in Lipetsk. We have a young group, mainly people from age sixteen to thirty-six. Something like that."

"I understand. You know, I predict that soon it will be easier to find tapes since Mr. Gorbachev is beginning to like rock music."

"Then things will open up, Mr. Maklarenko."

"Yes, indeed we are all looking forward to that day, but now the militia sometimes breaks into a show that features an underground band and kicks everybody out! That's the way it is! The government believes anything connected with rock and roll is an ideological threat, maybe because of the power of the music or because a lot of it comes from the West."

After Pavel and Natasha left the building, they stopped at a small restaurant for some hot soup and warm bread. Pavel was pleased with the tapes that he had purchased at the laboratory.

"This is good music, Natasha. I think it will go over well in the disco. Just..."

Suddenly, several people burst into the restaurant. They were talking in loud voices with the manager about a big demonstration in Red Square.

They finished eating, and Pavel quickly paid the bill. "Let's go and see what's happening!" He had grabbed her hand and started running down the street.

"Are you sure you want to?" Natasha asked breathlessly, but Pavel only hurried all the faster. Soon, other people had joined them. A truck was headed down the street, and they quickly jumped on the back.

When they neared Red Square, they saw a yellow bus suddenly pull up. It was filled with KGB men. Hundreds of people were beginning to gather in the street. They were yelling denunciations of the Communist Party. Their faces were filled with anger as they pushed through the crowds of people. The air was filled with tension as more and more people filled the square and began to demand more freedoms, the end to suppression.

Then, Pavel and Natasha turned in horror to focus on what was happening in front of their eyes, right in Red Square. Two people had poured gasoline over themselves and set themselves on fire. Before the KGB could reach them, two more people had set themselves on fire. The crowd was electric with emotion and terror. The burning people ran through the square, shouting and demanding freedoms and a new life. People were pushing to get closer to the demonstrations.

Some people in the crowd frantically rushed toward the burning people. Pavel joined them and tried to extinguish the flames from their clothing. They were able to save some of them, but others were burned beyond help.

The crowd grew angrier. People were yelling and shouting and pushing forward in the square. About twelve feet away from them., ten other people were holding up signs, "Down with Communism! Down with the Soviet party! We demand freedom of speech!"

Pavel started to move forward to get a better view of the protesters. Their eyes were filled with determination, but the KGB men's eyes were filled with a hardness and hate as they moved toward the demonstrators.

Natasha covered her eyes from the terrible scene in front of her. She had never seen such horror, such emotion in a crowd before. "What will happen now to those people that survived?" Natasha asked, her voice choking in fear.

"The militia will probably arrest them. I don't think there is anything more we can do. Let's hurry over to the next street. Maybe we can get through and get over to the train station."

They had to walk almost a mile through the city before they were finally able to get a bus over to the train station. As they glanced back, they could see the KGB men in their huge blue overcoats arresting the people who were still alive after setting themselves on fire. The militia was breaking up the demonstrators and the crowds of people.

"How often does this happen here?" Natasha asked later as they found a seat on the train.

"Quite often. Tokaloff talks about it. He has a family here in Moscow. These demonstrations show the strong feeling people have about the government. Soon, this will spread to other parts of Russia. But, at first, it will probably happen very slowly and then more people will begin to get involved."

The first night that Pavel played some of the underground tapes that he had bought in Moscow there was a large crowd of people. The disco had been doing very well over the past few months. Tokaloff was pleased. It was his first business venture, and the group could see a real future for other discos.

Tonight, was Pavel's turn to use the microphone. He started out with his usual greeting. "Good evening, everybody. And what club are you enjoying with us tonight?"

The crowd responded with a rousing, "Ulybka."

"Good. The best place in Lipetsk. Have you head of Aleksandr Solzhenitsyn? He is one of our own writers who has written about the terrible torture and conditions in the Russian prison camps. Yes, a famous writer. He wrote about those terrible times in his *Gulag Archipelago*. The archipelago in the book stands for a country consisting of an archipelago of islands all made up of a vast network of penal institutions, all designed as a huge machinery for police oppression and terror on all Soviet life. Look, he is a famous writer, and what happened to him? He finally had to leave the country and live in exile.

Just as Pavel finished speaking, he noticed a familiar figure standing at the edge of the group. It was Andrey Dimitri!

Pavel hurried toward him, but Andrey turned and quickly disappeared in the crowded room. What would happen now, he thought in sudden desperation. Would Andrey report what he had said to the party? He and Tokaloff had literally put their whole hearts and souls into the operation of the club.

During the past months, Pavel had continually spoke out to the young people about how the government had threatened its most famous poets and writers. He wanted them to think about their society. Now what would happen?

Pavel saw Tokaloff approaching and signaling him to get off the microphone. He knew that Tokaloff had no idea that a party member had been present in the club that evening. But then, was Andrey really a party member? Pavel wasn't sure.

"Give us a break, Pavel. Put on that new tape you just got in Moscow."

"You mean, Kono?"

"Yes, the one called, "In Our Eyes.""

111

Was this the right selection, he asked himself after all he had just said tonight? Well, to hell with it! He was no damn coward!

Pavel turned and put on the tape.

In our eyes you can see the sparkles,
In our eyes you can see the hope
that was dead for our fathers.
In our eyes you can find the fountains
that pour the water of life
on the dead land.
Somebody said we had no future
Well, now you can see it in our eyes...

The crowd loved it! They tried to sing along with the music even though most of them didn't know the words.

"I like that one, Pavel!" Tokaloff exclaimed, nodding his head and keeping time to the music with his foot. "I'm glad you went up to Moscow to get those tapes. It will really be a boost for the disco!"

Pavel noticed that Tokaloff always dressed very casually for these evenings at the disco. But when he had a business meeting with some of the other young businessmen, particularly in Moscow, he was particular to dress with a shirt and tie and jacket. Impressions and business promotions were now a part of his life. He thought of himself as one of the "New Russians." Now each evening, his ready smile greeted all the young crowd each weekend as they entered the disco. Everyone knew and liked Tokaloff.

On the way home, Pavel decided that he would stop at Dimitri's apartment and see if Andrey were at home. He had to talk to him.

Olga answered the door. She was surprised to see Pavel this late at night. "Are you looking for Andrey?" she asked anxiously.

Pavel nodded and looked beyond the open door.

"He isn't home yet. I don't know where he is tonight."

"Tell him I want to see him the minute he gets home. It is important."

Valentin and Marina were sleeping when Pavel entered the apartment. Valentin had been drinking a few beers as usual and had fallen into a sound sleep.

The sounds of his loud breathing could be heard throughout the room. Papa was a good man, Pavel thought as he studied his father's face. His lively sense of humor always brought laughter to any group. He was a hard worker and often proclaimed that every hard-working Russian man was entitled to a drink at the end of the day whether it was the old home-made wine or the occasional beer that his son brought him. Valentin was very proud of his son and often told him he would go far in the world. But then, he would joke and say that he liked it better when Pavel worked at the bottling factory when he was going to school. Then, he was sure of getting some beer. After a while he would say with a good-humored smile, "Never mind, I have a son that was educated at the university! I'm very proud of him!"

Pavel had just started to review the lessons for his classes the next day when he heard a knock at the door. It was Andrey with a KGB officer! So his supposed friend had told on him, Pavel thought, his forehead frowning in disgust.

"This officer wants to ask you a few questions, Pavel. He accuses me of being a spy. He searched the apartment again today. Tell him you have seen me at party meetings, and I'm a loyal member of the Communist Party."

Pavel looked in amazement at his friend's request. After all, he was certainly no Communist Party member himself, and what did he know about Andrey? Still, he had to keep the kid on his side. "Yes, of course, Andrey is a party member. I can vouch for him. After all, I am his close friend and neighbor."

"And you are a good party member, Mr. Lubov?"

"Not exactly, but Andrey is a loyal party member. I know that for a fact."

The KGB officer smirked at Pavel's declaration and walked quickly down the hall making a loud sound with his boots and arrogant manner.

"Remember, Andrey, I stood up for you, my friend. So you were at the disco tonight and heard what I had to say. What do you think? Were you ready to report me if this officer hadn't come by to accuse you?"

"What do you think I am? Some kind of a shit to tell on a friend?"

"I don't know, Andrey, but you seem to have changed. And I don't understand why you are going to party meetings either. So what's going on?"

"Nothing. So what if I attend party meetings? If I get them off my back, I can turn around and do whatever I want." Andrey's dark eyes flashed with defiance.

"Maybe you can and maybe you can't. The more you attend those party meetings the more they think you are following along with their line of garbage."

"Garbage? Honestly, I don't know what to believe anymore. I hear people talking about freedoms and multiparty systems and wonder if they really know what is possible here in Russia."

"You don't think changes are possible in Russia? I don't understand. Here, you saw how your brother's murderer got released through bribes, accused you of being a spy and now the KGB men are searching your apartment. What kind of a man can stand and take that shit and not work for changes in our system?"

"What choices do we have? I know where you're coming from, Pavel, but some people are talking about economic reforms where people can start up their own businesses and get loans from banks. It sounds crazy to me."

Pavel looked intently at Andrey. He was taller now, and his thick black eyebrows and dark eyes gave a foreboding look that he couldn't miss. "Tokaloff and I are hoping it will be possible to eventually open up even more discos."

"The disco," Andrey said with some scorn. "The more you talked that night the more I turned against what you were saying. I don't know. I just don't know whether it would work out here. People here aren't like the people in the West. They don't have the know-how."

"People are strong in their feelings and ideas. You should have been in Moscow with me. There were many demonstrators in Red Square. Some of them were setting themselves on fire to show their protest against Communist rule."

"The crazy bastards! I think they're just fooling around with our minds with their ideas. Anyway, believe me, I wouldn't think of reporting what you say at the disco to the KGB!"

"I hope you are telling me a straight story, Andrey, or there will be lots of trouble for all of us."

"No trouble. On my brother Ivan's head, I tell you the truth!" Andrey said, turning and looking Pavel squarely in the eyes.

114

But Pavel wasn't so convinced as he watched Andrey walk down the hallway.

Why didn't he feel he could trust this young man? There was something in his tone that made him feel that Andrey could be easily swayed from the propaganda at the Communist meetings. He could be following the path of least resistance with them just like many other people were doing. Still, he could be dead wrong about him. But there was the potential of a real danger that this man might bring into his life.

Chapter 13

Several months had passed since Pavel had gone to Moscow and had purchased the underground tapes. It was the late spring of 1987. The disco had been doing well up to this point, but it was obvious to Pavel that Tokaloff was beginning to be concerned.

"You are going pretty strong on your talks to the young people. You know, about how the Russian poets and writers were suppressed."

"You think I am wrong to say those things?"

"Not wrong. Maybe soften it up a little. Then, too, there is the underground music that we have been using a lot of lately. "

"What are you saying? Not to play those tapes any more?"

"No, but maybe just mix it with some of the more accepted music that we're suppose to play."

What disturbed Pavel even more was that Alex, the sound manager and Dnieper, the other D.J. agreed with him. They seemed to be worrying about their jobs at the disco. Pavel had a tendency to put himself last and just do what he thought was right in his own mind.

"Is there something more to this that I'm unaware of, Tokaloff?"

"Yes, as a matter of fact I received a call from the KGB office just before you came in. You'd better get over there. Tell them that we have had high praises from the Komsomol and that they said we were doing a great job here."

Pavel hurried out of the disco. Their worried voices clashed in disharmony in his ears, but he felt someone must be behind all of this. Was it possible that it could be Andrey who had reported him just to climb out of his own trouble? He tried to put the disgust out of his mind, but it kept moving through his body even though he couldn't be sure.

When Pavel entered the office of the KGB, a man motioned for him to sit down before a large over-sized desk. It was piled with papers and well-worn file folders. Pavel decided that this was their life, probing into every corner of other people's lives.

His personal fears of the disco were soon alleviated as the KGB man started to ask questions. "We called you in here to ask you about Andrey Dimitri. We understand that he is your neighbor. We want you tell us the names of his friends in Lipetsk."

Pavel was surprised. This was not what he had expected. He had fully expected the officer to question him about his work at the disco.

As the officer continued, it seemed to Pavel that this man had known him all his life. He talked about his friends—Andrey and Ivan and his friends Viktor and Grigori at the university. He knew all about his family, his Grandmother Karolina who had recently died and Natasha, his girlfriend. In fact, he knew everything about him. It was as though this man were looking through a magnifying glass at his life.

After the KGB officer had interrogated him for about an hour, Pavel realized that this was their typical method of operation. If they know everything about you, they believed they could control you. But still, it was to his advantage to tell them everything he could about Andrey—especially about Ivan and how he had been murdered in the streets, so Pavel emphasized that Yakov had lied about Andrey being a spy just to escape prosecution himself. Finally, the officer told Pavel that he was free to leave.

As Pavel left the office, he began to think about Andrey. Surely, he would stay on his side through all of this. Now, it was evident to Pavel that the KGB had a file on practically everybody in Russia. This man had talked to him like he had known him all of his life and that was one of their methods to put fear into a person—that there was no escape from their investigations—that there wasn't a thing that they didn't know about you.

These thoughts lingered in Pavel's mind as the weeks passed. He was busy with the end of the school semester. Now, he was looking forward to the summer and some time to think about his future. He had not enjoyed teaching as much as he had expected.

Tonight was supposed to be a break from school papers and preparations. His old friends Zhupey and Maksim were coming over to the apartment for a while. He hadn't seen Zhupey in a long time. Natasha said she would try to come over for a while. She was all caught up with her homework in her classes

Stepan was spending the weekend with the family. His favorite toys were scattered across the floor in the living room. "This is a picture I drew of you, Papa," he announced proudly.

"What am I doing in the picture?"

"You are talking into the microphone at the disco."

"Who told you that I talk at the disco?"

The boy looked around the room for some help, but saw only blank faces staring at him. He shrugged. "I don't know. Maybe I heard Andrey talking to Allery. But Papa, will you put on a record for me?"

"I will put a record on for you if you promise to go to bed now. This music will put you to sleep."

At that moment, Natasha opened the door. She picked up Stepan and hugged him. "What a good boy to go to bed as his papa tells him."

Stepan gave Natasha a quiet little smile, knowing that the praise was supposed to help him mind and go to bed. She carried him into the next room.

When she returned to sit at the table in the kitchen, Zhupey and Maksim were already having a beer with Pavel. They were deep into a discussion about the subjects of his talks when he had the microphone at the disco.

"The only thing that bothers me, Maksim, is that I can't be sure what Andrey is saying to people about the disco, and furthermore, what I have to say when I have the microphone."

"You say that Andrey has been to the disco and disagrees with what you are saying about the suppression of our writers and poets?"

"Yes, and he disagrees about reforms and ideas for more freedoms for people wishing to start their own business. And now, he's attending party meetings to try to persuade the KGB men that he's not a spy as Yakov has claimed."

"That's a crazy idea. The KGB will probably let him alone after a while, don't you think?"

"I hope so. They called me into their office a few months ago and asked me all kinds of questions about Andrey."

"What are his viewpoints on communism?" Zhupey asked leaning eagerly across the table.

"He doesn't think a multiparty system will work in Russia, and the protesters are crazy."

"Is that so? Well, just keep an eye on him. It looks like he can't be trusted," Zhupey warned.

Natasha glanced over at Pavel. "I can't understand why anyone wouldn't support trying to get new freedoms for the people here in Russia."

"Well, there are some people that don't agree with us. Mainly, the old people and others that are not ready for changes."

"The KGB is beginning to lose control, but still, Natasha, would you stand up in front of other people and talk against communism? That takes a lot of courage!" Andrey asked with a serious frown.

"Yes, absolutely. If I believe in something like changes in our society, I will stand up for my views. Absolutely, Maksim."

"The time may come, Natasha, when you will have to take a position or follow what the Communists and the KGB demand!" Pavel emphasized.

The last day of school, Pavel was supposed to meet Natasha at the disco. It would be kind of like a celebration for the ending of the school year. It was not his night to talk to the young people or ask them to read their poetry. It would just a special time for them to be together.

Pavel thought that Natasha looked particularly beautiful when she sat down at the table that evening. He could smell a light floral perfume that enveloped her dark hair and soft white shoulders. She was wearing a casual light blue summer dress with thin shoulder straps. When she smiled at him, he could see the warm flicker from the candlelight in her eyes.

"You are especially beautiful tonight, Natasha. How I long to put my arms around you and slide the straps from your shoulders. Then, I would explore your body with kisses."

"Oh, Pavel, you are really too much! I think you have been listening to a lot of poetry."

"Some of it is very good poetry. Still, Natasha, I wish we could find a way to be alone together."

"This summer when it is very warm in the park?"

"Yes, a summer evening when it is very dark and we are alone. I want you to be all mine."

"I am all yours, now."

"I mean I want to marry…"

119

A tall figure suddenly appeared near the doorway and motioned to Pavel.

"I will be right back. Dnieper wants me to put on a few tapes while he takes a break."

A few minutes later, Pavel returned. "I just put on Savage's "Tonight." It is a beautiful song. Do you want to dance?"

When they sat down again, Pavel asked, "Do you remember what I was asking you before?"

"You were talking about getting married." Natasha looked down into the wine glass in front of her as though looking for the answer as she swirled the dark, red liquid around and around.

"Yes. What do you think?"

"I don't know, Pavel. I'm kind of scared."

"Why? Why are you scared?"

"I have some friends who were in love like we are and then after they got married everything changed."

"Things change because you make things change. We are so much alike, Natasha. We would not change."

The music stopped and Pavel went to put on another tape.

"What is that song, Pavel?"

"It is a song put on by a French group called *Space.*"

"You know, Pavel, I have always wanted to go to France. I've heard it is a beautiful country. But of course, it would be nice to just be able to travel somewhere."

"Maybe that will come, Natasha. So many things are happening now. I think people are ready for more of the freedom that you talk about."

"Well, it would be nice to just be able to buy some tickets and have the freedom to travel. As it is, we can't even book a room in a hotel in some Russian city unless we have some connection."

"Next year, you will have completed your teacher training. Do you have any idea where you might be teaching?"

"No, not right now. But of course, I am worried because you know that after graduating in teacher training students have to go and work in the village that has been designated for them. The conditions in a village are horrible. I can't even choose where I want to go and work. I hope something else turns up. Still, I have a relative that might be able to help me."

120

"Well, we'll hope so. But now, I should see you to the bus. We both have to get up in the morning."

The next day all hell broke loose. First thing in the morning, Pavel got a call to go directly to the regional Communist Party's office. He was totally baffled. What in the hell was up now? he asked himself.

He knew something was up when he entered the party's office. All the highest level from the regional party, the Young Communist League and the KGB officers were there.

First, the representatives of the league got their turn on him. Zhores Ozaolas started out first. "Listen, we work very hard with the young people. It is our responsibility to organize some social life in the town for them. And we mean to entertain and teach them, not to brainwash them like what is happening in the disco that you and your friends are operating."

"You forget that at the disco the young people have the opportunity to read their poems and stories. Their paintings are on exhibit in the hall. We are capable of doing all those things," Pavel emphasized.

"You are not doing a good job. If we get any more complaints from parents, we will close down the disco."

Pavel thought there was no use to argue with those people anymore. The Komsomol and the KGB were obviously overreacting when Tokaloff and the rest were trying to have a place to entertain the young people. The whole thing would probably pass over and soon be forgotten.

But this hope turned back to despair again when Pavel returned to the apartment. The principal of the Plekhanovo High School called and wanted to see him immediately.

It was the same story. The director of the school said they had received some information about him from the KGB. They didn't think he should be allowed to teach the children because he might have some bad influence on them.

The whole world had suddenly closed down all around him. He had been fired from his job at the school. The authorities were threatening to close the disco. At this point, he was totally without any work.

Pavel looked out of the window thinking he might get some ideas as he watched the people walking down the street. It was almost summer and the new, bright, green leaves of the nearby trees stood out in stark contrast to the blue sky. In the distance, he could see the first hint of a few dark, rolling clouds. It looked like a storm was coming toward the city.

The darkness of the clouds stirred his feelings. Pavel felt the rising tide of anger filling his body. He was so angry, so damn angry he wanted to strike out and protest against what had happened. The fools, the fools, he repeated to himself over and over again.

He went into the lavatory down the hall and looked into the mirror. In one quick, sudden moment, he took a razor and shaved off his hair. This was his protest. Maybe it was crazy he thought, but at least he would show them all what he thought of their damn Communist Party and the KGB that tried to tell people what to think and what to do.

Immediately, he decided to take a bus to the university and meet Natasha as she left her last class.

It amused Pavel that Natasha did not recognize him at first. The other students leaving the school turned and stared at him.

"What did you do? Why did you shave your hair all off, Pavel?"

"Come and let's walk along the river, and I'll tell you what happened. The regional office of the Communist Party called me into their office, and several high-ranking people had their turn on me. Now, they're threatening to close up the disco, and the director of my school fired me this afternoon!"

"All because of what?"

"The Komsomol claims that they are getting objections from some of the parents. Obviously, someone from the government was there last night and heard me speaking into the microphone like I usually do. Damn them! Damn the KGB and the Communist Party!" Pavel's voice rose in anger.

Several students walking on the path ahead of them stopped and stared at him. "Skinhead. Stupid skinhead!" one sneered.

"Let's go, Pavel. Let's get out of here!"

When they got on the bus to go home, people turned and looked at him. "Say what goes with you? What's the big idea of shaving your head? You some kind of a skinhead or something?" one teenager asked.

Pavel tried to explain what had happened to him.

As the weeks passed, he was annoyed at all the different reactions people had to his views. Some understood and others thought he was crazy. Natasha sympathized with him. Pavel was totally surprised when she shaved her head to protest the actions that were taken against him. He told her she really didn't need to do that. He knew she was sympathetic.

When Marina came home from work, she was very surprised at seeing her son. As a rule, she was a very quiet person and never interfered with anything he did. This time, Pavel didn't know what to expect.

"I don't know whether this is a good way of showing your protest or not. You're a grown up kid, so you should know what you're doing. Still, I have to say you certainly look ugly."

But that didn't perturb Pavel. It seemed as though his friends gathered around and supported him. They told him times were changing, and pretty soon the Communist Party and the KGB would not have such influence over people.

And that was the thinking when some of his friends got together in the small coffee shop near the university. When Pavel entered the shop, they were talking in excited voices about the new movements in the country. He was pleased that Tokaloff was becoming more optimistic.

"Well, Pavel, how's your head doing these days? You must be pretty cool up there without all that hair?"

Pavel laughed. "I guess so, but I'm still pretty hot about the whole thing!"

"You should have kept your mouth shut up and just let the kids do all the talking. Maybe that would have satisfied that good-for-nothing Young Communist League."

"It was all the talk about the suppressing of our best writers and poets and the underground music that brought on the trouble." Pasaukhov stared directly at Pavel.

"What else could we do? We say we want to tell the young people how the government has been suppressing our greatest writers and poets and the people in our society. What were we supposed to do? Just go and hide our heads in the corner like a bunch of idiots? What kind of men would we be if we did that?"

"You're right. We did what we had to do," Tokaloff agreed. "Things are changing very fast now. We really can't cope with the

Communist regime any more. After all, a lot of us have business abilities, and look at the people in the West who have abilities. They can work hard, start businesses, and move ahead."

"Yes, Russia is a virgin, huge market which needs a lot of things."

"What are you planning to do now, Pavel? You lost your job at the school. Where do you go from here?"

"I've asked myself the same question over and over. I'm not all that sorry I lost that job. Teaching school wasn't what I really wanted to do. Actually, I don't know where I'll go from here."

"I think Valentin would like to have you go back and work at the bottling factory. I'll bet he misses that beer you used to bring home to him," Pasaukhov said with a broad smile.

"Yes, he likes his beer all right."

"Say, what happened to that Andrey Dimitri fellow? The one whose brother was shot down in the streets. Did he turn communist or what?"

Tokaloff sat up suddenly. "Wait a minute. Do you think he was the one who complained to the Komsomol?"

Pavel turned and faced him. "My God, I wonder! But the last time I saw him he swore that he would be loyal to us and our disco!"

"Is that so? You never can tell about some of these people what they'll do."

"If he's in on this, there's going to be plenty of trouble!" Pavel said angrily and started toward the door. He never looked back to see their reaction.

Chapter 14

Pavel searched through the folders on his desk for the papers that he was supposed to translate into English. He had been working as a translator and interpreter for the Lipetsk Steel Company for the past two years. Often, he had to interpret during important meetings since people came in from all over the world to negotiate contracts with the plant managers. As he had explained in the beginning to Natasha, this plant was one of the largest producers of raw steel in the world and was, in fact, a huge, iron and steel plant combined. The Lipetsk Steel Company was under the management of the steel ministry in Moscow. The ministry controlled the whole steel industry.

He had placed his anger toward Andrey on the shelf for the time being. Olga had told him that Andrey had abruptly moved out of the apartment soon after Pavel had been fired from his job. He told his mother that he was moving in with four other men in the top floor of an old reconstructed building across town. That's all she knew. He had refused to tell her anything more.

Pavel was suspicious that Andrey seemed to vanish right after they received complaints and threats from the Komsomol, but in the back of his mind he believed that Andrey would eventually surface. It was just a matter of time.

Still, the disco continued and had been having another very successful year. In fact, Pavel and a few of his friends had started a little business. In the past, they had tried to get some good music for the club, and now that they had established the channels of getting that music, there was a real demand for the tapes. On the side, they started a recording enterprise. Ironically, Pavel was making more money here with this company and the disco than he was at the steel plant.

After Pavel left the steel plant that afternoon, he headed for the disco. He knew he could pick up something to eat before he started to work. Now, he was in charge of the whole program—the music—the microphone that he used to talk about political concerns and what was going on in the country. Everything.

Tokaloff and Pasaukhov were full of good humor and jokes when Pavel walked into the disco that evening."Hey, Pavel, we were just talking about how the Komsomol threatened to close down our place back in 1987, probably for playing underground music. Now, look, they are playing a lot of the underground music on television," Tokaloff laughed.

"Yes, and now *Melodia* is putting out those underground bands on their records. Think about it. This company is owned and controlled by the government!" Pavel added.

"Times have changed," Pasaukhov emphasized. "Let's hope the KGB realizes they shouldn't pay attention to those things anymore."

That evening at the club, Pavel decided to put on the record, "Quiet Nights." The words were sung by Victor Tsoi with the Kino Band. Tsoi was openly calling people to rise up and stand proud to fight for what they deserved. People have to make a choice in their lives whether to go to sleep or go out into the streets and join the people who want to make a change.

Just as he was leaving the building that night, a familiar figure was lighting a cigarette under a lamp light. Evidently, he had just come from the disco. Nothing else was open in the surrounding neighborhood.

When he turned around, Pavel recognized the man's voice. His face had changed from a very boyish look to a man who had been living in very poor conditions. Yes, it was Andrey!

"So it is you? Did you just come from the disco?"

"Yes and I heard that song you played, "Quiet Nights." It doesn't make sense to tell people to fight for changes. We are better off under the communists. You will not survive under any other government."

"You like to have the KGB coming into your life and searching your apartment? Telling you that you are a damn spy?"

"No, but I no longer live with my mother, and I am no longer under suspicion."

"Why did you come to the disco?"

"I thought I might just listen to some hard rock, but instead, I heard underground music and your propaganda."

"I want to know something, Andrey. Did you turn us in? Is that why the authorities threatened to close the disco back in '87?"

"No. That is absurd. Your crazy disco means nothing to me," he smirked as he walked away. Up the street, he was joined by two other men. Pavel could hear them talking about the underground bands.

"They are no good for people to hear!" one said emphatically, his voice echoing against the buildings as they passed.

Pavel was very angry at those words. They were just parroting things that they had heard at party meetings. He had the urge to go after them. Confront them with their words, but he realized that this wasn't the time. He stopped and shook his head in disbelief. If only he could change their minds, especially Andrey. How had this young man's mind been so twisted? Did he owe it to Olga? Pavel was filled with dismay, but at the same time the anger began to build up within himself at the thought that this man and his friends might have been behind the threatened closure of the disco and the loss of his job.

While the disco meant nothing to Andrey, it meant a great deal to Pavel and his friends. The Ulybka was open five nights a week. Now, on weekends up to two hundred people patronized the club. Pavel and Tokaloff had kept in touch with the underground bands in Moscow and St. Petersburg. Sometimes, they invited those bands to perform at the disco. They were always a very big success. For Pavel and his friends, the disco was important.They saw things were beginning to happen with their business. So much was moving ahead in Russia at this time, and they wanted to be a part of this surge of freedom.

As Pavel watched Andrey and his friends disappear down the street, he felt the hand of Tokaloff on his shoulder.

"That was Andrey, wasn't it?"

"Yes. He disapproves of the music we play."

"So, I wonder if he doesn't mean trouble?"

"Still, I'll try to find out where he lives and have a talk with him. But, I sense lots of trouble ahead!"

As the months passed, the job at the steel plant became more and more demanding. Thoughts of Natasha often entered his mind often when he had a few moments to himself. How he longed to have an apartment of their own where they could be together, to hold each other and make love whenever they wanted. He missed seeing her. They could only spend moments together almost like trying to reach up in the air and catch a colorful bird and hold and caress it for a short time before it was time for it to fly away again.

Many foreign engineers came to the plant, and Pavel was responsible for their training. Most of the time, the engineers came from developing countries such as, Iran, India, Pakistan, Egypt, Nigeria or Indonesia. Usually, a delegation would meet about eight in the morning, and Pavel would take them to a certain section of the plant for training, such as steel making, steel rolling or the blast furnace. This day was no different than any other time. A delegation was due to arrive from Germany that morning. Pavel would take them to the blast furnace where some of the blast furnace managers would speak to them for a couple of hours. It was Pavel's job to translate for the foreign engineers.

This morning, Pavel was called into the KGB office before the delegation arrived. This was the usual routine. Every week, the KGB would call him into their room. He was used to it by now. So were the other interpreters who worked at the plant.

Today, their warnings seemed more severe to Pavel. What was up, he wondered. Maybe they just wanted to assert their authority.

"I'm sure you have been informed that a delegation is coming in this morning from Germany. You will meet them at the airport. They will be having lunch." The big man in the chair leaned forward across the desk and moved his finger in warning to Pavel. "I am telling you not to keep any presents from them. Not even a pen with advertisements on it. Whatever they give you, you must turn in to our office. You cannot accept any evening invitations. Your job is just to translate.

"Now remember to watch these men very carefully. Today, they will go to the blast furnace. Make sure, that's all they see. We have some furnaces at the steel-making shop which were developed for the military. The military rejected them, so as you know, we installed a couple of them at this plant. They are very advanced. Make sure, at all costs, that the foreigners don't see these furnaces."

Pavel knew that those warnings were stupid since the furnaces had already been sold to Yugoslavia and Italy, so they were not a secret in any sense of the word.

After telling Pavel those things, the man went on to tell him what he was to say and what not to say to the men of the delegation. "We just fired a man who did not obey our orders. Let that be a warning to you!"

It was like he was some kid that had to be lectured to every week. It was humiliating on the one hand and ridiculous on the other. Many times foreign engineers tried to make friends with him or meet him outside the plant. He had to make up different reasons for refusing, and they could see that he was obviously lying. Sometimes, he was frank and told them that the authorities objected to any socializing. But Pavel knew that if they caught him doing what they told him not to do, he would be fired, and there would be big trouble. Quite a few interpreters had been fired because they did not obey the orders from the KGB office. What next? Pavel felt like he was walking a very thin line.

It was in the summer of 1990 that a delegation came from Finland. It was Pavel's job to show them through the huge steel plant and translate for them as a plant manager explained the operation of the steel-making process and the machinery that was being used. Pavel was instructed not to let any of the Finish delegation out of his sight.

When it was time for lunch, Pavel again was required to translate, but as usual, he would be too busy to eat with them. There was all kinds of liquor for the engineers. It was often obvious that some foreign delegations viewed the training period as a vacation, so they let all the barriers down.

Today, was no exception. Pavel was supposed to accompany the engineers to the Sukhoboreie Resort about fifteen miles from the city. Here, they would enjoy the best of food, saunas and entertainment.

As they neared the large hall where they were to be entertained, one of the engineers, Don Peterson, turned to Pavel.

"I can imagine you get tired of translating all day long?"

Pavel looked at the man as he hobbled along the pathway. He was on crutches and had only one leg. "Not usually, Mister Peterson. I take it all in a day's work. It's my job."

It was obvious that the man had been drinking a lot at the bar, but so had the other men. Maybe it was because of the prohibition against drinking in Finland, Pavel reasoned.

They could hear the loud, blaring sounds of the band moving out toward them as they approached the hall. On the stage was a tall, slender girl singing into a microphone.

Peterson stared at the girl with obvious appreciation. His eyes roamed slowly over her attractive face and stopped at the low neck of her silver glittering dress which revealed large, voluptuous breasts and a deep cleavage. Her hips swayed seductively to the music as she sang. Often, she would lean down and hold out her hands to the men who sat in the front of the stage.

When she finished her number, Peterson rose from his seat and leaning on his crutches, managed to clap wildly for her. "Who is she?"

"She is a vocalist from the Ukraine and…"

"Well, I want her for the night."

Pavel searched Peterson's face to see if he were serious, but he wasn't sure. The man had been drinking pretty heavily. He pretended he didn't hear the man's request.

It was well past midnight when all the delegation was settled in their rooms. Sometime around one o'clock, Pavel heard a loud banging outside his room. It was up to him to handle the situation.

When he opened the door, he saw Peterson banging on all the doors in the hallway with his crutch.

"What are do doing out here, Mister Peterson?"

"What the hell do you think I'm doing? I'm trying to find my room. I can't remember my room number."

An hour later, Pavel was sound asleep when he heard angry voices out in the hallway. Peterson was out there again banging on all the doors with his crutch. Three men were fighting and yelling at him.

"What the fuck are you doing? You old suds head. You old fool."

"Don't tell me I've had too much to drink." His words stumbled over each other as he tried to get them out of his mouth. "I can drink any of you under the table and more."

His loud yelling woke up five other men. They started to push him into one of the rooms that was already occupied.

"Hey, fuck you! You son of a bitch! You don't belong in here."

"Don't remember my room number. What the hell do they put those damn fool numbers on the doors for?" Peterson said, his voice thick with confusion. "If you guys push me once more in this hallway, I'll cut off your balls!"

Pavel dragged himself out of bed and into the hallway to break up the fight and get Peterson back to his room. Finally, everything quieted down around three in the morning.

During the summer of June, 1990, many changes were taking place in Russia. Everyone was talking about them. Pavel was planning to stop off and catch up on the news with Tokaloff at their usual coffee shop.

"So what do you think of what is going on in Russia now? People are speaking up on television to the whole country about their points of view and their memories of what happened to them," Tokaloff began.

"This is actually the first time in Russian history that people could explain their points of view. Maybe they are thinking that they can get rid of the Communist regime and move on."

"Yes, I believe perestroika has begun. Look, it was apparent from the elections of 1989 and 1990 that millions of people, including millions of regular Communist Party members, were turning their backs on party leaders. In fact, the party has been losing members by the thousands."

"Then notice that letters from some of the defectors have been published in *Pravda*. It looks to me that the Communist Party is finally beginning to lose power. Look here at what was published in the paper today."

At the Twenty-eight Communist Party Congress on July 2, 1990, Gorbachev addressed the military and asked them if they wanted tanks again. He insisted that the military high command had previously agreed with his policies, but demanded that any dissident generals and colonels must be loyal to the government or resign from their posts. Then Yakov Yeltsin appeared before the congress and urged Gorbachev and the Party's moderates to join together in an alliance. He purposed that the Party rules be liberalized, get its cells out of the military and the KGB. Yeltsin demanded that the Party should now change to a parliamentary party. Its new name should be the Party of Democratic Socialism. Through all the disagreements during the congress, Gorbachev was able to strip the Politburo of real power over the government.

"It will probably be on television tonight. I also heard that before the congress was over, the Russian republic declared that laws passed by its legislature took precedence over laws passed by the central government. Now, it is expected that each of the other fourteen Soviet republics would make similar declarations. So, my friend, it looks like things are beginning to happen at last," Tokaloff said hopefully.

"That's true. It won't be long before we can start up our own businesses in Lipetsk. I'm going over to the disco," Pavel said as he made his way to the door. "I don't have to work, for a change. Natasha and I are going to spend the evening together."

That evening, many people had crowded into the disco. At least two hundred people were enjoying the music. Natasha was waiting for him at a table near the bar.

"You haven't told me yet about your job, Natasha."

"I was very lucky, I think. My uncle helped me get a job as a substitute in the high school, so I don't have to go to work in some village."

"Your uncle has some connections?"

"Yes. And what do you think of this? Some of my friends plan to marry people in Lipetsk."

"Because of the rule that in Russia if you're married to someone in the city you don't have to leave and teach in some little village?"

"Yes, that's right. I am also teaching part-time in a college, but the guys there are so rude. They don't want to learn anything. Another girl there teaches German. She is very strict and really tries to discipline them, but something terrible happened!"

"What was that?"

"Some of the guys threatened to rape her!"

"That's awful! Remember, you are about the same age as your students. You must be careful."

"Oh, I know. I realize that! So, put on a tape that we can enjoy, Pavel."

A moment later, the music of a beautiful song filled the room. "This song is called 'Moonlight and Vodka.' The song is about this man's stay in Moscow. He describes a cold, Russian night. He is sitting in some bar, and one of the girls is trying to attract his attention, but he is thinking that this girl might be working for the KGB."

"I think I have heard this song before."

"Yes, This is Chris de Burgh, an Irish singer. He performed recently in Moscow."

"I like his voice. So, tell me how everything is going for you? Now, you have two jobs."

"Well, it does help to pay the bills, and after a trying day at the steel plant, I can come here and really enjoy myself."

"I bet you make more money here than at the steel plant!"

"Yes, that's the beauty of being involved in a business. I make one hundred and twenty rubles a month at the plant and five hundred rubles here at the disco! Quite a difference!"

"Pretty soon, many people will be able to open their own business!"

Pavel nodded, but as they parted, he felt a doubt rising in his mind. It wouldn't let go. Everyone had so much hope, but the KGB and the Communist Party was still very powerful.

The next day, his fears became a reality. Again, he was called to the offices of the Komsomol. It had been two years since he had entered this office and been threatened with the closure of the disco.

This time, they claimed that they had more complaints from parents. Zess Duzola's tone was very damaging. "Your disco is not the place for our young people. They need a place where they can dance and be entertained."

The KGB officer had the next turn. "You are spreading anti-Soviet propaganda. Like the music you played last night."

Pavel turned in his direction. "What music are you talking about? 'Moonlight and Vodka'?"

"Like I said, you are not doing a good job," Duzola interrupted before the officer could answer.

"We just opened this little disco, and now as it turns out, it's the only place where young people can be entertained in Lipetsk, so what are you trying to tell me?"

Pavel was thoroughly disgusted. He was getting nowhere talking with these people, so he abruptly turned and left the officers. He wanted to go to the disco to meet with Tokaloff. The whole group was there sitting around a table. Despair was written all over their faces.

"Some Communist Party member or KGB must have been here last night. It's only because the KGB was mentioned in that little song, 'Moonlight and Vodka.' One minute they said our place was good for young people. Then all of a sudden, I play that song and one person objects, and then all the others fall in with them."

"Well, we're all closed up now," Tokaloff said despondently.

"And all we were tying to do was to wake up the consciousness of our young people. I guess it is a crime to think. If you are a thinking person, you're immediately in trouble because you are likely to question and dare to change things. And they don't like that!"

"Yes, that's true, but now look at us. We were making a good living here," Pasaukhov said, turning and frowning at the others.

"The party is overreacting just because of one innocent song." Pavel thought for a moment and then looked up. "I've got an idea. I see some hope."

"Hope? How do you see any hope here?"

"Because they are overreacting. They are panicking and maybe believing that the party is beginning to be in trouble. I think we can regroup and open up again in four or five months." Pavel's face was set with determination. "Things will be different by then."

"Maybe you're right. We'll see. More and more people are speaking out," Tokaloff said, the eagerness of business beginning to return to his face. "Now, they have to take care of their own survival."

"Yes, just think. In the past, the Communist ideological machine couldn't allow the underground music to be played before people because they couldn't afford to expose the general public to those ideas. They were considered very, very, dangerous! Mark my words, soon they'll be crawling around in their own squirrel cage with no one to feed them!"

But the next day, Pavel found that the squirrel was in reality more like a lion, trying to raise its head. The roles were reversed, but Pavel was determined not to yield to their demands.

First thing in the morning, Bule Hudhava, the head of the foreign relations department at the steel plant, walked into Pavel's office. "Come to my room. I need to talk to you right away."

Waiting for him, was an important party member and a person from the Young Communist League. Ivan Donovitch started the assertions. "Because of the incidents at the disco last evening, you will likely lose your job here at the steel plant."

"Let me assure you that there is no connection between what I do at the disco and what I do here at the plant. This is an entirely different job. They are not connected in any way," Pavel emphasized looking the man squarely in the eyes.

"We don't see it that way, Mister Lubov. Why should I have telephone calls from my party bosses telling me that I have an employee who is causing trouble? Here, he is working at a disco and talking about freedoms for people and playing underground music, and he is working closely with foreign engineers. He's a threat to your company," Mr. Hudhava said, obviously upset.

Pavel could see their reasoning. Since he had landed in trouble in one place, then he was not loyal to the whole regime. And all it took was one phone call. Probably, some KGB person was at the club the previous evening. The tape he played, *Moonlight and Vodka,* mentioned the KGB as something undesirable, a warning for the person who was watching the girl in the bar. And that's all it took. Just all it took, Pavel said over and over again in his mind. The more he thought about it, the angrier he became. Damn them all! Damn the party and their system! He slammed his fists on his desk when he returned to his office. He just wouldn't put up with it. Just one phone call by some party member or KGB officer to give him all this trouble. Damn them all! Was this the end of his career? If that was the case, he would get even with them all. He had to.

Chapter 15

Five months had passed since Pavel had been called into the office of Bule Hudhava, and for five months, he had felt swept up with the attitudes of his boss and the whole rotten situation. But he felt something was brewing because he suspected that certain people wanted to get rid of him because he was trouble. He knew it was just a matter of time before things came to a head.

Only one thing had taken the right turn. The disco had recently opened. The original group was back working again.

It was in the late fall of 1990, that Pavel was summoned again to Hudhava's office. This time it was for a different reason.

The man rose and shook Pavel's hand. "Sit down. Listen to this. I am offering you a job in India in Ranchi. Your contract is for two years. You will be working at an iron and steel research center and translating and interpreting, much like you do here."

Pavel could see immediately that this was not an offer, but a request to leave and virtually a way for them to get him out of the way because he had become trouble for them. The same thing had happened to other people he knew. So, in effect, they were offering him a way to go, and the offer on the table was not negotiable, so Pavel accepted and left the office. He would be leaving soon, well before the end of the year. The pay would be better than what he was presently receiving, but he considered the job somewhat like an exile from his friends and his country. He would be living in a Russian compound near the steel plant. What would it be like to live outside of Russia? What restrictions would be placed on him, he wondered. Here, he had been working with others for more freedoms for people. What direction would this job take him?

Anxieties began to build up in his mind as he approached the apartment building. He would have to begin sorting through his things and deciding what to take. Then, Natasha's face flashed in front of his eyes. Yes, he would need to talk to her today. Would she go with him to a strange country? Would she be willing to leave her family, her country and travel with him? She had never been anywhere before.

As he walked down the hallway, he heard loud noises coming from Dr. Korotch's apartment. He had few friends and rarely had visitors because of his ill health.

Pavel raced down the steps to the apartment below. In the doorway, were two men, the very same he had seen walking down the street with Andrey that night after the disco had closed for the evening.

"Shut up, old man! Shut up, you fool!" the one yelled. He had his hands around the man's throat.

"Tell us where you keep your money!" the other one demanded.

Pavel stepped quickly into the room. "Get your hands off of him! This man spent years in the Russian prison camps. He's got no money."

"That's not what we hear. Get out of the way, or you'll be next!"

When he refused to move, the man they called Yegor threw him down on the floor. Pavel felt the sharp edge of a knife against his throat. The blood slowly oozed from his neck and began to soak his shirt.

The man held him firmly to the floor while the other pushed Korotch back into a chair and started to tie the doctor's wrists.

Suddenly, there was a movement at the door. Pavel struggled to see who was dashing into the room. When he looked up, he stared into the eyes of Andrey.

"What the hell are you doing here?" Andrey demanded of the men.

"This man has money. He's dying anyway. The party will reward us for it!"

"Stand back, stand back! Where do you get the idea he has money?"

"Because he bribed the judge to let that fellow Ivan out of jail."

Andrey sat down on the couch, holding his head between his hands. "That fellow, Ivan was my brother, you fools! Doctor Korotch got the money from friends. He spent his life in those lousy prison camps and in the uranium mines."

"Yes, and remember, it was Doctor Korotch that gave you medicines and got you well after Yakov beat you up. You almost died!" Pavel said turning and looking squarely at Andrey.

"I will listen to no more of this nonsense!" Yegor yelled. "That's got nothing to do with getting the money! Who cares about anything else?"

"Let's kill them both!" the other man suggested, moving toward Pavel.

At that moment, there was a noise in the hallway. The commotion had attracted some of the other tenants.

Yegor turned quickly to his partner. They ran toward the door, motioning Andrey to follow.

Pavel stood up and faced Andrey. They stared at each other for a moment. Pavel saw only the pupils of Andrey's eyes, enlarging with fear. He moved forward as though to obediently follow the men. Then he stopped and turned back and slowly started to untie the doctor's wrists. He sat down next to the old man and put his arm around him.

"I will never forget what you did for me and my family. Those men are no good. I promise you they'll never bother you again!"

Pavel was about to say that it was about time he realized they were no good, but self-satisfaction was not the way to go. The important thing was to help this young man realize what he had been doing.

After they settled the old doctor in bed with some hot tea, they went upstairs to talk. A quietness settled over the apartment house. It was almost as though nothing had happened. Where did life begin and end? Where did the real meaning of life begin to stir in people's blood, Pavel questioned himself.

Andrey was the first to speak. "I can't understand those men. I've been living with them, but now I can see they just don't care about people, not the individuals that really count, like Doctor Korotch."

"Let me tell you something. The Communist Party is not concerned with people like you and me. They just want the system to work, for people to conform to their ideas and not to think what is really happening to our society. You remember how Yakov was released after killing Ivan?"

"And Ivan is dead. My brother is gone. He was such a good person," Andrey said despondently.

"Yes, because of our corrupt system. Now, Allery has no husband and Ivan has no father!"

138

"Say, why are you home so early? Most people are at work."

"Most, people, Andrey. Today was different. Tell me, where have you been working? Didn't you quit going to the university?"

"Yes, but I think I will go back. It was crazy for me to quit."

"You would be smart to finish your education."

"I'm going to have to get my things out of the apartment I share with those four other guys. Will you go with me?"

"You want to go back there after what happened?"

"They are sure to be back working now. They won't be home."

"Let's call up Maksim, Andrey. I think we can get a couple of our friends to go with us." Pavel turned to the phone to call Maksim. He was relieved to find him at home.

"Maksim says for us to meet him at his place, and he's sure he can get some other guys to help us out."

They hurried down the outside steps of the apartment building with just one purpose in mind: to get the unpleasant business out of the way. And fast.

By the time they reached Maksim's apartment, there were four others that Pavel recognized getting ready to leave.

"You're sure no one will be home over there, Maksim?" Andrey asked as he looked around the group.

"They work late and won't get home until after eight-thirty."

"Good. Then let's go."

They were lucky to have a way over to Andrey's place, Pavel thought as they climbed into Yaroslav's truck.

"I don't think we all need to go up there, Andrey, because I'm sure no one is home now."

But when they reached the top of the stairs in the apartment building, Andrey stopped suddenly and turned around. He stared at the others and tried to say something, but he could only shake his head in disbelief.

Andrey could hear loud voices coming from the apartment. The men were at home. He walked to the door and motioned for the others to come up.

"Maybe we should leave," Andrey began. "These guys are tough and will fight and kill anyone. They don't give a damn about anyone!"

"There are seven of us. Let's go! Open the door, Andrey!"

139

When the men saw Andrey standing alone in front of the door, they moved menacingly toward him.

"You son of a bitch! You fuckin' son of a bitch! What the hell are you doing back here?" Yegor yelled.

"I've come to get my stuff. I don't want any problems."

"Oh, you don't want any problems! You stupid coward. You ran away with your tail behind your legs over at Korotch's place."

"He gave me medicines after Yakov beat me up. He saved my life."

"Saved your life, you fuckin' coward. We'll show you what we do with cowards," he sneered.

"Yeah," yelled another man moving in toward Andrey. "We'll show you! Then see if your great Doctor Korotch can save your life."

The group moved quickly toward Andrey, but stopped suddenly when they saw six men coming in behind him.

"Oh, you have company. Let's take them on!"

To Pavel's surprise, Yaroslav whipped out a gun from under his jacket. "Stand back, you fucks, or I'll blow your heads off!"

The group moved back in complete surprise. He had apparently caught them off guard. "Get your things, Andrey and let's beat it!" He kept his gun trained on the men, ready for immediate action.

A few minutes later, they were off in the truck. They could hear the men yelling obscenities as they sped down the street; the tires of the car screeched loudly as they rounded the corner.

"That was a close one, Yaroslav! Without your gun, we might have had some fight in there!" Pavel exclaimed.

"That's right. You never know what might come up. That's why you always go prepared."

"Yeah, right, Yaroslav! But very few people have a car and a gun like you do. You have more connections than a electrical circuit!"

The rest laughed loudly at Pavel's remark. "Well, you've got to be in a position to defend yourself against these party members and their strong-arm ways of controlling people."

"You can say that again, Yaroslav," Andrey agreed. "Andrey found that out."

"Where are you going to stay, now?" Pavel asked Andrey after they had driven a few miles.

"Well, I quit my job a few days ago. They don't know that."

"You said you were going back to finish up at the university?"

"Yes, I never should have left. I guess I got upset over Ivan dying. I didn't know what I wanted to do. The KGB were after me all the time and said I was a spy! Then Bulat said he would protect me from the KGB and got me a job."

"I don't think it's wise for you to stay there with your mother. Those men know you used to live there. Is there somewhere else you can stay?"

"Let's go back and see if mother has some ideas. My uncle and his wife lives in the city near the university."

"That would be perfect for you!"

Yaroslav left them off near the apartment building and sped off with the others.

Suddenly, Pavel remembered what had transpired earlier that day. So much had happened that everything had been placed in the back corners of his mind. "Say Andrey, let me tell you something. The steel company is sending me to India to Ranchi to work. I guess they think I'm too much trouble for them. They want me out of the way."

"Whew! That will be some move! When do you go?"

"In a few weeks or so. I've got to find Natasha and tell her. What do you think she will say?"

"Listen, I don't know much about women, but if I were Natasha, I'd go along. She won't want to stay here without you!"

Pavel shifted his shoulders as he carried some bags of Andrey's clothes, but didn't reply. His mind was going in so many different directions. First, he wanted to check back with Dr. Korotch. Undoubtedly, the man needed some attention after the assault by Andrey's so-called friends.

As they neared the entrance to the apartment house, they noticed a few people had gathered at the steps and were talking in sober tones. Even the old women, the same ones who usually sat on the benches out in front, were talking excitedly and turning their heads toward the apartment building.

"What is going on?" Pavel asked one of the old women.

"It's Doctor Korotch. He's very ill. He's not expected to live past the day."

Pavel put his arm around Andrey who was breathing heavily with emotion at the old lady's words.

They hurried into the building toward the old man's apartment. They found him lying in bed. Several friends and an old aunt were standing by the bed.

"My friend, Pavel," he said as he saw him enter the room. He spoke slowly, the words came with difficulty as his eyes filled with tears and emotion. "I am going now. I have nothing to leave you, but I leave you with something more precious than money."

Pavel moved closer to the bed, so the old man would not have to exert himself to speak. "I leave you with my legacy, my passion for the people of Russia. How I have worked for the breaking of their chains of communism. For new freedoms, for democracy. I pass this on to you, before I die. Carry on, Pavel for me. I know you can do it."

Korotch held out his hand to Pavel. As Pavel accepted the transfer of the legacy and power, Korotch, realizing his mission had passed over, left the world that he had struggled to change and died satisfied that he had given his mission to reliable hands.

The room was quiet for a long time after Dr. Korotch had died. There were no tears, only a feeling among all that were present that his work must be carried on. His work must not have died in vain.

Finally, one older man spoke. "I knew the man after he came from the uranium mines. Many, if they survive, come back broken people. Broken in health and spirit. But not Valadimir Korotch. He worked for democracy all these years. Nothing would stop or break him. Even the KGB tried to crush him, but he sat here in this apartment and wrote accounts of his ordeals, the false accusations and his life in the prison camps. Now, they are finally being published!"

Another man bowed his head. "Yes, he helped me when I was beaten by the KGB. He got money from some of his friends and helped me get a job. Yet, he suffered every day from his illness from the radiation in the mines. He was a genius in medical research before he was sent away to the camps."

An hour later, Pavel and Andrey left the apartment. Andrey was grief-stricken that the doctor who had saved his life had died because no one could save him from what the soviet system had done to him.

Pavel knew he had to hurry to catch Natasha before she left her last evening classes at the college. First, he made a phone call to Andrey to tell him about Dr. Korotch. As he dashed out of the door, Andrey met him in the hallway.

"I'm leaving to stay with my uncle and his wife now. Here is their address." He handed Pavel a piece of paper.

"Keep in touch, old friend. And keep strong. Don't let anyone change your mind. I will let you know when I am leaving, but I expect you to keep Doctor Korotch's words alive here in Russia while I'm gone."

Andrey grabbed Pavel's hand. Then, they held each other in a strong embrace. "Until, the next time. Thanks for all your help today. Believe me, I won't forget it."

Pavel was filled with mixed emotions as he hurried to the school to see Natasha—fear that she wouldn't want to leave Russia and anger and resentment if she should refuse him. But when he saw her face fill with love at the sight of him, he quickly tossed away his anxieties.

"You didn't tell me you were coming by here!" Natasha said breathlessly as she hurried up to him.

"I have something to tell you. Let's walk over to that coffee shop near here and talk."

Natasha wondered what he had to say. His face was so serious. She hoped it wouldn't be bad news.

"Oh, that's better. That hot coffee tastes so good. It's so cold outside today, Pavel I can hardly stand it. But by the look on your face, I can see you have some news to tell me."

"That's right. Hudhava called me into his office today."

"Oh, no, not again."

"Yes, he's saying that he is offering me a job at the steel plant in Ranchi, India. In effect, of course, he is telling me to go. I will have a two-year contract. In a way, it's like being exiled and getting me out of the way because I have been trouble to him."

"You are going to In-d-ia, Pavel?" Natasha said in complete disbelief.

"That's the way it is. They didn't give me any choice. What do you think, Natasha? I want you to go with me."

"Go with you to India?"

Pavel watched the shock cross Natasha's face. "I realize this is a complete surprise to you. But think of it this way, we would be together."

"Is it possible for me to go with you?"

"Yes, if you are my wife." Pavel turned to draw Natasha closer to him. He held her hand and looked closely into her eyes. He was looking for a sign of her emotions. Doubt? Fear? How much did she really love him?

"We would get married?"

Now, he could see the warmth beginning to fill her eyes. "Natasha, we have to decide if our love is strong. Are we ready to make a commitment to each other? That is so important."

"I know that. Yes, I know." Her voice seemed to trail off as she thought of leaving Russia, her family and going to a strange country. "I'm thinking about going off and leaving everyone."

"We will be able to come back on leave sometimes. I love you. I guess I've loved you from the first time we met. Do you love me enough for this?"

Slowly, the little gold flecks in her eyes began to sparkle. "Yes, yes, Pavel, I love you. I love you very much."

"Will you be ready to go?"

"Soon?"

"Yes, in about a month or so."

"Mrs. Pavel Lubov?"

"Yes, you will be mine, Mrs. Pavel Lubov."

And so they were married.

When they boarded the plane for India, Natasha leaned her head back against the pillow after the plane had left the runway. The cities of Russia with their chimneys emitting tall columns of smoke into the cold, gray sky were passing swiftly past the window. And so was the life that Natasha had known since she was a very little girl. What was lying ahead of her, she wondered?

A group of friends and family had seen them off at the airport. It was heart-breaking to see Stepan as he cried and said goodbye to his papa. Pavel hugged him and promised he would get back to see him real soon. He was only eight years old. Then, mama whispered advice into Natasha's ears as they waited at the gate. Eat well. Be careful. Natasha's brother, Sergey had stood next to his father, Nikolay trying to be manly and helpful. Marina came forward for one last embrace. She appraised her son carefully. She knew he would be all right. He had always held firmly to his opinions and would back up for no one. Undoubtedly, he sure must have gotten this strong determination from his Grandfather Stepan, she thought.

Their last words, "Take care of yourselves," passed slowly through Natasha's mind. She had never traveled before or been away from her family. Would they be safe in India? They would be living in a Russian compound. Just the workers from the steel plant would live there. Something like a contained community, Pavel had told her.

Sensing how Natasha must be feeling, he brushed the side of her face with his lips and patted her hand. "Well, we are on our way to India. This should be a very interesting experience for us. I'm sure of that."

"You said you know of other people who have been sent to India?"

"Yes, some other people have been sent to India because they have spoken out against the Communist Party. The high party officials believe that if they get rid of some of us, we will not be around to support the democratic movements. Their idea is to send us away for a couple of years until things quiet down in Russia. I was just one person that they focused on."

"And that's what they think? That things will quiet down, and the party will strengthen and continue?"

"That's about right. Those who are sent away won't be around to stir up the movements in Russia."

"Well, time will tell what will happen. I, for one, think they will fail."

"I'm sure of it, Natasha."

"What about your job? Do you think you'll like the change?"

"I've been thinking about it. Of course, I had no choice. I would prefer to stay, but this change could be a very good thing in my career because I will be better paid, and maybe it will present more challenges for me as a translator."

He noticed Natasha's eyes looking very sleepy. "Get some rest," Pavel suggested. "We got up very early this morning, and we have a very big day ahead."

Who knows what might turn up during the two years in India, Pavel thought to himself as he dozed off to the droning sound of the aircraft's motors.

Once in India, Pavel found that the challenges came from places he would never have dreamed. First of all, he had to work very hard to prove his abilities as a translator. The expectations and the responsibility for this job were a lot higher than his job in Russia since this company was already on an international level.

About a month after they settled into an apartment in the Russian community, Pavel returned home, slamming his brief case on the table.

"What's going on, Pavel? What happened?"

"I am angry, Natasha. Do you know that we can't leave this community to go anywhere without the written permission from the party boss or the KGB? Everything here is under very strict control."

"That sounds much worse than in Russia. Maybe the party thinks they can continue to run things here the old way and then they can do the same thing later on back in Russia. What do you think?"

"Yes, they want to turn back the clock and have the same old Communist Party rule again. We've got to be aware of what is going on. Some of the party leaders here may try to return to Russia before long and stage some trouble. Mark my words, Natasha, something big is brewing."

"Soon? What have you heard?"

"I can smell it in the air like a sailor can smell land at sea from miles away. But this smell is not the sweet smell of virgin land. It's the fowl smell from the exhaust of tanks trying to take over people's lives!"

Natasha shuddered and walked into the kitchen to prepare dinner. What kind of trouble and danger had they walked into unknowingly? Well, maybe he was just exaggerating.

But it was not the season for exaggerations. They had been living in Ranchi for almost a month when Pavel was called into the plant office to talk to Lex Yoritch, one of the important managers and Zal Tyunin, a KGB officer.

"Pavel, I haven't seen you at the party meetings. We have requested that you attend them," Selyunin began.

"That's right. I don't want to go to the meetings."

"Well, now listen. You are a young man. You have your whole career ahead of you, and you have to comply with what we tell you."

"I understand what you are saying. You are my boss. I'm doing my job as an interpreter and translator here. If I perform my duties poorly, then in that case you have to call me to your office, and you have to tell me I am performing my duties poorly."

"And the party meetings?"

146

"I'm not a Communist Party member. I have never been one. And what's more, I believe that your Communist Party is a Fascist organization. I don't want to have anything to do with it. I've never been to any of your meetings, and I will never attend one of them no matter what you do. If you don't like me for that, okay. Send me back to Russia."

Selyunin's face became livid with anger. He continued to pace back and forth in front of Pavel, then completely lost his patience. "I see you're not taking this seriously." With one quick movement, he kicked Pavel in the groin and knocked him onto the floor.

Pavel doubled up from the excruciating pain. He looked up at Selyunin who was standing over him. The dirty dog, the dirty dog, he thought. The hate rose within himself and mixed with the pain that was piercing his body. These actions were the life blood of the KGB and Communism.

"Yes, that's the thing I'm going to do immediately," Selyunin continued with a smirk on his face. "I'm sending you back because I don't need people like you here, not only because you are trouble, but because the others will see that they can do the same thing, so I don't want to keep you here. I'm sending you back."

"Wait a minute. I was sent to India in hopes that I could help the Russian specialists here, and now in less than a month you are sending me back. The management at the Lipetsk Steel plant have spent a lot of money on my air ticket and paid for my moving expenses. The management back there will look at you and question what kind of a manager you are. Who cares about your party meetings in Moscow?"

Selyunin looked in bewilderment at the young man's audacity. He glanced at Borisov, hoping he would counter with something, but Borisov only looked puzzled and shook his head.

At that moment, the conversation was interrupted by a telephone call. Pavel could see that it was from some important official as Borisov motioned for him to leave. "I'll talk to you later, Mister Lubov. We are not through. I can promise you that."

After Borisov finished talking on the phone, he turned to Selyunin who was walking impatiently back and forth in the room.

"What did you think of that, Yuri!" Borisov said heatedly.

147

"I smell something, and it is not pleasant. Here, we have a new man who has just come from Russia. Something is going on back there that he feels free to talk like that about the Communist Party."

"Yes, the man is fresh from Russia. Here, in India we keep along straight and strict party lines."

"I hope this doesn't portend a change for the party. We must stand firm, Alexsei. We will not put up with this nonsense. I suggest you get rid of him."

"Moscow will not like that. He is one of their best. I agree that we should get rid of him, but I'll make arrangements and send him down to Bhilai. That will show him a thing or two!"

Chapter 16

It was early in 1991 when Pavel and Natasha arrived in Bhilai. This was in the State of Madya Pradesh. The plant here was the largest steel production plant in India. They worked with the Russians. Back in the fifties and sixties, Russia wanted India to go in the same political direction as Russia. The iron and steel industry was considered very important for the national economy. Russia built huge steel plants in China, India, Egypt, Korea and many other countries. The steel plant in Bhilai was built sometime in the fifties. The Indians didn't know how to run the steel plant, so they would go to Russian steel plants for training. The Indians depended on the Russian steel plants not only for technology, but also for the equipment. The basic equipment needed to be replaced every fifteen to twenty years, but some equipment had to be replaced every year or two. The plant in Bhilai was a self-contained plant, but they paid a lot of money for the services, the technology and the equipment.

At this time, Pavel was assigned to translate and interpret for a group of Russian consultants who worked in the iron and steel research center. The center was affiliated with the steel authority of India. The KGB was paid by the Russian embassy. The Indians paid money to the Russian Steel Ministry who in turn paid Pavel for his work.

They were given an apartment in the Russian settlement. In a way, it was like a smaller city in a larger city. About six hundred Russian families lived there. The compound had Russian schools and Russian doctors. The small city was run by the KGB.

Natasha was becoming more and more disgusted with the rules. "I can't understand this. Why can't I mail letters out to my parents whenever I finish writing them? Tell me, Pavel what is going on?"

"The answer is that the mail only goes out on Saturdays. We have to take our letters over to Setyako's apartment."

"Over to Setyako's apartment? Why over there?"

"Because supposedly, all in-coming and out-going letters are read at random. You've probably noticed that our letters are opened before we get them. I tried to drop letters off at the plant or at the Indian post office, and I got in trouble about that."

"What a pain! Why are we so controlled here?"

"The KGB wants to monitor everything in this compound. If you drop letters off at the Indian post office, you are disobeying the rules."

"Some people came by here today and asked me to join their committee. What is that all about? Are we supposed to go around this compound and ask questions of our neighbors? I never heard of such a thing!"

"Natasha, this is just the way the KGB tries to control things here. They may come to our apartment and ask you questions on the pretense that they want to know if you are making alcoholic beverages here. That is not allowed."

"Well, many people are making alcoholic drinks here. We all know this. It's all kept pretty well under cover."

"Yes, but the KGB is also interested in finding out what the people are reading, and they want the names of any people who are writing anything that relates to Russia or foreign governments."

"What should I do if they ask us to be on one of their committees?"

"Tell them your husband is away out of the city so much that he probably could not serve on any of their committees."

"You know, I never really understood why you were sent here to Bhilai. I was sick at the time from the change of climate from Russia."

"The KGB man, Zal Tyunin, was surprised at what I had to say. I told him that back in Russia, people's attitudes are changing. Here, the system tries to stay the same. Back home, people are saying openly that the Communist Party has to go. They are saying the party is a fascist organization. We don't want it. That's basically what I said. But, Natasha, I believe that the party is covered with blood. Their entire history is covered with blood. What right do they have to run our government?"

"Well, I know that you feel strongly about that, but it seems around here we are back in Stalin's time. So, you told them back in Ranchi that you did not want to attend the Communist meetings?"

"Yes, straight out. That was when Selyunin kicked me in the groin."

"And you were in terrible pain for a few days and had to go to a doctor. It was terrible!"

"Well, after that, I'm sure they realized that things have changed back in Russia. Otherwise, I wouldn't have spoken out that way. They thought they were punishing me by sending me here to Bhilai, but it has turned out to be a good thing in spite of the restrictions in the compound, because the plant is actually the center of the research center."

The next day Pavel learned that there were just three people on the staff, two engineers and himself. They reported directly to the Indian and Russian engineers in Ranchi.

In the beginning, the local Communist Party members tried to exercise their power and push Pavel to go to meetings. One party boss took him to one side and tried to persuade him.

Again Pavel said, "I'm not coming to your party meetings. You are not my boss. My boss is five hundred miles away. If he calls and says that I have to do this or that, I will do it."

"We will see, we will see," the man said as he shuffled some papers on his desk. He was not pleased with the situation.

Pavel thought that nothing would happen, since he knew that his former boss was aware that he was firm about not attending party meetings.

But as the weeks enfolded, he was not so sure. Doubts crowded his mind. The KGB often struck without notice. No one could be sure of their status within the compound. The atmosphere in the community was very heavy and depressing because people knew they were being watched by the KGB all the time. The KGB would just come to their homes and remind them that they were being watched and could only read certain approved books. They explained that since they had six hundred Russians living in this settlement they had to assure the people's security. But Pavel knew they were not concerned about security. They were concerned with keeping total control of the minds and thinking of the people in the compound.

There were secret KGB people among the other workers at the plant. After a while, Pavel could distinguish a few of the specialists from the secret police, because the KGB men weren't knowledgeable about the steel technology. One day however, their presence at the plant became very obvious.

"A very high official from the Russian government, Mr. Tozimino, is coming to visit the plant today," Turgov announced just as Pavel was entering his office. Turgov was the public relations manager at the Bhilai company.

"So that's what is going on. I noticed there was a lot of Indian military all around the streets this morning."

At that moment, the air was filled with a heavy chopping sound. Pavel shaded his eyes from the hot Indian sun. About six helicopters appeared in the sky. They had the markings of the Russian and Indian military.

"Look, Pavel, see who is coming out of the plant to give directions about which streets to block off here."

"Yes, the very men I suspected were not specialists are actually KGB men. Now, we can see them for what they are. The prisoners that were held in the camps in Siberia would love to get their hands on them and eliminate them like the exterminators spray the rats fleeing from a building." Pavel knew he could say this to his friend because he was sure that Turgov could be absolutely trusted.

"Don't you wish it could be that simple? I know how you feel about their fearless control. You were beginning to get out of that restrictive regime back in Russia, but here, it is the same."

"I think they would like to go back to Russia and enforce the Communist Party again."

"And maybe sooner than you think!"

"What do you mean? Have you heard something?"

"Come over here away from the building where we can talk. Pretend to be watching the helicopters. I worked late a few days ago. I heard several men, obviously KGB, talking. They didn't know I was in the next office looking for something in the files."

"What were they saying?" Pavel asked, his face filling with intense interest.

"They were discussing plans for a coup back in Moscow."

"When? Are they directly involved? Or are they talking about some other group here in India?"

"Well, they seem to be involved, along with some other people. They talked heatedly about taking over the Kremlin and Yeltsin! I don't believe it is imminent. But who knows? It happens when the time is right."

"I'm not surprised at hearing this. I felt all along that many Communist Party officials were holding out here in India just waiting for the opportunity to go back and take over. Look around, Turgov. Do you see any of those men that were talking in the office?"

"Yes, I see three of them. The heavy-set man and the other two that are walking together. You know their names, don't you?"

"Of course. We'd better split up. The helicopters have landed." Pavel turned away from watching the party officials. The anger was spreading across his face, but he knew he had to control himself. But later? He would give anything for the opportunity.

That evening when Pavel returned to the apartment, he found that one of the KGB men was there talking to Natasha. What was going on now, he asked himself angrily. His eyes darted around the room. Some of the books that Pavel had been reading were moved to one side on the table.

The officer had obviously been looking all through the apartment. As he walked into the living room, he continued to joke and laugh. "Ah, nice place you have here. You've really decorated it very nicely, Natasha. I hope you are comfortable?"

Natasha didn't return his smiles. "Everything is fine, Mr. Tafarevich. I'm pleased you like our apartment."

The man continued to move around the room as though what he was doing was just an everyday and expected occurrence.

When he finally walked out of the apartment, Natasha raised a defiant fist and mocked his voice sarcastically. "Yes, I'm so happy you are pleased with our apartment you big, fat pig. Now, just keep away from here and leave us alone!"

Pavel was amused at his wife's anger. "What did he do here? Just mess up my tapes and books?"

"And probably got his dirty fingers all over my parent's letters and our books."

"Be assured he will be back, or some committee members will come calling unexpectedly. Since I am an interpreter, I am one of the first to be checked because I can read English," Pavel answered with a deep frown.

"Yes, I know, but I still don't like it."

"So what have you been doing today? "

"I went to my Yoga class. And then I spent some time knitting."

"The sweater for your mother? The pattern you're using is very beautiful. She will be really glad to get that when you finish. They're having a terrible winter back there in Russia."

"That is one good thing about living here. Compared to stores in Russia, India is a shopping paradise. Mother wrote in her last letter that she can't find any decent clothes."

"Natasha, the family down the street is going back on leave to Russia next month. Let's buy some things for our families, and they can take it back with them for us. Maybe you'll have the sweater finished by then. That would be nice."

"Yes, I think I can. What happened at the plant this morning? I saw a lot of helicopters in the sky."

"That's right! Some of the men I suspected as being KGB men came out of the woodwork and greeted the party."

"What will happen now that everyone knows that they are the secret police? Will they be sent back to Russia?"

"I imagine so, but they are replaced quite often anyway. Still, we know that there are KGB in the plant and here in the compound all the time. Turgov heard some of them talking in an office a few nights ago when he was working late. They were talking about a coup that is supposed to take place in Russia sometime in the future—or soon, maybe."

"A takeover of Yeltsin and his advisors?"

"That's right! That's just what those dirty bastards have been trying to do!"

"Go back to Russia, Pavel and help organize the opposition! We can't go back to communism! They will take away all our freedoms! Saying nothing and thinking nothing!"

Pavel put his arm around Natasha. "I would love to go back and help fight for our freedoms and democracy, but I can't do that now! The time will come. It has to."

Natasha could see the defiance in Pavel's face. She smiled encouragingly. "The time will come, Pavel. I'm sure of it. We'll make it happen!"

She turned and went back to the kitchen to prepare the evening meal. They seldom ate out since most of the meals in the restaurants were very spicy Indian food. Most of the Russian families prepared their own meals at home.

154

From the window, Natasha could see the rows of apartment buildings. Beyond these, was a swimming pool that they frequently used for exercise and to escape the extreme heat. Other times, she would put a cool washcloth against her forehead when she stretched out to relax and read in the afternoon. Often, her thoughts drifted back to Russia, and the faces of her former college students moved slowly before her eyes. How different everything was here. How totally different, and she wondered if Russia would go back to the old order again, just as restrictive as it was here in the compound.

Now, if they wanted to go somewhere they all had to go together on a bus. Sometimes three or four buses would be assigned and take them out of the city to the waterfalls. Natasha figured the authorities did this so that people could be watched easier if they were all together. Still, the waterfalls were a beautiful place. The children in the compound could play where the water wasn't deep and fill their pockets with little pebbles. Families would bring picnic lunches and enjoy the coolness of the waterfalls.

Pavel would sit next to her, and they would try to pretend they were alone and surround themselves with their own world and the music they loved. Often, Pavel would read, and she would let her mind drift back to the days at the university when they would walk together along the banks of the river. Then he would stop and embrace her and kiss her softly on the lips.

"What are you thinking about? You seem to be miles away!" Pavel exclaimed in bewilderment as he entered the kitchen. The water was boiling away on the stove.

Natasha turned from the window. Her face relaxed in a slow, quiet smile that Pavel had grown to love and understand. "I was thinking about how we used to walk along the river near the university in Lipetsk. We would stop along the path, and we would embrace. Then you would pick a flower and hold it up to my face and trace my smile."

"Then I would kiss you like this." He held her closely to him until he felt her heart beating next to his. "Come, forget about cooking."

He led her into the bedroom and pulled back the cool sheets on the bed. He slowly began to undress her and touch and hold her until she cried out with delight, wanting more and more. Our life should always be like this, he thought. With the KGB watching and following them, their life could crumble around them. People talked about death now like it was an everyday occurrence. But he would fight for their rights with every drop of blood in his body. He was determined.

Chapter 17

When Pavel walked out of the office that early afternoon a man called to him. "Hey, friend, are you leaving now?" His voice was filled with a strange urgency.

"Yes, why?"

"I've heard some people talking in the office about some fighting between the Muslims and the Indians. It may be dangerous in the streets. Maybe you should check on it."

"Oh, I don't think it's anything." And Pavel walked with unconcern out to the car. He had been in Calcutta on business for the company for a few days. He was due at the airport in an hour.

There seemed to be no sign of trouble as his driver started down the street, but suddenly without any warning an angry mob appeared from around the corner of a building. They were joined by more people. Soon the streets were filled with a huge crowd that was hurling stones and shouting obscenities.

"Get down, get down in the car!" his driver shouted. He tried to move the car down the crowded street.

"Should we get out of the car and run for it? We have to be at the airport in an hour!"

"We would be massacred. My job is to get you to your plane safely."

Soon, Pavel could hear the sounds of clubs beating on the metal of the car. He was terrified! What had happened to cause all this rioting in the streets, he wondered.

Then the car started to rock back and forth. The crowd was yelling for them to get out. Was this the end? Was this the way he was going to die? At the hands of an angry mob in India? Pavel crouched down further in the back of the car.

More people joined the throng around the car and the one behind them.

"I think this is a fight between the Muslims and the Indians, Pavel, but they are so angry they will turn against anyone in the streets."

If the mob broke the windows in the car, they would be doomed, Pavel reasoned. All would be lost. No sooner did these terrifying thoughts race through his mind, then he could hear the sounds of breaking glass and the angry voices of the mob shouting through the broken windows. Pavel felt the flying fragments of glass covering his body. He tried to keep his face covered as he crouched behind the front seats.

Then he heard a whistle. A truck of policemen were driving down the street toward them. The people started to move away. It gave them just the right moment to turn and drive swiftly down a side street. For the moment, at least, they were saved.

That night, Pavel was never so relieved to enter the compound. Even the security guard at the entrance was a welcome sight.

Natasha opened the door at the sound of the car and embraced Pavel. Her face was filled with concern. "Oh, Pavel, I was so worried about you! Look, you have fragments of glass in your hair! And your arms are all bleeding from cuts!"

"Yes, there was rioting in the streets in Calcutta today! The Muslims and the Indians are fighting. Our car was surrounded. If the police hadn't arrived to help us, I would have been dragged out of the car and beaten by the mob!"

"And you were almost killed! How terrible for you! How awful! Let me wash the blood from your arms and get the glass out of your hair."

"I guess I didn't get all the glass off my clothes and hair. Have you heard what is going on in Calcutta on television?"

"I heard some official making a speech on television. He said there had been an interesting discovery. Some historians had discovered that a Hindu temple near Calcutta was first a Muslim mosque many years ago. I don't believe the man fully realized what trouble this statement would cause because his voice was very matter-of-fact, just announcing the news."

"Yes, I am sure the Muslims were undoubtedly furious to learn that their religious place of worship had been turned into a Hindu temple."

Late that evening, a KGB man came to the door. "Because of the fighting in some of the cities, everyone is confined to the compound. The streets are not safe now. No one is to leave, not even to go to the plant."

Pavel and Natasha turned and stared at each other. This was so totally unexpected. They sat in the living room and talked about the situation late into the night. More restrictions, more tensions were certainly not good news.

First thing the next morning, a committee member was at the door. "There is a party meeting tonight over at Tudorovitch's apartment. You are expected to be there."

Natasha watched the reaction on Pavel's face. She was surprised to see him nod in agreement.

After the man left, Pavel explained. "These are bad times right now. I suppose sometimes when I am home, I will just have to go and listen for a while."

Still, the fighting in the streets throughout India lasted for a whole week. No one went to work. Before it was all over, many people were killed.

As the days passed, the tension in the streets and in the compound began to rub heavily on Pavel's nerves. He talked about the restrictions with several close Russian specialists that shared his office.

"Ivan, I have been thinking about getting out of Bhilai for a weekend," Pavel said during a noon break. "Isn't it a shame that we have seen nothing of this interesting country? All we have seen is this little compound and the steel plant? We've never been allowed to go anywhere beyond the gate."

"So what do you have in mind?"

"First off, we have a free weekend coming up in two weeks!"

"You are up to something, Pavel! Getting out of here could be dangerous," Filipp said with a slow smile.

"Dangerous?" Pavel drawled, looking Andrey squarely in the eyes. "You don't get anywhere if you don't try. I suggest we just pack and buy some tickets and take the train out of town."

"I like it. Good idea!" Ivan exclaimed. "Let's organize a trip to Darjeeling in Tibet. I heard that it's a very beautiful place in the mountains."

"Then let's do it, Ivan. We'll tell only our wives. It would be too dangerous for them to go. This will be like a trial run." Pavel was pleased. He was itching to get out of the compound if even for only a weekend.

But when Natasha heard about the trip, she was worried. In order to go beyond the gate to go to the store or to the market, you had to have the written approval from the local Russian boss. Pavel and Ivan did not have that approval. Still, she always went along with his ideas. Usually, things worked out, she told herself, so she helped him pack a few things.

"Don't worry, Natasha. After all, this is just for a weekend. During the week, I have to do what my boss tells me to do. After the work hours, I'm a free man. Just because I'm in India, doesn't mean that I'm in prison. If I have a free weekend, and I feel like going somewhere, I go. Just remember, Natasha this is just a trial run, so you will see, I will be back Sunday evening."

The next day, there was trouble in the compound. The three men were missed. A few committee members came to the apartment. Natasha told them that Pavel had left to be with his Indian friends that he had worked with in Ranchi. But she knew they didn't believe her.

On Monday, Pavel went to work as usual. Before he had the chance to look over some of the inter-office mail, he was called into the office of the KGB at the plant. Ivan had already been summoned. When Ivan saw Pavel enter the room, he looked at him questioningly.

Mr. Tafarevich was very angry. He rose from his chair and faced the men squarely. "You had no right to leave the compound without written permission. Through these actions, you were violating all the rules and principles here. I'm sure that you are aware that we have the full power and authority to punish you."

"Yes, Mr. Tafarevich. You can send us back to Russia, but first of all, you're not our boss, so why are you talking to us like this?" Pavel watched the man carefully for his reaction.

For the next few minutes, the same angry words were tossed back and forth between Tafarevich and Pavel. Pavel decided to try and reason with Tafarevich. "All we did was go to Darjeeling. We had a free weekend, and we thought it would be an excellent opportunity to see this beautiful city. It's a shame to be here in India and not be able to see any of the country or the culture. It was easy to do. It was not at all complicated. You should go. All you have to do is buy a train ticket. It's easy."

Finally, Tafarevich slapped his hands against his sides in exasperation. "Enough of this. I never want to hear anything more from either of you about breaking rules and taking off without permission."

As the men left the office and walked down the hallway, Pavel nodded to the others with a slow grin. "I don't think we have to worry about this. If this conversation had taken place three years or even a year ago, we would all have been in deep, deep trouble."

"Yes, I think so," Ivan agreed. " Times have changed, Pavel. Let's hope so."

"You know, we have a contract with the Indians. I asked to see it when I first started to work here in Bhilai. The Russian bosses acted like the contract never existed. I'm going to demand to see it. I think we have a right to travel under the contract, but they don't want anyone to see it."

"That's right. Let us know what happens, Pavel, because if we have the right to travel, we'll go where we want."

Within a month, they got their contracts. They spread all three of the documents out on the desk in Pavel's office.

"Look here!" Filipp exclaimed. "Here is a little clause that says we are allowed eighteen paid days of travel in India to see the culture and the country."

"Yes, and you know why? It's because the Indians made up the contract, and the Indians are paying us. The Russians don't want us to know about it. They want to keep us under tight control in the compound," Pavel emphasized.

At that moment Ivan entered the room. "Just wait 'till you hear this. The big news is that four KGB party bosses are going to take the train to Darjeeling this weekend!"

Pavel doubled up with laughter. "The stupid goons. They bound themselves up with their own rules. Believe me, before the polish wears off their boots, let's go somewhere for our eighteen days of annual leave."

"You bet, and we don't have to flip on that one!"

"And we don't have to polish their boots to go, either!"

"Don't celebrate too soon!" a voice warned from the doorway.

They all turned to see who was entering the room.

"Turgov! Why all the words of doom and gloom?"

161

"Well, Pavel, I am hearing rumbles of a coup that is supposed to happen soon in Moscow."

"Where is this information coming from?"

"I heard some men talking. I can't say anything more. Keep quiet about it, whatever you do!"

Pavel looked questioningly at the others. Then, he decided to follow Turgov to see if he could learn something more. But Turgov shook his head and hurried down the hallway. When he saw that Pavel was still following him, he stopped and motioned for him to step outside in the pretense of going for a smoke.

"I heard two men talking in the office a couple of days ago. I don't know where they were from. It was late. They didn't know I was next door. There was a Mister Zhukovsky and a Mister Lomonosov. I believe they are from Lipetsk."

"Mister Zhukovsky!" Pavel exclaimed astounded at the news. "I didn't know he was here in India. He and a Mister Lomonosov gave me a bad time when I was going to school because I was visiting two foreign nationals at the time. They are strict KGB men. All the way!"

"Well, from what I can gather, they have been making plans with the KGB chief Vam Kurchakoff and Zakov Tylakov."

"I thought all along some coup supporters were hiding out here in India. Damn! I wish I could be back there in Russia right now!"

"Patience! Patience! You can't be in both places. You can't be working here in Bhilai and on the streets of Moscow at the same time!"

But Pavel didn't know that his friend, Andrey Dimitri was standing on the streets of Moscow at this very minute. He had taken the train earlier that day to buy some books for school. Now, he was taking some English classes like Pavel had done, thinking that a knowledge of the English language would be valuable to him in the future when he started looking for a job.

It was getting late, and he had to hurry and make his purchases at the book store. Suddenly, a car drove up to the curb and two men got out. When Andrey recognized them as Lomonosov and Zhukovsky, he quickly turned and moved behind a stack of books. Once, Lomonosov had searched his apartment, and both of them had given Pavel a lot of trouble a few years ago.

There was no one else in the book store, so the men began to talk easily back and forth.

"What did you think of our plane trip, Zhukovsky?"

"Not bad. One day you are in India and the next day back here in Russia!"

"I was getting tired of keeping a low profile in India. Now, maybe we can get in on some of the action here in Moscow."

"When will it all start?"

"In two days! In two days we will be in control at the White House, and those reformers will be warming their buns in prison!" Lomonosov laughed loudly at his joke. "Some vodka, my friend?"

Zhukovsky smiled at those words. His narrow Slavic eyes peered over his reddish, fat cheeks. He selected a few books and slapped his friend on the shoulder.

Andrey waited until he was sure that they were well down the street before he moved out from behind the narrow book stacks. Then, he pretended to be busy looking at some books in the back, so the shop keeper didn't remember he was in the store at the same time as the KGB men.

In two days, a coup would begin, Andrey thought excitedly to himself. How he would love to have a chance to get even with those two men and the ones he had lived with in the apartment. Because of them and Yakov, his brother and Dr. Korotch had died.

Andrey could feel the blood pumping rapidly through his body. He wouldn't go back to Lipetsk just yet. He had to be here when the coup began. He was determined and was ready for the action. In fact, more than ready! Allery was living in the city with her little boy now. Maybe he could stay with them for a couple of days.

It was early evening when Andrey arrived at Allery's apartment. She was excited to see him, but when she heard what was going to happen in the city, she tried to persuade him to leave and go home.

"Let me tell you, Andrey, it would be better if you did not get involved in any way with this take-over. Remember, the problems you've had with the KGB. Think of your mother. How terrible all this has been for her."

"The problems I had with the KGB were all this Yakov's fault. After the police arrested him, he claimed I was a spy just like he claimed Ivan was a spy."

"Where is Yakov now?"

An electrical shock moved down Andrey's spine. He had forgotten all about him, or had he? Perhaps, he had just pushed all those terrible memories in the far corners of his mind. Ivan's sudden death on the streets. His own beating. All by the hands of Yakov. "I don't know." Andrey's voice trailed off. Then he stopped and shook his head. "I have moved around so much it would be difficult for him to find me." Find me. Kill me. Accuse me. The memory of Yakov and what he had done to Ivan pierced his thinking.

"Be careful, Andrey. Think carefully before you do anything."

Andrey had several days to think about Allery's warning and spend some time with Ivan. How the boy had grown! He was already active in sports at his school and was becoming tall and strong like his father, Ivan.

On the morning of August 19, a neighbor told Andrey that someone was organizing a protest just outside the Kremlin in Manezh Square.

Andrey lost no time. He didn't have to account to anyone, so he raced down the street. By now, the news of a coup was spreading rapidly through Moscow.

Before Andrey could reach the bus, a familiar figure called to him from the entrance of a building. "Remember me? I'm Maksim Romano, Pavel's friend."

"I'm on my way downtown. I've heard something about a coup going on in Manezh Square. What do you know about it?"

"Plenty. I'm here in Moscow now working part-time for a weekly paper, the *Epokha*. The conspirators have ordered the closing of all newspapers that have been advocates of glasnost and reform. Our paper was just closed an hour ago. Probably because of an article that one of our journalists wrote."

"What was that about?"

"He wrote that Gorbachev was not ill, and furthermore, was removed from his post by force. Now, Gorbachev is being held against his will. He also wrote that this action is a serious state crime."

"Bravo, for him! Now what?"

"We ran off copies of this article before our offices were closed. We need help, Andrey. Our plan is to paste this article on the walls of the subway system where many people can see it."

"Okay, let's go. As I remember, you have an old truck?"

"Yes, that's right. Over there. We'll have to hurry because I'm sure crowds will start to form all over downtown very soon."

They drove swiftly to the entrance of the subway and raced down the stairs, stopping at all the possible places where they could paste up the article. They worked rapidly trying to accomplish as much as they could before the crowds of people or protesters arrived.

Suddenly, just as Andrey was putting up the paper, he noticed a policeman rapidly approaching him. Surely, he would be arrested and taken in for posting articles like this in the subway. Where could he turn and get away, he thought in desperation. The policeman stared at him and saw immediately what Andrey was pasting on the wall. And just as suddenly as he had appeared, the policeman deliberately turned his back and turned and walked away.

"What was that all about?" Andrey asked in surprise. "Why didn't he arrest me, Maksim?"

"Because they are with us. They don't support the conspirators! Let's head for downtown. We'd better take the bus."

As the bus approached the square, Andrey could see a large crowd near the square. He could hear sirens in the distance. Soon, police cars and fire trucks started to arrive. Then a column of armored vehicles came into view. They were coming from the direction of Detsky Mir, a children's department store that shared Dzerzhinsky Square with the Lubyanka, the headquarters of the KGB., about a mile from Manezh Square.

Suddenly, a man next to Andrey grabbed a megaphone and urged people to run to meet the vehicles. Some started to run and jump in front of the column. Others climbed on top of the armored trucks and yelled at the soldiers to go home. They would bring shame upon themselves if they became a part of a junta.

Another man shouted, "Don't shoot us! Don't shoot us!"

The soldiers responded telling him that they were ordered to just take a position and to maintain order.

By afternoon, the crowd had grown to almost fifteen thousand. Those around him, were talking about putting up a barricade. Andrey had noticed that a construction project was under way near the White House.

"Let's go on over there," Andrey suggested to Maksim. "We can get some concrete slabs, scrap iron and old pipes. Hurry up! We can do it!"

With so many people eager to put up barricades, they soon had placed huge amounts of debris at the intersections near the White House. Maksim knew that the barricades would not stop the tanks, but it would show the conspirators that they were willing to shed their own blood and actively resist any takeover.

Some people were gathered around small portable radios. One man who had been listening to the news reported that Radio M was off the air, and the Soviet stations were transmitting only the official statements of the conspirators. Another man claimed that no one was jamming Radio Liberty which was broadcasting from Munich. Radio Liberty was the United States' Russian-language station.

"Who is responsible for closing the radio studios, Maksim?"

"Probably the KGB agents closed and sealed the studio."

The people in the square were upset at the news that the station had been closed down. A depression seemed to settle over the people that were listening to the portable radios.

"You know, Andrey, I think the people here are beginning to believe that the conspirators will succeed. Then it will be a long time before we can get back to the reforms again," Maksim said despondently.

Andrey shook his head in disbelief at the way everything was going.

But in a few hours, the station got back on the air again. The rumor was that the Ministry of Communications was split into two factions. One supported the station and the other opposed letting the station back on the air. Finally, a deputy minister ordered that the connection between the studio and its transmitter be restored and the state radio, Radio M was back again on the air.

"How did all this start, Maksim?"

"As a reporter, I heard that there was a meeting late one evening at the Kremlin. Vice President Yanayev and Prime Minister Pavlov and many others got together. Kryuchkov told them that a catastrophe was taking place and that Gorbachev was ill from a heart attack or a stroke. Kryuchkov wanted everyone to sign a document creating the Emergency Committee. The document would make Yanayev the new president. Finally, after much persuasion, he signed. Then when Bessmertnykh, our foreign minister, arrived he was also pressured to sign. He refused, saying that this document would isolate the country and perhaps bring on sanctions from the West. So the group began to fall apart."

"Sounds like a lot of poor planning. Maybe the whole coup will fall apart."

"Not so fast, Andrey. Let's wait and see what happens."

By mid-morning, tanks had surrounded the Moscow City Hall and were taking positions at many key points of the city. People reported that there were tanks at the newspaper offices, Lenin Hill, the White House and the TV and radio stations.

"Look!" Maksim exclaimed. "The soldiers are taking down the Russian tricolor and are replacing it with the red Soviet flag! I can't believe this is happening! I'm going to make a call. I'll be right back."

A few minutes later, Maksim returned. "I just got up the nerve and called General Yevgeny Shaposhnikov, the commander of the air force. I was lucky to reach him. He said he had listened to Yazov's commands and explanations of the coup, but he told me personally that he is revolted by what had happened!"

"Did he say that?" Andrey asked in amazement. " Will your editor let you publish that in your paper?""

"I hope so, but I don't know at what point. Shaposhnikov also called the leaders of the coup, 'sons of bitches'!"

"Print it, Maksim, print it!"

"I'm for it! Anyway, let's move back to the White House. That's where we should see something beginning to happen."

Around noon, there was a pronounced stir of excitement in the crowd. They could see Boris Yeltsin walking down the front steps of the White House. He immediately climbed up on a T-72 Tank, No. 110 of the Taman Guards.

The people were amazed to see Yeltsin standing tall and commanding on top of the tank. His broad shoulders and shock of thick white hair were in stark contrast to the solders standing below.

"Yeltsin! Yeltsin!" the crowd roared as he faced the people in the square.

"Tell the soldiers to go home!"

The excitement grew as more people edged closer to get a glimpse of this man who had, without concern for his safety, climbed a tank.

"He is the symbol of our democracy!" one man shouted. "Listen to him!"

Yeltsin's face broke into a look of fierce determination. His gray-blue eyes closely searched the crowd. His voice thundered across the square as he spoke. He told them that the legally elected president of the country had been removed from power and that they were dealing with a reactionary and anti-constitutional illegal group. He went on to declare that all the decisions and decrees of this committee were illegal and asked the people to oppose their actions and demand a return of the country to normal constitutional development.

After this address to the people, Konstantin Kobets, Russian defense minister appointed by Yeltsin, climbed onto the tank and began speaking to the crowd and the soldiers. He promised to organize a military resistance and try to convince the soldiers and the troops not to follow the commands of the conspirators.

Around noon, Maksim and Andrey noticed some people gathered around one of the portable radios that someone had brought to the square. Yeltsin was addressing the soldiers, the officers, the KGB and the troops of the Interior Ministry. He told them that the country was faced with a great threat and reminded all of them that they had taken an oath to the people, and their weapons should not nor could not be turned against the people. He urged them to make the right decision and not bring dishonor to the country.

After he had finished speaking, Andrey turned to leave. "I have to get back to Lipetsk, Maksim. I hope things quiet down soon."

"Time will tell. It was a good thing we were here today, because we couldn't have seen it on television. The conspirators control the state television. I hope you can get through these streets. Anyway, call me tomorrow if you can. Here is my number."

Andrey tried to move away from the crowds that were pushing toward the White House. But he was not having any success in getting through the congestion. To make matters worse, he was not familiar with the subways in Moscow. He looked around for Maksim among the sea of faces around him. Fortunately, his friend had seen his dilemma and was trying to reach him.

"Let me help you. We will go the subways, but you may not be able to get out of here today. Stay with me until this is over. I live in a room near the newspaper office."

"You don't live in Lipetsk anymore?"

"I'm working here for a while. Part-time at the newspaper and part-time at a factory. My wife and I aren't getting along very well. She's back in Lipetsk."

"Well, I'm still going to the university. I got a letter from Pavel the other day. He and Natasha are living in a Russian compound in Bhilai."

"Are they happy?"

"Not really because there are so many restrictions there. And the KGB and the Communist Party enforce the rules like the old days here in Russia. They are very strict. Pavel got in trouble for leaving the compound one weekend without permission with one of his friends. They took the train to visit Darjeeling. And most of the time, he refuses to go to party meetings!"

"That sounds like Pavel all right! He never would let the KGB or the Communist Party tell him what to do!"

"Can't blame him. I'd like to get even with them, myself!"

Maksim noticed the fierce determination in Andrey's voice. "Take it easy, fella! I know how the KGB hounded you and kept searching your apartment, but their time will come."

Late that evening, Maksim showed Andrey the newspaper office where he worked. "I'm hoping this coup will be over soon, and we can begin to publish again. It isn't like one of the big papers, but I'm learning a lot here about the business."

Suddenly, a person appeared in the doorway. "Hi, what are you doing here so late at night?"

"Just showing the office to my friend here. Andrey. We spent the day downtown near the White House."

"I just got some hot news. I'm going to write it up and see if old Ruslan will publish it."

"Hot news!"

"Yeah, but it's my scoop. At six o'clock this evening, an assault on the White House by the Alpha force of the KGB was scheduled to start."

"The special Alpha force? I hear that those men are supposed to be better trained than the American Green Berets. So what happened?"

"Well, the Alpha force would have completely taken over everything, but I understand they refused to attack!"

"What a break for Yeltsin! He probably would have been killed!"

This statement crossed Maksim's mind with a cold feeling of reality. What terrible brutality could arise in the streets and invade the White House, the very symbol of their freedoms.

He clinched his fists in anger. "What is it going to take, Andrey, to put a stop to all of this?"

"Huge crowds. The stubbornness and the strong will of the Russian people, Maksim. We will paste up more flyers in the subway stations and bus stops tomorrow."

The next day Maksim and Andrey headed for the subways again in the old truck. This was the second day of the coup.

That morning a crowd of one hundred thousand people gathered in the square near the White House. Because of the information being spread in the leaflets, people were hearing more and more about what was going on.

Around ten-thirty, as tremendous crowds gathered around the square, Yeltsin appeared on the White House balcony. Above him was a huge Russian tricolor flag. In a deep, sonorous voice he told the people that the Russian prosecutors and the Interior Ministry had orders to prosecute anyone who obeys the commands of this illegal committee. He called for the people to stand together and support the troops who had steadfastly refused to follow the putschists. He told the people that he was convinced that this aggression would not win out. Democracy would triumph!

"What do you think of that speech, Maksim?"

"A good one, I think. People can see him as the symbol of democracy and what they have been asked to risk and defend."

"This time, Maksim, I have no choice but to get back to Lipetsk and my classes. I've missed too much already."

As Andrey made his way through the crowds, his eye caught a familiar face. It was Yakov standing with Lomonosov and Zhukovsky—the KGB men. Of all people to come across. The one person in Moscow he didn't want to see! Up to now, Andrey thought he was safe and had faded into in the streets of Lipetsk!

He hurried along trying to avoid a confrontation with any of them.

Suddenly, Yakov raised his fist and moved toward him, but Lomonosov restrained him, and he turned away with a leering smile spreading across his face.

"Damn him!" Andrey swore under his breath. "Damn, Yakov and the KGB! Sons of bitches!" If Yakov found out where he lived, he might die in the street like his brother. He had to get to him first!

Chapter 18

Several weeks after the coup, Pavel received a letter from Maksim. He called to Natasha who was just finishing up the dinner dishes in the kitchen.

"Look, I just received a letter from an old friend in Russia! It's from Maksim Romano! Do you remember him?"

"Of course! What does he say?"

"He is working in Moscow for a weekly newspaper, and he ran into Andrey the first day of the coup. They helped build some of the barricades at the intersections of the streets near the White House. Later, they saw Yeltsin climb on one of the tanks and address the crowd!"

"How lucky they were to be there. What was Andrey doing in Moscow?"

"Buying books for his English class. He saw Lomonosov and Zhukovsky in the book store. He heard them talking and kept out of sight. They had just come back from India and were talking about the coup that was about to take place!"

"Aren't those the two KGB officers that gave you all that trouble when you were friends with the foreign engineers? Then, they arrested and beat you and kept searching your apartment?"

"Exactly! Same damn KGB men! Then, Maksim goes on to say that he heard from Andrey after he got back to Lipetsk. Before he left Moscow, Andrey saw Yakov in the crowd with Lomonosov and Zhukovsky. Yakov raised his fist at him. Now, Maksim thinks that Andrey will go after Yakov and seek revenge for his brother's death."

"You'd better write to Andrey, Pavel. You know how much he hates the KGB and those guys that he lived with who attacked Doctor Korotch. No telling what he might do!"

"Yes, you're right. I'll get it right in the mail tomorrow." Pavel stretched out in the over-stuffed chair in the room and put up his feet. "Well, I'd better look at some of these papers that I brought home from the office."

A little later, he looked up at Natasha with a worried frown. She was sitting on the couch working on the sweater for her mother. "I'm concerned about something that came up at the plant. A few months ago, Doctor Turcostiva, the representative of the Russian Steel Ministry, came down from Delhi and met with some of the plant managers. Turcostiva proposed to the managers that we help an influential Indian with his doctoral degree. Now, my job over the past few months has been to translate the English to Russian and sometimes Russian to English. There is a lot of scientific information."

"Oh, Doctor Turcostiva? Don't you see Doctor Turcostiva quite often when you travel to Calcutta on business?"

"Yes, he knows many Indians, so, for example, if he got a call from Moscow wanting to know if he knew of a possible candidate for a doctoral degree, he would be able to make a suggestion. So, I believe he is the connection between the Moscow officials and the Indians, because he has been the representative in Calcutta for the past ten to twelve years. He knows all the Indians in the industry."

"What is the problem about this?"

"Well, all the research for this work is supposed to be conducted by this Indian engineer. Maybe he is doing it, but I have some doubts. And that's not all. Later on, I will be required to go back to Moscow and translate for the committee when the doctoral candidate defends his thesis." Pavel's face was filled with concern.

"But you're not sure about who is actually doing the research?"

"That"s right. I think there will be quite a few of these theses for me to translate as time goes on. Well, we'll see what happens. Maybe I can find out what's going on."

Natasha could see that Pavel was very troubled. She knew that he would be the last one to get involved in any kind of scam.

For the next few weeks, Pavel didn't have the opportunity to search out his suspicions. He was kept pretty busy translating the scientific papers. One day at lunch, the conversations turned back to the coup in Moscow.

"What do you think of the coup in Russia? Why do you think the people got so involved in trying to stop the conspirators?" Filipp asked.

"I've heard that many young people came to the White House because they were more interested in defending their right to go into business and get rich than anything else. Now, they've gone from commodities exchanges into banking. Many businessmen are making fortunes that would amaze you!" Ivan replied.

"So you think it's all money?" Pavel held up a newspaper. "Here, the Calcutta paper says that Radio Liberty interviewed the poet, Yevgeny Yevtushenko who was with Yelstin when he addressed the crowd from the balcony at the White House. Yevtushenko believes that the coming of glasnost has educated and transformed the people. He sees a new and different generation of Russians who are educated and unwilling to accept the old, strict Communist rules. Young people are becoming involved. They are not leaving reforms to the old people. They feel they have a chance for freedom."

"You mean read any kind of book they want and hear all the different songs and music they want, Pavel?" Ivan asked leaning forward to see the article.

"Yes, it's all here in the paper, what Yevtushenko said. He says the young people don't want to spend their lives behind the Iron Curtain, locked away from the rest of the world."

Ivan started to read the article and then suddenly looked up. "Say, do you remember, Pavel about those eighteen days of annual leave we're supposed to get? Are you planning to go back to Russia next year?"

"Actually, I hadn't thought about it yet. First of all, I want to get my passport. Remember when we first came to India the first thing they did was take away our passports?"

"Yes, that's right. Why do you want it now?"

"Well, just because it's my property. It belongs to me."

"Well, let us know what happens, because we'll need them when we go back to Russia next year."

But Pavel didn't have Russia on his mind. He wanted to go somewhere else. Still, he needed his passport before he could go anywhere. The more he thought about it, the angrier he felt. What right did they have to keep his passport?

Late in the day, he had a chance to go to one of the plant's offices. Officially, this man was supposed to be a steel engineer, but Pavel knew for a fact that Mr. Rennikof was a KGB officer. He knew next to nothing about the operations of the steel plant. His job was to just sit in the office and report anyone who had been causing trouble. It was his job to keep the passports.

Mr. Rennikof looked up from his desk when Pavel entered his office.

"I would like to have my passport back."

"What do you want your passport for?" Rennikof asked in a superior tone. "We keep all the passports locked up for safekeeping here in this office."

"Well, it's my passport. Why are you keeping it locked up? It doesn't belong to the government."

The man argued some more, but Pavel could see that he didn't seem to know what to do. It was obvious that he was stalling for time.

"After all," Pavel continued again, "It's my property. I want it back."

Two weeks later, Pavel finally got his passport. It was at the end of the day when he saw Filipp and Ivan just leaving the office. He felt relieved and jubilant as he waved his passport for them to see.

Ivan gave him the "thumbs up" and turned to Filipp and shook his head. "Just like Pavel to demand his passport! Leave it up to him; he doesn't take 'no' for an answer."

"He's one determined cuss. He gets what he's after, all right! I think he must have something up his sleeve.!" Filipp said, shaking his head.

Getting his passport was just the first step in Pavel's plans. He knew that Filipp and Ivan were anxious to go back to Russia, but he had other plans. He was seriously thinking about going to Thailand and Singapore. No one else had gone to other countries on their annual leave.

That evening, Pavel came home with a triumphant look on his face. "Look, Natasha, I finally got our passports!"

"For our annual leave to Russia next year?"

"No, so we can go to Thailand and Singapore!"

"You are crazy! We'll never be allowed to go anywhere besides Russia!"

"Yes, Natasha, we're going to Singapore! I told them that we have been to Russia. This time, I want to go to some other place."

"What did they say?"

"They said you can't do that. You can't go anywhere besides Russia."

"I'm worried about that, Pavel! What happens if we go somewhere else?"

"This is what happens!" Pavel exclaimed with a wide grin on his face."Look, Natasha, here are our tickets. I bought them myself. We'll leave in two months!"

Natasha sighed and collapsed on the couch. "Oh, this is just too much! I can't believe it! Just think! Singapore! Thailand! Is this really true?"

"Yes, we are really going, Natasha!" He reached out his arms for her and held her very close. Carefully, he wiped the tears from her cheeks. Natasha's tears of joy were moving down his face as he kissed her over and over again.

Finally, he motioned toward the next room. "Time for us to get ready and think about our trip!"

"What—to think about packing? Now? We're not going for two months!"

Pavel started to laugh. "No, this is the time for us to make love and think about our future together. Right now, I want to hold you with nothing between us. I want to feel your soft loveliness next to me."

"How wonderful this trip will be! " Natasha exclaimed as she moved toward the bedroom. Eighteen days! Just think of it! I can hardly believe it is true!"

But it was true! At first, it was going to be just the two of them. Then, Pavel realized it would look better and cause less trouble if someone else from the plant went with them. So, it was early in 1992 that Zadislof Trovati went with them to Thailand and Singapore.

"Look!" Pavel exclaimed as the plane took off for Thailand. "We are the first Russians from the compound to go to a foreign country!"

"Just remember, we will have to face the authorities when we get back to Bhilai," Zadislof warned. "You know, this is a dangerous step for us to take."

"Are you having regrets?"

"No, not at all. But we may be putting our jobs in jeopardy."

"I suppose we could be in trouble when we get back. But what can they do about it?" But Pavel knew they could do plenty.

Zadislof shrugged. "It will be worth it no matter what happens."

"It will be worth it just to get some time away from the compound where we are watched all the time. Now, we can say anything or do anything we please!" He stroked Natasha's hair. She had nestled closer to him, and he could smell the light floral scent of her favorite perfume around her neck and hair. How exciting it would be to see Thailand and Singapore together! To be free from the domination of the Communist Party's rules of the compound. Freedom! Pavel let the words pass through his mind. Then, he thought of the time that Natasha and he could spend together. Yes, free, from being disturbed by the sounds of knocking at the door from committee members coming to look through the apartment.

"Freedom," he whispered to himself.

Natasha heard the words as she stirred from her sleep. "Yes, freedom. We will have lots of freedom. Maybe we won't come back. Let's just stay up here in the air and keep flying."

"A good idea, right now!" Pavel kissed her lightly, so very lightly on the lips and let the time slip away.

During the next few days in Thailand, they let many hours slip away. Often, in the coolness and quietness of their hotel room, they made love with abandon. Natasha stood by the window with the last rays of the sun revealing the outlines of her soft, curvaceous body through the sheerness of her nightgown. Pavel set the wine glass down on the table and moved to embrace her. How sensuous she felt through the soft fabric! He had never wanted her so much!

"How lucky I am to have such a beautiful girl, such a beautiful wife!"

But the time passed by much too quickly. They bought gifts for their parents and mailed them off from Thailand. And Stepan—now, he was writing Pavel and Natasha letters. He was growing and learning so many new things. Marina reported that he was the best in his class at school. Pavel believed it. Anyway, it was the absolute truth. Of course his son was very intelligent. What else could he expect!

The evening they flew into Singapore, Natasha was amazed at all the glittering lights of the city. "I'm surprised that Singapore is so large!"

"Well, Singapore is not just one island, but a main island with more than sixty smaller islets surrounding it. There is lots to see here!"

"I'm sure there is lots to see here," Zadislof agreed. "I believe I read that Singapore is the melting pot of Southeast Asia. Arabs, Chinese, Europeans, Indians, and Straits-born Chinese came to live here. And these races with all their different religions all live peacefully together!"

"That's a lesson that people in other countries should follow."

"That's for sure, Pavel. Yes, so much of the world has been fighting over different nationalities and religions."

Natasha shuddered. "They call it ethnic cleansing. Sometimes, whole villages are massacred!"

The next day, they decided to visit Chinatown just behind the skyscrapers of Singapore's financial district. Here, they saw Chinese merchants doing business from the ground floor of quaint pre-war shops. Pavel bought a colorful kite for Stepan.

Late in the afternoon, they walked along the busy shopping belt that stretched from Orchard Road to Marina Bay. Here, shopkeepers told them that the only Russians they had seen were sailors who often visited Singapore.

It was in the third shop that they met several Russian sailors. They were trading vodka for some electronics because they had no money.

"Are you going to see Little India?" one asked.

"Little India!" Pavel exclaimed. "We just came from a Russian compound in India. I work as an interpreter for the Bhelai Steel Company. And there we live under very strict Communist rules. We can't leave the compound without special permission."

"So how did you get here, friend?"

"I told them I wanted to go to Thailand and Singapore for my annual leave. They didn't agree, so I bought the airplane tickets myself!"

"Well, good luck! You might be in for a pile of trouble when you get back. If you lose your job, you can look us up and join the Russian navy!"

Pavel shook his head. The words "navy" and "army" passed before his eyes. The old army days. Stealing, fights. Living like wolves in army barracks. The great Russian army that the media had fed the people.

He watched the sailors walk down the street. Another time. Another world. He had walked out of that world. Now, what would happen when he and Zadislof returned to India?

A week later, they found themselves in a big storm. The storm had blown in like a monsoon from the sea. It seemed to have gained in momentum as it swept in from the Indian Ocean. The source of the storm originated in Ranchi. Dalislov, Pavel's boss, had flown in from Ranchi. It was not a pleasant situation.

It was obvious that the whole system was in a turmoil. Neither the authorities in Bhelai or Ranchi had been confronted by their employees in this way before. Pavel and Zadislof were called into the plant manager's office. A few of the party bosses were there as well as Rennikof, the KGB officer, Zal Tyunin a party boss from Ranchi and Aleksei Bjorisov, the plant manager from Ranchi.

Rennikof walked around the desk and glared at Pavel and Zadislof. His face was livid with anger. "What did you think you were doing by going to Thailand and Singapore? Our policy only allows you to go to Russia on your annual leave. You were jeopardizing your jobs here and your whole career by deliberately flying to these other countries. You know, you had no right, no right, whatsoever!"

He started to pace back and forth in front of the two men, then stopped, to let Zal Tyunin, the party boss from Ranchi, have his say. "He's right! Look what you idiots have done! We were called here from Ranchi because of this situation that you have created! There is no excuse for this!"

After several hours of angry words, Pavel thought the path to take would be to claim complete innocence. "I have been doing well with my job. There have been no complaints. I didn't think it was wrong to go somewhere else on a vacation just as long as that was on my own time."

But Rennikof only shook his head angrily. "I won't listen to this nonsense! Clearly, your action was taken fully aware that you were going against policies."

"Rennikof is right!" Selyunin said, pounding his fist on the desk. "We will send you back to Russia with papers that say you are black-listed because many people decided at a party meeting that you are an ideological enemy. You have expressed these ideas and do not deserve to move ahead in your career. In fact, you do not deserve anything more in your life. Many people like yourself have had this happen to them when they disobeyed!"

"And do you know what that will mean?" Rennikof demanded. "Since the papers say that you are to be black-listed, you cannot find a job in Russia. Your whole career that you worked so hard for is now ruined!"

Each of the men took turns threatening Pavel and Zadislof for many hours. It was late afternoon before they had finished venting their anger. Finally after hours of threats and anger, Pavel was exasperated. He stood up and said quietly, "Okay, send me back to Russia with your bad references. Russia is different today. Your references mean nothing there. It's a different country now."

"Go! Go! Get out of here! Both of you! You'd better start packing your bags to leave!"

Later, in the hallway, Zadislof put his arm around Pavel's shoulder. They walked together to their office. It was empty for the moment. "What do you think will happen? Will they carry out their threats?"

"You know, in the past, the party could ruin a man as easily as swatting a moth—just with one little blow, they could ruin a person's whole career."

"And now?"

"I believe they are just trying to throw their weight around. Maybe I am wrong, but I think they are powerless to do anything, because we have been doing our work correctly. Besides, the situation is Russia is different now. The Communist Party doesn't have the power like before. Now, they are discovering they don't have the absolute control they used to have over many situations."

"You're probably right. But still, we can't be sure."

In the next few weeks, Pavel was restless and worried. The words of the party bosses tormented him. He felt sure that they would do nothing, but again, he was not sure. There was no peace in his mind. And evenings, he tried to console Natasha. He had not told her exactly what had taken place in the meeting. She would worry too much, so he held her closely at night and soothed her questions with soft assurances as he stroked her hair and kissed her over and over again.

Finally, it became obvious that the KGB realized that they should leave Pavel and Zadislof alone. Because Pavel was very good at his job, the Indians offered to extend his contract because they needed his services. The storm had passed. But he didn't know that a much bigger storm was threatening his life and Natasha's some miles out to sea.

Chapter 19

During the course of the next several years, Pavel was busy translating scientific theses for Indian engineers. There were also other interpreters who were also involved in the projects. Still, he had to deal with many different papers and different research which was supposed to have been done by Indian engineers. At first, the work seemed quite innocent, but as time passed, doubts began to move into Pavel's mind, and he couldn't find the answers.

In March of 1993, he was required to fly to Moscow once again to translate a thesis before the scientific community. The Indians paid for the trip to Russia. The whole event was supposed to take several days.

Pavel and Mr. Hadan, the Indian candidate, were met at the airport and taken to their hotel in a special car that was furnished by the Russian Steel Ministry. They conversed very little on the way to the hotel. Mr. Hadan spoke Russian with difficulty, so he leaned heavily on Pavel for assistance.

The next morning they went to meet with different officials and spent the whole day talking about the steel industry in Russia. Later, Pavel reviewed his notes and the thesis that he would defend for Mr. Hadan.

Prior to this time, Mr. Hadan and Pavel had worked together in Bhalai. They had met with scientists who explained different parts of the thesis to both of them. Mr. Hadan did not write the thesis, but supposedly did all the research. The whole project usually took about three years. When the research was completed and the thesis written, the scientists asked Mr. Hadan different questions that he might be expected to answer before the committee in Moscow.

Mr. Hadan was the manager of a large steel company. A few years ago, he had married the daughter of one of the ministers in the Indian Steel Industry.

The second day that they were in Moscow, they went before the scientific committee which was a large body of about forty people.

The committee was well represented by some of the top scientists of Russia. Here, Mr. Hadan was required to defend his thesis. The committee's job was to decide whether his thesis, based on scientific evidence, was important, significant and had any real scientific value. Otherwise, it would fail.

Pavel was required to translate for Mr. Hadan for four or five hours that day. As he spoke before the committee, his eyes trained on the people in front of him. They were all very well-known scientists. He had heard them speak on the radio and on television. They were men that were known throughout the scientific communities in the world.

Then when the scientists began to question Mr. Hadan, an alarm rang off in Pavel's mind. This man didn't have the knowledge to have been able to conduct this research himself! Pavel felt angry and upset. He had to get back to Bhilai and put the pieces of this together, but he strongly suspected that the whole doctoral program was a big fraud!

It took several months for Pavel to begin to sift through all the information he could find. First, some of the most influential people in the Russian and Indian steel authority would choose some Indian candidate who already was a manager of a large steel company and had hopes of moving up. They would ask him if he would like to have a doctoral degree and say, "We will help you, but we will expect that in return your plant will pay for our trips to India and other places." Then, the Russians would send some research and development people to India to work on the thesis. After they completed the project, the Indian would go to Moscow to defend his thesis. It was already agreed in advance that the committee would accept the thesis.

Pavel knew that he had to do something about this terrible fraud before real trouble started in the steel industry. For himself, he wanted no part of the whole scheme, but what could he do?

When Pavel entered the apartment that late afternoon, Natasha knew right away he was troubled about something. His fists were clenched and his forehead was a myriad of frowns as he began to speak.

"You know, Natasha, I've been concerned about the research that I have been assigned to translate for those Indian candidates. Today, I met the Russian person who was hired to do all the research."

"You mean all the experimentation and the actual writing of the thesis?"

"Exactly. For one thing, I know that this Mr. Hadan is not capable of writing about steel. His paper dealt with a different area of steel of which he has no knowledge."

"And today, you met the real author of the thesis and the man that did the research for Mr. Hadan?"

"Yes, Mr. Vokhanoff did all the experimentation and developed his ideas into that thesis. He was paid by the Indians to write the paper, and further, it was done with the approval of the Russian Steel Ministry. The ministry sent Mr. Vokhanoff to India for that very purpose."

"That's terrible! Have you and the other interpreters worked on other theses where the men didn't really do the research?"

"That's exactly what's been going on," Pavel exclaimed, his voice rising in anger. "It's a rotten, stinking mess! Once, the chairman of the Indian steel ministry was also involved. He had some good connections in the Russian government and would frequently go to Moscow for government meetings. He was planning to retire soon and didn't want to retire without a degree. He wanted that degree, so he told them he was in a position to pay for it. Then the Russian Steel Ministry sent a qualified man to do a doctoral thesis for him."

"The committee in Moscow who listens to this man defend his thesis knows that this man doesn't know anything about that area of steel making?"

"Yes, it's all part of the scheme. The scientists who listen to the thesis keep quiet because after they award this man with his doctoral degree, they are then invited to India where they are entertained at the best hotels for several weeks.

"Natasha, I have been piecing all this together for some months now. Gradually, I have discovered all these things. I learned more things in the evenings in Moscow after the candidate was through talking before the committee. We would all meet at a restaurant and talk. I would translate and interpret for them."

"I hope you're not going to do anything about it!"

"I've got to!"

"I'm afraid, Pavel. I'm afraid that you will lose your job. It would be too dangerous to say anything!"

"Natasha, it's something I've got to do! I'm going to talk it over with my friend, Turgov. He knows what's been going on. We've discussed this before."

It was a few days later before Pavel had the opportunity to talk to his friend who was head of the public relations department at the steel plant. They had discussed bits and pieces of the problem together before, but now that Pavel had talked to the Russian engineer who had done all the work for Mr. Hadan, he decided to put it all in front of Turgov.

They decided to meet in a small office that was being enlarged for a new Russian specialist. Pavel suspected he was a KGB man, but the place was safe for them to meet and talk. Tools and pieces of lumber were piled around the room.

Pavel entered the office in a storm of protest. "Turgov, I don't think this scam should be allowed to go on. I will not be a part of it any longer! The whole thing has to be stopped!"

"Stopped!" Turgov exclaimed. He was surprised at his friend's burst of anger.

"Yes, I talked to a Mr. Vokhanoff the other day. He told me he had done all the research and the thesis for Mr. Hadan. I've also got the names of several other Indian officials who have gotten phony doctorates."

"And to think of it, we are part of that whole scheme! That whole rotten scheme! Government officials are spending the taxpayers' money to get degrees that they don't deserve. I agree, this whole scam has to be stopped. Here, top Russian scientists are part of a plan that is virtually criminal!"

"So I believe we are the only ones who can stop this!"

"Okay. I have all the basic knowledge of what occurred. Let's put together an article and get it published in our local steel plant paper. I am close friends of the editor."

"*The Steel Times*?"

"Exactly. I will use my name as the by-line for the article, but I believe if your name is used along with mine, it will cause a lot of problems and real unpleasantness in both governments. After all, you are a Russian and getting paid by the Indians. Me, I'm just an Indian working here at the plant."

"Then it's agreed? We'll write the article?"

"Yes, turn in a first draft to me as soon as you can. Give me some names and all the details. You are the only one who knows these things because you were at all the meetings."

Pavel walked away from the meeting with Turgov. He was sure of their purpose. The scam was wrong. And all the people involved in the scandal knew it was wrong.

That evening, Pavel listened quietly to some of his music tapes. Natasha was over at a neighbor's apartment. She had left one of the old, soft Italian songs on the table. It would match his mood.

He rarely drank any wine, but there was a tall glass of home-made wine in the refrigerator that a friend had left for them. Maybe the wine and the music would sooth his nerves, he reasoned. He turned the glass slowly in his hand. The movement caused the red liquid to spill on his shirt cuff. It immediately brought to his mind the red flags that protesters often burned in Moscow in the old days. Things were happening in Russia. The old fire started to burn inside him. He wanted to be with the others. Expressing his views and talking about freedoms.

Suddenly, there was a loud knocking a the door. Damn it! It was probably another committee member coming to check the apartment. He walked quickly into the kitchen and emptied the glass and washed the wine down the sink. Damn, snoops. Why couldn't a man do what he pleased in his own place?

"Oh, good evening, Mr. Lubov. I hope you had a good day?" the man asked politely. His eyes searched quickly around the room. He paused at the desk and looked at the book Pavel had been reading. "Oh, an English classic, I believe."

Pavel nodded. He was thankful he had not started to write the article for the paper. But he hated these intrusions on his privacy. What right? What right has he to be here? The words moved in torrents through his mind. I hate the system. I hate it! He stopped and shook his head. There was nothing he could do. Absolutely nothing! At least not now. But...

"Well, everything looks fine, here, Mr. Lubov. Have a nice evening."

It was all Pavel could do to keep from swearing under his breath. Then, he noticed Natasha coming from the neighboring apartment.

"What! Another committee member?" Natasha asked. She was clearly disturbed. "And that isn't all. Someone was here earlier and said there was a party meeting at eight tonight."

"Looks like I'd better go, especially now that Turgov is going to publish an article about the Ph.D. scam!"

"What are you saying, Pavel? What's going to happen?"

"No, don't worry. It won't be on the article. Now, don't worry."

But Pavel knew there was plenty to worry about. If the KGB knew he was involved in writing the article, they would be after him and a whole avalanche of trouble will fall on them both.

Two months later in July, the article was published in *The Steel Times*. About this time, Turgov made a speech about the scam at a management meeting at the plant. A lot of high officials were present, including the steel minister from Delhi. Turgov's intention wasn't just to disclose the real shame of the doctoral program, but to show all those high officials that they should correct this situation and do it quietly within the steel ministry. He tried to present the problem, not as an insult to anyone, but to show them that the whole practice of doing research and theses by someone other than the doctoral candidate should be stopped. And everyone at the meeting listened carefully to Turgov because he was head of the public relations department, and it was part of his job to act on situations that involved relations between the steel ministry and the Indian government.

However, the whole matter didn't end that easily. Immediately, the Indian steel minister went back to Delhi and fired about seven or eight high officials in the steel ministry, including the chairman, who then had to give up his Ph.D.

A few days later, the whole scam hit the national newspapers. High officials like Sadrad, Donterjo, Vakosh, Ramaras, Acharya, Mangal, Singh, Bannerjee, Povano and Hadan were fired.

From that time on, Turgov was careful not to spend much time with Pavel. He saw him once just passing in the hallway just after the national newspapers began to carry details of the whole scam in the government.

"Did you see the Calcutta papers? They fired seven or eight high officials in the steel ministry. I mentioned just three names in the article. I understand that there was some opposition to the firing of these men, but they didn't dare to raise their voices. For some others, it was a good opportunity to get rid of some of their political rivals."

"Call me at home, Turgov. I'm afraid you will get in trouble if they see you talking to me. After all, I'm the only one who could have known all these names and details. I worked on the translations and attended the meetings."

From that time one, the Indian government started many investigations. There were articles in the national papers almost every day.

Turgov called one evening. "Did you see the news in the Calcutta paper today? Extensive investigations are going on right now. Doctor Sadrad was the first man to be fired. Did you translate his thesis?"

"No, Dr. Sadrad received his doctorate some seven years before I came to India. They really went digging to find him so soon. I believe he must have had a lot of enemies in the government."

Pavel stopped when he heard a sound at the door. He never could trust who might be outside—a committee member or...But it was just Natasha. She had gone for a swim at the pool.

"Natasha, I was just talking to Turgov about Doctor Sadrad. He was just fired. You remember that he has been quite successful on his own as well as working for the ministry. He owns some private blast furnaces."

"I think you told me that he has made millions in his own plants."

"That's right. I predict there will be a big storm and investigation about him. He's a very powerful man!"

In a few days, the storm broke with a tremendous furry. Soon, the national papers in India were filled with other names. Dr. Donterjo, who had a position with the Steel Authority of India, and Dr. Vakosh, chairman of the Steel Authority of India were dismissed in dishonor. Pavel had translated parts of their thesis. Later, more names followed, and they were dismissed.

Two weeks later, Dr. Ramaras, one of the deputy chairmen of the steel authority left his office. Right after the articles describing the scam appeared in the major papers, Dr. Mangal retired promptly although he was on the rise in his career. He had just received his doctoral from Moscow and immediately after receiving his degree, he was promoted to a very important position. Before, he was just one of the steel authority superintendents in one of the plants in India.

Then, suddenly, he was promoted to a position in the government. He had just gotten this position, and then suddenly, after this scheme was revealed in the steel authority, he retired.

Pavel personally knew another man, Mr. Povano, who was approached several times by the Russian Steel Ministry. He was the chief engineer of the Bhilai Steel Plant who was responsible for production. The Russians had made a lot of plans for him to move up in the Indian Steel Authority. At that time, even though he didn't hold a very high position, he was moving forward very rapidly.

Mr. Povano was working around the clock. He was very hard working; actually a workaholic. The Russians approached him several times. But he declined. He was aware of the scheme and didn't want any part of this fraud. Clearly, he knew what was going on between the Indian Steel Authority, the Russian government and the scientific community.

About this time, Pavel began to believe that the worst of the storm was over. It was late in the day, just as he was leaving the plant, that he saw Turgov hurrying toward him.

"What's new, Turgov? I hope there is no more investigations right now?"

"No, not right now. Not today, anyway."

"I found out that the Russian, Mr. Vokhanoff, who has spent almost two years in India writing theses, researching and doing experiments, was finally sent back to Russia. Nothing has happened to him. Looks like they figured he was just a ghost writer doing his job. I guess this whole thing will blow over now!"

"Don't depend on it, Pavel! All you need to bring all this to a boil is to have the KGB and the Russian Steel Ministry get involved! Then, watch out!"

Later, Pavel learned that the whole machine, the whole scam was finally stopped. There were no more phony Ph.D.s that were granted by the committee in Russia. Candidates for the doctoral then went to Germany and the United States where they studied, did their own research and wrote their own theses. But Pavel's mind was not at ease. The shadows of trouble began to invade his mind and his thinking and wouldn't let go. Something was about to happen! He was sure.

Chapter 20

By September, Pavel began to feel like he was walking along on the edge of a deep chasm. If everything went smoothly, he could avoid trouble. But if he lost his balance, he would fall, and his future would be in utter turmoil. He knew he was fencing with danger when he helped Turgov. So far, no one knew he was involved in writing the article; still, he was the only one who had such personal knowledge of the meetings and the names which were published in the paper. How long before they would find out? The thought of this revelation constantly plagued his mind

At the same time, he was planning to return to Russia with Natasha in October on their annual leave. Pavel could picture in his mind the reunions they would have with their families and friends. They were receiving a letter from Stepan almost every week now. He was looking forward to seeing his papa and bragged about how tall he was getting. How he missed his son! He remembered how it tore his heart to pieces to have to leave him, his only child, his only son.

About the middle of September, Pavel received a letter from Maksim. He had left the *Epokha* and was now working for a different newspaper, the *Novoye Vremya*, which had a much larger circulation. He and Karolina had recently divorced, but he mainly talked about the political scene in Russia. "I'm writing to tell you, Pavel," he wrote, "that after the 1991 coup, Yeltsin's team was far from unified. First, Yeltsin selected Aleksandr Turskoi, who had an excellent record as an officer in the war with Afghanistan and had been the leader of Communists for Democracy. Yeltsin thought that Turskoi would bring him the votes from the military and in the provinces, but as the time passed there was continual friction between the two. On top of all this, Yeltsin was faced with the tremendous job of creating a market economy and a political democracy."

"Things are churning again in Russia," Pavel said, looking up questioningly at Natasha.

"What will it be like back there? We will be there in a few weeks now!"

"Yes, and I've been thinking about Andrey. We haven't heard from him in a long time. I believe he is in his last year at the university now."

"Maybe no news is good news. As I remember, Maksim was concerned that Andrey was still trying to get revenge on Yakov."

Back in Moscow, Maksim was getting some breaking news in his office. Yeltsin was planning to issue a presidential decree to dissolve the congress and call for new elections in December. First, Yeltsin and his advisers decided to meet and issue the decree on Sunday, September 19. Rutskoi and Khasbulatov would not be in the White House. But soon after this, the news leaked out. Rutskoi and Khasbulatov found out about the plan and decided to call a special session of the legislature that very Sunday, so in turn, Yeltsin called off announcing the decree for a few days.

Maksim decided to hurry down to the White House to see if he could pick up some more news. Near the building, he encountered Khasbulatov talking with a few reporters. "Rutskoi and I are planning a new strategy," he announced, laughing as he wiped the perspiration from his face. "After Yeltsin has had a few drinks, he will sign anything!"

After a few remarks, Khasbulatov walked away from the reporters and refused to answer any more questions. The group talked among themselves for a while and offered ideas as what would happen next.

Later, the reporters found out that the opposition's plan was to oust Yeltsin the moment that his degree became public. They were sure they would be successful.

Maksim was hoping for more news as the days passed. Finally on the twenty-first, just as he was about to leave his office, he heard a special news bulletin being broadcast on the evening news. Yeltsin said that he was going to sign an Order Number 140 which was a step-by-step constitutional reform in the Russian Federation. He spoke with confidence that he was prepared to carry out his plan, dissolve the parliament and call for new elections.

Just as he was hurrying to grab a jacket and head for the door, Maksim spotted a familiar figure climbing the steps to the large newspaper office. It was Andrey!

"My friend, what a surprise to see you. What have you been doing with yourself? Now something more is happening! Do you always show up when there are political coups?"

"What do you mean? Political coups? What are you talking about, Maksim?"

"Exactly that, Andrey! Yeltsin was just on television. He plans to dissolve parliament and call for new elections!"

"And that means a coup is about to take place?"

"Maybe! I feel it in my bones, like when a storm comes in. Hurry! Get in my truck, and we'll drive as close to the White House as we can."

"Maksim, I came here to see if I could talk to Mr. Platonov. I was hoping you could put in a word for me. I will graduate in early spring and…"

Andrey was interrupted by the shouts of people crowding into the streets.

"Wait, a minute, Andrey. I'm going to park this truck over here on this side street, so we can get out of here later."

They walked several blocks before they reached the White House. About two thousand people were moving through the streets. Some of them were holding the red banners and the red flag of the old Soviet Union.

Maksim asked some of the people questions and took notes of their responses. "See, this is what you do as a reporter, Andrey. Maybe you can get a job as one of the editors with your university education. How long do you plan to stay in Moscow?"

"Well, I was hoping to talk to one of the editors tomorrow, but I don't think I should stay with you. Someone told me that Yakov was looking for me. The KGB has been questioning me again. Now, they seem to think that Yakov is part of some black market business. They got the idea that I might be working with him. Can you beat that? That good-for-nothin' son of a bitch!"

"How did they get that idea?"

"Because I bought a gun on the black market."

"Andrey, Andrey! You need to keep out of trouble, not look for it!"

"Well, wasn't it Yaroslav who pulled a gun and stopped those guys that threatened us at my old apartment? You need a gun to survive today!"

They drove rapidly away from the crowded streets. Maksim parked his truck in a space behind his apartment. He motioned for Andrey to follow him. It was dark outside by now, and it was difficult to move around the trash cans and debris outside the building.

It was almost uncannily quiet. A cat suddenly screeched as Andrey stepped on his tail in the dark. At that moment, a figure moved near one of the tall cans. Andrey saw the shine off the black gun that was pointed directly at him. Andrey ducked and pulled out his gun. With one quick movement, he fired at the dark figure. The body fell heavily to the pavement. His arms stretched out in front of him and his chest heaved as the last gasp for air wheezed from his body.

Maksim ran quickly to help Andrey. "Who is this man? Why was he shooting at you?"

"I don't know who he is, but I think he's probably Yakov's friend. I saw him on the train, then again in the station. I was lucky to get him first!"

"Probably followed you from Lipetsk. Hurry! Let's get him out of here!"

They pulled the body across the alley and lifted it into Maksim's truck. He wasn't sure where he was going, but suddenly a picture of the river flashed across his mind. "I'm heading for the river, Andrey. Thank goodness no one came out of the buildings. It's late. They're either sleeping or watching television."

"I shouldn't have left Red Square with you. People could have seen us. Now, you're implicated with me."

"Don't worry! There were thousands of people in the square. You'd better get out of town tonight. How many people knew you were coming to Moscow?"

"No one, really. I came to Moscow with the idea that you might help me get an appointment with one of your editors."

"It will have to wait now, but sure, I'd be glad to help you."

It was almost one o'clock in the morning when they reached the section of the river that was more desolate and covered with thick bushes. Thick clouds covered the dark sky. Maksim drove the truck down a short, sloping bank.

"Looks like not many people come here. That's good. Hurry! Let's get this over with."

"Maksim! Are you sure he's dead?"

"Look at him! He's soaked with blood now from the hole in his chest. Look at his face. He's not breathing. His days with Yakov are over!"

They pulled the body from the truck. "See if he has any I.D. on him."

"Here's his wallet, Maksim. His name is Zviad Gladkov. He's from Lipetsk. We should burn his papers." He leaned forward and gave the body a swift kick. "The dirty pig! He won't cause me any more trouble, the son of a bitch! The no-good son of a bitch!"

"Slow down. You have to keep your mind set right. You're not through with this mess yet. You have to deal with Yakov. And you must play it smart, or you'll end up like this guy right here!"

"I know. I know. " Andrey's eyes glared with defiance at the blood-soaked body. But his mind was trained on Yakov. He had to get to him first.

"So you think this gook knew you were coming to Moscow?"

"Followed me. Now, you can see why I needed to buy a gun!"

Maksim wired a large concrete building block to the man's feet. Together, they pushed the body down into the water.

"Now, let's wash in the river and get the hell out of here!"

An hour later, Maksim dropped Andrey off at the train station. Another time soon, he would arrange an interview for him with Mr. Platonov. He left him with the warning not to be walking around alone on the streets and the suggestion that he change his appearance—dye his hair or something. But Andrey only shrugged and walked off, swinging his arms and tossing his head with confidence.

For the next few days, Maksim was busy covering the development of the events at the White House. At first, reporters were free to ask questions and go in and out of the building. Khasbulatov continued to claim that Yeltsin's days were over. He and Rutskoi were sure of victory.

Then on September twenty-fourth, Maksim and some of the reporters heard that Yeltsin ordered the Moscow city officials to shut off the phone lines, electricity and heat in the White House. While he was standing by the building, Maksim noticed that many deputies were leaving.

"What's going on?" Maksim questioned one of the deputies.

"Yeltsin has offered to pay our salaries and benefits through 1995 if we leave the building, so to hell with it. I'm leaving!"

Maksim chuckled to himself. *I'll bet Rutskoi and Khasbulatov are furious to see these deputies leaving.*

Soon, the police arrived in a yellow armored car. They proceeded to play loud, blaring music and government propaganda. They had planned to continue the loud music and speeches day and night.

Maksim turned and hurried back to his office to write up the story. There was chaos in the Kremlin and chaos in the White House. It kept four reporters busy virtually day and night to cover the news.

By the time Pavel and Natasha arrived in Russia around the first of October, the situation was rapidly worsening. When Pavel saw on television people carrying signs supporting a monarchy, supporting Lenin and Stalin, and walking around the grounds of the parliament, he was furious. He made up his mind to contact his old friend, Yaroslav and see if he wanted to drive up to Moscow.

Yaroslav suggested that they go to the offices of the *Novoye Uremya*, but Pavel was impatient. He decided to call Maksim and ask him to meet them in Red Square, but was told that Maksim was already near the White House on an assignment.

A thousand demonstrators moved into the square. They tore apart a stage and used some of the steel parts as weapons to attack the police. Many were marching under the red flag.

At that moment, they spotted Maksim standing with some reporters near the White House. He embraced them both warmly. "My God, Pavel, what a surprise to see you! Are you here on your annual leave?"

Pavel nodded. "What have I come home to? What is really going on?"

"Khasbulatov and Rutskoi want to take over the government and oust Yeltsin. They are sure of victory. I believe they plan to take over the television and radio and even expect the army and police to join them!"

Pavel was filled with anger. "This can't be, Maksim! We can't let this happen. If this happens, we may be plunged back into communist times again!"

Suddenly, they were interrupted by loud shouting from some people marching toward the White House. They were carrying red flags and shouting, "Down with Yeltsin! "Support the Soviets!" Some were yelling to strike the democrats, the Jews, and the police.

By evening, close to twenty thousand had gathered in the streets. Maksim had been in touch with his office and was told to stay near the City Hall on Tver Street. He learned that Yegor Gaidar had spoken on the radio and urged the people to come and support the government.

Maksim turned and asked some people, "Why did you come?" He carefully wrote down their responses on a pad of paper.

"We had to come. We had to be here to support the democratic forces. Otherwise all will be lost!"

During this time, Yeltsin was miles away at his country retreat. Rumors began to mix through the crowds. Then, overhead the people heard the chopping sounds of a helicopter. It slowly descended and landed on the Kremlin lawn. It was Yeltsin, but what could he do to turn around the sweeping events that threatened his government and his very existence?

Pavel and Yaroslav stayed in the streets all night, joining with the protesters who supported the government. Maksim was busy talking with other reporters and calling back to the newspaper office. They waited anxiously for him to bring them some news.

"Have you found out anything, Maksim?"

"My boss told me that Ostankino, the television complex, has shut down Channels 1, 3, and 4! But some news people that support the government are using a backup studio across town. They interviewed many people who are strong supporters of the government."

"What is Yeltsin doing about all this? Have you heard?"

"Well, Grachev has promised army troops and tanks, Pavel. Still, nothing has arrived. Nothing!" Maksim said shaking his head in despair.

Just as the first rays of sunlight were beginning to light the square, they heard the rumbling of tanks in the distance. Maksim decided to go over to the White House and find out what was going on.

Many armored personnel carriers and T-80 tanks were moving into position at the White House. Suddenly, a shattering noise filled the air. One of the tanks fired a canon into the White House.

Pavel could see the fire spreading through the upper floors of the building. Black smoke poured into the air. At that moment, a reporter came running from the building.

"All hell has broken out in there," he yelled. "I think the whole building will come down!"

"What is going on?" Maksim asked anxiously.

"It is crazy! Some of the White House defenders are singing old Soviet songs! Khasulatov is going to pieces, and Rutskoi is yelling obscenities on the phone to the chief justice of the Constitutional Court, Marina Zorkin. He is commanding them to call the embassies!"

"I'd better get to a phone really fast!" Maksim shouted as he heard this news.

"You'd better wait a bit," the reporter advised. "More is coming! Look! The White House forces are firing back at the troops, but, see, they are no match for the tanks."

By the end of the day, the White House had become a "Black House," standing starkly like a defeated warrior brought to his knees. There was destruction in the building and bloodshed and beatings in the streets.

From the lobby of the Hotel Ukraine, Pavel and Yaroslav watched the final events of the coup on television. Some young boys were being interviewed on one of the programs. Pavel was amazed at the story. The boys were only seventeen or eighteen years old and had just been arrested.

"Look, Yaroslav, these boys were approached by a man in the street and were given a few dollars and a rifle to shoot people, just innocent people who were not fighting or anything—just crossing the street."

"You're right, Pavel. I can understand that someone might kill others to stand up for their own beliefs, but these boys had no idea what was going on!"

"Exactly. For just a few dollars they agreed to take the rifles and go against their own people. It is a sad day when we have a young generation that can be bought and paid off. They don't care which side they are on, and they don't know why they are fighting."

Later, on television, they saw that Khasbulatov, Rutskoi and the White House leaders were arrested. This time Yeltsin had won, but only by a very narrow margin. It was time for Pavel and Yaroslav to return to Lipetsk and Maksim to return to his office to write the biggest story in his career.

The Coup of '93 was not the same as the triumph of the Coup of '91, with Yeltsin standing on a tank. The Coup of '91 was shown on television throughout the world. Now, Moscow did not celebrate. Dark lines formed for funerals, and the vodka remained corked and forgotten.

Pavel returned to his parents' apartment realizing that another crisis might erupt at any time. So far, the authorities in India did not know that he was the co-author of the article about the scam. His name was not used.

Still, Pavel took comfort in the fact that Marina and Valentin were in good spirits and delighted to have their son home with them once again. Natasha left to visit her family for a few days.

Late that first afternoon, while they were sitting visiting together, the door suddenly opened and Stepan rushed into the room to embrace his papa.

"My Papa, my Papa! You're home!" His face quickly tightened up as he tried to hold back the tears.

Pavel picked him up and hugged him. Their faces were filled with emotion and feeling as they held each other.

"Don't ever leave me again, Papa. Stay here with me," he begged.

But Pavel knew he couldn't promise this to his son. He would spend as much time as he could with Stepan. Perhaps, they would go fishing. How he had grown in the last year! And he loved hard rock music just like his papa and enjoyed hearing Pavel tell him about the old days at the disco.

Everything seemed the same as he remembered in the apartment. The same sweet cakes on a plate on the counter and the same small packages of cheese. How his grandmother, Karolina, had loved the sweet cakes! She used to make them often, but now there was no one to make them. They came from the store these days.

"You still like your beer, Papa?"

"Still like it?" he answered in disbelief. "What Russian doesn't like a drink on his day off?"

Pavel grinned to himself. Valentin didn't need the excuse of a day off to have a drink. "Then, since you still like a drink, I have a surprise for you. I've got two bottles of beer for you!"

"That's great news! So you got your old job back at the bottling factory, hmm, Pavel?" he teased.

Before Pavel could answer, there was a loud knock at the door. Who could it be? He had been home for only two weeks. He opened the door to find a KGB officer staring into his face.

"You've been arrested! You must come immediately with me down to headquarters."

"What for? Why are you arresting me?"

"You'll find out down at the office," he sneered.

Pavel had no idea why he was being arrested. He had not been home for some time now. What possible trouble could there be?

The same KGB officer, Mr. Romanov, questioned him for several hours down at the headquarters. "Empty your pockets," he commanded. "Ah, just as I thought. You have one hundred dollars in hard currency in your possession. You know that when you enter Russia with foreign currency, you are supposed to exchange it for rubles. You know that, don't you!"

"Wait a minute! Part of my salary in India is paid in U.S. dollars. I am paid in foreign currency."

"Never mind all that! That's not important! You are under arrest! We are going to hold you here."

Immediately, Romanov rose from his chair and motioned to several guards to take him away. Pavel could feel the cold, steel gray eyes following him down the hallway.

The guards pushed Pavel into a room and began to beat him with their hands and fists, hitting hard on Pavel's heels. The pain was excruciating and radiated up to the middle of his back. Then while one of the guards held him, the other beat him with a police club until he fell over unconscious.

When he awoke, he found that the guards had thrown him into a jail cell with hardened criminals. He figured that the guards had hit him in a way that would not show any injuries. This must be part of their special training. But still, the pain continued to throb in his back.

He pretended to sleep. It was safer that way, especially in a cell with these murderers and professional thieves. Pavel knew the accusations were ridiculous, because everybody had dollars in Russia. People could buy things with Russian rubles or dollars. Everybody possessed dollars, because nobody had faith in the

Russian ruble because of inflation and the uncertainty of the future. The law had been the subject of a lot of ridicule. Initially, Pavel had planned to spend some dollars in duty-free shops in Russia, so he and Natasha bought some watches and souvenirs. He knew the KGB couldn't accuse him of being involved in the Ph.D. scam because they didn't have that information.

Two days later, he was released. When they were alone, he questioned the officer. "Okay, we're out of the official room now. You're not writing anything down. Can you tell me why I was arrested? Off the record, what was the reason?"

The man laughed as though Pavel was a very naive person. "The investigation is not over yet. Right now, we are setting you free because we haven't the evidence to hold you right now. But, you must sign this document before you leave. You are not to leave this town or Russia before the investigation is over. We plan to keep track of you, and we will call you."

Pavel felt the man's hard, staring eyes following him as he walked to the door. Now, what was he going to do? He had planned to stay in Russia for about two months, but he had to leave before they had time to put a case together.

During the next week, a KGB officer came and searched his parents' apartment. After this happened, Pavel and Natasha stayed with her brother and sometimes with her parents.

It had been a month since they had left India. Pavel decided they would leave Russia. He reasoned that the KGB would not imagine that he would run from them. Ordinarily, a person had to have permission to leave the country from the KGB. It took three months to get permission, and maybe then it was not granted. But Pavel and Natasha already had the permission, the visas and the passports. Everything was ready. Still, their parents questioned them about this decision and whether this was the time to return to India.

"I am concerned about you and Natasha," Marina said. Her forehead was lined with a worried frown. "Is the best thing to do, son?"

"I don't want to stay around here while they build up some foolish case against me. I don't think they have enough reasons to keep me in Russia. Besides, why should I stay here and risk losing my job in India?"

Marina did not reply, but hoped that Pavel knew best. She hoped that he could find a way out of all this trouble.

The most difficult part of leaving Lipetsk was leaving Stepan again. He spent hours talking and explaining to the boy what he had to do.

"I have to leave, Stepan. I would rather stay here with you, but it isn't safe for me right now. I will write to you as before. One day soon, we'll be together again. I promise you." But as he wiped his son's tears from his face, he wondered if he could keep this promise to him. God knew he wanted to.

The next day, they flew back to India and yet, Pavel knew they were actually outlaws. He knew that the KGB was after him and very soon they would be after him in India. It would not be difficult for the authorities in the steel ministry to figure out that he was the one who provided the details of the article. Pavel was the only interpreter who was involved at that time, and they also knew that he was very friendly with Turgov. Turgov would not know about some of the statements and some of the meetings that were described in the article.

Pavel knew he would have to think and move fast in order to escape the wrath of the government officials and the KGB. But was it too late? he questioned himself. Perhaps, the machinery to destroy him was already in motion.

Chapter 21

The storm hit without warning the next morning. Pavel left the compound as usual for work, but he learned right away that he wasn't working there at the plant anymore. To Pavel's utter amazement, he was fired! Fired without any warning! He was devastated. Where was he to turn?

Pavel decided to look for Mr. Syanova, his immediate boss. He walked rapidly to his office. His mind was filled with questions and anxiety.

"What's going on, Mr. Syanova? I don't understand."

"Well, your contract has been terminated. Maybe the Indian Steel Authority decided that they don't need your services anymore. You understand, of course, that you and your wife must move from the compound. The apartment was for you as long as you worked for the Indian Steel Authority. Take a few days and pack, but you must absolutely vacate the apartment in five days!"

Pavel was astounded. He had to find out what had gone wrong. When one side decides to terminate a contract, there must be some kind of notice, some reason given, so he decided to go and talk with Mr. Eugador, the Indian person who was responsible for his contract.

The man had a sour look on his face when he saw Pavel entering his office.

"What has happened here, Mr. Eugador? I don't understand. I have a contract with the Indian Steel Authority until the middle of July, 1994, and before I left for Russia, I was told that my contract was going to be renewed. They were going to ask the Russian side to provide more interpreters. They needed more people in this position."

Mr. Eugador looked annoyed. "Well, now we have too many interpreters. This happened during your absence. How could we find you and tell you all this when you were in Russia?" He handed Pavel his papers and turned to make a phone call.

What a bunch of lies, Pavel thought angrily. He knew what they were doing was against the law. They weren't supposed to terminate a contract without talking to him or without explanations. No one had mentioned the article that had been published in the paper, but he knew deep within himself that must be the reason.

Pavel immediately picked up his things from the office. Several of his friends noticed that he was cleaning out his desk and that he appeared very angry. Something went wrong.

Pavel swore under his breath. He had made the decision to refuse to participate in the doctoral scam and had decided to reveal the whole operation with Turgov in the article. Yes, but he had to do it. He resolved to get even with them. But which way to go?

When he reached the apartment, Natasha was just finishing up the breakfast dishes.

"What is it, Pavel? What's happened?" Natasha knew something was terribly amiss for him to be rushing into the apartment so early in the morning. Alarm and worry was moving across his face.

"I've lost my job here. I was told that first thing this morning!"

"But why, Pavel? Why?"

"Those sons of bitches! They gave me crazy answers. They said they have too many interpreters now! Before we left on our annual leave, they said they were going to hire on more!"

"Now, what happens?"

"We have five days to pack and move. The apartment was for us to use as long as I worked at the plant."

"What has happened to Turgov?"

"I understand that he was fired just after we left for Russia. Now, he is staying with his sister in Delhi."

Later that day, Pavel was informed that someone from the Russian embassy was coming to see him and was reminded again to pack and leave the apartment in five days.

The next afternoon, the man from the embassy arrived at the apartment. Mr. Hymogeyer was tall and slender and pushed into the doorway in a great hurry.

"Mr. Lubov, you are running into trouble here in India. There is some kind of an investigation going on in the embassy in Delhi. The embassy also received some information from Lipetsk back in Russia. We understand that there is some kind of a criminal investigation going on there about you. Now, you must return to Russia immediately. You are to go to Delhi and go to the embassy to get your papers. Those are your orders. You must obey them and return to Russia immediately!"

With those words, Mr. Timofeyev rose and picked up his briefcase. He gave Pavel a hard stare and turned to leave.

"I don't understand all this!" Natasha said as soon as the man had left. "I thought you had a contract with the Indian Steel Authority until July."

"Contract or no contract. They terminated it! I can't go to court about this because I'm still facing charges in Russia. Remember, we came back here on the run because I thought I still had my job here."

Natasha felt the full impact of his words. Charges! Charges! When the KGB got hold of a person, they shook the individual like a pit bull and didn't let go until it had devoured the bleeding body. She felt as though they were caught up in a whirlwind that could only end in the destruction of their lives together.

"What can we do?" Her voice was shaking and barely audible. Her legs felt weak. She had to sit down on the couch as she waited for Pavel to answer.

"We will pack all of our things and go to Delhi, but we will not go to the Russian Embassy."

"But where, Pavel? Where?"

"We will check into a hotel. Maybe we can get visas for another country."

"And if we can't?" She was too terribly afraid to cry. Her body felt cold, cold with an icy fear. "And if we can't?"

Pavel could sense the shaking in Natasha's voice. He went over and sat down beside her on the sofa and put his arm around her. "Don't worry, Natasha, we will find a way. We will be together. I promise!"

But Natasha couldn't help worrying as she hurriedly turned to pack their things. It was plain to her that Pavel couldn't answer the question what they would do if they couldn't get visas and leave the country. And how long would he be able to keep his promise that they would always be together?

"It's something like fencing, Pavel!" she said with a worried frown.

"Fencing? That's a strange word to use."

"Fencing with the KGB, yet trying to get along with them. Above all, you have refused to be intimated by them. You've maintained your position that you're entitled to certain freedoms, certain human rights. And you refused to go along with this Ph.D. scam."

"That's interesting, Natasha. Fencing." He pronounced the word very slowly and let it move through his mind. The swordsman of old fenced for their lives. Sometimes with their wits. What would he have to do? He knew that if they couldn't get the necessary visas, they might have to run for their lives.

Two days later, they checked into a hotel in Delhi. First, Pavel decided to contact Turgov. He valued his friendship and advice. And he certainly needed it now. They planned to have lunch together at a little Indian restaurant several blocks from the hotel. It wasn't like old times, he thought, because neither of them had a job to talk about. Nor could they visualize their future. But, in a way, it was their future. But, in a way, it was the same. They were friends. Just like before.

Pavel noticed that Turgov was thinner, but he walked with the same self-assuredness as before. His tanned face broke into a warm smile when he saw Pavel sitting at a table.

"I was hoping that I would hear from you before you made any decisions."

"Turgov, what do you know about all of this? What does the embassy know about me. About us?"

"I have a friend in the embassy. He told me that something suddenly came up. They know what happened to you in Russia, and they found out about the article and your involvement."

"My contract was good until the middle of July."

"Yes, but I think you lost your contract with the Indian Steel Authority because somehow the Russians from the embassy applied some pressure on them. The embassy found out about you, and so the Indians just terminated your contract."

"So this really blows the lid off of everything!"

"Yes, that's what happened to both of us, but because I am an Indian and have some physical disabilities, I was just let go. But you know there has been a general panic in the Indian Steel Ministry. Some high-ranking officers decided to take early retirement. They were afraid of impending investigations."

"It's been in the newspapers again since I left?"

"Exactly. All the major papers in India have been covering the story. Many important people have resigned or been forced to resign. The Indian Steel Authority and the Russian government were running a terrible, stupid scam. We did the right thing, Pavel, to expose them. We did the right thing, I'm sure."

"The last doctoral I worked on was with a Mr. Hadan. In fact, I went with him to Moscow and translated his thesis before the scientific community. It was at that time that I realized that the whole thing was a terrible scam, because this man wasn't at all familiar with the research that was purported to have been done. You can't imagine how I felt, Turgov, standing there before those men who were well known in their fields, standing there and knowing that the whole thing was a fraud. These men have appeared on television as experts in their field, and yet, they knew that this man hadn't done the work for this thesis!"

"I understand, Pavel, perfectly. That's why we wrote the article together. Did you know that Mr. Hadan was fired from his position? Yes, he and many others. It's been a big scandal in the Indian government."

"Somehow, that's not very consoling right now. You can imagine how Natasha feels. She's terribly scared and upset. Where do you think we should go, Turgov? I can't go back to Russia. I was beaten and thrown in jail once and forced to sign a paper saying I wouldn't leave the country."

"What was that all about?"

"Possessing hard currency!"

"Those crazy bastards! What did they expect you'd have on you? You were working in another country and were paid in hard currency."

"Yes, lots of people in Russia have hard currency."

He rose and put his arm around Pavel's shoulders. His warm, brown eyes reflected the sympathy he felt for his friend. "I'm sorry this has happened to you, but I think you should try and get visas for the United States. That would be the best place for you and Natasha to go."

Pavel nodded in agreement. He went back to the hotel for Natasha. They would have to get their visas and hurry to the American embassy before the situation got any worse.

However, they were forced to wait for hours at the embassy. "We just have to get the visas, Pavel," Natasha said in a worried tone. "We have nowhere to go! If we go back to Russia, they'll throw you into jail."

Her words circled around and around in Pavel's mind. Were they going to end up like trapped animals? As the hours passed, his mood slowly changed. First, it was anger, then anxiety, then slowly to despair. He couldn't understand the reasons for his feelings. They had not been refused, but as time wore on and the hands on the clock moved slowly toward four o'clock, he thought he knew. The uncertainty filled every corner of his being like molten lava pouring down a mountain side leaving the people nowhere to go or to escape.

Late that day, when Pavel walked away from the embassy's office, Natasha immediately knew he had not been successful. Anxiety was plainly written all over Pavel's face. It was not good news.

"What did they say?"

"If we want to get American visas we have to apply in Moscow, our country of residence. That seems to be the policy in the majority of embassies."

"And of course, we can't go back to Russia! We don't have time to apply in a lot of embassies. What can we do?" Natasha asked in despair.

"I have an idea. Tomorrow, we will go to the Australian embassy and see what they say. Some of the embassies, I understand, will issue you a visa if you know some people in the country, and they invite you to visit them. We know a couple of people who live in Australia. Your friend, Mary, that you studied yoga with in India, lives in Australia. And remember the man I met in Calcutta? He lives in Sidney, and once he invited us to visit him."

The next day, Pavel went to the Australian embassy and was told he needed a written invitation from someone in Australia. He immediately telephoned his friend, Mr. Milton, who agreed to fax him an invitation to their hotel.

Natasha was relieved, but she wondered what lay ahead of them in Australia. Pavel kept reassuring her they would be all right.

"Remember, we'll be together. Australia may hold the future for us. Wait and see, Natasha. Wait and see."

His words that they would be together comforted her. That was the important thing. To have him close and to feel his arms around her.

It was several days before they were scheduled to leave. In the remaining time, they withdrew from everything around them where they allowed no one or anything to enter their own special circle. Time stood still. It was their world. Their own private world where they clung to each other. They reached down within themselves and found renewed strength from each other.

On the way to Australia, Natasha laughingly reminded Pavel that they hardly left the bed the whole two days before they left.

"Oh, we did get up once in a while to eat something!"

"Yes, once in a while!"

"Well, it was all your fault. You were a terrible tease!"

They laughed together, and Pavel held her closer as the plane slowly circled and descended to the Sidney airport. It was late afternoon, and the fading sun shown brilliantly on the wings of the plane as it taxied down the runway.

Mr. Milton met them at the airport. The couple thought it was reassuring to see a welcoming friend and to be miles away from all that trouble.

They stayed three weeks in Sydney. The Hamptons were a warm, friendly people, but Pavel knew they must immediately take some action to stay in the country. They went to the immigration office and explained to the officers that they needed to stay in Australia, because the KGB would beat him and throw him into jail again. He was told that if you are a refugee you must apply back in the country where you lived, and that meant going back to Russia. That was absurd. Pavel knew they couldn't go back to Moscow, so they waited and tried to think of alternatives.

Up to this point, they had begun to think or perhaps hope that all the turmoil they had been through was surely a thing of the past. Then George Hampton received a letter from a diving and scuba resort in the Philippines. George was a scuba diving instructor, and he was invited to teach for a length of time in the Philippines. They would be leaving in a few days.

Still, Pavel kept reassuring Natasha that they would find a way out of their problems. They would go to Canberra, the capital of Australia and stay with Jane Marcel and her family.

The second day, Pavel decided to try again at the immigration office in Canberra. After all, this was the capital city. Maybe it would be different there.

But when Pavel returned to the house, Natasha could see the bad news filling his face as he spoke. "I got the same answer, Natasha. The same answer. We have to apply in Moscow!"

Natasha felt the despair rising within her, a dark uncertainty of nowhere to go, no hope. "What can we do?"

Pavel sat down next to her and wiped the tears that were slowly moving down her face. He wished that they could just hold each other and let their tears mix together, but he couldn't allow himself the luxury of letting go. He had to remain strong. For Natasha. For himself and their future. But what future did they have ? he wondered.

"I am determined, Natasha. I am determined to solve this problem."

"Where? How?" Her voice shook, and she trembled with the same troubling despair and fear.

But Pavel could only answer, "We will find a way, and we'll stay here as long as we can."

It was March, 1994 when they secretly returned to India. Nobody knew they were in the country. They were fortunate that they could stay with Turgov in Delhi. Still, they knew they could only remain in the country three months. That's all the Indian government would allow.

But to Natasha and Pavel the three months moved too rapidly. There was not enough time to think, but there were hours and hours to feel the pressures and inevitable dangers they knew lay ahead of them in Russia.

Finally, when the three months were over, Pavel bought tickets for Russia because that was the only country that would admit them at this time. They had Russian passports, but they did not want to go to Russia. Neither could foresee or foretell what might happen when they got back to Lipetsk because they had run from the KGB. Pavel had refused to stay in the country and let the authorities put together a case against him.

On the flight back to Russia, Natasha worried that they would arrest Pavel again. Then how could he keep his promise to always stay with her? Not let go of her? They had been so close. She desperately needed him.

They had spent the last few weeks talking about the situation. "I feel like we are cattle going back to be killed, to be slaughtered. I'm terrified."

Pavel tried to comfort her, but down in the depths of his very being, he felt the same way. He had no idea what might happen, but experience had taught him that when it came to the KGB, it was bad news. They were capable of the dirtiest things in the world. He had learned this from the stories of his grandparents and the accounts of the great writers and poets of Russia. He finally fell asleep to the drone of the plane's engines as he thought back to the days of the disco in Lipetsk. Then, he had tried to show the young people what the Communist government had done to the Russian society and how they had suppressed the true stories of the great Russian writers. Now, what could he do? How could he fight for freedoms now? Then he felt a slight movement like a soft breeze near his ears and the words of his Grandfather Stepan speaking to him. "Don't give up! Believe in what you do!"

Chapter 22

It was the early summer of 1994 when Pavel and Natasha returned to Lipetsk. They had nowhere else to go, no other alternative. But this was not the alternative they wanted. In fact, they were living on borrowed time, and the creditor was the KGB.

When they first got back, life seemed to revolve around a normal day of visiting with friends and family and eating meals together. One day, they decided to take a chance and ride the bus to the university. Pavel wanted to walk along the path near the Volga River where he and Natasha had spent those precious moments discovering each other and finding the beautiful love that began to grow between them. Yet all their old friends had moved long ago through the school and were out working someplace. Even Andrey. He had just completed his last year.

Suddenly, a figure stepped out in front of them from the tall bushes that lined the river bank. "Hello! Aren't you a friend of Andrey Dimitri's?"

"Yes, do you know him?"

"Of course. We're old buddies. I haven't seen him lately. I thought I'd run into him around the university. Does he still come here for classes?"

"I don't know. I haven't seen him in a long time."

"Maybe you could help me find him if he still lives in Lipetsk?"

There was something about the man, something about the way he pronounced the words, "old buddies" that sent an alarm through Pavel's mind. "What is your name?" Pavel asked studying the man's face as he responded.

"Zaviad Gladkov," he replied, his eyes hardening into a coldness that Pavel had not seen since his last encounter with a KGB officer. He repeated the words again, taking care to notice Pavel's reaction to his name. Then, he immediately turned and walked quickly down the path behind them.

"What did you think of him? Wasn't it strange that he asked if you could help him find Andrey, then walk away like that?" Natasha asked in bewilderment.

"Yes, very strange, and I don't believe he's a friend of Andrey's. Did you notice that hint of a smirk on his face when he said they were old buddies?"

One evening, several days later, Pavel's old pal Yaroslav called and said that his friends from the old disco place were asking about him. They planned to meet in the coffee shop around seven-thirty. Just like old times.

The former manager, Sergey Tokaloff, and the sound manager, Igor Sviatoslav were already sitting at a table when Kiruyha and Pavel walked into the shop.

"Hey, you're looking good, Pavel. Just a little frayed around the edges and toasted from that climate in India! Welcome back! Have a beer," Tokaloff said as he offered Pavel a foaming glass of the cold., amber liquid.

"He just got back from a Russian compound in India where the KGB absolutely forbids the drinking of alcohol! Even the homemade stuff. They would come around to the apartments and check them out!" Kiruyha informed them.

"That's true, but the truth of the matter is I usually don't drink anyway. It was just their damn fool rules and their committees coming around to my place checking on what we were reading and what we were doing that got to me. But, in my frame of mind, I'm ready for a beer!"

"Here's to your return! Enjoy the beer! Say, what goes anyway, friend? Yaroslav tells us that you've got a pack of KGB trying to throw you back in jail here in Lipetsk, and the Indian government is going to pieces because of an article that you wrote exposing some big scam in the Indian Steel Authority. It looks like you haven't changed a bit. You're so red hot, I'm afraid to light a match around you 'cause I might blow up!"

Pavel tried to wipe the anxiety from his face. "Get off it, Tokaloff! The day you quit smoking because of me, will be the day! Tell me, what happened to the disco after I left."

"It's finished. There's just a movie house there now. Sergey Dnieper, the only one that stayed on for awhile, says that after you left

210

things started to go down. The economy here started to change. After perestroika and the break-down of the Soviet Union, the economy was in shambles. Nobody has any money to buy those things, so you see, the factories are having a hard time selling their products. And the inflation is tremendous. You've probably noticed that?"

"Yes, but I've noticed that there are a lot more consumer goods in the market then when I was here before. I understand that a lot of German companies and Western European companies have moved in. People seem to scrape the money together and still buy things. I guess they want to try out new things, like Coca Cola."

"Tokaloff is right," Alex continued. "A lot of people can travel easier than before because they don't need a visa to go to some countries like Poland or China. Now, they go to China, India, Singapore, and other places and bring back items to sell in the flea markets. My brother, Sergey, was able to get to the United States on a visa. He thinks he has found a way to stay there."

"Back when we had the disco, there was a lot of interest in new democratic movements and programs. What is going on now, Alex?" Pavel asked anxiously.

"Yes, what you say is true. There was a very strong movement among the young people. The movement was fueled by some very good, noble ideas. We still want to make things better in Russia, like setting up new businesses and supporting new economic programs."

"Is there a leader now, so that we can move forward?"

"Yes, Yavlinski is the man. He has formed a party called the Yabloko. He is an economist and an excellent man. You should go and meet with him. I believe he is scheduled to be in Lipetsk next month."

Tokaloff nodded in agreement. "But now, tell us about Natasha. And how is your son?"

At the mention of his son, Pavel's face winced in pain. "It is so hard for Stepan. I try to explain to him, but I know he just wants his papa home with him."

"How is Natasha dealing with all this trouble you've both been through?"

"Not very well. She's visiting with her parents now. And she's really upset and worried about what we're going to do."

"And what are you going to do? You won't be able to stay here very long."

"I'm going to Moscow as soon as I can and apply for visas for the United States. If I can't get visas for both of us, I'll get one for me, and Natasha can come later."

"We'll work out something. Anyway, I've got to go to Moscow next week. We'll drive up together, Pavel," Yaroslav promised. "We may bump into Andrey. He's been trying to get a job at the paper with Maksim."

"Sounds good. I'll take you up on it!"

But it was two weeks before Yaroslav could get away from his job at the factory. They left very early in the morning for Moscow so that Pavel could apply for the visas and hopefully be able to pick them up late in the afternoon. Andrey was expecting them. They planned to meet at a restaurant for a late lunch.

Yaroslav would join them later. He wanted to see his brother who had been in an accident. Pavel hadn't seen Andrey since the October coup.

Later that day, as Pavel was approaching the restaurant, he noticed Andrey hurrying across the street with a familiar person. It was Maksim!

"What a surprise, Andrey! Are you working at the *Novoye Uremya* with Maksim?"

"Not yet. The first of next month, Pavel."

They found a table in a back corner of the restaurant. "This way, we won't be overheard," Andrey said glancing quickly around the room.

"Does it have something to do with Yakov, the man who killed Ivan?"

"It is because of the man Andrey killed who is a friend of Yakov!"

Pavel stared at his friends. Was this some crazy joke? he asked himself.

"I can see you are amazed. Yes, a friend of Yakov tried to kill Andrey behind my apartment. He had a gun. Andrey got him first. We dragged his body into my truck and dumped him into the river!"

"What a nightmare that must have been! Then what happened? Has the body been recovered?"

"Don't mention that. We weighted his body with cement. Fortunately, the guy was a loner and a drifter, so no one has reported him missing."

Pavel turned and looked questioningly at Andrey. "Natasha and I were walking along the river near the university the other day. A guy stepped out suddenly in front of us from the bushes. He said he was looking for you and thought he might see you around the school. He wanted to know if I could tell him where you lived."

"Did he tell you his name?"

"Yes. Zviad Gladkov. That's what he said."

"Zviad Gladkov!" Maksim and Andrey almost shouted the name in amazement.

"You know him?"

"Know him?" Andrey echoed. "He's the man I killed! The man who tried to shoot me behind Maksim's apartment, and..."

"Wait a minute," Maksim interrupted, noticing Andrey's face growing white with terror. "That wasn't Zviad! What did he look like?"

"He was tall and muscular, very muscular. Big broad shoulders. Light hair and very narrow eyes. When he said you both were buddies, I thought I noticed a slight smirk on his lips."

Andrey turned suddenly to Maksim. "Then that wasn't Zviad Gladkov! That man had very dark hair and a short, rough-looking beard."

"Who was it then?"

"It was Yakov. Yes, it was Yakov who was looking for me, Maksim!"

The three sat and stared at the table in front of them. They were amazed at this discovery. No one spoke until the waiter brought them their lunch.

"So now, Yakov is looking for you. What will you do now?"

"Yes, Yakov is looking for me, but I think Yakov is getting into big trouble. Right now, he's too busy to look for me. Tell Pavel the story, Maksim."

"There is so much for sale here in Russia. The mafia, bureaucrats, and even the KGB all want a piece of the action. Some of the sales are approved by the government, but others are not. I have been following Yakov very carefully. He is part of a group that is working with foreign brokers to sell everything from highly sophisticated conventional-weapons systems to rare and strategic metals."

"I've heard that scientists now earn less than one hundred dollars a month. I guess the big worry is whether nuclear material might be sold because scientists and workers need the money," Pavel suggested, his forehead lined with concern.

"Exactly. Yakov is part of a mafia group who won't stop at anything to make millions, probably billions of dollars on anything he can get his hands on. And they are heavily armed. They have Russian-made submachine guns, powerful enough to pierce bulletproof jackets!"

"If you are on his trail looking for a story, it seems like Yakov will be looking for you just like Andrey."

"He doesn't know me, but he knows Andrey. I've told Andrey he must change his appearance. Dye his hair. Grow a beard and maybe get some glasses."

"What are you trying to tell me, Maksim! The girls won't go for me then!"

"Don't be stupid. Forget the girls. Your life is at stake! Right, Pavel?"

"Yes, the mafia is no joke. This man will stop at absolutely nothing now that he's part of organized crime."

As Pavel left the restaurant, thoughts of Yakov's involvement with the mafia worried him. Andrey was clearly in danger.

Yaroslav had just driven up to the restaurant. He waved at Maksim and Andrey. Pavel told him about Andrey as they drove off in the truck.

"Andrey is clearly in danger. He's in deep with both feet!" He turned around and looked directly at Pavel. "And you don't look so good either!"

"I'm beginning to think the KGB might just drop my case."

"You're kidding, yes?"

"The police maybe turning away from internal affairs. I've heard that since the agency was renamed the Federal Counterintelligence Service, they are concentrating more on foreign affairs."

"Most Russians still call them the KGB, but I wouldn't trust the sons of bitches, Pavel! Not on your life!"

As they passed through the streets of Moscow on their way to the government building, they could see evidences of the 1993 coup in the streets near the White House. The railings on the bridges had been broken in the demonstrations and were not yet repaired. The work of the restoration of the White House was slow and disappointing to most Russians.

Yaroslav waited in his truck for Pavel to return from the embassy building. He came back with the news that he needed an official invitation from some friend in the United States. Also, the authorities would not allow him to get a visa for Natasha, because there was the danger that both of them would not return to Russia. Every person must leave some family behind, a job or some property to guarantee that they wouldn't stay in the United States more than three months. Pavel was determined to make things work out.

But early the next afternoon, he received a call from Edward Domannov. Pavel recognized the name immediately. He was the man who had interrogated him about possessing hard currency down at the office of the KGB last fall.

"Listen to what I have to say," Romanov began. "We know that you are back in Lipetsk. We haven't forgotten anything about you. I want to meet with you privately."

"Where? When?"

"Tomorrow morning at the park over on Lenin Street. You are to sit down on the bench near where the children used to play and wait for me. I will be there at nine-thirty. Is that clear?"

"Yes, I will meet you there," Pavel said evenly.

No one was at home when Pavel received the call. He decided just to tell Marina, so someone would know where he was going. Still, he couldn't figure out what the man wanted. If he wanted to talk about his file or an impending case against him, why would they be meeting at a park? Why not down at the KGB office?

The next morning, Pavel arrived at the park a little early. Children didn't come here to play anymore. The equipment was rusty and broken. The nearby apartment buildings had been deserted years ago. People left the buildings because there was no heat, the roof leaked, and no one seemed or wanted to be responsible for the repairs.

Not even the old people came here to rest or talk with their neighbors. A few squirrels ran around the ground searching for something to eat, but in a short time, they returned to the trees that were growing along the street several blocks away.

Deserted, desolate place, Pavel thought as he sat down and waited for Edward Domannov. The past few years pierced his thinking. The troubles in the compound in India. The scam in the Ph.D. program. The problem with the KGB and his being beaten and thrown in jail. Losing his job in India. Their unsuccessful attempt at staying in Australia. He probably could tolerate this himself, but when the problems invaded his world with Natasha and his son he could not bear the pain. He often thought about the beatings he had suffered at the hands of the KGB, but this pain did not compare with the mental suffering. The beatings were of short duration, but the mental suffering just continued on and on with no end. They spiraled around his life. How could he reach out and stop the agony?

At that moment, he could see the figure of Edward Domannov slowly approaching him. A moving feeling of hate rose within him. Perhaps, it was an accumulation of all the past years, all the harassment of the KGB which now invaded his system.

Romanov sat down next to Pavel on the bench. "Listen carefully to what I have to say to you. I have access to your file. I have the ability to do anything I want with that file. I can delete it, or I can give it some additional boost which can hurt your case. This could land you in prison for the rest of your life. It's up to you to chose."

At this point, Pavel started to object. The whole point of this man's accusations seemed unreal and unbelievable.

"Wait, a minute," he continued, seeing Pavel was about to object. "You must pay me ten thousand dollars to erase everything out of your file. Be assured, I have the ability to do this." His eyes were filled with a cruel determination.

The man's cold, calculated words hit Pavel with an icy thrust. What choice did he have? "All right, but I don't have ten thousand dollars. I'm willing to pay, but I don't have that kind of money. If you will give me some time, I'll see what I can do."

Romanov agreed, but left with the warning, "If you want to keep out of big trouble, you must pay this money!" He rose from the bench and walked defiantly across the park.

What was all this about? Pavel wondered as he searched his mind for some answers. He doubted that the man could delete his file. After all, this was not his personal file that he could do with it as he wished. It was still in the office with the KGB. And besides, this was not an official meeting, so he decided he would play for some more time and try to think of some way out of the situation.

Pavel decided to call Sergey Tokaloff. Sergey was a smart businessman. He might have some ideas, so they decided to discuss the situation at Pavel's apartment where they would not be overheard.

That afternoon, Tokaloff listened carefully to Pavel's description of the meeting with Romanov. "Are you sure this man doesn't have criminal ties with the mafia, especially since he is trying to extort money from you?"

"I don't believe so, at least not at this point."

"This could be just a simple case of extortion, but don't depend on it."

"I can't believe that I would be the object of real extortion. I know some businessmen who have dealt with these criminal elements, but after all, I'm not a businessman. I'm not in any kind of business here at all."

"Well, time will tell what this man is up to and if he has any ties with a criminal group. I have a friend who has a grocery store. He was supposed to pay the mafia for protection. One day, he didn't pay the fees, and they came and smashed all his windows and set fire to his store."

"Maybe you are right. I don't think he's acting on the behalf of the KGB. If this were just KGB business, he would call me and send me an official notice to come to the office for more interrogation. I'm going to try to stall for more time."

"You could tape some of this man's conversation or take someone along with you as a witness."

"Good excellent idea, Tokaloff. Maybe I can do that."

"Keep me informed, and be careful, Pavel. If this man is involved with the mafia, you could be in for real trouble!"

Two more weeks passed before Pavel received another phone call from Edward Domannov. It was in the evening, and Pavel had been showing Stepan how to set up cassettes and program some of the end-of-the-year dances that were being scheduled at his school.

Pavel hated the interruption with his son. He put these moments with Stepan away in his mind where he often drew them out to remember, especially when times were bad and trouble came pushing down on him.

The sound of the man's voice swept over him like the cold, calculated beat of a metallic machine. Again, Pavel was requested to meet him at the Pobeda Park across the city, early in the morning. And again, the demand was the same. This time, the man appeared to be more threatening. Pavel repeated what he had said before—that he just didn't have the money and didn't know where he could get that kind of money. Still, he promised Romanov to keep trying.

Natasha was seriously worried about the situation. What could they do, how could they be safe with all these threats invading their lives, she wondered.

She found out where Olga was living and decided to go and talk with her. Olga had endured so much in her life. Yakov had killed her son. Now, he was trying to kill Andrey. To avoid trouble with the KGB, Yakov had told them that Andrey was a spy and writing against the government. Now, it was a matter of which one would get to the other first.

The apartment was sunny and attractively decorated with some of Olga's handicrafts. She looked well, but Natasha knew that hidden within her gray blue eyes, there was deep sorrow, a sorrow and worry about Andrey.

"What do you hear from your son? Do you see him very often?"

"He is working for a big newspaper, the *Novoye Uremya* in Moscow," she said proudly. "Maksim helped him find a job. He seems really interested in reporting and the newspaper business."

"Yes, Pavel said he saw him in Moscow. There was talk that he should change his appearance so that Yakov wouldn't recognize him."

"That is a terrible thing. A terrible thing. First that man kills my Ivan, and now, he is after my son. My only son. Their hate for each other is terrible. When Andrey was home, that's all he talked about. Getting even with Yakov for killing his brother. I'm afraid for Andrey, Natasha. I'm afraid. One of them is going to die."

Natasha tried to comfort Olga, but no words seemed to bring any relief or encouragement for the woman. As Natasha left the apartment, she put her arms around Olga and promised to come back real soon, but she wondered what freedom she herself would have in the days ahead. Every day seemed to bring her closer to a danger that she could feel rising within herself.

On the way back, she stopped at the store for some bread and sausage. It was late July and getting very hot in the city. It was time for Marina and Valentin to be home. Valentin would probably be cross from the heat unless he had some wine or beer to drink. She couldn't be sure if Pavel would be able to get any for him today since money for food was scarce and inflation was so high.

As she walked down the hallway, she heard loud laugher coming from the apartment. They must have some company. It was Sergey Tokaloff, the former owner of the disco, the *Ulybka*. He had brought Valentin some beer.

"I told you he was one smart businessman, Papa."

"You'd better believe it! Always remember, beer is the staff of life!"

"I thought bread was the staff of life, Dedushka," Stepan said, looking up from the television set.

"So it is, Stepan, so it is. For you, it is bread. For me, beer. Also, beer." Valentin raised the bottle to his lips and smiled contentedly.

"I understand that you met with Edward Domannov again. What happened this time, Pavel?"

"The same thing, Tokaloff. Same demands as before."

"What do you think you're going to do about it?"

"You know, I wonder about this guy. After I went back to India, their attention shifted from cases like mine to restructuring their own intelligence. If it weren't for Romanov, the whole KGB office would probably not bother with me anymore. That's my impression."

"So what goes with this guy?"

"I think he's acting on his own and on his own initiative. He has had access to the files. Then, apparently, he decided since I've worked abroad I probably have some money."

"You plan to just stall him along?"

"That's right. What the hell else can I do? I don't think the KGB is connected with criminals, but I could be wrong. From what I see on television and the newspapers, the KGB is fighting this emerging criminal element, and for now, maybe they have the situation under control."

"I'm not so sure that the KGB has everything under control," Natasha said coming over to the table. "I just heard on television that a woman in Moscow started up a new business a few years ago. She noticed some street cleaners sweeping up the snow. They were warm and comfortable in their jackets while she was freezing just shopping in the city. She decided to buy a street sweeper's jacket at a local market for thirty rubles. Then, she sewed some flowers on the jacket and sold it to a friend for much more. Now, she has a million dollar business and exports these jackets for fifty dollars to France and the United States. She employs about one hundred and fifty seamstresses!"

"Looks like she really hit onto a good idea, hmm, Pavel?"

"But listen to this! Recently, she was held up at gunpoint four times, so now she has an armed bodyguard. That's what I mean. It looks to me that crime is on the move, at least in Moscow."

"Well, there is an upside to this story. At least where else in the world could a person start a business like this with no capital? You should go and listen to Grigory Yavlinsky, Pavel. That man has some excellent plans for the economy here in Russia. Who knows? He may run in the presidential election in 1996!"

It was almost fall when Pavel had the opportunity to hear Yavlinsky speak at a meeting of young liberals in Lipetsk. He was impressed with the Yabloko party. Most of the people there were his age, and he found that they were progressive thinking young people and open to new ideas.

Yavlinsky talked forcefully to the group. He described detailed proposals on how to carry out new economic reforms.

People in the group asked him many questions. Some said they believed that life was better now in the large cities, so why was it that so many people at the State Duma elections voted for the KPRF or the Communist Party?

Yavlinsky moved closer to the group and answered them directly. He agreed that some people were living better than before, but others were not. A large number of people lost their basic benefits that they had under socialism. Now, with inflation, the little money they have doesn't go very far. That's the reason they support and vote for the Communist Party.

The man continued to talk for about another hour, and then he said he would take one more question. Pavel asked him what course he thought the government should take to improve the economy. Yavlinsky's suggested that the Russian government should work to attract more private foreign investments as well as to encourage Russian investors. But to achieve this, the Parliament must amend the legislation in order to encourage more investors.

It was at this meeting that Pavel saw Igor Popov who was the representative of the Yabloko party in Lipetsk. He knew Igor because they had often studied together at the university. Pavel was impressed with the party's ideas and invited Sergey Tokaloff to go with him to talk with Popov.

They met at Popov's office in downtown Lipetsk. On his desk, were pamphlets about the Yabloko party.

Igor greeted them warmly. He had a personality that reached out to people. "What do you think is going on now, Pavel? There seems to be a lot of confusion."

"Well, many people in 1991 did not understand transition and change. Now, the older people are dissatisfied. When there was Communism, they were promised that in a few years if they worked hard they would see this paradise. But that paradise didn't happen. Many have lost their jobs. I think people have lost their belief in what they were doing."

"Yes, that's true," Tokaloff agreed. "It is especially tough for the old folks because ten years ago with communism they were getting some kind of retirement, some kind of pension. It wasn't much, but it was something that was guaranteed to them. They didn't have to worry that maybe next month they wouldn't see their money. Now, with inflation, their buying power goes down."

"And what do you believe the young people are thinking, Pavel?"

"The young people, like myself, are mostly happy with the situation because it presents us with more opportunities to establish ourselves in some kind of activity or business."

"This is Yavlinsky's position," Igor emphasized. "He is one of the few people on the political scene today who can tell us how to cope with these problems and how to achieve these goals. He is an expert on economics."

"Igor, do you think Yavlinsky will run in the 1996 elections?" Tokaloff asked.

"He can count on support from the intellectuals in the larger cities, but winning the election is another matter."

"I understand that Moscow is the number one, important city," Pavel continued. "I heard on television that more than eighty percent of the country's capital is centered in Moscow."

"Yes, Moscow is the heart and soul of Russia. Most of our politicians who are worth their salt agree. Yavlinsky believes that Russia must establish a place in the world, find its own identity, and be free of Western pressure. Still, Russians need Western business skills, and they need Western investment."

"I remember some of the words of Alexander Solzhenitsyn," Pavel said reflectively. "He warned that the future of the world would be determined largely by Russia's ability to avoid being destroyed in the rubble left from communism's collapse. Personally, I can see there's much that must be done here in Russia."

As they left Igor's office in downtown Lipetsk, Tokaloff turned and asked, "Well, what do you think of the party? I am impressed with them, myself."

"If I stay on in Russia, I would join the party. Igor is completely truthful and carefully analyzes the situation. Other political leaders are not that truthful because they are either involved with the criminal element or are communists and want the old order back. This movement believes that we shouldn't try to westernize our country, but should take care of our economy first."

"You say if you could stay on here in Russia? Do you have hopes of that this KGB officer will quit threatening you?"

"I've been hoping this man will give up and leave me alone. Otherwise, I will try to go to the United States, but I need an invitation from my friend, Sergey Dnieper. You remember, he is the twin brother of Alex who was the sound manager at the disco."

"An invitation to visit?"

"Yes, that is the first step. Then, I will need to find a job and arrange for Natasha to come over to be with me. It won't be easy. But I would much prefer to stay here and work for more progressive programs and more freedoms."

But it wasn't that easy. Romanov would not give up. He smelled money like a pit bull lurches for red meat. And soon, Pavel could sense that Romanov was relentlessly after him. The next time he called, they were supposed to meet at the Sokol cemetery.

"The cemetery? " Pavel questioned. This was unbelievable. What was this man trying to tell him? If he didn't have the money, he would shoot him and throw him into some makeshift grave?

"It is a quiet place. No one is around. Just be on time. Nothing will happen to you. Remember, I want your money!"

When they met at the cemetery, Pavel repeated what he had said before."My family is poor. You can kill me, but I don't have the money."

Romanov was not moved by these words. "If you don't have the money, then get the money from some place, from your friends. But let me tell you, you'd better get the money. I will call you in a few weeks. Don't give me the same story again," he snarled. He raised his fist threateningly as he walked away.

There was no doubt in Pavel's mind now that Romanov would carry out his threats. He was tormented day and night with worry. What could he do? After all, ten thousand dollars was a tremendous amount of money. The idea of raising that kind of money for the average Russian was ridiculous. He expressed his fears to Tokaloff. He didn't know where to turn. They decided to drive up to Moscow and try to get some ideas from their friends.

They met at Maksim's apartment. He had a couple of rooms down the street from the newspaper office.

"You're really dealing with a bastard, Pavel. What do you think he will do if you don't come up with the money?" Maksim asked.

"I wish he would go to hell! And I'd like to send him along real fast! I thought he would give up after a while, but he is becoming more and more threatening. I may have to leave Russia on the run."

"And that would leave Natasha here. What would happen to her?"

"If bad comes to worse, she could take her visa and go to India for three months. I'm very worried what could happen to her. They could arrest her. I don't know what they would do to her! It's a terrible situation!"

"I have an idea," Maksim said, leaning forward with determination. "First, let me know when you're supposed to meet with Romanov again. I have a friend who is a champion boxer. He will go with you and beat this man up. I guarantee he won't bother you again. Besides, he will be a witness for you and could carry a recorder on him and tape everything!"

"Good idea! Just as soon as the bastard calls me, I'll get in touch with you. I'd sure like to get a tape of his threats and fix him real good!"

It was late September when Romanov called him again. This time, there was no mistake in his tone. He was definitely threatening Pavel to bring the money with him. They would meet at the Sputnik Park. "And listen here, do not pull any tricks or bring anyone with you. We're meeting alone. Be assured that I am armed, so come alone, or you will not leave the park alive!"

Pavel knew he was not joking. There was no way that he could bring Maksim's friend along with him to beat up Romanov.

Romanov warned him again, but now, there was an edge and anger in his voice. They talked for a while. Romanov suggested ways that Pavel could raise the money. He stressed his words and glared at Pavel as he spoke.

"Sell all you have. Ask your family and your friends for money. I don't care how you get the money, just get it, and fast!"

Pavel left the meeting with a feeling of danger creeping up his back. He was desperate. He had to reach Sergey Dnieper in California to write and set up an official invitation for him. And it had to happen fast! His time was running out!

In the meantime, Pavel decided to try and sell off a lot of his personal things, like his television set and stereo system. His stereo system was very advanced since he had a huge collection of rock music tapes that he used when he worked at the disco. But in the back of Pavel's mind, he still hoped to use the money to begin a new life in the United States. Now, where was his life taking him? He still desperately wanted to stay and join Yavlinsky's party and work for economic reforms. He certainly didn't want to give his money away to that swine, Romanov. But would he have any choice?

Chapter 23

Maksim was just finishing writing a news story when Andrey Dimitri burst into the room and threw his jacket in a chair.

"Listen to this! I got this story from a good source in St. Petersburg." He held out several pages of notes in his hand.

"You got a story! Wait until you hear mine!"

"Just hold off a minute, Maksim. This will hit all the front pages. This person claims that the mafia has taken away his car and home. This happened when he was driving his car, and this mafia gang staged a traffic accident. Some of the police are involved with this scheme."

"What's he going to do? This can't be any ordinary citizen. Most Russians don't own a car."

"That's right, but this time they picked on the wrong guy. The scheme was to get the police to warn the man to settle up the accident claim. The sum of money was enormous. The mafia gets the money, and the man doesn't know where to go. He's dead broke. And law enforcement is a big joke. Evidently, the mafia has more guns and weapons than the police. Even soldiers are selling their guns to the highest bidder."

"But you say this time they picked on the wrong man. Who was he?"

"Arkady Kozyrev!"

"No fooling! He's an important government official. They'll be plenty of trouble over this! Where did you get this story from?"

"I have a friend, a gal, that works in his office."

"Be sure and get all the facts, Andrey. Make sure you can back them up with quotes and so on. Then write it up. I'll take a look at it. But, listen to this scoop. Igor Sviatoslav was just in the office. He said he was supposed to be repairing some pipes in the basement of an old hotel downtown when he heard some guys talking. He slid down behind a pile of rubble, so they wouldn't see him. They were talking about a big deal with some German and American brokers who work out of Switzerland."

"What are they selling?"

"Precious metals, like the highly restricted materials and boron 10, which is used in reactor control rods, and osmium 187. The osmium 187 is a non-radioactive isotope that can sell for more than $100,000 a gram."

"This is big news, Andrey?"

"The big news for us is that one of the guys was Yakov! That's why Alex came here to tell me. It happened late yesterday afternoon. They are going to meet there again in a couple of days. I'm going to ask Alex to help me with this."

"Alex! He's no reporter!"

"I need him for something else. They won't suspect him if they did see him there. He's been hired to do some plumbing. And they don't know him. He was always behind the scenes at the disco."

"So Yakov is in on this! But, what's so big about buying and selling this stuff anyway?"

"That isn't the big story. Just before they broke up, they were talking about setting up a deal with a whole network to sell some plutonium. They think they have a way to do this. "

"They must have some big connections! Don't you think it's pretty dangerous for Alex?"

"I've got a friend who knows about electronics, and he's going to put a recorder in that room in the basement. Alex would just go with him when he sets it up. Then, all he has to do is pick up the tape next week."

"Be careful about working on this kind of story. A friend of mine, a newspaper man in St. Petersburg, said he knew a reporter who was killed by a briefcase bomb after writing up a story on the mafia and illegal arms trading. You don't want to end up all blown up or carved into pieces and thrown into the river just to write a story!"

"Don't mention throwing bodies into the river, Andrey. I don't want to even drive by the stinking place! But still, if we're going to beat Yakov at his game, we've got to move before he makes his move on you, and we've got to move fast!"

"He won't get me, Maksim. I'll get to that son of a bitch first!"

But Maksim wasn't so sure. Yakov apparently had many connections. He had gone from being a common street ruffian, to being a murderer, and now was connected with a criminal network

226

that was ready to make money selling the deadly plutonium. Still, the story itself wasn't the whole issue. They had to get to Yakov first. When it came down to it, it was either Andrey or Yakov. Andrey vowed it would be Yakov.

A few days later, Andrey was in Lipetsk to check on a story. He decided to call Pavel. As they talked, Andrey could sense discouragement in Pavel's voice when he mentioned the meetings with Romanov.

"I have made contact with Sergey Dnieper. He's going to send me an official letter, an invitation for me to go to the United States. Once, I get that I can go up to Moscow and get my visa."

"You think you're going to have to leave the country? Is Romanov that serious about the money?"

"Yes, I think so. Remember, you suggested that I take along that friend of yours who's a boxing champion and let him beat up Romanov? Well, the guy warned me not to bring anyone with me. He said that he is well-armed and would not hesitate to use his gun if I disobeyed and brought someone with me!"

"I'm sure this man is connected some way with the Russian mafia! We got rid of communism, but now the Mafia has risen. And, let me tell you, this monster has learned to work hand and fist with some of the former high officials in the Communist Party, the KGB, and criminal bosses throughout the world."

"One other thing. I noticed something the last time I met with Romanov. He was wearing small diamond cuff links! Believe me, I was really surprised! How could this guy afford to buy something like that?"

"That's what I'm saying. The son of a bitch is getting money from somebody that's connected with the Mafia. Right now, it looks like it's extortions. Extortions are everywhere."

"I guess you hear a lot about that since you're a newspaper reporter."

"That's right! People can't stay in business without paying money to the mafia for protection. Others are afraid to advertise when they are opening up a new business because they might attract the mafia, and for sure, they would move in and start demanding money for this and that. They are sucking people dry, just like this Romanov is trying to suck you dry by demanding that you sell off everything and give him your money!"

"What can I do about it, Andrey?"

"Do what Andrey and I are going to do about Yakov!"

"Yakov!" Pavel exclaimed in amazement.

"Yes, we are moving in on him. He is working with a network of criminals who are planning to sell plutonium! We know where they are meeting, and my friend is going to set up a recorder to tape their conversations!"

"That's pretty risky! Good luck."

"And good luck to you. You're going to need it! Keep in touch, Pavel and be careful. That man and his people are dangerous! Take him seriously."

The next week, Alex called Andrey and told him he had the first tape of the recorded meeting from the hotel basement. At the same time, the electrician had placed a new tape in the recorder. Alex was supposed to meet Andrey at a designated newsstand and just pass the tape over to him. They thought it would be safer and quieter that way.

That evening, they played the tape in Andrey's apartment. Soon, they discovered that the voices on the tape were those of three dealers. Two were Spaniards and one was a person from Colombia. A businessman, evidently a buyer from Bavaria, was meeting with them.

"First, here is the sample that you wanted. It is in this small lead container," claimed the man with the Spanish accent.

"What exactly does it contain?" the Bavaria asked in a high-pitched voice.

"A tiny amount of plutonium-23 and highly enriched uranium-238 oxides, a reactor fuel known as mox."

"When can I pick up the next sample that you talked about before?"

"We will have it here in three days."

Andrey could tell from the voices that the buyer had left the room. Then, another man began to question Yakov.

"I'm sure I can get enough of the stuff to make us rich for the rest of our lives. Listen, I know that the top atomic scientists are paid less than Moscow bus drivers. They can be bribed. Also, getting the stuff from the plutonium-production plant in Krasnoyarsk is a possibility, but I know someone who can get it from one of the nuclear research institutes."

"Is that so? Bring the sample with you to our next meeting."

The recording picked up again with the second meeting. They could tell from the conversations, Yakov was able to get the plutonium. This time, it was a sample of an H-bomb component, lithium-6. The Bavarian was told to expect a large shipment of mox at the Munich Airport from Moscow the following week. It would be shipped in a metal container inside a black vinyl suitcase. This time, the three dealers would buy directly from some scientists who worked at a submarine-research reactor plant. The sale was worth millions of dollars.

The next voice they heard was from one of the Spaniards. Evidently, the buyer had left. "Are you sure this man can be trusted?"

"He was highly recommended to us. His background and records are impeccable. What do you know about him, Yakov?"

"About the same thing. I'm positive he can be trusted. Absolutely!" The tape ended with Yakov's statement of assurance.

"Well, what do you think of all that Andrey?"

"It's hot stuff, but what do we do with it? Warn the authorities in Munich?"

"Exactly. That's what I intend to do, and I'll have to act quickly before it is too late! This may be just the beginning of a serious leak. You can imagine what can happen if certain countries continue to buy this material!"

But even with the tape, Andrey was having difficulty convincing his own editor or the authorities in Munich.

"I think this is just a bunch of irresponsible talk, Andrey," Mr. Efimov said, looking at Pavel skeptically. "I don't believe they are getting any plutonium from Russia. I've been told that not one single gram of plutonium-239 has been reported missing from Russian storage. What happens, Andrey, is that members of this criminal network are putting up a pretense that they can get this material just to make millions of dollars. Money is the name of the game. Here, every day in Moscow, the mafia is extorting money from businesses, and we both know the KGB and the police are in on the whole rotten business!"

Andrey was listening to this whole conversation, but said nothing. Having just started working with the newspaper, he felt his only recourse was to keep quiet. He glanced over at Andrey and could tell that he wasn't buying Mr. Efimov's story. But what could he do?

The following morning, Andrey tried to call the authorities in Munich, but he had absolutely no luck in trying to convince them. He began to feel desperate. Here, he had evidence, taped evidence, that these men were going to ship deadly plutonium out of the country, and no one would listen to him. What damn fools they were!

During the next week, he was upset enough over the whole situation that Efimov came around to Andrey's desk and asked him why he didn't have that story he covered in Lipetsk in on the deadline. Finally, he said, "Well, it's in, anyway. I think you need the afternoon off. You don't seem to be very alert today. Go for a walk and get some coffee!"

Andrey left his desk, but decided to do some research of his own, especially after listening to one more tape that he received from Alex early that morning. Perhaps it was a reporter's instinct or just plain good luck that he decided to browse through the newspaper clip file. He was startled and amazed when he pulled an article about Yakov from the file. The story collaborated what he had heard on the tape. He carefully removed the newspaper clipping from the file and took it back to his apartment.

"Listen to this!" He showed the story to Andrey that evening. I found out from our own files that Yakov was once an aviator in the army. That's what Yakov was saying on the last tape. Look, I took this clipping out of our newspaper files. He's shown with another aviator. Evidently, they rescued a pilot that went down during the war in Afghanistan."

"I see that he has put on some weight since that time. Look how skinny he was then. What do you plan to do with this information?"

"Just this. Alex slipped me this tape today. I listened to it here this afternoon. There wasn't much on it, but they discussed one very important thing. Yakov was saying that it would be easy and economical to ship the material by plane. Evidently, that's what he wants to do. He says he can fly a plane from the Chkalovo Air Base to Leipzig and avoid the customs' inspections."

"Will he be able to get a plane to fly?"

"With bribes and that kind of money, you can do about anything. Now, I have to find out when he's going to make that run."

"What good will that do?"

"Stay with me, Andrey. I've got a plan. If it works out, you can bet that will be the end of Yakov!"

Andrey walked back to the office to work on the Arkady Kozyrev story. But he also had his own idea what to do about Yakov. He would do it his way. An hour later, he was on the phone. He was successful with the first contact. The meeting place was the old run-down food store two miles away. He was told to come alone.

On Monday morning, all hell broke lose at the newspaper office. It all started around ten o'clock. First, there was one very important phone call; then more phones started ringing.

The editor, Nodar Efimov came rushing into the room waving some sheets of paper. He had just been talking to a newspaper in Munich.

"Why didn't we get this story first?" he glared fiercely at the reporters who were making phone calls and moving rapidly around the room. "Look at this leading story! A one-pound canister of mox—poisonous isotopes was intercepted at the Munich airport late last evening."

Then he turned abruptly to Andrey. "Come into my office right away. I want to talk to you."

Andrey knew immediately what he wanted to talk about. Why hadn't the man listened to him before?

Efimov wiped his forehead with his handkerchief and sat down before his desk. He shook his head in disbelief. "The police got tipped off. They were waiting when this Colombian's suitcase came out on the airport conveyor belt. The paper here says that inside the suitcase was a metal container that held a pound of mox. This is reported to be the largest seizure ever made of the poisonous isotopes."

"Yes, and this amount of plutonium is enough to poison a whole city's water supply or make what they call a 'dirty bomb' that could disperse radioactive particles in the air. And worst of all, almost enough plutonium to make a bomb."

"You seem to know a lot about this plutonium," Efimov began and then suddenly began to stare at Andrey in astonishment."Is this what you were telling me about a week ago? Oh, my God, what a fool I was! I just couldn't believe what you were saying."

"I had the tapes and everything, Mister Efimov! I tried to call some officials in Munich to warn them, but to no avail. They wouldn't listen! Who tipped them off that this shipment was due to arrive at the airport?"

"A detective who was posing as a Bavarian businessman."

"I have the tapes with their conversations about the sale and the shipments. No names were given. I know there were several dealers, some Spaniards and a Colombian and the Bavarian that they seemed to trust who was prepared to buy the mox."

"Well, they wouldn't listen to you in Munich because they already had the tip that they needed. Did they ask your name?"

"Right. I gave it to them."

"Good. They'll probably call you. Let me know. We'll get the rest of the story right here! Next time you get some information, and I brush it off, you have my permission to give me a whack on the head!" He got up and walked over to Andrey and put his hand on his shoulder. "You're the best reporter I ever had. Sure glad I took you on. Old Shlapentokh has bad heart problems and is going to leave next month. You'll move up to his position. I promise you!"

The promises didn't mean much to Andrey at this point. He had plenty on his mind to think about. Still, he was pleased that he left Lipetsk and had the opportunity to get a job on this paper. He enjoyed meeting and interviewing people Yes, there was the excitement that raced in his veins when big stories broke like the two coups right here in Moscow. Now, all this was in his blood, and he lived for the breaking stories and the rush to meet the deadlines.

Andrey smiled to himself. Then, slowly, his mind focused back to Yakov, and he began to make plans for his next move.

But Andrey wasn't waiting for him. He was on his way to meet his contact in Pago's run-down store. The old man had been having a hard time getting the supplies for his place. The store wasn't anything special, but if you needed anything, Pago usually had it. He knew exactly where it was. All the shelves were piled high with boxes of all sizes and shapes. Pago would climb slowly up a ladder and produce the exact item that the customer wanted. Andrey always wondered how the man could find anything in all that mess.

Andrey waited a half hour for his contact to arrive. As soon as the man appeared in the door, Pago turned to leave. It was obvious that they knew each other.

"So you are Andrey Dimitri? You work at the *Sovoye Uremya* newspaper office? Okay, I checked you out. What do you want me to do for you?"

"I want you to kill this man. Here's his picture. It was taken when he was an aviator in the Afghanistan War."

"His name is Yakov. Why do you want to do away with him?"

"He killed my brother, Ivan. First, he beat me up because I was ahead of him in a crowd trying to get some things at a food store. Later, my brother heard him talking and joking about what he did to me. They got in a fight in the street near where I live. Ivan was arrested. Then a friend of ours bribed the officials and Ivan got out of jail. Yakov told the authorities that my brother was a spy and worked against the government. Later, he killed Ivan. Next, he sent a person to kill me. I killed him first. Now, I want Yakov killed because I know he is after me."

"A real fucker, eh? Where can I find him?"

"Yakov is involved with the black-market nuclear selling. He plans to fly a package of the stuff from the Chkalovo Air Base to Leipzig in East Germany. That way, he avoids the inspections at customs. The plane will be empty of any material coming back. Get one of your men to put a bomb on the plane and let him blow up in it on the way home!"

"I can't promise that, kid. But I can arrange to have him shot as he gets off the plane."

"Okay, do that. Maybe I can watch him get shot!" Andrey said. His eyes were filled with hate and anger.

"For a kid, you've sure got a lot of rage in you! I can't say I blame you. The son of a bitch deserves to be killed! I need to know when. And I need four thousand dollars to do the job. You call me when."

Andrey agreed, but he had no idea how he could come up with that kind of money. Still, he knew he had to get the money. It was either Yakov or himself. And he vowed that Yakov would not kill him. Then, he could walk down the street or go home at night without looking in the shadows or listening for footsteps behind him as he walked.

For the next few days, he didn't say anything about the matter to Andrey. He knew he was busy working on the Munich story. But one late afternoon when Andrey was just finishing up at his desk, Andrey told him he wanted to talk something over with him. They walked to a bar a few blocks away and ordered a couple of beers.

"How is the Munich story going?" Andrey began.

"Right now, the authorities believe the plutonium that was seized in Munich may have come from a submarine-research reactor or perhaps a plant that was preparing isotopes for civilian use."

"And who stole the stuff?"

"Well, we know that Yakov had something to do with that, but I'm sure he knows some senior lab technician who was able to steal the plutonium. I don't think you'll have to worry about Yakov much anymore. The authorities will catch up with him and arrest him. His time is running out!"

Andrey wasn't convinced. He didn't want to wait any longer. "Do you have any more tapes? I'd like to know when Yakov is planning to fly with a delivery into Leipzig."

"I haven't talked to Alex recently. I thought we had all the information we needed."

"Are you kidding me, Andrey? If I have a definite date when Yakov is going to make the trip, I'll know exactly where he is going to be—and when!"

"What do you plan to do then? Certainly, not try to kill him!"

"No, I won't kill him. I'm planning to hire someone to do the job for me! He's connected with the mafia."

"Oh no, Andrey! For God's sake, don't do that! That's crazy. Those guys want a lot of money. Leave it to me. I'll ask our editor, Efimov, to contact all the authorities in Leipzig and alert them about the delivery. Then, they'll arrest Yakov and that will take care of him!"

But Andrey wasn't so convinced. Yakov had a way of slipping through the fingers of the law. He could slip through the cracks of any system like a slimy snake. And this man's poison could shoot off like venom and kill anyone that got in his way.

"How are you going to find out the date and time of delivery?"

"Let's go and call Alex now. I'm sure he's home by now."

They went back to Andrey's apartment and made the phone call. Alex was just getting home from work. He promised to put another tape in the recorder, but he wouldn't be able to pick it up for a few days because he was working on another job right now.

Andrey took the receiver. "We need the information. We have to know the exact time when Yakov is going to make this delivery."

"I'll see what I can do. They plan to meet tonight. It will be late before I can call you back."

Alex was not pleased with the situation. First off, he wasn't working at the hotel anymore. His job was finished. He had no real excuse to be there, but if they needed the information right away, that meant he had to go back there, set up the recorder and try to get out before they arrived.

It was close to seven-thirty when Alex got down to the basement of the hotel. The group usually met around eight. He would have to hurry. Just as he set up the recorder and hid it near their table, he heard their voices. Luckily, he had brought his plumber's tools with him. That way, it looked like he had some legitimate business in the basement. He moved a distance away where he could hear their voices and still be out of sight.

The Spaniard spoke first. "What are we going to do? They got the Colombian at the Munich Airport. And that stupid fuck that we trusted will turn us in for sure."

"He doesn't know where to find us. This is our last meeting," Yakov emphasized. "We'll get our money after I fly a few of these shipments into Leipzig. But let me tell you, we can't meet here in Moscow anymore!"

"Certainly not down here in this sewer place. When do you make the first trip, Yakov?"

"Next weekend. I will be returning to Chkalovo around eight in the evening."

"Are you taking a bodyguard?"

"No. I don't want no bodyguard. Then I got to pay off the son of a bitch!"

"As though you aren't getting enough money, Yakov."

"That's all right. I can't trust nobody. Those bodyguards are all a bunch of crooked fuckers. Wait a minute!" He turned around and listened for a moment. "Someone's in here. Let's get him!"

The three men rushed through the basement and cornered Alex. He pretended to be putting some tools away.

Yakov pushed him up against the wall and grabbed him by the throat. The Spaniard started beating him in the ribs.

"You dirty sneak. What the hell are you doing listening in on our business?"

Alex struggled to speak, but Yakov had his hand tight on his throat. The man's eyes were wild with anger. At this moment, he seemed ready to kill as he moved in on Alex.

"I'm a plumber working here. You can ask in the hotel."

"What do you take me for? Some fool? Plumbers don't work at this time of night. What the hell!"

"I didn't want to come back again. I left some tools here."

"You're no plumber. Who sent you to listen to us? "

"Oh, let him alone, Yakov. Look at his hands. They're worn and dirty like plumber's hands."

"I'm going to kill the bastard. I tell you, I'm going to kill him. I hated him the minute I laid eyes on him!"

The Spaniard shrugged. "Well, kill him, if you've got to!"

Alex grasped wildly for some way out. "My boss is supposed to inspect this work tonight. Listen! He's on the steps now."

An unmistakable sound was heard in the room.

"Come on, Yakov, let's get the hell out of here!" The two picked up their papers and case and dashed through the basement to the outside door.

Suddenly, two cats came rushing through the dark rooms. Alex grinned in relief as he watched them chase each other. "Thanks, pussy cats, for saving my life. I always knew cats were good for something. Come on. I'm taking you both home with me for good luck." He picked up the recording tape and headed for his truck that was parked behind the hotel.

Andrey had fallen asleep on the couch when the phone rang. It was Alex. He vividly described the meeting between Yakov and the Spaniard.

"I almost got knocked off, Andrey. If it hadn't been for those two cats, I'd still be rotting there on the floor with all my bones crushed and beaten."

"That was terrible, Alex! Just terrible! Listen, I appreciate the information. I'll make it up to you. I promise!"

Andrey turned with a triumphant look on his face. "Now, we have the information we need."

"That's right. Now, we have the exact date of the delivery to Leipzig. I'll tell our editor. The police will take care of Yakov!"

Andrey could see that his friend was relieved, but he was sure that he would get even with Yakov himself. Yakov must be killed. He was positive that Yakov would slip past the police. Ideas and plans began to swirl around in his mind. Now, he had to figure out how to get the money and give all the information to his contact.

It was late when Andrey got back to his room, but he decided to make the call anyway.

His contact answered the phone almost immediately. "A week from this Saturday, you say? That's pretty fast. Now, I can't arrange to put a time-bomb in a case on the plane or to shoot him just as he arrives back at the airport in Chkalovo. Too many risks, especially since you can't pay me the five thousand."

"Can you just kill him? Say one thousand?"

"Okay. For one thousand, my man will follow him and shoot him when he gets to his car. That will be outside the air base. Bring the money to the store, same place, nine o'clock, Thursday evening."

Andrey agreed, but now he had just a little over a week to get the money. This weekend, he would go to see his mother and Tokaloff in Lipetsk and borrow the money. Maybe he could make some extra money on the side helping to stack and deliver the papers around Moscow and the nearby cities.

Olga told him that she was worried about what he was doing. It just wasn't safe, she said over and over again. But finally, she relented. At least there wasn't the threat that Yakov could kill her son. She would borrow some money from her family and Ivan's family.

He found Tokaloff at a small nearby bar. Andrey thought that was a good omen. The man would be in a good mood. But, he was surprised to find that Tokaloff was filled with warnings and caution.

"What if the police pick this guy up in Leipzig? You pay this guy all this money. Then, Yakov's arrested, and where are you then?"

"I guess I'm taking that chance. These traffickers slip in and out a lot these days and get away with it!"

"You're talking about drug traffickers. That's a whole different story. This is nuclear smuggling. Material that can blow up a whole large city! Just realize they aren't playing any little games. This smuggling is dangerous and deadly."

Andrey was beginning to think the whole deal was off. What was he going to do? Then, suddenly, he made a quick decision. To hell with this. He would kill the man himself!

But then, Tokaloff slowly reached into his pocket and pulled out two hundred dollars."Here, I was saving this to pay off the mafia to leave my store alone. Maybe they won't be back for a few weeks."

"Thanks, anyway, Tokaloff, but I think I will wait on the whole thing right now. I've got another idea that won't involve all that money. It will be quick and easy. I'm sure of that."

Tokaloff began to question Andrey, but got no real answers. A half hour later, he watched him walk out of the bar. What was this kid up to? he wondered. Maybe Andrey had some crazy idea in his mind. Maybe he should have pressed him more and found out what he was planning to do. Of course, he wanted Yakov dead just as much as Andrey did, but was killing the man the way to do it? He had serious doubts. Still, he figured you had to take some risks in life. If he didn't believe this, he would never have gone into his own business. His thoughts traveled to Pavel and how he was the object of an extortion scheme. He was also in grave danger. Now, it seemed as though the mafia was taking over all of Russia. Everyone was greasing palms, and the smell was slowly creeping through the streets, the government and the KGB.

It was Monday morning when Andrey gave the recorded tape to Mr. Efimov. This time, Efimov believed that an actual meeting had taken place and the men were planning to ship plutonium. Immediately, he telephoned the authorities in Leipzig.

"This is a big story, Andrey. When the arrests are made, you shall write the story, and you will get your by-line!"

"Let's hope we can stop this sale. These leaks are too dangerous for all the people, not just Russians and Germans, but all over Europe."

"And more than that. Some men in the Monterey Institute of International Studies in the United States now believe there is much nuclear material that's unaccounted for. It's a very threatening, dangerous situation."

Andrey went back to his desk to proof-read the story he had written just yesterday. "It has been reported that some plutonium was found in a garage in Baden-Wurttemberg, Germany. Now, German scientists are using chemical 'fingerprints' obtained from the samples to try to trace the thieves who stole the plutonium." The article went on to state that the authorities believed that the material was probably stolen from an assembly plant in Russia.

It was at the end of the week that Andrey said he needed to talk to his friend privately in his apartment that evening. Before he left Moscow, he told his mother that he had changed his mind and didn't need the money. He could sense the relief in her voice. The plan was too dangerous, she kept saying. He was glad he had changed his plans. Now, he was the only one involved in the killing.

"What's going on? Something wrong?" Andrey asked anxiously.

Andrey walked quickly through the door. Wrinkles from a tight frown etched his forehead, and his dark eyes were flashing with determination. He began to speak rapidly. The words seemed to slam with defiance around the room.

"I've already decided what to do. Tonight, I'm leaving for the Chkalovo Air Base to be there when Yakov arrives back from Leipzig. I'll follow him to his car and kill him. A hit-man wanted one thousand dollars to do the job. I called the whole thing off. I will do it for myself for free!"

After these words, Andrey turned and moved swiftly down the street.

Andrey knew he had to stop him before he did this crazy thing, but Andrey was faster and disappeared into a small warehouse and vanished in the darkness.

"Stop! Stop! Andrey, listen! I've got to talk to you. I'm your friend!" But his words only echoed through the cavernous building. Andrey was gone!

Andrey decided to leave for the Chkalovo Air base later that night. He was sure he could find Andrey before it was too late. A frightening story had come into the newspaper the day before. In Moscow, a person had left a Minatom lab with about ten pounds of highly enriched uranium and had taken it home with him. What would stop Yakov from returning with some of this material from Leipzig to sell? If Andrey shot him and Yakov had some plutonium on his person, Andrey also could blow up in the attack. He had to reach Andrey in time before it was too late!

It was almost five o'clock before Andrey saw his friend. He was walking around near the runways at the air base.

Andrey saw a plane taxing down the runway. In the evening twilight, he couldn't make out the person who was climbing out of the plane. Was it Yakov or had he been caught in Leipzig?

As the man crossed the airstrip, Andrey could distinguish his features. It was Yakov! He had escaped the authorities in Germany! He appeared to be carrying a package. It might be some plutonium or highly enriched uranium. If Andrey riddled his body with bullets, what might happen? He shuddered to think of the outcome!

Yakov rushed cross the field to get to his car. He was totally alone.

At that moment, Andrey saw Andrey beginning to follow Yakov. He knew he had to get to him before it was too late.

He called out to him. "Stop! Stop! Wait a minute!"

Andrey heard Andrey's voice off in the distance, but he was determined to move ahead and kill Yakov.

Just before Andrey raised his gun, Andrey shouted, "He may be carrying plutonium!" He had to stop him before it was too late!

For one brief moment, Andrey stopped and turned around.

"Stop, stop!" Andrey shouted again. "For God's sake, stop!"

But this time, Andrey couldn't hear him. The only sounds in his ears was the pounding and rhythmic beat from within himself, "Shoot, Shoot! Kill him!"

Quickly, he raised his gun. At that split second, Yakov saw Andrey. He saw Andrey, his old enemy, and he knew it was all over. Andrey began to riddle Yakov's body with bullets. And Andrey stared into the man's cold, steel-blue eyes and saw a reflection of himself and all that had passed between them.

Yakov fell onto the pavement. The blood streamed from his body.

Much to Andrey's relief, there was no evidence that the man carried any nuclear material. He turned and shouted to Andrey.

"Hurry, hurry, you've got to get out of here! Jump in my truck. We'll go and get lost someplace in Moscow for the night!"

Chapter 24

It was the middle of October. Pavel was returning to the apartment house when he noticed a strange car that he had never seen before parked on the street. Some men appeared to be sitting and waiting inside. Maybe they were just visiting some friends, but still the car didn't look familiar to him because he knew all the people who had cars in the neighborhood.

For the moment, his mind was filled with thoughts about getting the money. So far, Pavel had not been very successful. After all, ten thousand dollars was virtually an impossible amount of money for the average Russian to raise. And he needed whatever money he could scrape together to get started in the United States.

Suddenly, as Pavel entered the apartment building, he felt strong hands reaching for him and shoving him against the wall in the darkness. One of the men thrust a gun to his head. Pavel could feel the object moving through his hair against his scalp while the two other men held him against the wall.

"Listen, you fool. If you keep on playing dumb with us, we'll shoot you! We want the money!" one of the men shouted as he pounded Pavel against the wall.

"Why me? Why are you asking me for money? I don't have any money. I don't even have a job, for God's sake!"

"You know what we mean. Romanov has told you that you must come up with ten thousand dollars. You know exactly what we're talking about."

At that point, Pavel realized that these men were not acting alone. They were working with the KGB officer.

"Listen, Romanov is very serious. You don't want to play any games with him, so if you care about your life and your family, you'd better get the money. And fast! You have just ten days. This is your last chance. We know where you live, and there is no way to escape us!"

The men turned to leave. Again, two of them pushed Pavel harder against the wall and against a radiator. The pain was excruciating.

He walked back to the apartment. The pain from his back radiated across his shoulders and neck. He sat down and looked around the apartment. This had been his home for many years except for the years he had spent with Natasha in India. Up to a certain point, things seemed to have been going well for him. The marriage had been a good thing in his life, but now it seemed that his life was crumbling around him.

He rose and walked over to the window. People down there were walking to the store or taking care of a little business. The old women were sitting on the benches talking about people they knew and catching up on the latest gossip. Yes, life went on as usual, Pavel thought. But in his life, the turbulence of the past few months began to pound in his head. He was filled with despair. Those criminals wouldn't let go of him. They invaded his life like a mad dog on a rampage. He had no peace, no safety. Just constant torment. He had to find a way out.

What would happen to his parents and his son? For a moment, fear crowded all other ideas and plans out of his mind. He was thankful that Natasha was staying with her family. She would be much safer there. But what about their future? It was obvious that the men he was dealing with were not just simple ruffians out to make some money. Romanov was connected with the KGB and probably the mafia. They were looking for big money, and he was convinced they would kill to get it. He had to stall for time. He had to stall for time so that he could sell a few things and have a little money when he left the country. That was his only way out. But still, he felt like he was confronted by a terrible danger that kept looming up in from of him, relentless to let go.

It had been a long night. When they left the air base, they knew they would have to drive all night and into the early morning hours to reach Moscow. They stopped at a friend's apartment to stay for the weekend in case they needed an alibi. But he doubted that they would have to prove their whereabouts, since the police would probably think it was a rival gang member who shot Yakov.

Monday was a different story. Much was unfolding at the newspaper office. First thing, Efimov hurried over to Andrey's desk.

"Well, here are the results that we wanted. The authorities heeded our warning and seized the plutonium in Leipzig. They are trying to trace the package. All they have to go on now is that some plane out of Chkalovo delivered the material. I'll put you on this story. Maybe you can find out what the authorities know about the plane and the pilot that was shot here in Russia."

Andrey stared in disbelief at the page of notes that Efimov had just given him. This was the last thing he expected. He knew who the aviator was and the person who shot him. What would Efimov think if he knew that his name was Andrey Dimitri, and he worked in this very newspaper office!

"Check with the authorities here first, and then call out to the base. See what you can find out."

On the way out the door, Andrey almost bumped into Andrey. "You won't believe this! Efimov has assigned me the story about the plutonium that was seized in Leipzig! I've got to find out more about the plane that was used and the pilot that flew the plane."

"Take a photographer with you, Andrey. I want a picture of Yakov dead and frozen in the morgue."

"That's all right for you to say, but the burden is on me to find out the name of the so-called gang that killed him. What am I going to come up with?"

"You know the name of the pilot. That's simple. Yakov's mafia will think that their rival gang shot their man. They'll be all hell bent to try and get even with them. And what's more, they won't be coming for me!"

"I hear you, Andrey. You may be right on that. But still, we've got to hope that this current seizure of plutonium at the airport in Leipzig will curtail their sales. This dirty business has got to be stopped before it infiltrates into our very lives and government!"

Andrey could see the determination in Andrey's eyes and realized that his friend was a true journalist and crusader. It was in his blood. But for himself, he worked with tangible things, things that he could reach out and maneuver. People that he could talk to — like or dislike. Or hate, like he hated and removed Yakov. He was not interested in ideas like Andrey was, but he knew he could "cut it" as a reporter, covering the beat on the street or a demonstration in Red Square.

Some of Andrey's work was already cut out for him. He knew the name of the aviator and already had a copy of the old clipping from the newspaper file telling about Yakov's rescue of another aviator during the Afghanistan War.

He stopped at the KGB office to get more information to add to his story. There were some notes in the file about Yakov's involvement with the Ivan murder. But the report did not state that Yakov was charged. His record in the service was, on the surface, admirable, especially after his daring rescue of the pilot during the war; however, on one occasion the report continued, he became very angry with another person on the base and almost killed him. Once, during maneuvers, he nearly wrecked his plane as he came in for a bad landing, swerving off the runway and skidding into one of the buildings. Evidently, those events were forgotten after he saved the pilot's life. He drifted around after he left the service and often got into street fights.

After gathering this information from the files from the KGB officer, he stopped to talk to some men in the front office.

"Who do you think killed this man? Was it one man acting on his own or some rival gang retaliating against Yakov and his mob?"

"Most likely some member from a rival mafia. What motive would one single man have to kill Yakov?" the officer sneered at such an absurd idea.

Andrey was pleased with this answer and decided to ignore the man's superior attitude. As far as he was concerned, he had the information that his editor wanted. Then, he would call out to the base and get a description of the plane and when it had left the air base.

By early afternoon, Andrey had an outline of the story for Efimov. Evidently, Yakov had bribed someone on the base to get a release of the plane.

"Good work, Andrey! That was clever of you to search our own files and find that clipping on Yakov and his rescue of that pilot during the war."

A few hours later, the complete story was on Efimov's desk. He called Andrey into his office.

"Good article, here, Andrey! You almost write as though you knew the man. I read some animosity between the lines that builds up the interest of the story. Just be careful and don't overdue it."

244

The editor's words moved through Andrey's mind. It was difficult for him to write the story as objectively as usual. The difference was that he was a part of all the action, directly involved, and he didn't like it. He hadn't planned on it.

It seemed as though Andrey was up to his neck in trouble ever since he met him. Bad luck seemed to follow him around like a black cat. First, there was Ivan's death, then his fraternizing with those criminals who almost killed Dr. Korotch, then his killing of Zviad Gladkov, and finally his killing of Yakov. Was this the end of the murders? And for how long would Andrey be able to avoid the KGB before it found the scent of his trail and reached out and devoured him?

When Pavel read the account of the shooting and the seizure of the plutonium in Leipzig in the paper, he sighed in relief for his friend. Yakov had been shot! Now, someone had done Andrey the favor of getting rid of Yakov. And to top it all off, Andrey's by-line appeared under the title of the article! He was pleased that Andrey was getting along so well at a job that he really enjoyed.

Later that morning, Natasha came over to the apartment. Pavel had warned her that it was not safe for her to be there, but she said she had missed him and would stay just a little while. Besides, she had been over to see Olga and had some news.

"She is so relieved that Yakov was shot. You can't imagine, Pavel, how relieved she is now that Andrey is out of danger! Olga confided to me that Andrey was here in Lipetsk about a week ago and was planning to hire a person to kill Yakov, but he would need money to do this, so he ended up changing his mind!"

Pavel frowned at this news. It wasn't like Andrey to back out of a plan. Still, what were his alternatives? Hire someone or—the thought was unnerving. Natasha interrupted his thinking.

"Why don't we go into the bedroom for a little while?" she suggested, trying to coax him out of his serious mood.

He smiled and picked her up to carry her to the bed. "I think you're getting heavier or I'm getting weaker."

"You'd better not be getting weaker, Pavel!" she laughed as she began to undress. "Hurry! Lock the door before someone drops by!"

After they made love, Pavel put on a tape of soft music. He reached over and smoothed Natasha's hair and kissed her softly. How precious she is to me, he thought as he watched her eyes becoming heavy with sleep. He wanted her close to him always. Once, he promised her that they would never be apart. We'll always be together, he had said. This is what Pavel wanted most of all, and he hoped and sometimes prayed in the middle of the night that nothing would ever come ranging out of the shadows and tear them apart.

It was around two o'clock when Pavel received the official invitation in the mail to visit Sergey Dnieper in the United States. Now, he could go to the embassy in Moscow and get his visa. This time, instead of asking Yaroslav to drive up to Moscow, he decided to take the train. He needed some time by himself to think over his next move.

It had been five days since the men had grabbed him and threatened to kill him if he didn't come up with the money. Since then, he had been selling off some of their things, but he still didn't have the ten thousand dollars. He told his friends that he had some things to sell like his expensive stereo system and a television set. Natasha sold some of her things like sweaters, some jewelry that she had bought in India and a leather coat. Still, Pavel was far short of the ten thousand dollars, and he needed the money to cover expenses when he got to the United States. If he could just hold the thugs off a little until he got out of the country! That's what he had to count on.

While Pavel slept on the train moving toward Moscow, he didn't know that a situation was brewing in the KGB office. The Spaniard, Mr. Velasquez, who was involved in the plutonium sales, was making plans with his friend, Manuel to go to the KGB office.

"Do you see this man here in this photo? His name is Andrey Dimitri. Yakov told me about him once. This man claims that Yakov killed his brother several years ago. That is a lie. The man lies. I want you to go to the KGB this morning and tell them that you saw Andrey kill Yakov out at the air base on Saturday. That will fix his ass, real good."

Manuel rubbed his pocket with the palm of his hand and looked up at Velasquez expectantly.

"Okay. Here's the money. Now remember, you don't let them try to change your mind about it."

"Well, I didn't see him do it, but I will say so."

"You're damn right you'll say so, or you can tell your priest you're going to need the last rites. After all, you were working at the base for the past few weeks weren't you?"

"Yes, sir, I was working there. I will tell the officers what you say."

"Also, remember to positively identify him from all the photos they show you. Look carefully here at his photo. Be real sure about it to them."

Velasquez watched the man walk down the hallway of the apartment building. He had picked this man because he knew he would keep his mouth shut. Sometimes, he bought drugs from him, but otherwise, his record was clean. Manuel had stern, dark eyes and could tell a convincing story. Velasquez wanted to either blame Andrey for this shooting or a rival gang who had been invading their markets. Right at this point, he wanted to get even with Andrey for Yakov.

Several hours later, Manuel was at the KGB office. An officer showed him about ten photos, and Manuel identified Andrey Dimitri's photo as he was instructed without hesitation.

Then Officer Levada shuffled the photos and added a few more. He asked Manuel to identify the shooter again.

This time, Manuel pointed to another photo.

"You're positive now; this is the man?"

"Yes, sir. I'm sure. I just got a little mixed up."

This time, Levada noticed that the man was extremely nervous. "Okay. That's all." the officer said. "If I need any more information, I'll get in touch with you."

Manuel walked out of the office with a quiet grin. Now, he had some money. First big money he had seen in a long time. Velasquez was a real sport.

Officer Levada searched for Andrey's file and the other person that Manuel had identified. The second man was in jail now. Then he found Andrey's file. At first, he thought he had found a gold mine. Andrey had accused Yakov of killing his brother in the streets of Lipetsk several years ago, but no charges were brought against him. He knew that Yakov had connections with a large mafia gang in Moscow. Velasquez was one of the important men. They had been fighting with a rival mafia over drug trafficking, brokers and customers. He had Andrey's address and decided to check him out.

But Velasquez's mob had the money. Levada licked his lips appreciatively. They would pay him to put the heat on their rivals.

Andrey had worked late that day at the newspaper office. Andrey had given him a couple of stories to write, and he had decided to stay at his desk to finish them. Efimov had recently praised his reporting. This was the first praise he had received since his university days. If he just kept out of trouble, Andrey thought, he was sure he would move up to a good position, maybe an editor.

But trouble was waiting for him outside the old building where he had rented a room. Just as Andrey got off the bus, he noticed the car, and he noticed the man following him into the building.

"What do you want?"

Levada showed his credentials. KGB officer. "Is this where you live? Then let's go upstairs and talk."

At that moment, Andrey felt the perspiration growing on his skin. He felt damp and cold as he led the way to his room. The evening was quiet and still with low clouds hanging over the city threatening an early snow.

"Where do you work?"

"I work at the *Novoye Uremya*. I'm a reporter. My editor is Nodar Efimov."

Levada was surprised. He knew that was a very good job. Andrey's answer took him somewhat off guard.

"I see. I understand that you were out to the air base at Chkalovo last Saturday." Levada watched Andrey's reaction carefully.

"Chkalovo? That's a long way from here. I don't have any business out there. I was staying with friends this weekend. Here, I can give you their names and addresses." As Andrey said these words, he stiffened so that he could answer the officer with force and determination.

"Okay, I'll check this out. If I need some more information, I'll connect you. Be assured of that!" Levada turned and walked down the hallway. Hell, he thought, this kid can't be connected with this killing way out at that air base. He's pretty settled down with this newspaper job. Besides, I can't make any money off of him. I'll contact Velasquez or one of the important men in the mob and tell him their rival mafia is responsible for the killing. Velasquez's group will pay me to put the heat on them. The fat jowls on his face moved with anticipation. He could taste the money already.

But Andrey didn't know that Levada was already counting the money and forgetting about his connection with Yakov. He went to bed thinking about the KGB officer and his relentless questioning. In his mind, he could see Levada's eyes sunken and cold above his fat, pock-marked face.

Andrey had to get to work early the next morning. As he entered the newspaper offices, he almost expected to see a KGB officer waiting for him. Instead, he noticed Andrey talking confidentially with some man. It was Pavel!

"What a surprise!" Andrey exclaimed."What are you doing here in Moscow?"

"I'll tell you about it. When do you get another break here?"

"In a couple of hours. Good. We'll go out then for some coffee."

Andrey left the office to go on an assignment. The photographer grabbed his camera gear and hurried after him.

"I've been worried about you, Pavel. I've been concerned about your safety. Have you heard anything more from Romanov?"

"Yes, unfortunately. About a week ago, just as I was entering my apartment building several guys grabbed me at gunpoint. Evidently, they work with Romanov because they mentioned his name and warned me not to play games with him. The man was dead serious, they said. I was told to get the money. They gave me ten days. One of them held a gun to my head as he talked! They had a car waiting out in front for them."

"These men are evidently working with some mafia group. I guess you have no choice now but to get out of the country!"

"That's right. I'm picking up my visa this afternoon. We've been selling off all we can."

"How much time do you have before the ten days are up?"

"About five days now. But, I don't think they'll do anything. They have to give me some time, and I hope by then, Natasha and I will be out of here!"

Around nine o'clock, Andrey returned to the newspaper office. Andrey had phone calls to make for a story that was on deadline, so Pavel and Andrey walked to a small coffee shop down the next block and found a quiet table in the corner.

"I read in the papers that Yakov was shot. What do you know about it?"

"Well, Andrey and I knew that Yakov was going to fly the material to Leipzig from the air base in Chkalovo. I think he told you that Alex planted a recorder in the basement of the hotel where the mafia leaders were meeting. We had all the information. The time, the place, everything. Yakov bribed a person at the base so that he could use the plane for the delivery. Andrey found an article about Yakov in the newspaper files. He was an aviator during the Afghanistan war, so that explains how he could get the plane."

Pavel was beginning to become impatient listening to all this round about information that he already knew. "Yes, I read the article that Andrey wrote in the newspaper. But that isn't what I'm asking you? Did you shoot Yakov?"

Andrey hesitated and looked carefully around the room. They were alone. "Yes, I shot the son of a bitch! I tried to hire someone, but they wanted too much money, so I decided to do it myself!"

"You what? Andrey, aren't you in enough—"

"Listen, Pavel. It was either me or him. It was just a matter of time before he got to me. I had to."

"Someone probably saw you. I doubt you can get away with this!"

"I have an alibi. Andrey followed me out to the air base and tried to stop me. Then we drove all night and stayed with some friends of his in the city."

Pavel shook his head. "Okay, but remember the KGB has a file on you, and they know that you accused Yakov of killing your brother."

"Yeah, I know. A KGB officer was over to see me the other day. I gave him my alibi. He seemed real impressed that I worked for the *Novoye Uremya*. He sort of walked away unconcerned, so I quit worrying about it."

"Let's hope so. You've got a good job. Work hard and stay out of trouble. Forget your grudges with the KGB, Andrey."

A short time later, Pavel said goodbye to Andrey and Andrey at the newspaper office. His last words to Andrey came back to haunt his mind. "Forget your grudges with the KGB." It was good advice, but he couldn't take the advice himself.

Before he left Moscow, he had the visa for the United States in his possession. He took the train back to Lipetsk. As he rested his head back on the seat, he remembered Natasha's words when they were flying back to Russia. She said she wished that they could just stay up there in the plane and keep flying forever. There, they were safe and free from trouble. Now, her words took on a special meaning. He almost wished that he could stay on this train and ride into infinity, ride on in safety. But, he wanted Natasha by his side. They needed each other. Somewhere, somehow, he had to find a way, he had to find the answers.

A few days later, Pavel received a phone call from one of the men who had grabbed him in the hallway. It was evening, and the family was sitting at the table. They could tell by the sound of Pavel's voice that it was not a friendly call.

"Do you have the money now? Remember what we said."

"I don't have the money yet. You know that my family is poor. You can kill me, but I don't have the money. Just give me some more time and—"

Pavel shook his head in despair. The man had hung up on him.

"Why are those men threatening you all the time?" Stepan asked. "What have you done, Papa?"

"You don't have to have done anything for the KGB to be after you, Stepan. Don't worry. I'll find a way out of this."

Valentin and Marina sat and ate their dinner in silence, but their eyes told Pavel that they were concerned and afraid for him. Stepan sensed the tension. He could tell that his Papa was in some kind of danger.

When they had finished eating, he decided to coax a story that would maybe make his Papa forget all the trouble and feel better. "Tell me the story of how the fisherman saved my Great-grandfather Stepan, Papa."

"Well, Grandfather Stepan said he found himself dying of hunger because he was very poor and had no money. He told me that he was lying on some tall grass on the bank by the river and had already prepared himself to die. He prayed to Jesus to give him some strength and give him some food because he didn't want to die. A fisherman appeared who had been catching fish on the bank of the river. He gave my grandfather a fishing rod and said, 'I know you are dying. Here's the rod. Now you go, and if you catch any fish you will live. It's up to you.' Stepan was half-dead at the time, so he sat there on the

251

bank and caught some fish. To my grandfather, the fisherman looked like Jesus. The man appeared to have a halo around his head. Maybe he was hallucinating, I don't know. But that's how he appeared to him. Then Stepan caught some fish, and they made a fire, and they ate the fish. They did that for some time, catching the fish and eating it. After eating the fish, my grandfather became stronger."

"That's a good story, Papa. I'm glad you named me my after my grandfather. He sure had a lot of courage."

"Yes, courage is very important. Always remember, Stepan to remain strong and determined."

"Like you, Papa."

But Pavel didn't answer. He gazed proudly at his son and thought how often Stepan probably needed courage when they were separated and how often he, himself, had called on all his strength and determination to get him through all the recent troubles. And he was still in the thick of it. Danger hung on him like a leach he had once seen, sucking the blood out of its victim.

During the next week, Pavel sold some more of his things. He told Natasha that they couldn't see each other until they went to Moscow to the airport. It wasn't safe for her.

During the next few days, Natasha was filled with terror. What would happen to her if Pavel couldn't get the money? And how could he get that kind of money?

The whole terrible thing had happened so fast. She remembered that she had just gone out for a short time to go to the store when they grabbed her and pulled her into their car.

"Get in here, you bitch. You shut up and do what we tell you!"

There were three men. One of them tied bands of cloth across her eyes so she couldn't tell where she was going, but it seemed as though they drove for a very long time.

When she got out of the car, she realized they had taken her to a house outside of Lipetsk. There were only a few rooms with just a bed for her to lie down on and probably a couple of cots for the men in some other room. She could see sacks of old garbage along the wall in the kitchen. Maggots crawled among the discarded food. The sink was filled with dirty dishes and cigarette butts.

The men told her that nothing would happen to her as long as her husband gave them the money. Later, they let her talk to Pavel.

"They have kidnaped me! I've been kidnaped, and they are holding me here in this house! Her voice was shaking and her words were hardly distinguishable as she spoke. "I'm so frightened, I'm so frightened. I don't know what they will do to me!"

Then one of the men got on the phone. "We've got your wife here. Now, you know we mean business! This time, you must get the money. If you don't get the money, we will kill her!"

Pavel was thoroughly shaken. He could hear Natasha crying uncontrollably. He never thought they would touch her, but evidently they had grabbed her and pushed her into a car near her parents' home.

They told him they would call back and make arrangements for them to meet and get the money.

Natasha hardly slept that night. It was very cold in the house. Sometimes, one of the men brought her some food, but she couldn't eat. She was too terrified to eat.

On the second day, Pavel talked to her on the phone. He told her not to worry and that he would get the money. She didn't know that he was filled with panic himself. He was beside himself with worry wondering and fearing what they would do to his wife. Would they rape her or beat and cripple her? He knew that these men were criminals and could not be trusted. Almost every hour he was on the phone desperately trying to get the money. He contacted all of his friends and Natasha's family for help. They knew the cruelty of the KGB and their recent mafia connections.

Natasha turned in fear on the bed and watched the early morning sun filtering through the stained window. This was the third day! What would happen? Would this be the last day of her life? Was this the way she was going to die—away from Pavel, away from her family?

She felt her heart beating faster and faster in her chest. From the next room, she could hear the men talking. Sometimes they were arguing and their voices became louder and louder. Natasha imagined that they were deciding what to do with her. How they would kill her and dump her body. Maybe they would tie her up and set the whole place on fire!

They didn't offer her any food that day. Then she heard them talking on the phone. One of them came into the room and told her to get up. He looked at her as she trembled with fear and showed no compassion. Suddenly, another man came into the room.

"Everything is settled. We will let you go, but do just as we tell you," he said with a sneer.

As they led her out to a car, one of the men put the bands across her eyes again. They drove for a long, long time. Finally, they stopped. She could hear voices. One of them was Pavel's!

There was some talk about the money. Evidently, they were satisfied, and a few minutes later, they took the bands off her eyes and opened the door. They told her to get out of the car. It was dark now. One man that she hadn't seen before gave the orders. Immediately, the car swung away from the curb and drove rapidly down the street. She had no idea where she was, but it didn't matter because Pavel was waiting for her!

"You don't know how wonderful it is, what a relief it is to see you and have you hold me!"

Pavel felt her trembling as he held her tightly in his arms. They wiped the tears from each others' cheeks. They stood there holding each other for a long time, not wanting to let go.

"I was so worried about you. The men told me they didn't touch you or hurt you. Is that right, Natasha?"

"Yes, that's true, but all the time I was there I didn't know what was going to happen to me. I knew you would do all you could to get my release, but I didn't how you could get that kind of money. I was so frightened, Pavel, so terribly frightened!"

"And so was I. All kinds of thoughts kept racing through my mind. Finally, I got the money together. My friends and family really worked hard to get the money. Everyone did what they could."

Pavel glanced up and down the street. He noticed a coffee shop. "Come on, let's get some hot soup and a cup of coffee. It will help you. You need to get something hot in your stomach."

They stayed in the small coffee shop for a long time. Natasha watched Pavel's eyes slowly moving across her face as though he were trying to memorize the shape of her eyes, the narrow lines of her nose and the softness of her cheeks.

My beautiful Natasha, Pavel thought. He never wanted to lose her!

"There's something we just have to face. I don't like it, but what else can we do? We must make plans to leave Russia. I have my visa now. Maybe your brother can take you to Moscow so you can get a visa for India. You said once that if it were necessary you could go to the Ashram in Bihar?"

"Yes. The Ashram is offering an extensive course in Yoga. I could continue to study and be out of sight of the KGB."

"It will be safe for you there."

"Who was the man who took the money? It seemed like he knew you. Something passed between you like a mutual hate and dislike. He wasn't one of the men at the house. Who was he?"

"His name is Romanov." Pavel let the name roll off his tongue like the bitterness of sour food. "He is the man that has called me many times on the phone. We've met at different places. Yes, he's the one who has been trying to extort the money from me."

After a while, they called Natasha's family to tell them of her release from the kidnappers. They were relieved and overjoyed. Her brother said he would come to take her home to her parents. Later, he said he would take Natasha to Moscow the first of the week to get her visa for India.

Pavel didn't want to upset Natasha with his feelings about Romanov that afternoon, but during the next few days, the feelings toward Romanov grew more and more intense. He was the one who had continually threatened him ever since their arrival back in Russia, and he was the one who arranged for Natasha to be kidnaped. And he would have been the one to tell the others to kill her if he couldn't get the money! What right did this evil man even have for existing? Now, he could begin to understand Andrey's feelings about Yakov. He could feel the desire for revenge growing within himself.

During the next week, Pavel planned to sell the remainder of his tapes and records that he had left at the disco. His friends at the disco sold some of their own tapes and records. His father sold his watch. This would pay for his plane ticket to the United States and a little money in his pocket. Natasha sold some jewelry and clothes that she had bought in India. Finally, she had enough money to buy a ticket for Calcutta, and she already had her visa.

Now, they were ready to leave, and it was important that they leave quickly. Pavel knew they couldn't take any more risks, and they didn't want to take any chances that their families would be hurt.

Pavel began to believe that maybe now they could think ahead to freedom, until suddenly one morning, he received a phone call from Romanov. He thought he would never have to hear his voice or see his face again.

"What do you want?" Pavel asked harshly.

"What do I want? What do you think I want? You took too much time before to raise the money, so now you have to pay some more. Five thousand dollars for taking up so much of my time. We will not hesitate to find you and kill you if you don't come up with the money. I'll give you ten days."

Pavel was so filled with anger that he wanted to find the man and kill him, but a sudden streak of caution warned him to say nothing to incite the man. He agreed to the money and left the phone.

Now, he was absolutely certain that they would have to make a run for it and get out of the country as fast as they could. He hurried down to the building of the former disco to pick up his money for the sale of the tapes.

At first, no one seemed to know anything about the sale, but then a familiar face emerged from an office. It was his old friend, Alex Dnieper who was the former sound manager at the disco and was now a plumber in Moscow.

"You didn't know that I was the one who bought your tapes? When I heard they were for sale, I decided I didn't want anyone else to have them. Too many memories. Right, Pavel?"

"There's no one else I'd want to have this collection, Alex! I'm surprised to see you here. I thought you worked in Moscow."

"Yes, I'm working as a plumber for a company. Not doing too badly, either. Say, I've got news for you! Andrey and Andrey are down here working on a story. Come on and have a beer with us!"

Pavel started to say he didn't have the time to talk and have a beer, but something he never could explain later seemed to pull him down the street, some force that wouldn't let go.

The bar was dimly lit, but he could make out the faces of Andrey and Andrey at a table near the back.

"What a surprise to see you both! So you are both here out of the big city to work on an assignment?"

"Exactly. The authorities have picked up a man who walked out of a Minatom lab in Moscow with some highly enriched uranium. Then, he and another man, his accomplice, I guess, packed the material into glass jars. One took the train to St. Petersburg and placed those jars into a refrigerator. He was caught trying to sell them on the black market to a businessman from St. Petersburg. The other man came here and has been detained in this city."

"Did he bring any of the uranium to Lipetsk?"

"We don't know. That's our job to find out. Andrey is with me to learn more about investigative procedures. And of course, to see his mother."

"Well, Natasha and I are getting ready to leave the country. We are so thankful to all our friends and family and to both of you for helping us get the money together for Natasha's release. It was a terrible ordeal. I was terrified that they would hurt her or kill her!"

"We know you were. And believe me, Pavel, we were sweating it out, too. No telling what those bastards would do!"

"And that's not all! I got a call from Romanov again!"

"Romanov! What the hell does he want?" Andrey asked in astonishment.

"He said I took too long to pay him the first time. Now, he wants five thousand dollars! There's no doubt about it. We've got to get out of the country before one of us is killed or our families are hurt!"

"You've been harassed and beaten by the KGB ever since you were going to the university! And Andrey, too, I guess?"

"Yes, ever since Yakov killed Ivan and told the KGB I was a spy."

At this point, Andrey rose from the table and explained he had a couple of phone calls to make and also had to check in with his paper.

Five minutes later he returned. "Stay, a few minutes more, Pavel. Tokaloff is coming over to wish you well before you leave."

"What did the office say back there?" Andrey asked.

"I found out that there is going to be a top-level meeting at the KGB office in Moscow the first of next week. The dirtiest dogs in the business will be there—Lomonosov, Zhukovsky, Selyunin, and Romanov! What they decide will be important news! They have been searching for ways to get more power!"

Pavel scowled, but Andrey's eyes lit up with excitement. "What an opportunity! All the rotten sons of bitches will be in one room!"

"What are you getting at?"

"You want to get rid of those bastards just like I do! This is an opportunity to stop their dirty business. We knock them off, and it will disrupt the whole KGB organization!"

The group leaned across the table and stared at Andrey. "How in hell are you going to do that? You certainly don't propose to go in there, a KGB office, and shoot them?" Andrey exclaimed.

"No. Hell, no!"

About this time, Tokaloff walked into the room. He listened as the conversation darted back and forth across the table.

"I have an idea," Alex began. "I heard a lot of the discussions that we taped of the mafia group. They talked about some of their other activities like the possibility of delivering bomb packages to their rival gang members."

"Why not set off a bomb in the building?" Andrey asked.

"It would be hard to do and difficult for the person to get away."

"What about a car bomb? They will probably all go in the car to the airport? What about that, Alex?"

Andrey waved his hand impatiently."Identify these men, Pavel."

"Lomonosov and Zhukovsky are high up in the KGB. They continually threatened and beat me when I refused to stop seeing those foreign nationals when I was going to the university. They came and searched my apartment repeatedly. Zal Tyunin was the KGB officer in India. He beat me and tried to force me to go to party meetings. And Romanov, the worst scum of all, acted on his own to extort money from me and ordered the men to kidnap Natasha!"

The rest in the group could see that Andrey and Pavel were eager to do something. "All right. So we settle on moving a bomb into the building. What group can we get to do the job?" Andrey asked.

"What about that political group that is strongly anti-communist?" Tokaloff proposed. "They call themselves, "Kurkovas," after their leader. They have organized and put on protests in Red Square."

"Good idea," Pavel said rising to go. "But, I think my time is running out. I've got to go. The day of that meeting, I will be in Moscow with Natasha. I have a ticket for the United States, and she will be leaving to hide out in an Ashram in India until I can send for her."

"I wish you could stay here and help support the democratic forces, like Grigory Yavlinsky's party. You aren't afraid to stand up and speak against the old communist society. Yavlinsky is an outstanding economist and is working on new economic plans," Andrey emphasized.

"Yes, I have heard Yavlinsky speak once at a meeting. Ideally, I would like to live in Russia and support the democratic movements. Now, because of all the threats from the mafia, I have no choice. I have to leave. It is too dangerous here for Natasha and me."

"You and Natasha will be safe in the United States. Every time you stood up and fought for your rights, there was trouble from the KGB. Same with me. Someday, it will be different," Andrey added with determination.

"A beer for all of us," Andrey ordered. "Here's to a safe trip and an end to all your troubles! And don't worry. We'll take care of the bastards if we have to kill them ourselves!"

But Pavel was not so sure. It would be difficult to organize this move in such a short time. Still, it was a prime opportunity, but on the other hand, a wrong choice, could bring certain death to all of them.

A week later on November 21, a small van slowly approached the delivery area of the KGB located in the dingy Lubyanka building in central Moscow. Inside, a high-level staff of KGB officers were meeting. Top on the agenda was how they could get more control. Most of them believed the market system was not working and wanted communism back. Then, they could regain the power they had in former years.

About twenty officers sat smoking at a long table in the conference room. They were totally oblivious to what was going on in the parking area below them.

Zal Tyunin began the meeting. "This was the way it was in India. We ran the party with an iron fist. And it worked, but then things started to weaken in Russia. About that time, the party began to lose its power."

"The party was strong in India, Yuri?" Romanov asked with interest.

"Yes, let me tell you about the Russian compounds that were built for the people that worked in the Indian steel plants. Here, the people strictly obeyed our rules. They weren't allowed to leave the compound without our permission. They were required to attend party meetings. We had committees that went to the different apartments to see what the people were reading and doing with their time. Yes, the rules were strictly enforced."

"And no one caused you any trouble?"

"Well, there was one or two, maybe." A light of recognition passed through his mind as he spoke. "There was this Pavel Lubov who opposed us in every way. We lectured to him and beat him. We finally got rid of him and sent him down to Bhilai to work."

Romanov leaned forward with interest. "Then what happened?"

"I understand that his contract was terminated. He got into some trouble here in Russia. Do you know him?"

"Well, his name sounds familiar," Romanov said with a sneer. "A real rebellious dog." As he said those words, an explosion rocked the section of the building where they were meeting. The walls started to cave in, and the ceiling fell down in huge pieces on the men at the table. Romanov rose quickly, stumbling over the debris, clutching his chest and throat as the blood spurted out between his hands.

A few miles away, Pavel and Natasha were spending their last evening together at the Ukraine Hotel in Moscow. It was November 20, 1994. The next morning, Pavel would be taking a plane that would take him across the globe to another country.

They spent their last evening talking and drinking vodka together in the hotel lounge. The walls of the long narrow room were of a rich, warm cherry wood that reflected the soft flames of the candles on the tables. It was late, and it was quiet. The last few customers had left about a half hour ago.

As the time passed, Natasha knew it was getting late and their time together was running out. But neither of them wanted to talk about leaving each other. It was a moment, a time together, that Natasha wanted to hold within herself and never let go.

They sipped vodka very slowly, leaning across the table and drawing the love they saw from each other's eyes into their own private world. It was here that they found love and comfort and a direction in their lives.

"I can't think what it will be like without you, Pavel. It will be so hard." She had promised not to cry.

"We both need to be very strong," Pavel said, looking very intense. "One day we will be looking back on all of this, and we will be far away then. It will be a place where we can be safe and together. Believe me, Natasha. I promise you."

Natasha looked down at the liquor shining in the prisms of the cut-glass and tried to etch his words into her mind. She smiled up at him, but her eyes were filled with tears. "I know. I trust you."

For the next few hours, they talked and tried to laugh at the little things they used to do together. The walks along the river near the university. Listening to Pavel's tapes and sometimes dancing at the disco. Somehow, all the memories wove together, blended and became one.

In the morning, they walked through the lobby of the hotel and were surprised to find a group of people watching television. They were exclaiming with excitement as they watched the terrifying news flashing before their eyes.

Pavel noticed a familiar figure standing at the end of the group and walked over to talk to him. It was Grigory Yavlinsky, the leader of the Yabloko party. He was obviously interested and pleased with the news.

"What's going on?" Pavel asked Yavlinsky.

"There was an explosion in the KGB building in Moscow! Many high-level KGB bosses were killed at the meeting!"

"How much of the building was destroyed?"

"Just a very small section. You probably can remember when a similar event happened just after the 1991 coup?"

"Yes, I was in India at the time, but I remember hearing that the crowds gathered in front of the building and toppled the statue of Feli Dzerzhinsky. Feli was known as "Iron Felix." He was the founder of the Bolshevik secret police which later evolved into the KGB." Pavel emphasized the last few words with obvious contempt.

"Well, my friend, you feel the same way I do about the KGB and the communist system. Because of the KGB, many dissidents were tortured and imprisoned. As you remember, they also established a network of labor camps where millions of people died."

They talked together for a few minutes, then Pavel hurried to find Natasha. As he told her the news, they fell into each other's arms.

"Just think, our friends were successful! Their plans worked! Their plans worked!"

Natasha started to cry and laugh at the same time. Excited and relieved, they reached for each other. They could hardly believe the reports as they were flashed on the television screen.

" This is the best news I've heard in a very long time, because in that room was the alpha and the omega of all the mental torture I have suffered for the last twelve years."

"Longer than that, Pavel. There were so many others. Think of what both your grandfathers suffered under the hands of the KGB and the communist authorities."

"Yes, I know; there were many others who were tortured and killed."

"Then does it mean no one will be looking for us anymore?"

"No. Romanov belonged to a mafia. The men that held the gun to my head and kidnaped you were part of this mafia. They are looking for me for more money. I am certain they would kidnap you again to force me to pay. They are dangerous criminals and will kill to get what they want."

Pavel glanced at his watch. It was time for them to go to the airport. They sat in silence in the taxi, just holding hands and quietly embracing, during the long drive to the airport. They were too filled with emotion to talk.

Two hours later, they had to say goodbye. It was the most difficult thing Pavel had ever had to do in his life. He could not bare to leave his beautiful Natasha. She was the real treasure of his life.

Somehow, they found the strength to turn away and walk to their separate and distant boarding areas in the vast hallways of the Moscow airport.

Natasha felt Pavel's last words encircling her as she walked away. "We will be together again very soon." But she also remembered the words that they told each other a few months ago. They would always be together. He would never let go of her. Now, they would be separated by miles of ocean, and all they had between them was a hope, a hope that someday they would find each other again.

Chapter 25

A few days later, the Andreys were sitting in a bar in Moscow congratulating each other on the success of the bombing on the KGB building. It was late. Soon, they could make out the features of Dmitri Kagarlitsky in the dimly lit bar as he moved slowly toward them. He was carrying a large mug of beer in his hands.

Andrey rose quickly and raised his beer mug to salute the man. "Here's to the great Kurkova Party! You did it, friend! You guys were the men of the hour!"

"The men that made history!" Andrey corrected.

"Well, we haven't taken credit for this, but it's widely rumored. You wanted those KGB bastards killed. And that's exactly what happened. Just like clockwork!" Dmitri started to laugh at the joke. "Yes, the bomb went off with the precise ticking of a clock. Exactly. When they were all together at the board meeting! Every damn last one of them!"

"I wish I could have seen their faces when the ceiling came down on the sons of bitches! Too bad Pavel couldn't be here to celebrate with us. How he hated those men who continually threatened him and his wife!" Andrey exclaimed.

At that moment, a very beautiful girl entered the bar with a tall, slender man dressed in the usual, heavy workman's clothes. They walked over to the table where the group was sitting.

Dmitri turned and greeted them warmly. "This is my sister, Karolina, and my brother, Eldar. Eldar was in on the plot from the ground up."

Andrey smiled at them both, but his eyes rested on the attractive young woman. She was very fair, with long blond hair and high cheek bones and talked excitedly about the success of the bombing. So she was also a member of the Kurkova Party! The more he saw of this party, the more he liked it. It suited his temperament. If a job needed to be done, get it done fast! Like he did with Yakov!

"What do you do for a living, Andrey?" Karolina asked after carefully listening to his conversation at the table.

"I'm a reporter for the *Novoye Uremya*. I'm just new at the job. But listen! Andrey, will soon be promoted to take an editor's place!"

Karolina seemed clearly impressed. "Where are you from? Your last name is Dimitri, but you look Italian." She pronounced the word, "Italian" very slowly.

"Well, you are right. I am part-Italian. I graduated from the University of Lipetsk and came up here to Moscow. I was lucky to get the job." He moved over next to Karolina as he spoke. They continued to talk until closing time, and the group began to move away from the table.

"Looks like you were really impressed with Karolina. She's beautiful, Andrey. Better make your move before someone else takes her away!" Andrey suggested.

The next day tips began to come into the Moscow newspaper office like the opening of flood gates. Editor Efimor was excited as he paced around the large office. Telephones were ringing, and the reporters were busy taking the calls and rapidly writing notes as fast as the news came over the wires.

As soon as Andrey entered the office, Efimor motioned to him. "We are beginning to get tips that a party, perhaps the Kurkova party, was responsible for the bombing of the Lubyanka building. See what you can find out about it, Andrey. This is a breaking story for you!"

"What happens if it turns out that the Kurkova party is responsible, and we expose them? What happens to them?"

"What?" Efimor exclaimed in disbelief. "What happens to them? Who gives a damn! We just cover the news. Remember that, Andrey!"

Andrey nodded and picked up his notebook, pretending to be busy working on the story. A few minutes later, he left the office, but instead of trying to get more information on the party, he headed for his apartment.

For the next half hour, he made many futile calls trying to reach Dmitri or Eldar, active members of the Kurkova party. Finally, he decided to try one more place and one more telephone number.

"What goes, Andrey? How come you're home and not working today?"

"I've got a problem here. My editor has given me the assignment to get more information on the Kurkova party and find out if they were responsible for the bombing. So what can I do?"

"What can you do? Are you trying to fool me? Remember what we did for you, friend! Don't double-cross us!"

"Don't worry. Don't worry. You can trust me. I'll figure a way out of this."

But Andrey wasn't so sure, and he was clearly worried as he walked back to the newspaper office. He decided to spend some time searching through the files and look for information on the background of the Kurkova party. He called Igor Popov, the important Yabloko Party member, to find out what he knew about this political group.

"They are a very pro-democracy party and sometimes become quite violent to get their viewpoints across. I think the Kurkova party tends to go more for action than words and actual proposals," Igor added.

"What is your party saying about the possibility that the Kurkova party was involved in the KGB bombing?"

"A real possibility. If they are involved, I think they might claim responsibility, but if they do, it would put them all in a very dangerous position."

"If you have any more info on them, send it on over, Igor."

"Will do, but I doubt it. Anyway, if they are responsible, they did us a favor by getting rid of those leeches!"

Andrey turned away from the phone and stared at the notes in front of him. Yes, the party did them a favor. A tremendous, life-threatening favor, but where did he go from here? It was this job that put him in this position. He couldn't do what he thought was right and still work here as a reporter. Andrey was resolved. He would have to quit his position here at the paper.

At the noon break, Andrey caught his friend just as he was returning from an assignment. "Come over to my place for lunch, Andrey. I've got to talk to you."

The minute they entered the apartment, Andrey turned and spoke with vehemence. "I'm going to quit my job. I've got to!"

"What! You can't do that! Why? Why do you have to quit your job?"

"Because I can't be a newspaper reporter and do what I think is right. My life away from the office is too involved. First, it was the Yakov story! Now, because of our desire to get even with the KGB for Pavel's sake, I'm in a stinking mess. I'm too involved with the Kurkova party to write about them!"

"Those were important causes, Andrey!"

"Yes, but a reporter isn't supposed to get personally involved."

"You couldn't help it!"

"Maybe not, but that's the way it is! I'm going back and quit my job!" Andrey exclaimed angrily.

Andrey was astounded. Andrey was not one to become angry. He was the one who was always so cool and collected.

"You can't quit your job. You know how much it means to you. We've got to figure a way out of this!"

"I already have! I'm quitting!" Maksim shouted as he dashed out the door.

No! No! Andrey thought in despair. He just can't do this. I've got to stop him.

He hurried after him into the newspaper office, but Maksim was ahead of him and already walking into Mr. Efimov's office.

"You want to see me about something, Maksim?"

"Yes, I have to tell you..." he began. Then the phone rang, and Efimov motioned to Maksim to wait a minute.

In that one, brief minute, a torrent of words flooded Maksim's mind. Words that he felt he had to say. To give up the job. Then suddenly, there were no words—just a blank space that began to fill with all the feelings he had for his work as a reporter. Soon, words began to fill his mind, like when he started to write a new story. They were always there, waiting for him to use and express on paper. Writing had become his life, his blood. How could he quit?

Efimov finished talking on the phone and turned to Maksim.

"Never mind. I figured out the answer to my question. Thanks anyway, Mister Efimov."

But Maksim knew he really didn't have the answer. He glanced at Andrey as he came out of the office and shook his head. He spent the afternoon making some more calls and inquiring about the activities of the Kurkova Party. Maybe he could figure a way out of this mess.

It was late in the afternoon when Andrey left work. He knew Maksim had not quit his job, but he didn't know what had happened in Mr. Efimov's office.

Maksim's apartment was just up the street. He had to find out. After all, his future was tied in with Maksim's, and they had become close friends.

"So what did you say to Efimov?" Andrey asked as he moved through the doorway. "I figure you didn't quit."

"I planned to quit. Then, the phone rang. While Efimov was talking on the phone, I realized I couldn't quit. My work means too much to me!"

"I didn't see how you could quit. It's in your blood. The words come for you like music comes to a composer."

"Oh, come now, Andrey!"

"That's the truth. You have the ability to write and write well. I'm more for going out and interviewing people—just getting the story and writing it up."

They were interrupted by a knock at the door. It was Dmitri! He was bleeding! The towel that he held next to his shoulder was filling with blood.

"You've been shot! What happened to you?"

"Well, Maksim, evidently, the bartender heard us talking the other evening. He told some of his friends about our party."

"What friends? Who are they?"

"His fellow members that were fighting in the streets to overcome Yeltsin during the '93 Coup."

Maksim and Andrey looked at each other in amazement. "What are you going to do?"

"I am not the leader of the party. But the leader and his committees have decided to take responsibility for the bombing. Here, take this. Here is the information on how the bombing was carried out. Take it and use it."

"What? Are you sure? You've got to be sure, Dmitri."

"Yes, I'm sure. We all plan to leave and stay in Bulgaria for a while, reorganize and come back with a new name, new ideas! Just promise me one thing!"

"Anything, anything, Dmitri, for all that you've done for us."

"Work on the story, but don't turn it in for two more days. We'll be gone by then. In fact, we're leaving tonight."

"All of you?" Andrey suddenly asked. "Even Karolina? Here, I was going to ask her out, but now…"

"No, she isn't going. Karolina's not really so involved with the party or the party meetings. Go ahead and call her."

"Wait a minute! You've got to take care of your shoulder."

"I'm on my way before I bleed all over your rug!"

"Remember, it is blood for Russia!"

"Yes, I am proud of the blood I have given. Many times. For a democratic Russia!" He turned and glared at the group as he raised his fist with determination.

Chapter 26

It was mid-January of 1995. Pavel had learned from his friend, Turgov, that Natasha had arrived safely in India. But that's all he knew and that was back in November. It was virtually impossible to make calls from the Ashram, so he constantly worried about her. He knew that she was in a dangerous position even in India. They had left Russia on the run from the mafia, who were threatening to kill them if he didn't come up with more money.

Now where was Natasha? Christmas had come and gone. And no word. He had spent New Years alone, tormented and worried. They had always exchanged presents at Christmas and enjoyed special celebrations at New Years together. What had happened? It was almost as though Natasha had died.

Died? Died? Pavel stirred in his sleep. Natasha's face appeared before him in the darkness of the room. The KGB had found her in India and arrested her! The room was filled with her screams. They were torturing her!

Pavel sat up in bed sweating and breathing very hard. It was three o'clock in the morning. He rubbed his head and tried to focus his eyes on the reality of the room. But there was no comfort here. The nightmare continued to stalk the room. Was Natasha trying to reach him? Was she crying out for help? He had seen her face so clearly. So terrified. So alone!

But what could he do? He called Turgov and begged him to find out what had happened to Natasha. He had to know. He just couldn't live anymore with these thoughts torturing his mind. Still, it would be difficult for Turgov to get information since Natasha was supposed to be staying quietly in the Ashram, trying to keep her identity a secret. The mafia would not think to look for her there. But perhaps, they had found her after all.

Several times, Pavel had called home to his parents and her family. Some men that Natasha's parents could not identify were continually coming to the apartment asking for Natasha or for her whereabouts.

They told the men that they didn't know where she was and that she hadn't told them where she was going. But she had probably left the country. This harassment caused the family constant worry. They believed that the men wanted to find and kidnap Natasha, threaten her and extort more money from Pavel.

Marina and Valentin's said that they had been receiving mail requiring their son to report for possible military duty, but Pavel knew that this was an attempt to force him to appear since he had already served, and none of these men had been called at this time. Sometimes, men came to their apartment asking for Pavel, but they refused to identify themselves.

Still, no one had heard from Natasha. It had been quiet. The men had stopped coming to the apartments. Did that mean they had arrested Natasha? What had happened to her? And Pavel could find no peace. He couldn't eat. He couldn't sleep. The nightmares had become so real. He was convinced that Natasha had been arrested and that she was being tortured. He could see her terrified face before him night and day, crying out to him to save her. Please save me, Pavel! Please save me! Oh my God, how he wanted to reach her and save her!

Through all this torment, Pavel was finally able to find a job, loading lumber in a builders' supply yard in San Francisco. He had located his friend, Sergey Dnieper, who had formerly worked at the disco in Lipetsk. Then, he rented a room and took up the long arduous task of trying to locate an immigration attorney in hopes that he could receive political asylum. The next step would be to try to get Natasha over to the United States. But through all the many weeks, he didn't know if she were still alive or if he would ever see her again.

When Natasha first arrived at the Ashram in Munger Biltar, India, she was filled with worry and concern for Pavel and her family. She felt so alone. At first she was relieved to get out of Russia and come to India. But now, she felt so desperate about her future. But what could she do?

She often cried and felt very miserable. Then slowly, the peace and the quiet of the Ashram began to fill her mind and quiet her body. People in the Ashram told her that a person's system becomes purified through the silence.

She was not supposed to talk during certain hours. Her teachers explained that when you talk you expand a lot of energy, so to keep that energy you must stay within yourself. You need to just keep silent. The quiet time was from four in the morning to seven or eight. You weren't supposed to talk during meals. Then you are quiet again in the evening. At this time you study and chant the mantra by yourself.

Natasha enrolled in a Yoga teacher training course at the Ashram, a part of the Bihar School of Yoga. Thirty people were enrolled in the Yoga Asana course, mainly from Europe and Australia. One of the subjects was Swara Yoga, the science of breathing. After this, she had a one-hour class, Yoga Nidrra that taught people how to relax. The teacher said that when you are between the conscious state of mind and in between sleep, your body is relaxing very deeply and your mind is not sleeping. When you are in this state, you receive rest, the best rest for your mind and body, so you actually become energized after this. It took Natasha a long time for her to learn to keep her mind focused and not drift away or fall asleep. But later, she realized that those courses of relaxation and meditation were the only things that kept her sane during the long weeks of separation from Pavel and her family back in Russia.

Still, Natasha didn't actually have the money yet to pay for the course. The course cost two hundred dollars. She had no money, so she went to talk to Swami Niranjanananda Saraswatai. He told her that she would not have to pay right away, so she tried not to worry about that.

During the next few months, Natasha met people from all over the world who had come to take different workshops. One older lady, Adele Muller, was especially kind to Natasha. She was from Germany and had come to take several yoga classes. Just recently, she had sold all the furniture in one room in her home and decided to start a yoga studio.

They confided in each other and became close friends. Natasha could speak some German, and she helped Inga with her English.

Several weeks after Inga left, Natasha received a letter in the mail from her. Inside, was a check for two hundred dollars. She knew the story about Natasha's flight from Russia and was aware that Natasha had no way of paying for her yoga courses.

Tears came to her eyes when she read the letter. Such wonderful kindness from someone she had known only a few weeks!

During the courses, the teachers didn't want the students to leave the Ashram or go to the city, so the gates were closed. But this did not work out for Natasha. She continually worried about Pavel and how he was doing so many miles away on the other side of the world. Would she ever see him again? Often at night, her pillow was wet with tears. Then, she would remember what usually brought her comfort and recite the "Om Shanti," ending with "May none be unhappy! Oh peace, peace, peace." This seemed to give her some measure of peace, but it didn't replace the longing within herself.

Once or twice, Natasha was able to leave, and she rushed to a place to try and call Pavel. She was sure she would be able to talk to him. First, she had to give a person at the desk some money. This was a very small business where people could make copies, send faxes or make calls. One of the managers would dial the number, and Natasha had to pay whether she reached her husband or not. That's the way the system worked. Today was the same situation. She talked to someone that was renting another room in the same house and asked him to give a message to Pavel. Maybe he would get the message. Maybe he wouldn't. So she turned away. There was one consolation. In two more weeks, her course at the Ashram would be over. Turgov had asked her to come and visit with him and his wife. He said he had a plan that he hoped would work for her.

Turgov lived in Delhi. He and his wife lived in a modest apartment, decorated with the warm, rich colors so typical of India. They greeted her warmly and offered some chai, a hot, spicy tea that she especially loved. How good it seemed to Natasha to be with friends and to be able to talk about her life and the experiences that she had been through recently in Russia.

"I have talked to Pavel quite a few times. He misses you terribly and constantly worries about your safety."

"What is he doing now? The last I heard he was trying to get a job."

"Yes, he is working in a building and supply yard. Certainly, not up to his education and capabilities, but I am sure things will work out better for him in the future. It will just take him some time."

"What should I do now, Turgov? If I go back to Russia, I will be going back to where the KGB can find me. I'm terrified of that!"

"I have a plan. I will take you to the American Embassy here in Delhi. You can say that you have been traveling with some friends here in India and now would like to get a tourist visa and visit the United States."

"Oh, do you think it will work?" Natasha was beginning to feel relieved.

"Let's hope so. We have to try, so we must arrive at the embassy early in the morning."

Natasha entered the American Embassy building with hopes that she would soon be able to join Pavel in the United States. But all she had were hopes. There was nothing else left—not encouragements, not assurances, not promises.

It was four o'clock in the morning. There were long lines of people already ahead of her. Turgov had given her twenty dollars for the application. She had to try, but she had been turned down at the embassy in Calcutta. They didn't give her any reason—just the application stamped in bold letters, "REFUSAL."

What would she do if she were refused again? Natasha tried to put these thoughts out of her mind, but they wouldn't go away. She had to have some kind of plan. It wasn't safe for her at her parents' apartment back in Russia. Time wouldn't wait for her to decide. Without notice, the KGB would undoubtedly be at the door with a warrant for her arrest or perhaps the extortionists would find her on the street when she was coming back from the store and drag her into their car like they did before. This time, there was no money left to pay them. Not from anyone. Their families and friends had sacrificed so much to help them before.

Two hours later, Natasha finally approached the window with her application.

"Well, you applied once already in Calcutta. You weren't supposed to apply again here, so we cannot give you the visa." Quickly, the clerk stamped the application, "DENIED," and Natasha turned away bitterly disappointed. There was nothing left for her to do, but return to Russia.

Her return flight ticket was from Calcutta. Turgov bought her a train ticket from Delhi to Calcutta. From there, she would fly to Moscow.

As the plane soared into the sky, Natasha remembered how, a little over a year ago when she and Pavel had flown from India to

Russia, they had promised each other to always be close together. But still, they had felt that they were like cattle going back to be slaughtered. The feeling never left them. They had been on the run from Russia to India to Australia to India and back to Russia again. Then, Pavel had been threatened by Romanov and the extortionists, and she had been kidnaped. It was the fear. It was always the fear.

Here, above the clouds, Natasha felt safe. All the danger was below. Down below, people were acting out their aggression, their hatred and their violence. She couldn't sleep because she knew that soon the plane would land in Moscow, and once again, she would be part of the turmoil and the danger in her life.

Hours later, her brother, Andrus, greeted her at the airport. She was glad that he didn't say anything to her about how thin she was or how much the strain of worry showed in her face.

It was good to get back. Her parents were overjoyed to see her.

"I know you feel bad that you couldn't get a tourist visa, but it's so good to have you home with us, if even for a little while," Marla said, embracing her daughter. She knew that Natasha was very anxious to leave the country to join Pavel. But the future did not seem hopeful for them.

Natasha went over to the window. It was dark now, and she could see only a few people walking on the streets.

"You say people have come here asking for me, Papa?"

"Yes, and I don't mean the friends that you know. Since we don't have a phone, I have described their appearance to Pavel's parents. They talked to Pavel, but he doesn't recognize the men from my description," Zal emphasized.

"Have men been coming to Valentin's and Marina's place, too?"

"Yes. And a policeman once and..."

He was stopped by a loud knocking at the door.

"Hurry, hurry! Go and hide!" Marla whispered and quickly pushed Natasha toward the closet in the bedroom.

A tall man stood in the doorway. "I am looking for your daughter, Natasha," he said in a loud voice. "I want you to tell me her whereabouts. Where is she working now?"

"I've told the authorities many times that we don't know where she is now. I believe she has left the country."

"Is that so? Well, we are keeping a watch on your building. Maybe Pavel will show up here. Let me tell you, we are losing our patience!"

There was another man waiting in the hallway, and they left together.

Natasha came out from the bedroom. She could see the fear in her parent's faces. "I'm so sorry for all of this. It must have been terrible for you!"

"It has not been easy. We live in fear. It starts up again every time one of them comes knocking at the door."

"What am I going to do, Mama? I can't live in hiding in the bedroom."

"No, we've got to think what to do. Let's decide in the morning after you get some rest." Marla and Zal talked long into the night about their daughter.

"I have an idea, Marla. I think she would be safe with my mother in Butyrki. What do you think?"

"That's a good idea. Butyrki is about thirty miles south of here. It is a very tiny village. They wouldn't think of looking for her there."

"I'm sure she can ask one of her friends to drive her down there. If they see her on the streets around here, they could kidnap her again like they did before."

Late the next afternoon after her mother returned from teaching in the kindergarten, Natasha embraced her parents and her brother. She didn't know when she would see them again.

Her grandmother's house was back down a short dirt road from the main street of Butyrki. Dianna was about eighty years old, but very active.

"What a nice surprise to see you, Natasha! Come and sit down. I'll make you some hot tea right away."

Natasha smiled to see her grandmother so well and keeping busy. She had not seen her in over a year, but she seemed the same as always.

"As you've probably heard from Papa, some authorities are looking for me. If someone should come here asking about me, tell them you haven't seen me in over a year."

"Don't worry, child. Everything will be all right. We are so far away from the cities here. You will be safe."

Several weeks passed. Natasha had been content to stay with her grandmother, hidden away from the glances of the villagers or the danger that lurked in Lipetsk. Still, there was little to do to keep busy.

She couldn't work or then the authorities would find out that she was back. Then, all the anxieties of the day seemed to flood and overpower her at night. She cried softly in the darkness of her room, often, almost giving up hope. Sometimes, she thought that this would be the end of her life, just existing in seclusion away from people.

Then one day, a car pulled up in front of the house. Natasha ran and hid in the shed behind the house. After a while, the door opened. and revealed a very frightened young girl trying to hide her face from the men who were standing in front of her.

In a minute, her face broke into a wide smile. She flung her arms around the young men. They were Andrey Dimitri and Maksim Romano!

"Do you remember me? I used to live down the hall from Pavel's parents."

"Sure, I remember you. You're Andrey. I heard that you both are working for the *Novoye Uremya*, a newspaper in Moscow. That's a fine position!"

Andrey grinned and glanced at Maksim. "I know you are staying here out of sight, but Pavel called Andrey last evening. He has been calling everywhere looking for you. Your parents don't have a phone."

"You could go to Marina's and Valentin's apartment tonight. Pavel said he would call there early in the morning, our time. Andrey and I have a story to cover in Lipetsk, so we can get away this afternoon."

Natasha agreed. Just to be able to talk to Pavel would be worth any risk.

An hour later, they arrived in Lipetsk. It was early afternoon. Andrey promised to call in the morning after she had talked to Pavel. "Let me know if there is anything I can do," he had said.

Marina was expecting her daughter-in-law and embraced her warmly.

"Look, I have bought some fine sausage for us at the store."

But Natasha did not feel hungry. All she could think about was the phone call from Pavel.

"Oh, come and eat something, Natasha. Here, I have some home-made wine that my neighbor brought over. I'll tell you what I'll do! I'll share the last with you! It will make you feel better," Valentin coaxed.

But Natasha only smiled and ate a little bread and vegetables. That night she decided to sleep on the couch near the phone.

When the call came through, it was early morning. Her hands shook as she lifted the receiver. "Oh, Pavel, is it really you?"

"My God, how wonderful to hear your voice! Papa says you are staying with your grandmother in Butyrki."

"That's right. I've been there for several weeks now. But Pavel, I'm so lonely. I have to keep out of sight. I can't work or anything."

"I know it's hard for you. But soon it will be all over. Believe me! I want you go to the US Embassy in Moscow and apply for a tourist visa. I'm trying to get political asylum, but it will take some time."

As they talked, a warm feeling began to sweep over Natasha. The weeks of anxiety seemed to pass from her body. Perhaps, there was hope again with the visa. Then, she would be free to leave Russia.

Andrus drove her to Moscow to the American embassy. Again, the news was bad. The embassy refused to give her a visa, so she went back to Butyrki, completely crushed and disillusioned.

It seemed as though each night she went to bed feeling like all hope was gone; then, she would wake up and decide to start all over again. Finally, a friend who had connections with different tourist agencies said she might be able to help. They decided that Natasha could apply through these agencies and get a tourist visa. Again, she was hopeful.

Four months had passed since Pavel had left Russia. Whenever he talked to Natasha, he felt somewhat relieved. He was relieved that she was safe. In between times, he felt that he was going crazy. There were times when he couldn't reach her. There was no phone in her parents' home or in the village where she stayed with her grandmother. He would call one friend, then another. Some would say they didn't know where she was, and the anxiety would start building up within himself all over again. Maybe she had been picked up. Or the extortionists were back planning to kill her for more money.

If he did get the political asylum, Pavel planned then to apply for Natasha. So far, she had not been successful in getting a tourist visa from any of the agencies. Finally, a lady, who was a friend of Sergey Dnieper's, said she would try and get Natasha a Mexican visa and could go to a university in that country. She met with some university official, and then, the university made some inquiries in Moscow at the Mexican Embassy. Again, nothing seemed to work for Natasha. People told her to hope. Hope and hope. But there was no hope. The world was crashing all around them.

Chapter 27

Maksim was relaxing on the couch in the living room when he heard a knock at the door. He could hear Andrey's voice calling out to him.

"Come in. Come on in. Say, what do you have in that bag?"

"Some vodka, Maksim. Vodka!"

"Whom did you steal that from?"

"Me steal? I'm clean, man. Clean."

"The bottle's only half full!"

"What do you expect? A big bottle and a linen napkin? Igor gave it to me."

"Who's Igor?"

"Karolina's brother. She has two brothers. I helped Igor get some advertising at a reduced rate in the newspaper."

"How are you getting along with Karolina? Does she seem to agree with the other radicals in the Kurkova party?"

"Karolina is a fine girl. But remember, don't knock the party. That party is the one that blew up those KGB bastards!"

"Yes, I know, but I don't go along with their encouraging people to protest and set themselves on fire."

"Okay, but Karolina tells me that the members of the party are long gone from here. The Kurkova party is no more. Still, they claim they will come back again with a new name, for a new Russia."

Maksim had been watching television. A face flashed on the screen. It was the face of Zadislof Listyev. He was casually dressed and wearing gaudy suspenders and no jacket, quite similar to CNN's network host Larry King.

"Have you seen this show, Andrey? This is the *Chas Pik* show. It is supposed to be like the Larry King Show that people watch in the US. He interviews different people."

"Well, I've got no money for a television set!"

"No money or time, huh, since you have Karolina? Have you gone from part-time to full time with her?"

"Jealous aren't you? About time you found yourself a woman and quit sitting around here by yourself!"

Andrey ignored his remark. "Sit and watch this guy awhile. He's fantastic! He was one of the former co-hosts of the *Vzglyad* before it was banned for a while in 1990. Then, he went off to start a game show and later an audience-participation show. Recently, he's become very active in television advertising."

"Yeah, that guy must be loaded with money. And he did it on his own. He gets big, big money for the advertising slots. But have a drink before I go. I'm meeting Karolina at a disco tonight."

A half hour later, Andrey was just entering the disco when Karolina entered the room. Every time I see her, she seems more beautiful, Andrey thought. She would be beautiful to hold in his arms.

"Look what your brother, Igor, gave me, Karolina. Some vodka!"

"It's over half empty!"

"Well, I shared some with Maksim before I got here."

"Igor is busy working on a deal now. You remember, last November, Yeltsin decided to issue a decree that changed Ostankino into a semi-private holding company called ORT."

"Ostankino? Isn't that the largest state-controlled channel?"

"Right. The state held on to about half the shares and then sold the rest to a consortium—I don't know all their names. Then, the consortium hired Listyev to be the general producer of ORT."

"You mean, Zadislof Listyev? I watched him on television just a while ago. That guy is loaded with money!"

"My brother says he is a channel for new ideas for Russians."

"A channel for new ideas? He sounds like Maksim. Andrey has a real way with words. But enough of words, let's have a drink and dance." Andrey loved to dance with Karolina. She felt so good close to him.

An hour later, the bottle was empty and some of the people started to leave the disco. But he didn't want to leave Karolina. Not now.

"You've never seen my room, Karolina. Come! It's not far from here. I'll show you my trophy that was awarded to me for winning the university speech contest!"

"So this is what a young reporter's loft looks like!" Karolina exclaimed as she entered Andrey's room. "But you should have some large soft pillows on the couch or your bed. Maybe some brighter colors!"

"I need a woman's touch," he said drawing her close to him. He reached down into her sweater to feel the softness of her breasts. Slowly, he pushed the sweater up and unfastened her bra and began to lick her pointed nipples.

"You are too much for me, my Italian lover."

"Then come to bed with me, and I'll show you what I have for you!"

She unfastened her long blond hair and let it fall across her breasts.

Andrey slowly parted the hair and began to kiss her neck and the softness between her breasts. He felt her quiver and sigh as he licked her nipples again.

"I want you, Karolina. You're so beautiful!" He reached down and touched the warm place between her legs. It was moist, and he knew she was ready for him.

They slept in each other's arms until early the next morning. Neither wanted to move, but Karolina had to go to work at the beauty shop, and Andrey had an assignment that was due by four o'clock that afternoon.

The next time he saw Karolina, she was just finishing up at the shop. Andrey hadn't been able to get her out of his mind. He seemed to see her at every corner. Every time he turned on some music in his room at night, he would see her face, her beautiful face looking for him, smiling at him.

Today, he thought he might catch her before she left the shop. Her brother, Igor, had dropped by to see her.

"Where are you going?" Andrey called.

"Over to the bar down the street. Come on and join us. This is a new place."

Andrey was amazed to see such a beautiful bar. Large soft, colorful prints in gold frames hung on the walls. There was a huge long, ornate mirror over the bar. At one end of the room, there was a polished black grand piano with a circular bar around it. Quite a few people were sitting around the piano on stools and drinking beer. They were very well-dressed.

As they entered the bar, Andrey glanced down at the clothes he was wearing. Karolina caught the look.

"Don't worry about what you are wearing. We know the person that owns this bar. Besides it's early yet. Not really time to dress for evening."

"Not time to dress for evening." The words startled and penetrated Andrey's mind with a jolt. Did people really change their clothes for the evening? he wondered. He considered himself lucky just to have a few changes of clothes, let alone more clothes just for the evening. Must keep them busy changing all the time. What a different life!

"These people are wealthy, Andrey," Karolina whispered.

"I didn't realize that there were so many wealthy people in Moscow! I thought the only people that made money were those connected with the mafia."

At the word, "mafia," Karolina gave him a direct hard glance. "Not at all. That's the reporter side of you coming out. The person that owns this bar started up this business on his own."

Andrey noticed a tall, slender man approaching their table. Igor and Karolina greeted him warmly. His name was Geidar Fedotov. He was obviously the owner of the bar since many people spoke to him as he walked through the room.

"What do you think of Listyev's declaration of a moratorium on all the advertising for ORT for five months? Or maybe longer? That is costing a lot of people big money!" Igor exclaimed, leaning across the table.

"He claims he has to do this in order to straighten out the mess and corruption—a lot of illegal funds," Geidar said with a smirk.

"Is that so? By the time he gets done moving things around, we'll all be closing our businesses."

"Say, by the way, Igor, are you going ahead with your Mexican project?"

Igor started to answer then glanced with a worried frown at Andrey."Maybe we should go into your office and talk. This guy is a reporter!"

"And he's your sister's boyfriend?"

"Oh, you two stop this! Andrey is completely trustworthy. He's a new reporter and just does local news. Isn't that right, honey?" Karolina pursed her lips and rolled her eyes up at Andrey for approval.

"Well, he won't get any story off of this one. Someone connected with the large Gazda bank will pay me to go to Mexico and buy some soap operas. Then, I will give them to Ostankino with the understanding that only my client's advertising will be used."

"And how much do you expect to make on this deal, Igor?"

"The soap opera serials will cost me maybe ten thousand dollars, but listen to this. The commercials will bring in close to thirty thousand dollars a minute!"

"Just as long as Listyev doesn't close the pipeline. He's making a lot of enemies. People feel they don't want to wait for him to shuffle funds around. Opportunities that are here today may not be here tomorrow."

"I think Vlad Listyev is too smart a businessman to make big mistakes."

"I don't know about that! A lot of people are against him. They are hungry for money, and they want it now!"

Andrey noticed the warning in Geidar's voice and the dark determination in his eyes. He felt that something deep and ominous was taking place here in the conversation.

"When do you leave for Mexico?"

"Day after tomorrow. Then, I return the next day. The arrangements have already been made."

"Good. I'll see to it that nothing happens here until you get your money."

Again, Andrey could see the look of a dangerous agreement taking place behind the words. But his thoughts turned away from the discussion when Karolina moved over and whispered into his ear. "Let's say we have to leave and go over to your place."

Andrey was eager to make love to Karolina. It had been over a week now. They made excuses and left.

"Is your brother really flying to Mexico?" Andrey asked as they left the bar.

"Maybe he will. But maybe it won't work out. Don't worry about it, sweetheart." She moved closer to him and gave him a slow, sensuous kiss.

Her kiss and closeness moved Andrey, and soon all he cared about was getting in bed with Karolina.

Early the next evening, Maksim invited Dimitri to come over and eat some spaghetti with him. He had been back to Lipetsk the previous weekend, and his mother had given him some leftovers to take home.

"Say, I noticed that you've been coming in to work kind of tousled lately. Somebody keeping you up at night?" Maksim said with a grin.

"That Karolina is some babe! She looks even better with her clothes off, and that's saying something, the way she fills out her sweaters!"

"Looks like you got it real bad, Andrey." He reached over and turned on the television. Vlad Listyev's show was on. "Watch him, he's really good."

"I understand that a consortium hired Listyev to be the general producer of this holding company that's called ORT. Then he stopped all the advertising until he could straighten out all the funds. That has angered a lot of people."

"Where did you get all this from?"

"Karolina and her brother, Igor, invited me to go to this new bar where all the wealthy people go. Oleg was talking to the owner of the bar. He claimed that Vlad is making a lot of enemies. Oleg represents someone connected with the Gazda Bank and plans to go to Mexico, buy some soap serials, and give them to Ostankino on the condition that all the advertising will go to this man. Geidar promised that he would hold off on any movements until Oleg got back and received his money for the soaps."

"That sounds like some dirty business going on! Then what happened?"

Andrey stopped and suddenly realized what had happened. "Karolina suggested that we make excuses to leave and go up to my room to be alone."

"She got you out of the way so the men could talk and make plans. I hope you don't get caught up in some dirty business. You don't need that. I advise you to be careful when you are with Karolina. She might be involved with some criminal activities!"

"Karolina! I can't believe it!"

"If her brother is involved, she's also involved in some way. Just watch it! She could be dangerous!"

A week later, Karolina and Andrey were together again. He had long since put Maksim's warning out of his mind.

"What do you think, honey, Oleg is back from Mexico and made a lot of money off those soaps. Would you like to go with us to Mexico on another trip?"

"Why, I can't do that Karolina. I have my job with the newspaper."

"The job we have for you would bring in a lot, lot more money," she teased, then she began moving her tongue around in his mouth.

A warning began to sound in Andrey's mind. He could sense that something was wrong, and this time it wasn't Karolina's seductive perfume, but the lurking danger behind her words.

He decided to act as though he were considering the idea, but in the mean time to try and figure out how to avoid any trouble. The fact was that he wanted Karolina, wanted to be with her, but he was concerned about some of her brother's friends. Still, there might not be any significance to their activities other than just to make the money like a lot of other Russians.

The next evening while Andrey was eating a late night snack, he heard Maksim's voice shouting to him outside the door.

"Come on, Andrey. Hurry! I just got a call from the newspaper to come quickly to the office. Let's see what's going on!"

When they walked into the office, they found that the place seemed to be on fire with reporters making telephone calls and then dashing out into the street. Maksim stopped to talk with one of the reporters.

"What has happened, Maksim?"

He had difficulty getting the words out. "The reports are just coming in that Zadislof Listyev was shot by two unknown gunmen as he returned home this evening around nine!"

"Shot! I can't believe it. What else is in the report?"

"He was shot twice, once in the head and once between the shoulder blades in the stairwell of his apartment building. Let's go over there and get more information Andrey." Maksim called to a photographer to go with them.

They hurried over to the apartment building on Novokuznetskaya Street which was rapidly filling with squad cars and ambulances.

The photographer took several photos of Listyev as he lay sprawled across the concrete steps. Then, he dashed back to the newspaper office with the film.

Maksim questioned several police officers. He was told that the murder, most likely, was carried out by professional hit men who used silencer-equipped Browning 7.65-mm pistols. Then they drove off in a late-model BMW sedan.

Hundreds of people brought flowers and placed them at the Ostankino Broadcast complex. Later, people laid a carpet of red carnations in the courtyard outside Listyev's apartment building.

That evening, the news of Listyev's death was shown on television to millions of people across Russia. The atmosphere was one similar to the grief of the passing of a beloved king.

The next day, March 2, all the state-run and private TV outlets suspended all regular programming. All day, they showed only Listyev's photograph or current reports. At seven that evening, the television channels ran a two-hour program, similar to a memorial service. Everyone knew this man and had seen his programs. He had been admired and revered. His closest friends and colleagues spoke about this man whom they admired so much. Many expressed outrage at the government's failure to control the rising crime in the cities.

Maksim heard that Yeltsin was going to speak at a memorial service in the main auditorium at the broadcasting compound. Maksim and Andrey decided to head out over to the building to cover the story.

The auditorium was packed with Listyev's colleagues. Yeltsin told the gathering that he had fired Moscow's prosecutor general and chief of police because they had not worked efficiently in the war against crime. At the close of his speech, he stopped before a huge video image of Listyev onstage and bowed his head.

When Maksim returned to the office with the report, he asked Efimov for permission to write a piece that would reflect his thinking on the murder. It would be his first attempt at an article that would state his personal viewpoints. At first, Efimov was reluctant, but then changed his mind. The man was clearly a valuable asset to the paper and had a unique way of expressing his opinions.

As the days passed, Andrey became more and more concerned about Karolina's insistence that he quit his job and go to work for her brother and his friends. They had offered him a lot of money and for a young man that sounded pretty good. He decided to go over to Maksim's and get his opinion.

"How is the article going?" Andrey asked as he looked over at Maksim's desk.

"It was a little slow at first, but now it's really picking up. What's on your mind? How are you getting along with Karolina?"

"That's the whole trouble! She and her brother. They want me to quit my job with the paper and work with Oleg and his connections."

"I'd say that's pretty risky from what you were saying about Oleg's friend who said that he would hold off making any move until Oleg got back from Mexico. And also, some of the other things you said about Oleg's connections."

"What people do you think are responsible for Listyev's murder?"

"It seems as though no one knows anything. But I don't believe it! It all started when Listyev banned the advertising from Ostankino's programs. He claimed it was necessary because there was a lot of skimming from ad revenues reportedly worth about ten million each month."

"Well, the motive is there. But who is responsible?"

"Someone or some men who crossed his path and are getting rich on commercial ads on television. It could well be two men who have a huge vested interest in ORT, like Andrey Levada and Boris Bocharov!"

"And all they had to do was hire a hit man?"

"That's right."

"Are you going to write that in your article?"

"Something like that. Just enough to heat the pants of some of them."

Maksim was worried that the article could cause a lot of trouble, but he figured if Efimov had given the "go ahead" it would be okay.

A week later, Maksim's article was published in the *Novoye Uremya*. The reaction was tremendous. Some words were quoted on national television. It stirred a great deal of controversy. Efimov had not expected such a reaction to the article. First off, it was good publicity for the paper, but then because Maksim had criticized some of the vested interests in ORT, there could be real trouble. He decided to ask Maksim to write another article, suggesting another opinion of the reason for Listyev's murder.

Maksim decided to give it a try and took the work home with him. It was very late when he finally started writing at his desk. He knew he wanted to bring into the article that if Listyev could be killed, so could anyone else. Who was safe? Now Russia had a homicide rate of twenty-two deaths for every one hundred thousand people, one of the highest rates in the world. It was rumored that Listyev feared that he would be assassinated. Now, it was true.

The words began to flow on the page, tumbling over each other to be expressed. Maksim was thankful he had this gift. Writing was in his blood. He wrote because he had to. He loved the moments when he was alone and could write what was on his mind.

Suddenly, there was a loud banging at the door and some splintered wood fell into the room. Maksim jumped to his feet. He was terrified at the sight of a masked man holding a gun directly pointed at his head!

In one quick moment, the man fired the gun at Andrey, once between the shoulder blades and once in the head. As he lay sprawled across the floor, blood poured from his head and circled his body. The man kicked him to one side as he fled from the room. The contract was completed. The job was done.

The next day the office of the *Novoye Uremya* was busy but solemn. Grief was etched on the faces of all the reporters who knew Maksim.

When Andrey entered the newsroom that morning, he wondered why no one spoke to him. They turned away with sorrow because they knew that Maksim was Andrey's best friend. Maksim had always called Andrey "his buddy" because of the difference in their age.

Efimov motioned for Andrey to enter his office. "You probably haven't heard about Maksim?"

Andrey stared at Efimov. He felt a sharp coldness moving through his body. Suddenly, he started to shake with fear for what might have happened to Maksim. "No-no."

"This is going to be hard for you. He was shot in his apartment last night. We are sure it was a contract shooting. Shot in the same places as Listyev—once in the shoulder and once in the head. There was no hope for him when the neighbors came to his place." Efimov waited a moment, then added, "I'm sorry."

For a few minutes, Andrey was caught off balance, Then, all he saw through his tears was the darkness moving around the room and Efimov trying to find ways to console him.

"Maybe I should quit the newspaper business," he said shaking his head despondently.

"You're afraid that the same thing could happen to you?"

"No, because I could never take Maksim's place or maybe continue on without him. He was so gifted with words. I admired him."

"You have a future here, son. Come and sit down. I can understand your grief, but I'm sure Maksim would want you to continue here. I believe he was killed because of the article he wrote about the ORT holding company. Perhaps we should have been more cautious? What do you think?"

"I'm not afraid to stand up for what I believe. No matter what. I've done it before, and I'll do it again!" Andrey didn't want to explain. There was Yakov and Yakov's friend. And he would do it again, if he had to.

"Good! That's good. We need a man with conviction. How would you like to finish the article that Maksim was writing at the time he was killed?"

"Me? How could I touch it? I couldn't begin to write like Maksim!"

"I'm not so sure about that. Do it for your friend, and I believe the words will come for you."

Andrey took the papers home with him. At first, all he could do was stare at the hand-written pages. Then, he felt a strong light moving across his shoulders. Soon, the words started to come to him. Slowly, then very quickly. He could hardly keep up. When he had finished, he knew the article was good, but he knew that he couldn't have done the writing by himself. He had been guided. Still, the words were not Maksim's. They were his own. From that time on, he vowed that he would never again doubt his ability to write.

The newspapers and magazines around the world carried the story of Listyev's assassination. It was a shocking example of what was happening in the streets of Russia. Contract killings were common. People were being killed and robbed of their purses or some jewelry, just for a little money.

After Pavel heard about the assignation of Listyev, he wondered if anyone was safe anywhere. And he was concerned about Natasha's safety. All these worries kept building up in his mind until he thought he was becoming paranoid. Then, he would talk to Natasha again and would feel somewhat relieved. Still, he continually warned her not to spend any time on the streets.

But this was difficult for Natasha. It was so terrible for her to be away from people. She felt locked up in the tiny village of Butyrki, and she knew Pavel felt in prison in the US because neither of them could see each other. Still, her friends would often come for her and then she could visit with them and see her parents in Lipetsk.

Once, Natasha decided to go to the store. It had been so long since she had been in any shop. As she walked home, she passed a man standing by a car. Suddenly, she felt frozen with fear because of the way he looked at her. Maybe he was one of the men who had kidnaped her. He looked like one of them. She was terrified and started to walk very fast.

Her mother happened to glance out of the window and saw her daughter hurrying down the street. Something terribly was the matter. Was there another man following her?

Marla ran to the door. "Come in, come in. Hurry! Is someone following you?"

"I think so, Mama. I'm not sure."

"You will never be sure until you get out of Russia. And yet I don't want you to leave. It's so hard without you!"

Suddenly, there was a loud knock and a man's voice calling through the door. Natasha shook with fright. What should she do? She had to escape somehow. It was probably the KGB and would search every room in the apartment.

Then Marla recognized the voice. She opened the door. It was Andrey! But she could tell by the look on his face that it was bad news.

"Maksim was murdered in his apartment! We think it was a contract killing. He died with the same bullet wounds as Listyev. He was shot in the same places! You must get out of Lipetsk, Natasha. It's not safe on the streets here, especially with the mafia members looking for you. One day they will find you!"

Chapter 28

Andrey found it difficult to come to the newspaper office and not see Maksim working at his desk. He used to ask him for advice on writing his articles and often went out with him to cover a story. Maksim helped him learn "the ropes" of newspaper reporting. Now, he was mostly busy covering the stories of crime that were occurring almost daily in the streets.

A month had passed since he had last seen Karolina. For his hot-blooded nature, it had seemed like a lifetime. To his knowledge, she didn't have a phone. Sometimes, he would drop by the shop where she worked. Lately, there were more stories, more news that continually kept flooding into the newspaper office. Still, he didn't want to argue with her when she kept insisting that he quit his job. After all, he wasn't in a position where he had to support her, but still, Karolina couldn't seem to understand why he wouldn't change jobs and work for her brother since he would be making so much more money.

Late one afternoon, Andrey decided to see if Karolina was at the shop. He wanted to go with her over to a bar and have some beers and then walk over to his room. How he missed her sensuous body! Sometimes, he asked himself if that was all she meant to him. Maybe so, but he just couldn't seem to keep away from her. Something like a box of candy. The more you ate, the more you wanted.

A beauty operator at the shop told him that Karolina had already finished working and left about fifteen minutes ago. Well, he decided to stop by the fancy bar that she often went to after work. The bartender recognized him. He promised to give Karolina the message that Andrey was looking for her.

It was an hour later when he heard Karolina's voice just outside his door.

"You got my message?"

She moved closer to him and reached for his lips. "Yes, I've missed you terribly. What have you been doing?"

"More work. It's kept me pretty busy, I'll tell you."

"Too much, Andrey. You don't even have time for me!"

"Well, let's make up for lost time!" He took her hand and led her toward the large bed that was framed with big, colorful pillows. Karolina had helped him select them at a flea market. This bed was his prize position because, he reasoned, it brought him so much pleasure.

Suddenly she drew back and asked defiantly, "Are you going to quit your job and go with us to Mexico?"

"Karolina, what are you saying? You know how much my job means to me."

"And what do I mean to you?"

" You know how much you mean to me, but I just can't quit my job!"

"You're crazy! You'd make a lot more money!"

At that moment, there was a noise at the door. Karolina raced across the room. She was expecting her brother.

"Come on in, Oleg," she called out as she opened the door.

"Yes or no?"

"He says no!"

"Well, what kind of a fool are you?"

"Ever since Maksim was killed, I feel like I am sort of taking his place. I used to think I didn't have any real talent for writing, but then my editor asked me to finish the article that Maksim had been writing. Something seemed to be guiding me as I wrote, and the words came out all mine. And they were good. Now, I know I have the ability to write."

"Maksim was no example for you. He supported Listyev and denounced the people who were against the ban on advertising for Ostankino. You see where it got him? In a pool of blood!"

The picture of Maksim sprawled across the floor flashed in front of Andrey's eyes. He felt his own blood boiling at this man's accusations against Maksim.

"Maybe that's where your money is coming from—the money skimmed from the ad revenues!"

"So what? Karolina, I think this guy has a problem. He and his snoopin' friend, Maksim, poked their noses into the Ostankino situation. Maksim's article tried to expose all of us!" Oleg drew a gun and pointed it directly at Andrey.

"You'll do what we tell you or else!"

Andrey stared at the gun, and he stared at Karolina. Her face was filled with a hardness that he had not seen before.

Andrey reached behind a pillow and pointed a gun at both of them.

"I'm not afraid of guns! I have a gun, and I've shot two men and I'll shoot again if I have to!"

"Come on Karolina, let's get out of here. If he's killed people, he must be a hot number with the KGB."

During this time, Natasha was getting more and more upset because nothing was working out for her. It seemed as though all her applications for a visa to the United States had been refused. It was terrible. Some people had told her to forget Pavel. Look for someone else with some kind of a future. But she couldn't think of doing that. She loved Pavel, and he loved and cared for her.

As the days passed, time seemed to stalk across her life with no concern for her feelings. Nothing happened. Sometimes it seemed that no one cared. The faces of the embassy clerks and her applications marked with "DENIAL" moved before her eyes. There seemed to be no hope.

During the early summer months, Natasha had decided to plant a vegetable garden near her grandmother's house. Maybe it was out of desperation to find something to do. Dianna had shown her what to do since she used to have a garden when she was younger and was able to do the work.

This morning, Dianna called to her from the backyard. "Come on out here, Natasha! I think you have some tomatoes getting ripe here!"

"Already? It's only July. I thought you said they wouldn't be ready for picking until much later."

"That's for picking, child. You always have to keep a strong eye on them or they won't get ripe!"

Natasha heard a noise, like tires moving on gravel, out in front of the house. She looked at her grandmother questioningly.

"I'll go and see. If I don't come back right away, you know I'm detained, and you can hide in the shed."

Soon, she heard her grandmother's voice cry out, "Come here, Natasha!"

Natasha waited a few minutes not sure what to do.

Then suddenly, a tall figure came around the corner of the house. "Natasha, what are you doing out here? Come and see my truck. Andrey's mother gave it to me. She said her son would have wanted me to have it."

It was Pavel's friend, Andrey! She hadn't seen him since last March.

"I have news for you! Pavel just received his political asylum in the United States! Now, he plans to apply for you to join him!"

"Oh, I'm so relieved!" Natasha voice shook with emotion. "How long does he think it will take?"

"It takes a while. Pavel has sent the application papers to Washington D.C. They consider the case. If they approve, they will send the paper work to the US Embassy in Moscow and then notify you at your parent's home in Lipetsk."

"I can hardly believe it! It's been so long and so hard!" As Natasha spoke the words, "so hard," her voice started to break, and she began to cry.

Andrey took her in his arms. He felt sorry for this young woman who had been through so many ordeals and terrible danger.

"Soon, this will be all over, Natasha. Enjoy all the moments you can with your mother and father. They will miss you."

Natasha nodded, but the word, "miss," filled her mind, and all she could see was Pavel's face searching for her. Perhaps, they would be together soon.

As each day passed, Natasha had the feeling that she wouldn't have to wait much longer before she would leave Russia and rejoin Pavel in the United States. Once in a while, she went with her friends to Lipetsk, but her parents while pleased to see her, continually worried about her safety. They said that crime was so prevalent that people could hire someone for a small amount of money to kill anyone they wanted to put away. More and more men who were solid communists to the bone were moving into power.

Before, when she talked to Pavel, he seemed disheartened. He wanted to be there to support the democratic movements, but how could he? In Russia, the place of his birth, he could not even stand up and fight for what he believed or the mafia would hold him at gunpoint for more money, or the KGB would arrest him and put him away in some prison for many years to come. There were no alternatives. And, he owed it to Natasha to try and get her to safety.

During those times, Natasha reminded him that he had spoken out for freedoms to the young people in the disco. He used to talk about how Russia's fine poets and writers had been suppressed. Then, later, in his own life, he had refused to obey the orders of the KGB. Even when they beat him, he remained resolute and never gave in. But what about the future? Neither of them had the answer.

It had been over a year since Pavel had received his political asylum and still the waiting continued. Now, it was August of 1996. Finally, about the time that Natasha had about given up hope, her brother arrived at the house early one morning with a message from the American Embassy in Moscow. They had just contacted her parents. She was now free to leave Russia!

Natasha's hands shook as she reached for the letter from Andrus. After all this time. After all this time. "Free to leave. Free to leave" She kept reading the words over and over again, hardly believing it was true. Then, her eyes filled with tears, and the words blurred on the page.

While Andrus and Natasha were embracing each other for joy, Dianna came hurrying out of the kitchen to see what the excitement was all about.

"My dear child! How wonderful for you. Now, you can join your husband in America! When must you leave?"

"She can pack now, Grandma. Then, we'll drive into Lipetsk, so she can say goodbye to our parents and make plane reservations."

"Yes, she must go before those men who have been looking for her do something to stop her."

But the KGB and the Mafia were the last thing on Natasha's mind. She was free to leave. Free! She even liked the taste of the words as she pronounced the words over and over again to Andrus on the way to Lipetsk.

"You have nothing to worry about, Natasha. Remember, the important KGB men were all killed in the bombing in Moscow! Even Romanov!"

Natasha nodded, but she wasn't so sure. What about the men who kept coming to look for her at her parent's house?

A few weeks later, about forty miles away, a black sedan rolled out from the KGB office building parking area in Lipetsk and headed for Butyrki.

"You think the girl is hiding at her grandmother's house?" Leonid asked the man sitting next to him in the car.

"Yes, we got a tip yesterday from a very good source," Gavriil answered.

"If we pick her up, how much money do you think we can get for her?"

"I think her husband is around some place. He worked in India for quite a few years, you know. Once before, Romanov got ten thousand dollars! Remember? Maybe we could get five or seven thousand this time."

"It should be seven, or we'll bump her off!"

They arrived in Butyrki early that morning. Dianna was terribly frightened at the sight of the two men. She had hoped all the danger had passed, and Natasha could get out of the country in safety.

"We are looking for your grandchild, Natasha? Is she here?"

Dianna shook her head. "No, she left yesterday to visit some friends in St. Petersburg. I believe one of the names is Kira Tudorovich." She desperately hoped they would believe her lie.

"Okay, old lady. We'll still look around here a little bit."

When they were coming back from searching the house and the yard, Dianna heard the men talking about kidnaping Natasha and getting some money.

About a half hour later, Dianna watched the car drive away. She hoped they were on their way to St. Petersburg, but she knew that their search would not end there. It would probably take Natasha some time to get a plane reservation out of the country.

Dianna didn't know where to turn. Then, she remembered there was a person in the village that had a telephone. She had to try and reach Andrey at the newspaper office. He might be able to reach Natasha before it was too late.

Andrey was out working on an assignment. Dianna asked the office to have him call back. It was an emergency. She sat and waited and waited. Still, the phone remained silent and cold and totally indifferent.

She prayed the old orthodox prayers. Then, she added, "Please, dear God, help us to reach Natasha in time."

Just when Dianna decided to give up and leave her neighbor's house in despair, the phone rang. But the voice was not Andrey's. She was told that Andrey had left the office and gone to Lipetsk because his mother was ill. He gave her another number to call.

Dianna's hands were shaking as she dialed the number in Lipetsk. This time she was lucky. Andrey answered the phone, and Dianna told him about what had happened that morning.

He was worried. "I'd better drive over there right away and warn Natasha! They will go to her parents' apartment when they can't find her in St. Petersburg. Maybe they won't believe you that Natasha went to St. Petersburg."

"If they don't go to the city, there may not be enough time!" Dianna said in despair. "So hurry, hurry, Andrey. Please hurry!"

Andrey felt the pressure as he raced his truck through the streets. What if it was too late? It was afternoon now. They had plenty of time to get there ahead of him.

Just as he was climbing the outside steps of the apartment house, he noticed a strange car just pulling up in front. Was it the KGB officers? He wasn't sure, but he couldn't take that chance.

Andrey rushed down the hallway to Natasha's apartment. He pounded frantically at the door.

"Tell Natasha to pack and keep out of sight, Andrus, while I try to send this mafia bunch somewhere else!" He desperately hoped they could escape before these men forced Natasha into their car.

A few minutes later, two men knocked at the door. Andrey told Andrus to tell them that Natasha had gone with some friends to the Kruchina Coffee Shop in downtown Lipetsk. They seemed satisfied, and Andrus watched them drive off down the street in a great hurry.

"We have to leave now!' Andrey warned. "Just pack what you absolutely need, Natasha. And let's get the hell out of here!"

Just as they were about to leave, Marla and then Tolik returned home from work. They didn't expect that their daughter would be leaving until much later that evening.

"Will they stop Natasha at the airport?" Marla asked anxiously.

"I don't think so. These men are KGB, but they are not on official business. They are extortionists. She is safe as long as we can get into the airport and past all the security checks," Andrey assured them. But he knew it wasn't all that simple. He had no idea what was ahead of them.

Andrey placed Natasha's suitcases into the truck while she said goodbye to her parents. It was difficult. When would she ever see them again?

Her legs shook unsteadily as she climbed into the truck. She felt choked with tears and a terrible invading fear.

While Andrey was racing to the airport, he asked Natasha and Andrus to keep watching the road behind them to see if they were being followed.

Once, Andrus called out, "I think there is a car behind us that has been following our truck!"

Quickly, Andrey took an immediate exit, then drove rapidly through some streets and circled back to the highway again.

"Did we lose them?" Andrey asked as he pressed down on the accelerator.

"So far. I'm still looking for them"

It was late at night when they finally reached the airport in Moscow.

Andrey raced up to the terminal in his truck and motioned for Andrus and Natasha to make a run for it. The men who had been searching for Natasha could be close behind them.

"Tell Pavel we will all get together one day and fight against the crime and the communists here in Russia. And we will win! My God, we will win!" Andrey said with fierce determination. Then, he turned and moved rapidly toward the highway that led away from the airport.

Natasha had been very lucky to get a ticket so soon, just two weeks after she had left her grandmother's house. Now it was a ticket that led her to freedom and if luck was with her, would save her life from the KGB extortionists.

It wasn't until the plane soared into the sky the next afternoon that Natasha felt really safe and secure. Somehow, it didn't seem real that this was happening after all the years of fear and hiding in India and Australia and then with her grandmother in Butyrki. The tears ran down her cheeks as she watched the plane reach its altitude, move past the airport, and leave the huge metropolis of Moscow below. Would she ever seen her homeland or her parents again? Would she find Pavel in the strange land that awaited her?

The next day, the giant plane landed in San Francisco. Natasha had been too excited to sleep. Two years had passed since she had last seen Pavel.

And then it happened. For Pavel, his first sight of Natasha was when he saw her passing through the gate at the airport. He had been standing on the second floor of the terminal and watching the throngs of people going through customs. He rushed to meet her and took her into his arms. For a few moments they stood there, just holding each other and looking into each other's eyes, hardly believing that this was happening, finally happening to them.

An airport official started to request them to move on. They were blocking the way for other passengers leaving the area. But immediately, he could see that this couple could not move away from this moment. The tears were running down their faces, and for them, nothing or no one else existed. Time refused to move on.

"Pavel, it's been so long, so long. I've been so frightened," she said crying and shaking uncontrollably.

"And I have been so worried about you, always wondering if you were safe."

He held her closely, still not quite believing she was really back.

Later in the car as they drove toward San Francisco, Pavel turned to Natasha and said, "So many times, I have looked over at the empty seat beside me and wondered when you would be sitting next to me again. I feel like it was a miracle that we came out of all this trouble. We're not victims any more!"

"Yes, we're finally together, and we won!"

Then, it was August in California, and the sun was warm, and Pavel told her that the snow had melted long ago at Tahoe, but they would go and walk among the tall pines. And it was there that their troubles were swept away in the mountain streams. It was time to start over.

Printed in the United States
65261LVS00004BA/67-99

9 781424 134267